The Squad

A Thriller Novel

by

Phil Mac Giolla Bháin

First published 2018
by Frontline Noir, an imprint of Books Noir

Text copyright © 2018 Phil Mac Giolla Bháin

Print edition ISBN: 978-1-904684-33-6

A CIP record for this book is available from the British Library

1 2 3 4 5 6 7 8 9 10

Typeset in Garamond by Park Productions

For my parents.

Best wishes

Pól

mac Giolla Bhain

Acknowledgements

Several people were of huge professional assistance to me to in the preparation of this book.

Firstly, my publisher Bob Smith has consistently showed huge belief in this project and also in me as an author. Although the original creative impulse took place many years before we started working together, it was he who saw the merit in pushing The Squad to a conclusion. This is our third book together, although The Squad is a very different work to the previous two non-fiction titles. Throughout it all he has been there for me.

It is a given that writing means re-writing and in this I was hugely assisted by an awesome all-female editorial team. As my words blinked to life here in Donegal they were dispatched, in the first instance, to West Cork. Once down there in Tom Barry country my work was analysed, parsed, improved and returned to me with a list of suggestions and, on occasion, instructions! Míle buíochas Katie! This is our first collaboration as author and editor and I hope it won't be the last.

Outwith the professional team, many others helped, mainly by being themselves and being aware that I was working on this novel. In that regard I owe a massive debt of gratitude to Eugene McEldowney, a brilliant writer in his own right, for providing me with regular supplies of advice and encouragement. It seems such a long time since I reviewed his wonderfully evocative novel The Faloorie Man for An Phoblacht. That's how we met and I'm lucky to call him a friend.

A massive go raibh míle maith agat is also due to Danny Morrison. He is himself a highly successful novelist with a distinctly authentic literary voice on this island. In typical fashion, he said to me that he didn't think he merited "a mention in dispatches" for

The Squad. However, his input towards the final strait was a sort of tipping point for me. Also re-reading his atmospheric work The Wrong Man helped me to reconnect with the hidden paranoid world of 'the operator'.

The Squad was originally created as a film script in 2006 and for many years it was left unattended and unfinished until my writer's voice was reawakened. That is largely down to the collaborative work that I first undertook in 2013 with Mark Williamson and the Sweet For Addicts theatre group in Glasgow. They staged my play 'The Flight of the Earls' and I then wrote two bespoke plays for SFA in 2014 and 2015. After the second piece was performed in March 2016 I was finally ready to journey back into this novel. I am certain that without these works being written and performed I would not have finished this book.

Very special thanks go to Angela Haggerty for being there for me and giving me a nudge when I really needed it. She was invaluable to me at many important points on this journey and for that and for many other things I will always be in her debt.

This story has an important Stateside component and I therefore must send my gratitude across the Pond to Nirah in Philly just for being herself.

Thanks are also due to my brother Omar, Scotland's very own Pharaoh in the Celtic end, for his unflinching friendship and for reminding me of the wonderful complexity of the Ummah.

I will always be grateful to Natalia for sharing her story with me and, of course, for her smiles over the years. Muchas gracias chiquita.

Writers are difficult people to live with. The creative process is a type of emotional quicksand that sucks you in. Consequently, it can often entail a retreat from any meaningful human inter- action while ostensibly being in the same abode with signifi- cant others. Therefore, I'm lucky to have an understanding and loving family who are always there for me when I come up for air. To all of these people in the foregoing I give my heartfelt thanks.

Without this wonderfully eclectic coalition I wouldn't be able to do what I do. In their own unique way they all helped me to be able to get this novel across the line. Of course, any errors contained here are mine and mine alone. I do hope you enjoy the journey upon which you are about to embark. At the end of it all you, the reader, are the most important person in this entire endeavour.

Phil Mac Giolla Bháin
Ireland
2018.

Monday

Big Jack Dempsey was wide awake before his phone told him to get up. He had slept only in instalments. He had always been a light sleeper, but this was different. His brain wouldn't let him rest because of the day that was in it. This was THE day and he hadn't been able to put that out of his mind when he had finally turned in the night before.

Jack scanned the contents of the room from his horizontal vantage point. It was class all right. The furnished apartment in Temple Bar was just what the judge had ordered, in that the little fella had a room of his own. He explained to the social worker that he needed to be in that area for his work, but that he could spend a whole weekend with him there. Well, he hoped that the social worker's report would say that he had made the effort under difficult circumstances.

The place he had been in before in Arbour Hill was a kip, but it had suited him. It was a couple of hundred yards from where he had first seen the light of day in 1958. His granny had told him that it was a freezing February morning and himself was yawning as soon as he was out in the world. The place still had some of the original Dubs.

He stumbled through to the toilet to empty his bladder and caught a glimpse of himself in the mirror. He wished he hadn't…

The kitchen might have been like something out of a Sunday supplement, but he certainly wasn't. The social worker had looked jealously at the quality of the place when she had visited him. Stupid middle class bitch would be impressed by all this designer shite, thought Jack. Dempsey reckoned that she was probably from somewhere in Wicklow by the sound of her. Jack had met her kind before, trying her best to be English.

"Fucking West Brit," muttered Jack to himself.

In the fridge there was some salvation for his battered throat. The

Innocent orange juice was as smooth as it said on the label. Tesco all night shopping suited someone like Jack. Even the automated checkouts. There were times when he didn't want to face anyone. Anyone at all.

Solitary confinement in prison was meant to be a punishment, but sometimes he missed it. The screws had been trying to break him with isolation and no human contact, but after what had happened to Dermot it was the kindest thing they could have done for him.

He turned on the TV which was attached to the wall and had come with the apartment. It was Sky News. Those bastards in the Middle East had another poor bastard in orange pyjamas. The man looked utterly terrified as he read out a statement. The worst he ever had to put up with was the RUC Special branch in Castlereagh. They got fuck all out of him, but those Islamic boyos didn't play to any rules.

The man in the orange jump suit was a charity worker from America, Edward Joseph Hennessy. Ah, there's more than a drop of Paddy in there, thought Jack. One of yer own over there trying to help those people. The video stopped and they went back to the studio a still image was in the background partly pixilated out, but he could see the figure of a man in the orange rig out lying on the ground. He couldn't see the top half of him, but the newsreader woman said that rest of the video showed Mr Hennessy being beheaded.

One thought jumped into Jack's head: 'Shankill Butchers'.

Then there were various talking heads having their say about the severed head. Americans, Brits; all spouting shite...

Then there was our fella.

Christ what an embarrassment that gobshite was, thought the big Dubliner as the Sunday supplement-approved coffee maker burbled on the work top. That wanker was in love with himself for sure. He even looked like a Blue Shirt, which was all that Gareth Scully was. This fecker had so much of a hard on for himself that he had set up his own party: "Ireland Renewed." A whole seven TDs and now the bollix was Justice Minister. He had made a name for himself as a celebrity lawyer. He was a showman. Certainly not a star performer in the court, but the camera loved him. So, they had given him his own radio station and then a TV show. It had given him a platform to build a base among the West Brits south of the Liffey. He had been elected as an Independent, then he'd gone full-on.

It was hardly a tough interview. The Brits loved him. The wee girl who was meant to be there to ask the questions just let him ramble on.

"We are, all of us, in Ireland, in the United Kingdom and, of course, in the United States, in a changed world post-Nine Eleven. Now we are all threatened by the new horror of ISIS."

He let it sink in like he was the brainiest fecker on the planet and he had to let the rest of them catch up with his quicksilver brain.

"These new tools that science has given us must be utilised in the fight against global Islamic terrorism."

Finally, the wee journalist girl realised that she was meant to actually ask some questions.

"Some are concerned about civil liberties being eroded? What do you say to people who think that a national DNA database would compromise traditional freedoms?"

Scully looked at her like she was the backward girl in the class who was trying her best and was awaiting the mark in the exam. He tried to be kind to her, but you could see his heart wasn't in it. He just didn't do kindness.

"Yes, that is an important issue," he sneered. He didn't mean to sneer, but it just came out. His top lip was like Dr Strangelove's hand, thought Jack. The right hand kept wanting to do Nazi salutes to the US president. Maybe everyone has a bit of their body that betrays them? It curled up. With Jack he was betrayed by his dick – every fuckin' time. Every time he fucked, he seemed to fuck up. Maybe if he had been out of prison when he was young then he might have been OK now and not behaving like this and him nearly sixty. Fuck it. Yeah Jack, that's how you got to here you bollix, he thought.

The coffee gave him a lift. He needed it. He sat and looked around the gaff. It was class. This was where you lived in Dublin if you were doing kinda well for yourself. However, he would have swapped in an instant for one of the flats in the Ballymun towers in the eighties. That's where he had lived before he was scooped. He didn't have the price of a pair of new shoes back then, but he knew who he was. He loved the 'Mun. Sound people among the skangers.

He could deal with them; then again Big Jack Dempsey never had any trouble on the street.

It was the bedroom that fucked him up. If he could be with the wee fella long term then he would get something out towards Swords. A gaff with a garden. This would be OK for weekends, he hoped. In fairness what they had said about his flat in Arbour Hill was reasonable enough. Not that there was much fairness in the Family Courts in Dublin if you were a bloke and happened not to be married to the bitch that hated you.

The TV was still on and Jack heard a voice he knew well. He walked round to stare at the screen on the wall. It was a demonstration at Shannon Airport. Liam McMillan, Sinn Féin TD, was speaking to a crowd of several thousand. These demos were usually held on a weekend, but a demonstrator, a young university student from UCD, had been crushed by a Garda vehicle only two days before. Niamh Keane, who had only come along to the demo because several of her friends thought it would be craic, had become a martyr for a cause that she knew little about. Her happy smiling face from her Facebook profile was the most shared image across much of the social media in the last forty-eight hours, and not just in Ireland. Her Instagram account told the tale of a carefree university student with her whole life in front of her. Her death was a genuine tragedy and there was no suggestion that the young policeman who had reversed the riot control minibus knew that she was there. However, that didn't matter. The state had blood on their hands, and Jack watched as McMillan played the crowd's anger like a piano.

The militarisation of this airport in neutral Ireland was a national disgrace, said the Dáil Deputy. He called out Scully as a devious war-mongering hypocrite. The crowd cheered and Jack experienced the uncomfortable feeling of realising that he agreed with every word that McMillan had said. There had been a time when he never thought there would be any disagreement between them. Times change, thought Jack.

Then his phone vibrated with a text message. It was Tommy. Jack smiled. Always there for you, he thought. Sound man. He picked the phone up and called, "Howya?"

"Grand so," said Tommy.

Jack could hear that he was on speaker.

"You're out early."

"Ah, the young one let me down. So, this thing has to drive. No rest for the wicked."

"You must be bolloxed."

"I'm grand. Anyway, you want a lift? I'm coming past Trinity now. This is your big day for the wee fella?"

"It is. You're some man for one man for minding that buddy."

"Ah, away with ye Jack!"

"Take your time. I can park up. I'll meet you at Nico's. Buzz me when you're ready. I'll have the hazards on."

"Ah, you're grand Tommy. Appreciate the call though. I need a walk. I've time till I get there. Look, I'll see you at Walsh's after this. Need to clear the head and I don't want to get there too early. I might bump into that bitch."

"You sure buddy?" Tommy's voice crackled with the noise of the car's engine in the background.

"I'm grand buddy. But see you at Walsh's after this shite?"

"Ah hundred percent big fella. You'll be grand now. You have a strong case there."

It didn't take Jack long to get ready, largely because there was no time consumed by wardrobe dilemmas. He had one suit, one pair of dress shoes and three shirts, all white. All he had to do was rummage for a tie.

Tommy Noonan was a sound fella. One of the old guard. He would be there for ye till the end. Then he made an instant decision, not that he could have told you why. He hit the button on the phone and Tommy immediately answered.

"Howya Jack?"

"Change of plan. Can you pick me up or you in the other direction now?"

"I'm grand big fella. I'll be there in ten minutes, tops I'm in the flow round past Trinity. No bother. I'll buzz you when I'm back outside Nico's."

Jack sat down and poured another coffee. He considered stiffening it up with some Jameson's, but that would be a bad idea. Or would it? The old conversation started in his head again. It wasn't a secret chat anymore. It was something that he spoke about at his meetings. If that bad fecker were to win the argument it was sure to be on a day like this, thought Dempsey. He compromised. He walked into the spare bedroom in the apartment and there was a grip inside the walk in wardrobe.

Fuck, this place was fancy.

The holdall was ancient and one of the few things in this gaff that was actually his. He shoved his big paw into the bag and came out with a stainless steel hipflask. Jack unscrewed the top and had a sniff. It was as full as the time he had put it into the bag. The whiskey smelled better to him than anything imaginable. Only alcoholics would get that, and the aroma lured him in and told him that everything would be OK. Just one sip. No harm at all.

The other voice; that of his sponsor, John, roared in his head. He could hear his soft Sligo brogue shouting at him. Dempsey screwed the top back in a panicked fidgety way like a pubescent boy hastily closing a laptop. The Gobshite had won a tactical victory. Jack slipped the hipflask into the inside pocket of his suit jacket. If Sound Fella had been completely victorious then the flask would have never been taken out of the holdall. This was a row that would be had later.

The phone vibrated on the kitchen table and Dempsey moved surprisingly quickly for a man of his size to pick it up. His meaty paw was not designed for smartphones and he had to be very careful that he swiped in the correct direction. Dicey had fixed the phone up for him in the office and talked him through it. She had tried her best to explain what it could do. Basically, all the things that he did in the office he could now do on the move, but it still seemed to have mind of its feckin' own every time he touched it. He had developed a technique using the deftest of touches with his right thumb while holding the iPhone in his left. He sometimes appeared to onlookers to be in slight trepidation of the device. There was no one to see him in the Temple Bar apartment so he held the phone to his ear and it was Tommy.

"Heading your way buddy if you're ready."

"I am surely. Be down in a second."

Dempsey clattered down the metal stairs to the controlled

entrance that let him out onto the cobbled lane in Temple Bar. As soon as Jack stepped out onto Dame Street Tommy was there with the precision of a veteran ambusher.

"The Four Courts?"

"No. Heuston Station."

"You OK?" Tommy was puzzled.

"Drop me at Heuston and I'll get the Luas. I can pick up a paper there."

"Jack I can drop you at the door of that place no bother."

"I have to see a man first, Tommy."

"You sure buddy?"

"A hundred percent. Appreciate it Tommy. Good to see you buddy." Jack tapped his shoulder from the back seat.

"Proceed, driver," Jack said in a put on Dublin Four accent.

Tommy smiled and played along.

"Very good. Seán Heuston Station it is, sir!"

Tommy always liked to give the station its full name and this pleased Jack. He had been in a cab in the centenary year and the Dub driving the yoke had no idea who the station was named after or why. Big Jack Dempsey couldn't confide to Tommy the real reason that he wanted to be dropped off at Seán Heuston Station. The place itself was a touchstone for him. His father's father had been a guard on the trains for decades and this is the station he worked out of for years. Dempsey's grandfather had died two years before Jack was born and everyone said that Jack was the image of him. Tommy could have quite easily dropped him off at the courts, but Dempsey wanted to pick up the vibe of the oul fella just by being under that roof.

It was a secret ritual that he had never told anyone about. Despite his gregarious back slapping nature in the pub, Big Jack Dempsey was a very private man who had been excellently suited to the line of work he had been in throughout his youth.

Jack walked through the ticket queues and onto the concourse itself. This station had changed so much since his childhood, but was still familiar to him. It had been the largest covered area in Europe when it was built.

His grandfather had been a guard on the railway here coming up from his native Galway carrying dispatches from the Division there for GHQ. Right under the noses of the Brits! For a moment it gave him a little smile. He was of good people. Smart, resourceful and, well, brave. He just might get a victory at this court thing today, he thought.

When he got into the small Eason's he went round to get a couple of papers and a copy of *Phoenix* magazine. It seemed appropriate given where he was going. He walked out of Seán Heuston Station onto where the Luas stopped. From here it would take you into town or out to Tallaght.

The Luas wasn't designed for people his size. The doors swished open and more got in than got out. Jack reflected that the only other time that people in Dublin got this close to each other was in a night club when it was getting serious. Somehow he got in without asphyxiating anyone. It was the usual snapshot of the Dublin commuting classes in the second decade of the new millennium.

He could hear a collection of foreign languages. One he clocked right away was Polish. He had a lad working with him from Poland and he knew the word for grand, good and no hassle: "Dobzah." Well, that was how it sounded to his Dub ears. For his fella everything was always "dobzah." He reminded Jack of himself at that age. A good lad was young Stan. He'd left him in charge of a job today and he knew that he wouldn't let him down. He could do with a few more of his kind.

Dublin's Luas light rail system meant that Tallaght had lost its "end of the world" status for Dubliners. It was the end of the line for Luas, but that meant that getting into town was no big deal now. Any Luas on any day was a snapshot of modern Dublin. Young girls from private schools heading to Connolly Station to get the "Dort." Standing beside Polish cleaners called Anya and skangers from Ballyfermot called Anto.

Until the Luas, Dublin was the only capital city in Western Europe without a metro or light rail system. The tribe of brain surgeons that ran Dublin city decided to have two Luas lines that didn't connect. Cross-City was just an admission that they had buggered the thing up to start with. The Port Tunnel had been a case in point of a big infrastructure project being totally ballsed up from the start. Even

8

the day it was opened it couldn't take the biggest lorries; entirely defeating the purpose. Still, in fairness, the Luas had been a hit. Especially with the non-car owning population of Tallaght. That was where Jack had been reared since he was twelve when the family moved from Arbour Hill. It was the Soweto of Dublin and for long enough it had been a case study in social exclusion.

He then remembered it was on the last Luas going out to Tallaght that he had first bumped into herself. Actually that night was a lot of bumping into herself upstairs at her place. She said she was safe and he hated Durex. Even at his age he could still fuck it all up, he thought. And that was why he got out at Smithfield, the stop before the Four Courts.

Big Jack Dempsey was no stranger to courts. Diplock courts in the north, special criminal courts in the south. Now it was the family court in Dublin. The last round of this war had been at Dolphin House. Dolphins are meant to be friendly fuckers, thought Jack. There was nothing friendly about that place. Today was Phoenix House near the Four Courts. This charade today was all about her. She walked in a few minutes after him. She was walking her angry walk. Her pert little tits straight out like fixed bayonets. Her breasts had been different when he met her years earlier; all jiggly and giggly. Bunched up like two cushions inviting a weary head. His head. That was then. This was now. Angry women deal in shame, Jack thought. It is their main weapon against you. They shame you in the eyes of the world. They tell everyone that you're no use. No use at anything. No use in bed, no use as a provider. No use as a human being. He had provided his solicitor with his side of events. He was, of course, willing to pay for the support of wee Pádraig. However brief the liaison with the mother he was the kid's father and he hadn't missed a payment. He gave her cash payments, but they had been denied in court last time out. After that it was cheques. Which really pissed her off. That's when the tits came out swinging. He was nearly sixty and he was way too old for all this shite. Still, he had enough left in him to totally mess things up for tits like the ones angrily drawing a bead on him across the foyer of the court building.

Phoenix House was modern and purpose built. Dolphin House was a crumbling red brick affair on East Essex Street on the other side of the Liffey. The reception desk at Phoenix House would not have looked out of place in an Ibis or a Best Western. They had a policy of not calling out names but just the initials of the people involved in a particular case. He was told that the idea was to provide as much anonymity as possible to the participants in the farce that was Family Law in the Republic of Ireland. There were rows of fixed wooden seats along the walls and a square of bench seats in the middle of the floor. Jack sat down on the corner of the square nearest to the door and facing the reception desk.

His solicitor skipped past him holding a pile of thick paper files. She was trying to get across the open ground and avoid every one of her client's eyes like a waiter trying to have a quiet shift. Eye contact means you are caught. This was the third time she had avoided his gaze. He stood up and moved towards her. She had to acknowledge that. She was busy for sure. Every Joe Soap there was cash money for her. The least she could afford him was a little eye contact. For the €800 he was paying her down Temple Bar a Latvian Bond Girl would you more than a look.

"Mr Dempsey. Hello!"

"It's Jack, Clodagh. Always Jack," he smiled.

"Sure, great. I've had a look at your affidavit of means. That's fine, perfectly fine. I don't think the judge will need any more clarification of that. I've read the social worker's report and it is very positive about you and your new accommodation. I'm sure we'll be fine. Honestly."

"What about the guardianship? I need to know that I can get to see the wee fella."

"This judge is very good on that, Mr Dempsey. Now, if you'll excuse me."

She didn't look him in the eye at that point. She was lying for sure. He was fucked, but she would still get her €800. He suddenly didn't have any fight left in him. He went back and sat down. He hunched over and tried to make himself smaller. He studied the cracks round the toecap in his only pair of good shoes. Well they weren't that good, but they were what he used as good shoes. He didn't hear the case being called, but for once the bould Clodagh gave him full eye contact when he looked up.

He was lost in thought and not listening when he was jolted by Clodagh's voice.

"The case is called, Mr Dempsey."

All business she was, which was only fair for eight hundred feckin' euro, he thought. Just like in earlier court appearances he was hung, drawn and quartered before the judge even sat down. There was an essential honesty about getting brought before the Special Criminal Court in the 1980s. No one really had the pretence that any justice was involved. It was a war and the enemy captured you and they threw you in Port Laoise with the rest of your comrades. It was very similar to Internment in the North in the 1970s. The Brits couldn't defend their position as a democracy if they were scooping guys up into camps without a trial. So they invented the H Blocks. It was all a farce, but they thought they could convince the world that the men inside were criminals. They failed.

He could see why any man involved in this circus could get bitter about things. Much like Internment, you could get caught up in the craic for pretty much minding your own business. Even if you weren't involved when you were scooped a few months behind the wire tended to get you to see the world the way the lads viewed it. Long Kesh was a volunteer factory, but the British could never see that.

His grandfather had the same experience in Frongoch. The oul fella had attended some route marches with the Volunteers down the country in Galway, nothing more. He had been in the Fianna, but it was really just a bit of craic for him. After the Rising he had been lifted and put in an ex-Whiskey distillery in Wales with some of the most hardened revolutionaries in Western Europe, including a young fella from West Cork called Michael Collins.

The room, like the building, was all new and shiny. The old guard in the corner looked like he should've been on a drip in a care home. Jack was sure he was about to keel over. There's always someone worse off than you. Just find the fucker and you're on the way up! A Kerryman told Jack that during his first few days as a teenage POW in Port Laoise. The court clerk read out the details. The application for guardianship was in there all right. Fair play to her. Well, for €800 a day you gotta get something right. Yer one's solicitor stood up and started the spiel. Her client was willing to facilitate supervised access for the child's father despite his inappropriate behaviour in the past. She was frightened of the child's father who had a history of violence. With regard to guardianship, the mother did not think the child's father an appropriate person, due to the fact that Mr Dempsey was a convicted murderer. He was out on license as part of the Good Friday Agreement. Bingo! Magic bullet, end of story! No point in holding back. It was, in their world, all true.

"Mr Dempsey was serving several life sentences in the United Kingdom for numerous counts of murder and other serious offences when he was released under the terms of the Good Friday Agreement in 1998."

The judge looked over his specs and took a good look at Jack. She was then called up to the witness box and Clodagh girl gave him a weak smile. This was not a case study that she had come across in law school. She was duly sworn in on the good book. Nothing but the truth now, Jack thought.

"Please state your name and address for the court."

"Pauline Duffy, 106 Kilkenny Avenue, Killinarden, Tallaght."

"You are the mother of the child Pádraig Duffy, date of birth 08/11/2013?"

"Yes I am."

It was Oscar-winning stuff. Poor little helpless Pauline said she was in fear of her life from him and she had nightmares about what big bad Jack Dempsey would do to the little child. As she snivelled through her performance Jack looked up and could see the oul judge slowly falling in love with this tearful damsel from Tallaght. He was, at that stage, royally fucked and he knew it. There was nothing hard, concrete laid against him as a parent.

He had always paid for the kid, always wanted to. The wee fella knew Jack was his Da. His name was on the birth certificate, but he'd learned that in Ireland that meant jack shit. He wanted guardianship so that he could have an equal say in the wee man's upbringing. Were the women not always banging on about equality?

The only facts were that he was a Provie lifer out on licence. The bould Clodagh did her best for her €800. She told the judge that since release from prison in the United Kingdom her client had come back home to his native Dublin and had established a thriving security company. He had always financially provided for his son and wanted to co-parent with the child's mother. Moreover, there was no medical evidence or third party corroboration to substantiate Ms Duffy's allegation of domestic abuse against her client, Mr Dempsey. In fairness, it was a good a gloss as she could put on things.

The judge leafed through the papers, occasionally glancing up. When he finally spoke it hit Jack like a good dig in the solar plexus.

"Application for guardianship denied. Access to be supervised in consultation with the HSE," said the judge, and that was that.

Prison visits for his kid! He felt the temper rising in him, his old friend. The tubby old guard looked nervously at Jack. It was no contest and both of them knew it. There were another two guards out in the foyer, one of them seemingly constructed out of pipe cleaners. He could have decked both of them, but this system he couldn't beat. Jack turned and left the courtroom before he did some damage. The lovely Clodagh skipped out after him to make sure that her fee, sorry, client, was OK.

"Well that went well, just like last time."

Was that the only thing Jack could think to say to his utterly useless solicitor? She had been highly recommended to him by a father's group in Ballymun. Thanks lads!

"Mr Dempsey. I'm so sorry. There is the possibility of an appeal to the High Court, however."

"Is that it?" growled Jack? "I had a fairer hearing when I got sent to Port fucking Laoise!"

"Please, Mr Dempsey." Clodagh wasn't used to this level of aggression.

"Send me your invoice," were the last words he ever said to her as he walked away.

Going to the Four Courts would be a waste of time and as much of a mistake as when his grandfather had taken over the place with his comrades in 1922 during the Civil War.

He was about to properly explain to the lovely Clodagh just what a shite lawyer she was when he saw the little fella. It caught him in the gut. He didn't think he would be there. It was her sister handing him over to the bitch herself. The wee man spotted his dad instantly and that was that.

"DADDY!"

The child's mighty little voice bounced off the walls. Jack's legs automatically took him over to the child even though his head said that this wouldn't end well. Pauline saw him and decided to get the hell out of there. Pauline Duffy finally yanked the child and dragged him through the automatic doors. It would have been an affecting sight to any onlooker with a heart.

Outside Phoenix House was a small paved area with a coffee kiosk next to the Luas stop.

In that instant Big Jack Dempsey forgot everything about being angry at his useless €800 a day lawyer, the Free State, and that stupid oul judge. He just wanted to see his son. He moved towards the child and the child instantly struggled to get to his dad. Pauline was having none of it. She pulled the child back into her side.

"Pauline," he said, pleading. All the fight was out of him.

"It isn't your contact time," she snarled and kept walking. The child started to drag his feet and wail.

The only thing he could do was walk away from his only living son and it broke his heart. After that, the only thing he could think of was to shut his brain down. He walked away from Phoenix House, oblivious to the pitying looks that several people had directed towards him. He could still hear the wee fella howling. He had been a fighter all of his life and in this, the most fundamental one, he was beaten.

He was disgusted with himself and the voice in his head, the Gobshite, told him that there was a way to make it all go away. Just one glug and it would all be grand. He turned right into Burgess Lane where there were some roller shutters with yellow fuck-off lines painted in front of them. He didn't notice the minibus at first that was parked on them, he was too busy listening to the Gobshite. He reached into the pocket of his suit jacket and with the sun beating down on his big red face he took the first hit. The whiskey cascaded down his gullet and it felt wonderful. One was never enough, it never ever had been enough. He walked a few more steps up the lane and saw the front door for a touristy thing about the history of Ireland.

The history of Ireland could go fuck itself, thought Dempsey. It was the history of Ireland that had got him into this mess. The

Gobshite loved it when he felt sorry for himself. He looked up and saw some young lads getting out of a minibus. It was brand new. Kildare registration He was taking a swig out of the hip flask every few steps, all resistance to it gone. The Gobshite had won and his name was Seán Patrick Dempsey. Jack had a word with himself and he didn't hold back. He was the Gobshite and he was fucking rubbish. No wonder they won't let you look after your kid. There was no other way to stop this pain but to administer the medicine.

He was in mid glug from the hip flask when he crashed into this young fella with a backpack on his shoulder. Dempsey was born with the clumsy gene and he had the unfortunate gift of walking into things that he hadn't noticed were there. There was a row of young lads, hardly invisible, who were having the chat when Jack walked sideways into one. It set off a chain reaction, knocking one into the other.

The hip flask almost fell out of Dempsey's big hand, but Jack righted himself and saved the day. However, in doing so some of the precious liquid arched out of the stainless steel canteen and a few drops landed onto the nearest young lad. The youth jumped back like Jack had spilled sulphuric acid onto his bare skin.

"Ah sorry lads. Good luck!" was all that he could manage in the circumstances as he headed past them.

Dempsey instinctively raised the hip flask in a 'sláinte' type gesture. This seemed to make it worse for this gathering of young men. They took a few steps towards him as one and two of them moved around to the side of back in what felt like an encircling movement. This could kick off, thought Jack.

They were all foreign. Jack could tell that, but little more. Young fellas with brown skin, but not blacks. One of them shot Jack a look. The big Dub didn't speak their language, but he knew hatred when he saw it. The tension was unmistakable and even Big Jack Dempsey knew he was outnumbered for this one. All of these lads had the 'no holding back' look. Dempsey was an expert at spotting this.

The big Dubliner tensed himself for what was about to happen. The young kid that had been splashed with the precious liquid let a yelp out of him in some lingo. He was foreign, but that could mean just about anything in Dublin these days. The kid stared at

Jack with a real vengeful intensity. Immediately Dempsey knew it was about to become physical and there was a crew of them getting out of the van.

"Sorry fella."

The kid just stared at him and he was joined by a few of his mates. For a moment Jack thought that he might have to deal with all of them. This situation didn't fill Big Jack Dempsey with the fear. For sure it would have terrified any normal man, but then there was little that was everyday about Jack in such circumstances. Under the blubber of a takeaway diet remained the remnants of a promising heavyweight thirty years earlier. He was a frequent enough visitor to a battered gym down in Ringsend, run by an old buddy. Dempsey could still manoeuvre round the heavy bag like a pissed off dinosaur. When he let the right hand go the foundations of the building shook.

There was a time when he'd had a real chance of a top-class career before he'd decided to go down another road. That direction of travel meant that he couldn't see his own flesh and blood when he wanted to. The six foot four Dubliner reckoned it was one dig apiece for these youths, but given the day that was in it, scrapping didn't seem appropriate.

Jack had stopped counting at nine or ten. There was certainly a crew of them. He conceded the possibility that this could get interesting. All of his street fighting instincts told him that this about to ignite when there was an intervention. An older guy stepped out of the driver's seat and said something and they all stepped back. He was clearly in charge. One word from him and this young crew would obey. Either way. Dempsey spotted that yer man was a bit taller than the rest, in his forties he reckoned and the only one who was bearded. It registered with Jack that there was something else about him. What was it?

The top man said something in their lingo and they all backed off without a murmur. Anyways, it was over and Jack turned and walked away. Something told him to look back, he didn't know what, but when he did the young man he had bumped into was still staring at him. Suddenly Dempsey felt unsettled and he had no idea why.

He was still thinking about those fellas when he was suddenly faced with the Law Society of Ireland across the road from him. To his right were the offices of the Probation services. It was like someone up there was mocking him. However, the Alco Nav in his head was guiding him to Walsh's. The Gobshite was now in charge.

This was the part of Dublin where he had first seen the light of day. His mother's people had been Dubs for generations. The Bradys were well respected folk in Stoneybatter. He walked past North King's Street and he heard the voice of his Dubliner granny telling him what had happened to her young brother Danny in Easter Week. He was involved in nothing. The British Tommies had found him in a cellar with his mother and two sisters. They put bayonets into him. His mother never recovered from her broken heart. Dempsey's granny witnessed the butchery and never ever forgave them. She made sure this was passed onto her grandson.

He had tasted his first pint in Walsh's back when he was too young to drink. Now he should have been too wise to gargle, but he wasn't. This wasn't a good idea; he knew that as he looked at the Jameson's upside down on the gantry. Time to be serious. How long had he been off it? Like most alcoholics he knew exactly. The last drink had been three years and seven months ago until that swig in Burgess Lane. Fuck it! Why be sober? He thought to himself. The higher power could go fuck himself, and those clowns at AA. That swig from the hip flask had unlocked the door to the madness. Now he needed more. A lot more.

"Jameson's. Double."

The barman obeyed silently. That was exactly what Jack wanted. The whiskey arrived and the bartender lad asked him for something, but Dempsey couldn't make him out. Double whiskey? A tenner should cover it. He threw him a twenty euro note. He didn't care. He could now smell the whiskey, really smell it. The Higher Power could fuck right off!

Dempsey threw it down his throat like he didn't want to acknowledge he was drinking it. He didn't want to drink it. This was defeat. The whole day was a defeat. There as a day when Big Jack Dempsey didn't think anything other than victory was possible; as long as we stayed united and chipped away, then victory would come.

Wrong. Utterly fucking wrong. Defeat was the natural order for Paddies. Defeat or collaboration. Great choice. That gobshite Scully seemed born for the oul collaborating; his type always were. They were fucking good at it, too.

He managed a hand gesture to the barman that meant 'another'. The change was still on the bar and he helped himself to some of it as the second double was put in front of him. Jack's right hand moved with a swiftness that unsettled the man sitting on a bar stool beside him. Dempsey didn't even notice. It was only him and the Jameson's in there. The barman came back with his change and Jack rummaged for another ten euro note. The barman knew to just go and get another. There was clearly no need for chit chat.

This time Dempsey took the whiskey and sat down in the back area. The pub had been renovated some years back, but they had managed to keep the same character as the original part. As he walked under the arch that led to the jacks and sat down in a little alcove Jack was making it clear enough that he didn't want company. No one inside the bar had any desire to explore how serious Big Jack Dempsey was on that matter. No one at all.

Pauline was at the end of her tether with wee Pádraig. Just like his father, she thought, he can kick off for Ireland. The doors of the Luas opened and she stepped out at Jervis and her life saver was standing there.

"Siobhán!" said Pauline, who was startled to see her bestie.

"You heading home?" asked Siobhán.

No sooner had she said that than she could see that Pauline was in some kind of fix. The little fella was trying to pull away from his mother with tears staining his little face.

"I was in court with his D. A. D. D. Y." whispered Pauline conspiratorially to Siobhán.

"I want me Dah!" yelled Pádraig.

The child's wailing made people nearby wince. He certainly had a decent set of lungs on him. A pair of elderly women on their way to the shopping centre were looking and quietly tut–tutting at the immorality play being performed for them. The absence of a wedding ring was the first thing that the ladies had spotted. Pauline sensed their old judgemental eyes and shot them a look. They old ladies scuttled off in search of desperately needed cardigans.

"You look wrecked!" said Siobhán.

Pauline felt the tears welling up, but battled them back. She hated that big bastard and she was trying hard not to hate his kid. She was at the end of her tether. Then a desperate light bulb went off.

"Siobhán, would you do me a big favour, a real big favour?"

Before she could explain Siobhán did the mind reading and they both knew that she was on for doing the decent thing.

"Take him for a while?"

Pauline's knees nearly went under her.

"Would ya?"

"Sure I'm heading out to me Ma's now. Our Kevin's lad is there, same age about. When do you need him…?"

"Oh? A couple of hours. Just a couple…"

"Look, come over for him tonight, he'll get fed at me Ma's place. Take it handy girl. I just have to head into town to pick a couple of things up. He'll be grand with me, then I'll head back to Tallaght with him. Where you going now?"

"I'll just head back to mine. I need a bath and a drink…"

"Look girl, just turn the shaggin' phone off and have the rest of the day to yourself."

"I will. Look, thanks honey."

"Ah, go on. It's nothing. Look, me and this wee fella will have a great time."

Pauline wasn't even going to try and talk to her son, she had nothing left. Thankfully Siobhán did all of that. She bent down to wee Pádraig and said, "Do you like playing X-Box?"

Silence.

"My nephew Kevin is your age and he's got the new X-Boxy yoke. You wanna see it?"

Siobhán got a sullen nod. Pauline gently let go of his little hand and stepped back. Siobhán glanced her a 'feck off, it'll be grand' look. The Luas doors opened and she stepped into one going to Tallaght without a second glance. Pauline couldn't believe it had been that easy. She needed some peace and quiet and Siobhán had saved her life. Again. Some girl that!

Pauline got the Luas back to Tallaght. Siobhán deserved a feckin' medal. Talk about great timing! She had done the trick. The wee fella would be glued to the X-Box game he would be playing this afternoon while mammy was chilling out. Long bath. Scented candles. Phone switched off. After all that shite at court she couldn't face anything else. It sounded brilliant. On the way home she looked around the carriage. She was glad she didn't see anyone who knew her. As soon as the Luas got to the terminus she was out. She jumped on a taxi and was at her front door in no time.

Pauline Duffy couldn't normally rest if anything was out of place. Given that she shared this house with wee Pádraig that was sometimes an onerous task. The little fella could mess up for Ireland. Toys strewn everywhere! However, she didn't even look near the living room or the kitchen. It could all wait. She flicked the water heater on – it would take an hour.

She went into her bedroom and took off the suit jacket and skirt she'd had on for court. Navy blue. Her solicitor had told her to wear something "sober." She knew the form. No heels. Dress flat shoes. The smaller she looked the better. At five foot four she could manage that. The suit was put away in the fitted wardrobe. She closed the mirrored door and looked at herself for a second. She was convinced that her nose was too big, but she was mildly satisfied with her body. Pauline Duffy knew that she could still turn heads anytime she felt the need.

Her big make over earlier in the year had been a great success. Gone was the big hair that needed so much attention. That Polish girl in Blanchardstown was a genius with scissors. Everyone said that she suited her hair bobbed, but the clincher was the change of colour. Her own blonde colour either needed lightened or it had to go she'd concluded. Pauline had thought long and hard and then had finally decided on black. She knew it had been a good choice when some young lad told her in Coppers that she looked like Lily Allen. Then again, Copper Face Jacks did seem to have a numbing effect on otherwise sensible folk once they entered that den of stupidity on Harcourt Street.

She rummaged through a bedside drawer to find something that had, for once, a decent use… A small black satin blindfold courtesy of Ann Summers on O'Connell Street. She really loved that shop. All the girls knew her there. Nothing naughty about this for a change though. She slipped on the blindfold and it was instant darkness.

Then she remembered that feckin' phone. One more time, the motherly panic and guilt. She called Siobhán. Herself answered right away. She sounded her chirpy self. "Hi honey. We're in the Jervis centre and himself has a massive ice cream. All over him it is. He's gas. I've a something to pick up for me Ma then we'll be out to sunny Tallaght and the little man here can get X-Boxing with my nephew. He's grand, now switch off that feckin' phone missy and let auntie Siobhán take care of business. I don't want to hear from you till tonight at the earliest. He'll get dinner in ours. OK?"

"You're a fucking saint, so ye are Siobhán."

"If the child wasn't here I'd have some answer to that, Missy!"

Pauline creased into laughter for the first time that day.

"Love you, kiddo," said Pauline and she signed off.

On the screen of the phone was the face of little Pádraig in a Liverpool top that her father had got for him. He was two in the picture and a little handful even then.

She switched the iPhone off and laid back and put on the shades. Usually when that happened the little man was sleeping next door and she tried to make as little noise as possible as another product from the Ann Summers range did the business for her. Today she was nowhere near that mood. She drifted off for a while. When she awoke she wasn't sure how long she had been out and if the water was ready for a bath. She walked down into the kitchen and looked at the clock. She had been out for two hours! The water would be boiling!

She turned the heater off and skipped up to the bathroom. Pauline Duffy loved baths. Really loved them. She had this bath fitted two years ago. Cost her plenty. The taps were on one side which meant that it could comfortably accommodate two people at the same time. The last guest had been that guy from Cork. Nice guy, well built, but she couldn't abide his accent after a while. He worked for a car dealer in Kildare and that meant had a lovely new one. A Mercedes. Pure class! She didn't mind that he was married. That meant he was easier to get rid of. He had texted her last week and she was wee bit tempted, but not enough.

She had some new candles, a pal of hers had bought them on the Aer Lingus flight coming over from London. They were in a little box with two postcards of thatched cottages and all that shite. A present from dear oul Ireland for the tourists all the way to feckin' Tallaght!

She had something nice from the Body Shop to put in the bath. Not bubbles, just something that smelled soothing. She went into the bedroom and grabbed her laptop. She set it down on the loo and kicked up the tunes. Nothing heavy, nothing loud. The bath was nearly there. Only one thing was missing. Vodka! She took the first lusty gulp of Smirnoff and she was ready to slip beneath the waves. Immediately she needed a refill.

Pauline stood in front of the mirrored doors of her wardrobe as she took the rest of her clothes off. The vodka was already making her head tingle. She'd had nothing to eat all day except for a bit of toast. She stood looking at herself in matching black bra and thong. Nothing sober about this get up she thought to herself. The rest of the first glass of vodka was downed and full of Russian courage she went up on the balls of her feet and twisted from side to side looking at her butt and her waist. Not bad at all for twenty nine she thought. Pauline took off her bra and turned around looking over her shoulder at her back and her arse. The Smirnoff convinced her that it was not a bad sight at all. She slipped off the thong, picked up the empty glass and headed back into the bathroom.

The sound of Simply Red filled the smallest room in the house. She had liked them since she was a kid and got slagged by the girls about it. She carefully positioned the full glass of vodka on the side of the bath and then lowered herself into the water. As always she had it too hot, but there was no turning back. Getting quietly hammered in a warm bath was one of the great things about life.

It was about two weeks since her last period, so she reckoned this should be ovulation time. Which meant that she was usually mad horny for about three days. However, this month there was nothing, not even a twinge. It was all because of that big bastard at the court, she thought. Of all the fuckers to get knocked up by, it had to be him.

Hammered she was that night. Fucking hammered.

In Walsh's Jack relaxed into the next Jameson's. The Gobshite had been right. It all felt better. He started to laugh to himself. One fella coming back from the Jacks spun round and saw the big fella sitting in the alcove sniggering. Dempsey was startled out of his mirth and shot the man a look. That look. The man moved back to the bar and kept his head down; he wanted to keep it attached to his shoulders. After that there was no chance that anyone in that Stoneybatter pub would bother him that day.

The glass was empty and Jack had a brilliant idea. The hip flask! Even if the barman saw him, he wasn't paid enough to go over and complain that the big man in the corner was subverting the very basic premise that every public house is based on. It wasn't a money issue for Dempsey, it was that he just didn't want to move from that little alcove and spoil the moment. He also thought that for the first time that day he was beating the system. It was pathetic, but the Gobshite could always convince Jack Dempsey of the most awful shite. He sniggered to himself as he emptied the contents of the hip flask into the glass. It was him, the Gobshite, and the drink. In that moment it seemed to work perfectly.

The phone in his pocket wobbled and he knew that it would be about work, but he couldn't think about that right now. The thing wouldn't stop so he dipped into his pocket to find it, switch it off and at that the vibrating stopped. There was a missed call and it was from someone that he would give the time of day to any day that was in it.

Jimmy Brennan! One of the old crew. He had settled down in Bray years ago, recalled Jack. Jimmy must have wanted something, but that wasn't a problem. Despite the whiskey, Jack was somehow able to touch the correct part of the screen and the thing called Brennan back.

"Howya?" roared Jack.

"Mighty big fella. Mighty! Look, between the jigs and the reels. I was down the country and now I'm up in town. I'm in a session here in the Ashling Hotel. Bit of party here. Me and two fine things. Foreign. Jaysus! Long story. You about?"

Dempsey and the Gobshite knew EXACTLY what Brennan was on about.

"On me way, Mr Brennan. On me way."

"Mighty!" The voice on the other end of the phone was delighted.

Jack's basic plan was probably all that he could manage at that point. He walked out of Walsh's and turned right towards the Centra. There was a bus stop there, but he wasn't a bus fella. Dempsey knew that Tommy the taxi driver worked that end of the town. Then in an instant the shame hit him, it was the first setback that the Gobshite had suffered all day. He didn't want Tommy seeing him like that. Tommy went to the meetings too, after all. Those fucking meetings! He thought that he might have a card in his wallet, another taxi firm. His brain was trying to process things through the whiskey.

Then he spotted a yellow bubble on the top of a four door saloon. He simply walked out in front of the taxi and the front of the car lunged down as the driver hit the anchors. In an instant Dempsey was in the taxi. The driver was about to give out when he saw what was sitting beside him. A large shaven headed man with fine scar tissue lining through his eyebrows. It was clear that this passenger was no stranger to fighting. A twenty euro note was dropped beside the handbrake.

"Ashling Hotel. Keep the change."

Dempsey's words had the magical effect of propelling the car forward. Even better the driver didn't utter a word. Jack's brain, full of whiskey and the chatter from the Gobshite, didn't stop to wonder why Jimmy Bee might have been at that spot. It didn't matter. Nothing much mattered at that point except the next drink, and maybe one of the ladies keeping his old comrade company. Dempsey didn't say a word to the driver as he got out at Parkgate Street and walked into the hotel.

He could hear Brennan laughing. No one else let rip like that, thought Jack. No one. Little Jimmy Brennan was sitting in a large sofa with two young women as book ends. They were both very pretty, very blonde and dressed for a night out even at that time of day. Brennan saw his old buddy and was utterly delighted. It was something of a struggle for Brennan to get out of the deep sofa. Jack waved away the effort as unnecessary and Jimmy relaxed back between the two Latvians.

"Well this is a fine day!" said Brennan.

"Mr Dempsey, may I introduce Anna and Katya…"

They both lithely raised themselves from the sofa and shook the big Dubliner by the hand with a certain amiable formality. Each of them planted a peck on Jack's cheek. Anyone walking past would not have noticed anything out of the ordinary, but each of the girls locked eye contact with Dempsey. He knew that the look meant: 'a blow job, no condom, swallow, one hundred euro'. Jack was sure to take them up on their kind offer. He was, after all, a sucker for a bargain. All that Jack wanted to know was which one Jimmy had decided to rent out for the day. Dempsey was happy either way, they were both lookers. They didn't have the demeanour of anguished trafficked amateurs either. There were too many of them on the game in Temple Bar. However, these two were the real deal.

It was only then that Jack fully noticed just how much weight Jimmy had lost.

"You back in the gym, Mr Brennan?"

"Ah you could say that Jack. Fighting fit!" Jimmy was his cheerful self as ever.

Almost as if the ladies realised that there needed to be a chat between the two men, they both temporarily absented themselves to powder their noses. Jack leaned forward in the chair to ask Brennan which one he wanted for himself.

Dempsey didn't notice the waiter standing for his order until the windows came in and blew him back over the couch facing the one Jimmy Brennan was sitting on. After the bang there was silence. A horrible silence for an eternity of perhaps thirty seconds, at most a minute. A very long minute indeed.

Then the screaming started to pierce the hissing in Jack's ears. Jack raised himself from the thick pile carpet and realised that he was sober. The first sign of trouble and the Gobshite had fucked off. Typical.

He got up on all fours and checked on Brennan. The couch that he couldn't get out of had saved him from the shower of glass.

"Jimmy? Jimmy? You grand?" Jack gave his buddy a shake on the shoulder.

After an age Brennan responded. "What the fuck was…"

Jack then knew Jimmy was sound. "Look you stay here Jimmy boy. I'll be back. You're grand here. OK?"

"Sound man Jack…" Brennan seemed dazed, but otherwise OK.

At around five foot two, being collapsed into that huge sofa had worked out well for the little Corkman.

Jack got to his feet and walked out onto the street to his right he could see smoke reaching up into the afternoon sky. One thought flashed into Dempsey's head. "Heuston Station!" As he walked as fast as he could over to the bridge following the Luas lines he could already hear the screams of people and the wailing of sirens. In all of his years Seán Patrick Dempsey had never seen the aftermath of a bomb explosion. Finally he got to see up close and impersonal what a well-placed explosive device could do.

As he crossed the bridge his eye caught something on the ground. It was a human finger, the fingernail was painted. This had been an intact living woman a few minutes ago. In the centre of the road and strewn across the Luas tracks were some shining red entrails oozing blood. He knew instantly that these too had been part of a person. Big Jack Dempsey staggered back and launched the contents of his stomach over the road. The daycent fella in his head waited for him to stop retching. "Not so tough now are we?" was the whisper.

Jack shook his head quickly like he was back in the ring trying to shake off the effects of a good dig. He was there and he had to help and so he walked towards where the Luas stop had been. Dempsey had every intention of giving help until he got nearer to the where the explosion had taken place. There would be injured people there. He ransacked his memory for a First Aid course that he had been on as part of the security course that he had been required to take.

Where there had been a Luas train full of people there was tangled and wreckage and just… meat. Dempsey couldn't take another step towards the scene. He just couldn't. His legs would not cooperate. The screams were now at head splitting levels, some people must have been alive in there, but he couldn't do it. He turned and walked away back towards Jimmy Brennan as quickly as he could. If he helped Jimmy then he could still be a good guy. An ambulance roared past him as he stepped across the bridge back onto the north side of the Liffey.

Gareth Scully had the largest office in the building. When he became minister he'd checked. Just in case. A left wing blogger had submitted a freedom of information request and had made hay with the amount that the office redecoration had cost to be fitted out to Scully's precise specifications.

"Yes, yes, I fully sympathise." The lip curled again. He couldn't help it.

"Yes, yes, fully sympathetic, but the law is the law. They will be in Lagos tomorrow. What? The child? Yes, the eldest child is disabled. That is in the file. Yes. Don't they have wheelchairs in Africa? Hello? Hello?" Scully was slightly flustered that someone would have the temerity to hang up the phone on HIM! THE MINISTER! Nonetheless it was a satisfactory piece of work. Operation Vigilant had seen three hundred illegal immigrants, mainly Nigerian, rounded up across the country. His new fast track scheme would have them back in Nigeria or wherever within two weeks of arrest. The civil liberties lot were squealing, but legal representation and a Legal Aid fee had kept the lawyers onside. There was a knock on the door.

"Yes."

The door opened. It was his PA, Niamh Murphy. A fine looking woman of indeterminate age, perhaps a very well preserved early forties. Slim with short dark hair. Her nose was too big for her to be considered classically attractive. She was always very prim at work. Hardly a hint of a heel. Usually trouser suits. Small steel rimmed glasses. She looked what she was: A hyper efficient woman who seemed to live at her work. She was unmarried; that was for sure. She had been in the Department since her early twenties and had read for a degree in Public Administration by attending evening classes. She was now spending her evenings and weekends reading for a degree in Psychology with the British Open University.

"Sorry Minister," she almost whispered. She wasn't a loud woman, but this whispering was accompanied by an ashen face. Even Scully noticed.

"What is it, Niamh?"

She gathered herself.

"Minister…" she paused. "Minister, there have been three explosions on the Luas. Connolly Station, Jervis and Heuston."

Scully was rooted to the spot. He heard and understood, but didn't know what to do. There was a whole lot to be done. He had taken part in major incident exercises in the past. These drills helped to test the readiness of the police, the defence forces, civil defence, and the health authorities. The exercise scenario always looked at some major incident that caused mass casualties.

Now this was real. It was no exercise. People were dead. Lots of people.

"Minister? I said…."

"YES!" Niamh Murphy jumped back slightly then stiffened in anger.

"Are there any causality figures?"

"Minister. All we know so far. Three explosions. Multiple causalities…"

"When?"

"About twenty minutes ago, Minister. The bombs went off almost at the same time."

"Get me Keegan."

"The Commissioner?"

"YES!"

"Minister, he'll be…"

"Get me him NOW!" She turned and started out of the office when he called her back.

"Get me the Taoiseach as well, but Keegan first."

"Yes, Minister." The door closed and Scully stared at the picture on the wall of himself in Brussels with the EU Justice Ministers.

He suddenly felt very alone and very afraid.

Garda Tony O'Gorman was just walking towards Store Street Station to start his shift when he was blown off his feet. A keen GAA player, he'd had plenty of practice in being knocked off his feet, but this was of another magnitude.

The twenty-six year old from Galway lay on the ground next to the Busáras Luas stop for an eternity as he tried to grasp what had happened. It didn't help that he wasn't able to hear a thing, except for the hissing noise in his ears. Pat Walsh, from the same shift, was first out from inside of Store Street Station. He saw his mate on the floor and went to him straight away. The training made certain things automatic and every Guard out of Templemore was a trained First Aider. Fortunately, despite his almost complete loss of hearing Tony O'Gorman was alert, but his speech was slurred. Walsh couldn't see any blood or major deformity. The man from Galway had been lucky; whatever it was that had caused that bang outside. By the time he was helping O'Gorman to his feet there was a mad rush out the door by a posse of uniformed Guards, the next shift that had been getting briefed.

There no real plan, just a cavalry charge over to the scene of the blast. You didn't need to be CSI bloody Store Street to work this one out, thought Mick Boyle as he charged across to a pile of crumpled wreckage that had, until about five minutes before, been at the terminus at Connolly Station.

When Boyle got there, nothing prepared him for what he initially saw. At first he thought what he saw strewn about the ground was someone's shopping. It was a stupid thought. He was looking at body parts and what had been part of living human beings seconds before the device detonated. They later found out that another bomb had also gone off on the concourse of Connolly Station itself.

Boyle saw one man, his own head bleeding, going to the assistance of a badly injured man who was screaming out like he had never heard any living thing before. Boyle froze and was suddenly no use at all; he wasn't protecting or serving anyone. In that moment he was yanked back into the world of duty by Liam Murphy, a big Sergeant from Cork and one of the best on the shift. Mick Boyle stooped down to try and assist an injured person. He grabbed their arm by the wrist, but it simply slipped out of the sleeve. He stepped back, looking at the limb and then dropped it like he had just realised he had extricated a poisonous snake from a laundry basket. He started to shake uncontrollably.

"Boyle! Boyle!"

Murphy's Cork brogue snapped him back to the present.

"Sergeant…" said Boyle.

"Get over to Inspector Smyth there. He's incident Commander. Get yourself a task," said Murphy.

"OK…"

It looked as if the Luas carriage at Jervis had been attacked by an angry giant armed with a huge chainsaw who had then stomped off in a rage. This giant had ripped open the roof too so as to get inside at the soft squishy humans. When Fire Brigade Paramedic John Kerrins arrived, only one question occurred to him. "What kind of bastard could do this?"

As per usual, Ambassador Chuck Brannigan was drinking in the middle of the day. Although he was exhilarated by being a Station Chief, Jerome Pelfrey detested this part of his new position. He was obliged, in some ways at least, to keep the Ambassador in the loop, but he tried to keep these interactions to an absolute minimum.

Pelfrey had spent the morning digesting an 'eyes only' communique from Langley. He had also been looking at a real time feed from a drone hovering with lethal intent over a compound in Northern Waziristan. He was patched through to the Operations Room and heard Herb Stricker's voice in Langley authorise the operator outside Las Vegas.

"Arm…take the shot."

The screen was then blotted out with a flash and all that could be seen was the cloud from the explosion. When the smoke cleared, the building inside the compound was gone. There was very little chance that anyone inside that structure could have survived. The missile had been launched with Presidential authority. This was how Uncle Sam preferred to deal with any clear and present danger in the 21st century. Pelfrey joked to himself that while his utterly useless Ambassador believed in hellfire and damnation, the Bonesman believed in Hellfire missiles and damn the rest of it!

He would have been happy to leave Brannigan completely out of the loop, especially for plausible deniability, his favourite phrase. However, Ambassador Brannigan had to know of the developments in Dublin. At least to some extent. He entered the Ambassador's office without knocking. He was probably the only person in the building who could do that. It was clear that Brannigan had started early. He might have found Jesus, but he hadn't parted company with Jack Daniels, thought Pelfrey.

Jerome Pelfrey was born into Yale and the CIA. He became a Bonesman like his dad. A blueblood. He was a bookish type, physically slight, but imbued with an inborn sense of exceptionalism. The CIA analyst from Philadelphia had spent his whole working life at Langley. Although Pelfrey was genetically engineered to thrive inside the Beltway he knew that his lack of field experience was a problem. An entire concerto of strings had been yanked to get this posting and this was his chance to shine. He had to go back to Langley with that on his resume. Major favours had been called in to get him Station Chief without the appropriate field experience. He has his eye on the top job in Langley. He considered it his birth right.

Pelfrey's paternal uncle was a semi-mythical hero in the Company. Herbert Walker Pelfrey was in the first intake from the Office of Strategic Services (OSS), the forerunner of the CIA. His work in Berlin in the 1950s then later on in Italy was the stuff of legend. Pelfrey's assets were still yielding product even after he had passed away. The guys at the top of the tree in Langley were wet behind the ears when he was running agents across Europe both sides of the Iron Curtain.

When Jerome Pelfrey first joined the agency his surname had been a huge plus, but in time it had become a burden. He had a hell of an act to follow and that was why he was in Ireland.

"Oh say can you see?" Jerome Pelfrey could hear Brannigan down the long corridor as he approached the Ambassador's office. He had started drinking particularly early on, thought the CIA man. Or maybe he hadn't started early but had carried on from the night before.

"Oh say can you see a dead Eye-rack-eeh?"

Brannigan chuckled at his own joke. The CIA Station Chief entered without knocking. Pelfrey tried to conceal his contempt as he started to brief the Ambassador in the slow sleep-inducing monotone that was the only way that the man from Langley could speak. He suddenly had Brannigan's attention:

"Any Americans?" asked the clinically rotund Texan.

"Not that we know of, sir. The Irish cops haven't got a full list yet. Seems mainly locals and some foreign workers; Poles, Latvians, that kinda thing."

"Works for me!"

Pelfrey should have brought him up to speed on other matters. Like the Sig Int (Signals Intelligence) traffic being provided by the National Security Agency (NSA) in Fort Meade, Maryland. However, he exercised his judgement on the matter. He didn't tell the Ambassador the details on the ISIS unit that were now established and fully operational in Dublin. Pelfrey could have told his Ambassador that the Jihadis in Dublin were getting a lot of text messages from Aleppo in Syria and some from Peshawar in Pakistan. All he said was that the NSA and Langley were on it and that there would be no surprises.

"Collateral damage should be minimal Mister Ambassador, with a great prize at the end."

He probably should, in adherence to the protocols, have appraised Chuck Brannigan further. However, he thought better of it. One, he didn't really NEED to know; and two, given his infatuation with Jack Daniels, Pelfrey simply didn't trust Brannigan. If this operation went south then that would be the end of the road for Pelfrey's advancement in the Company. He simply finished the briefing by saying to the Ambassador: "It's all in hand. Going to plan. There's a statement being prepared for you by political. It will be released within the hour."

"I should see that first," growled Brannigan. He didn't like the idea that he was a complete stuffed shirt.

"They're top class professionals, Mister Ambassador, it will be fine."

Pelfrey's use of the term 'Mr Ambassador' was laced with derision and he left it there to sting Brannigan. The Texan was reduced to ad hominem jibes.

"Anything else from your tight Ivy League ass Pelfrey?"

"I'll keep you fully apprised of all relevant developments, Mister Ambassador."

The politeness of Pelfrey in the face of personal insults just served to further put Brannigan in his place and they both knew it. As Pelfrey travelled back towards his office he knew that he was treading a fine line with his Ambassador. He had to be in the loop as the representative of Uncle Sam in Ireland, but he wasn't an intelligence professional.

Chuck Brannigan was a serious Texan business operator. He was the major Democrat campaign contributor from the Lone Star state. When his guy got into the big chair in the Oval Office he was asked what he wanted. Chuck Brannigan loved his Irish roots. And how! He was the archetypal self-made American billionaire from central casting. Physically, he was a very big man, loud and brash. He could fill a room in more ways than one.

Brannigan had spent decades in a bottle, but had finally found Jesus when he was fifty. Like the rest of his newly-found evangelical congregation in Austin, he didn't believe in evolution. He did believe though, in the manifest destiny of Americans, preferably Texans, to rule the planet. To do that Uncle Sam needed to control as much oil as possible.

He had never gone to college and could be rather defensive about it at times. This was especially the case when an Ivy League tight ass like Pelfrey started using pussy words that he'd never heard of. The little prick did it deliberately, thought Brannigan. Despite that, Chuck loved the idea that he was the boss of Ivy League types with bits of paper from Harvard and Yale. He did not trust the guy from Langley.

When he had come to Ireland as US Ambassador he had miraculously decided that Jesus and the sauce could co-exist. Wife number three was with the program so there was no one to question his behaviour. His Montana gal was of good Irish stock and she was along for the ride. They had met at the last Democrat convention. Her father was a registered Republican and she had gone the other way to spite him. Mary was a spirited one and she loved being Madam Ambassador. So basically he could do what he wanted on a daily basis as long as he didn't make a public asshole of himself. State thought he was doing OK and his guy was now in the Oval Office via the Dealy Plaza route. Chuck Brannigan had never been happier.

Jack Dempsey stumbled back towards the Ashling Hotel like he had been on a three day bender, but he had never felt more sober in his life. The effects of the booze had vanished when he had chucked up all over a crime scene. A combination of Jameson's and concussion had propelled him towards the station, but he was no use there. He needed to check on Jimmy Brennan. He shouldn't have left him like that. That was a mistake, but Jack was good at them mistakes so he was.

Dempsey was shocked at the state of the hotel as he focussed on it. Every window was gone, but he should have known that. He was there when they came in. It was a bomb, thought Dempsey. A fucking bomb!

The foyer of the Aisling hotel was chaos. Some people were walking around like a bunch of drunks at closing time who had been splattered with tinned tomatoes. The thick pile carpet now crunched under his feet, the broken glass that had ripped through vulnerable flesh was everywhere underfoot like confetti from a bottling plant.

Dempsey was shocked at the state of the couch that Jimmy Brennan had been sitting on as he approached it from the back. It had been utterly lacerated and the little Corkman was very lucky that he was buried into the upholstery by the blast.

The unfortunate Brazilian waiter had shielded Jack from the worst of the blast as he had stooped over to take his order. He was still lying face down his white shirt now completely red. Nuno Da Silva was very still the way dead people were immobile. Jack was no stranger to sudden death happening right in front of him. He had seen it too many times.

Jimmy Brennan was back on the big couch that had undoubtedly saved his life. The little Corkman was dazed, but looked like he would be OK. He perked up when he saw Dempsey.

"Jaysus Jack!"

"Jimmy Bee. You well?"

"The best, Jack. Jaysus! Look at ye!"

Dempsey had no idea when Jimmy was referring to, but the little man gestured towards Jack's head.

"You're in a state Jack. Your head buddy."

It was only then that Jack started to be aware of the wetness down his back. The deceased Brazilian hadn't taken all of the flying glass into his back and a shard had hit Dempsey just above and behind his left ear. If it had been a larger fragment then the Dubliner might well have been lying down beside the 22 year old lad from Barcelos. Jack lightly fingered the part of his head that he couldn't see. In a moment he thought about finding a mirror, it was almost amusing. Dempsey felt OK, whatever it was it probably wouldn't kill him, he reckoned.

"I'm grand Jimmy. I've had worse in the Ring. You OK there yourself?"

"I'm dying, Jack," said the Corkman.

"Ah in your arse you are! Not a scratch on ye. Lucky fecker! "

"It's in me pancreas, big fella. They can't operate. They told me today when I was over in James's there. I wanted a shag with one of them foreign girls. Lovely. Aren't they? Did you see where they went?"

St James's Hospital was just one stop on the red line from Heuston Station. Suddenly the Aisling hotel made sense. Jack was still processing this information. He had known the Corkman since they had met up at a camp in Moyvane in North Kerry. That wasn't yesterday. Brennan was a top "blowey man" in them days. There wasn't anything he didn't know about explosives. In the midst of all of this carnage, Jimmy Brennan who didn't have a scratch on him was a dead man sitting in a couch.

"Jimmy…" this day had sucked all of the words out of Seán Patrick Dempsey. He couldn't make sense of any of it. Because at the end of the day, thought Jack, there was no sense, no order. It was all chaos.

"Six months, tops. Might be less though."

Jack just looked at him and now it all seemed very clear to Doctor Dempsey. Jimmy Brennan's face had that tight birdlike appearance. He had seen cancer before in several family members. It was a proper bastard of a disease.

"It's good to see you big fella," said Jimmy.

Dempsey looked up and around the foyer stood several yellow-jacketed paramedics attending to the most seriously injured. The screams seemed to be getting louder, but it was just that Jack's hearing was getting back to normal. Unknown to the ex-bomber there were trained personnel all over the city en route to where they were urgently needed.

In that moment Volunteer Seán Patrick Dempsey felt a stab of guilt that had been building up inside him for thirty years. It was a far worse feeling of remorse than anything that the Twelve Steps had been able to prise out of him. The truth was that Jack had never really wanted to make amends. He was lying to them sad faced bastards in AA like he was being interrogated by the Branch back in the old days. Still he wanted, somehow, to be the good guy. He used to be one of the good guys, he was sure of that. Jack Dempsey's head was beginning to clear and the idea seemed perfectly sensible to him.

"Jimmy. You're kipping in my gaff tonight. It's in town. Over in Temple bar. You can call Bray, tell them you're grand and you're stopping here."

Jimmy Brennan smiled at Jack's assumptions.

"Sure there's no one to call in Bray, young Jack. Herself fucked off six months ago."

"Ah. Sorry Jimmy...."

"Not a bother young fella, but you need to get that..."

As he said that Dempsey became aware of a presence beside him. It was a young woman, young enough to be his daughter. She reached up to inspect his head. She hadn't asked permission. It was that kind of day.

"Be still, please," said the paramedic.

She had short blonde hair in a ponytail. Jack pulled his head away instantly.

"I'm grand girl. There's hurt people here."

"Yes, you're one of them." She clearly took no shit from anyone, even the big bleeding house of a man in front of her.

"Sit down please. Here." She gestured to one of the big armchairs in the foyer. It was covered in glass fragments so she lifted the cushion and threw it on the floor. It was the day for improvisation. Jack complied and was suddenly looking at her Hi-Vis midriff. She seemed fascinated with the side of Jack's head.

"I'm grand..."

"Be still please. You've got a glass fragment in your head, it isn't too deep."

This was what Jimmy Brennan had been referring to, but Jack couldn't feel a thing. That was, until Aoife Watson's the little fingers started to prise out the shard of glass that was sticking out of Jack's head. Then it fucking hurt!

"Please be STILL." This little one wouldn't stand for any nonsense, thought Jack.

He sat still. When her hands stopped moving she spoke.

"A doctor will need to see this Mr…"

"Dempsey," said Jack.

"If you go out to the front there will be transport to one of the hospitals, I don't know which one you'll be going to, but…"

"Look, I feel grand."

She wasn't for taking any of this. "You've had a head injury. It's minor, but it will need looked at by a doctor. This came out of your head."

Her little latex covered fingers held a nasty glass fragment about two inches long.

"You were lucky, Mr Dempsey," said Aoife.

Jack felt he needed to bargain with her.

"If I promise to go myself to one like a good boy can I…"

At that point an elderly woman started to scream. Her husband who she had been cradling had lost consciousness and stopped breathing. Aoife Watson left her walking wounded casualty, leapt up and in one motion lifted the square plastic box she had been using as a stool to treat Jack Dempsey. Inside this tool box type container she had the devices that could save lives, but only if she got there quick enough.

Dempsey turned to Jimmy Brennan. "Come on buddy, let's get out of here."

"You've to go to hospital Jack."

"Ah, in me arse I am, Jimmy," said the big Dubliner, "I've had worse off the Branch."

"Jaysus."

"You good enough to walk Jimmy?"

"Fighting fit, big fella!" said the little Corkman.

"Grand. The town will be at a standstill because of this shite. Over the Ha'penny Bridge and we're nearly there."

"You're the man with the plan Mr Dempsey." Jimmy forced some cheerfulness.

"You didn't see those girleens Jack?"

Jack smiled to himself that his old Cork comrade was still lamenting his lost opportunity for a shag amid the carnage and the chaos. For Dempsey that showed an indomitable spirit rather than a callous disregard for suffering. The very day Jimmy Brennan had been told by a clinical team that he cancer in him was inoperable and would kill him within months, all he could think of was giving it to a couple of Latvian Bond girls.

"They were in the jacks when that thing went off. They'll be grand. I reckon they fucked off Jimmy. Working girls. No business in this butcher's shop."

"Jaysus Jack…"

The scene outside of the Ashling hotel sucked the breath out of Jimmy Brennan. There was a traffic jam of ambulances shunting into each other as they struggled to find a rectangle of unoccupied tarmac. The paramedics were loading people into the back of their vehicles and then leaving. It looked like chaos, but actually ambulances were being methodically filled with living causalities who needed to get to hospital, any hospital and the vehicles were heading off.

Jack gently tugged Jimmy by the sleeve of his jacket and steered him away from the scene. They walked left and headed down the Luas tracks towards Museum. They walked silently for a while and Jack appreciated that. For a big man he didn't have a large stride so there was little chance of him steaming ahead of little Jimmy Brennan. As they got to the Smithfield Luas stop Jack found himself outside Phoenix House for the second time that day. He wanted to say something to Jimmy about it, but he let it go.

The area outside the court building next to the little coffee kiosk was full of people who hadn't quite realised that there would be no more Luas activity that day. Jack could have told them, but he was on autopilot and still processing both what he had seen at Heuston Station and the news that Jimmy had given him. As he left Phoenix House behind him he considered that what he thought would have been THE event of the day had almost slipped his mind. Jimmy Brennan, always a chatty type, had been silent long enough.

"Jaysus Jack. The gobshites. Doing this all over the place today. Cunts!"

"What?" Jack didn't understand what Jimmy was on about.

"That wee ambulance girl told me. They didn't just hit Heuston.

There was one that went off at Jervis, Connolly as well. Fucking bastards," spat Jimmy.

Then Dempsey felt like he had taken one in the gut, a proper hook up into the solar plexus that stopped him in his tracks. Panic shot through him like electricity, encapsulated in one terrifying question that he needed answered right that second. Where was the wee fella? He rummaged for the phone in his pocket, but it wasn't there, wasn't where it should be. Dempsey's world stopped until he could find his phone. It wasn't there.

"What is it Jack? Lost something?"

Dempsey didn't answer him. Jack's big hands rummaged in each pocket until he slowed down and felt something hard inside his jacket. Slim, light and well designed, the iPhone was elusive to a panicked fumble by huge hands.

Dempsey got the device into his hand and took a breath. He touched the screen to bring up numbers and hit the one he wanted. It started to ring in his right ear. It rang only twice before it went to her voicemail. He hit the red button on the screen.

"Phones might be banjaxed, big fella…" Jimmy was trying to be helpful.

Jack stood motionless as his brain whirred, juggling and assessing various scenarios.

"Jack?"

"MINUTE!" It was a command to be silent.

Jimmy Brennan just stood there looking at Jack.

"OK Jimmy, look… Sorry buddy…"

"Ah stop it big fella. You're grand."

"Cheers Jimmy Bee." Jack had a grip of himself again.

"Look Jimmy I have to find out if my wee fella Pádraig is OK. I saw him this morning with his mother. He's probably grand, but she isn't answering her phone."

Jimmy Brennan read his mind and immediately knew that Jack's offer of hospitality to him was now a problem. The last thing the Corkman wanted to be to Jack Dempsey was a problem.

"Look Jack. I'm grand. Not a bother. I'm off to a hotel that hasn't been totalled by these gobshites. I'll try the Gresham and Jury's in Parnell Street, or whatever they call it now."

Dempsey was more grateful than he could express for Brennan absenting himself from his mental 'to do' list. In the instant after he felt gratitude he also suffered some guilt. Jimmy Bee the mind reader was on a roll.

"Don't you think any more of it, big fella. Look, if you need anything phone me. I'm still on active service!"

"Thanks Jimmy. Good luck."

Jack watched as the terminally ill little Corkman walked along the Luas lines towards the centre of town. He did so with as purposeful a stride as he had when he had walked up that muddy farm lane in North Kerry more than forty years ago.

He tried her phone again and it was still going straight to voicemail. Useless bitch. Although he fought it, the panic was starting to rise up in him. Was the wee fella OK? He listened to the sound of ambulance sirens and it seemed to him that they were bouncing off the walls of buildings on both sides of the Liffey. Then he did something that did not come naturally at all to Jack Dempsey, even after all these years.

He went to seek help from a policeman.

Jack stretched out and lengthened his stride as he headed for somewhere that he knew the inside of very well from his younger days. The Bridewell Barracks was the first place he had ever been taken to when he was arrested for Army business. As usual they got nothing out of him and he'd had a worse going over in the ring, but still, going to that place on a voluntary basis just made this day more mental.

He followed the Luas lines up to the Four Courts and he thought that he might catch up with Jimmy Bee, but there was no sign of him on the empty tracks. On Chancery Street any pretence at traffic management was gone. There were Garda vehicles all over the place, like they had just been abandoned. He saw one van with the driver's door lying open. Someone had got out from behind the wheel in a hurry.

His plan was to go into the barracks and ask if there was any list of the… If there was any list of the people hurt today. It really wasn't that much of a plan, but it was better than no plan. He was ninety-nine per cent certain that the wee fella wasn't within twenty miles of any of this shite. All it would have taken would be for that daft cow to answer her phone and…

Her landline! Yeah. She had a landline! The mobiles might be down with towers and all that craic, but what about landlines? They're underground cables, they'll be sound, thought Jack. What was her landline number? Did he ever have it? He had seen her phone on the breakfast bar in her kitchen. A hands-free yoke. Did he phone it once when her mobile was off? If he had he had never saved it to his phone. Fuck it! Back to Plan A.

He weaved through the triple parked Garda vehicles and a midget in a yellow hi-vis vest caught him by the arm.

"Can I help you?"

She was female and even shorter than the paramedic in the Ashling.

"I'm – I'm wanting to find out about my son. He might have been on…"

"There isn't a casualty list as yet." She cut across him. "Well, not as far as I know. It's very early for that. We're still getting people to hospital. Which Luas was he on? Your son?" she asked.

Suddenly Jack felt ridiculous and in the way in the midst of all of this chaos.

"I don't know. He might not. I think he got on the Luas at Smithfield."

"Going to Tallaght or into town?" she asked.

"I don't know," he admitted.

At this stage Garda Róisín Lynch realised that her time might be better employed elsewhere, although the big middle aged man standing in front of her did seem utterly genuine.

"Look. I'm sure he wasn't anywhere near any of this. But check the media later. We'll have a helpline number up. I'm sure your son is grand." Róisín knew she wasn't talking to a skanger. "Thanks, thanks for your time."

Jack felt simultaneously grateful and totally in the way. He couldn't think of anything to do but walk back to his apartment. He walked past the Four Courts and down onto the Quays. It was traffic chaos like he had never seen in all of his days in Dublin. Ambulances shouted abuse with their sirens to get past gridlocked vehicles of every make and shape. On the pavement there was a football crowd type density to the throng, but the faces had terror and confusion painted on them.

In the midst of all this, all he could think of was the wee fella.

As he walked over the Ha'penny Bridge in Dublin that homeless fella was still there begging. He had the look of a pure bred North Side skanger with hardly a tooth in his head. He looked about fifty, which probably meant that he was around thirty with most of his life already past him. Jack had noticed him the day before. Right then as the sirens screamed all over Dublin he felt it was rather comforting that in the midst of all of this chaos in Dublin yer man was still in business.

Temple Bar was designed for tourists to wonder around looking for new ways to lose their money. This place was an unknown quantity for the visitor, but somewhere they had been told to go to. In the past fifteen years Jack had made this corner of Dublin his very own parish. He knew the faces and stories in many of the bars, shops and restaurants. There was a transient workforce in the place for sure, but there were also some established heads in the place that had been doing business when he had first set up his firm. He would be stuck to think of a nationality that hadn't made this part of his city their own.

He convinced himself that his kid was OK, that he was worrying about nothing and that he could go back to being sensible about things. That was what the Gobshite was saying right at that moment. He was back.

Jack turned the key in the door and he was happy to be back in a space that only he controlled. He slumped onto the couch facing the wall with the large flat screen TV on it. The best idea in the place was a conservatory type roof in that part of the gaff that allowed a lot of light in. The wall with the TV on had a sort of mural depicting New York life. The city that never sleeps and all that shite. If he wasn't just renting the place then he would have painted over it on Day One.

He reached over to the other end of the couch to get the remote. The Gobshite told him to chill the fuck out and get something strong into him. He rummaged for the hip flask in his jacket pocket, but he had emptied the contents into him in Walsh's before Jimmy Bee had phoned him. There wasn't another drop in the place.

Roscommon John at AA had told him to be very careful about that, especially as he lived alone. He has a daycent enough cratur, but the Gobshite couldn't stand him. Yer man was from Ballyforan on the River Suck and Jack thought that being reared there probably meant that alcoholism was unavoidable. Still, he had guided him through the Twelve Steps and put up with a lot of the big Dubliner's shite with patience and good grace. Crucially he never believed any of Jack's lies about the drink, chiefly because he had told all of those lies himself again and again. Just having the soft sound of that Roscommon voice in his head drowned out the Gobshite and Jack pushed the button on the remote.

The plasma screen came to life and it was on RTE One. All normal programming had been binned and the news room was giving by the minute updates. Jimmy Bee's info had been pretty much spot on as he had told it to Jack. There had been almost simultaneous explosions on Luas trains at Connolly, Jervis and Heuston Stations. There had also been an explosion on the concourse at Connolly. The confirmed death toll so far was seventy-eight, but it was expected to rise. Across the bottom of the screen there was a help line number.

There was no landline in the apartment. He checked the mobile without much hope of a signal. He tried her number again and it was still going to voicemail. Now, Jack decided, that was deliberate! He phoned the office and it rang a fair few times before he heard Dicey's distinctive voice.

"Jack! You OK?"

"Grand not a bother."

"I was worried about you," Mary Reilly's voice betrayed genuine relief as she spoke to her boss of ten years.

"I'm grand," said Jack.

"Were you near any of…"

Before she could ask the rest of the question Jack gave her the answer.

"Near enough, but I'm grand Dicey. Anything I need to know at your end?"

"No. Stan called in. He got to a payphone. All the mobiles were down. Too much traffic with this shite."

"Is he OK Dicey?"

"Yeah. Not a bother. Has that job under control. His usual Superman act," joked Mary.

"Yeah. I could use a few more like him."

"That's a fact."

She liked that Jack had nicknamed her that from the first day. He knew her uncle. He'd had been in Portlaoise with him. Usually having such Provo family associations did you no employment favours in the Republic of Ireland, but for Jack it was a top class character reference. He hadn't been wrong. For ten years she had run his office with a calm brilliance. It had always nagged at him that she was too good for what she was doing and that he wasn't paying her enough. One day she would get a decent job offer and she would be gone, thought Dempsey. Until that day arrived he was very fortunate indeed.

Then he had an idea.

"Look I need you to do something for me Dicey. It's about the day that's in it," said Jack, rather hesitantly.

"Ah' course ah will. What is it?"

"It's my wee fella. Pádraig…"

"Oh Jaysus! Was he on the Luas?" Mary Reilly shrieked at the thought of it.

"Look, he probably wasn't, but his mother has her phone off and…well…"

"Put your mind at rest?"

"Exactamundo." With Mary Reilly in his corner, Jack was beginning to feel better.

"I'll try that helpline number they've set up. If I get anything then I'll get back to ya. Now you've had a day of it. How was court?"

"Usual shite, different judge."

"Sorry Jack."

"If all the mothers were like you the lawyers would be outta business girleen."

Mary Reilly was rearing a son on her own. He was now a feisty eleven year old, but although the father was a local guy he had played little part in the life of his son. Even though this was the case the door had remained open to him to step in and be a dad. It was the opposite of his own situation, thought Dempsey.

"Thanks Jack. I was hoping you'd get a result. I know you dote on the wee fella. Look I'll get onto this information line and I'll call you right back. The mobiles should be OK now. "

Dempsey touched the off button on the screen and Mary Reilly's voice was gone.

Jack worked the remote again and the volume bar crossed the bottom of the screen. In the time he had been talking to Dicey the official death toll had risen. It was now eighty-six confirmed killed. The talking head in Donnybrook said that the Guards reckoned that at least three, possibly four suicide bombers had detonated devices. Given the nature of the attacks Islamic extremists were suspected, although no group had yet claimed responsibility.

Jack's smartphone buzzed. It was the office landline. He fumbled to touch the screen properly. It was Dicey. Dempsey's heart was racing as he answered it.

"Yeah?"

"Sorry Jack, I'm a Muppet. I forgot to ask you the wee fella's full name and all that craic."

Dempsey's anxiety subsided and he felt himself getting angry, but he pushed that away. He should have made sure she knew that information and she was trying her best.

"Pádraig Duffy. Date of Birth 8/11/2013," said, Jack, not commenting on the fact that his son wasn't a Dempsey in name.

"Thanks Jack. I'm on it."

"Thanks pet." Jack was genuinely grateful that Mary would do this for him.

For the first time today he started to relax slightly. He tried to tune out the sound from the TV, but that didn't work, especially when they said the Justice Minister Gareth Scully would be on in a few minutes. On hearing that news Jack hit the power button on the remote. He slid down onto his side and closed his eyes.

The bath and the vodka had worked a treat for Pauline. She was better now, mended. Sitting on the bed, she looked at herself in the wardrobe mirrors. Her hair was still gleaming wet from the bath and she stretched out a leg, pointing her toes downwards. Not bad kiddo, she thought. Not bad at all.

She was in a short black satin-effect kimono with a big angry dragon on the back. Two weeks ago she had to go to the door and sign for something from Amazon and the lad nearly fainted. Yeah, not bad Pauline girl, she thought.

However, it was time to go back to being a mammy, so she powered up her iPhone and called Siobhán. Her number went straight to voicemail, which wasn't like her. The iPhone was going mental with Twitter notifications, a lot more than usual. She touched the screen and #PrayForDublin was trending worldwide. It took a long minute for her to get the gist of what had happened and then the feel-good vibe from the bath and the vodka evaporated in an instant of cold terror and maternal panic.

She called Siobhán again. It went to voicemail immediately. Again. Fuck it! She would be at her Ma's with the wee fella, thought Pauline. Chill, would ya? Her Ma had a landline, but she had no notion what it would be. It was over in Springfield. She could be over there in minutes and the little man would be at the X-Boxing.

She sprang off the bed and quickly dressed. Sensible knickers, jogging bottoms, a tee shirt and a hoodie she got from that big rugby lad who was at UCD. She slid the wardrobe door to one side and grabbed a pair of runners from the shelving unit inside.

Pauline tried a couple of taxi numbers in her phone, but there was no answer at either of them. She looked out of the bedroom window and saw that her neighbour's car was there. Ordinarily she wouldn't have dreamed of asking him, but this was an emergency. She could have walked, but the panic was rising in her; she needed to see her son and Siobhán's phone was off. And that wasn't like her. He was glued to that feckin' phone. Always on it. Tweeting, Instagram, Facebook.

She grabbed her phone and the bag that she had taken to court, a small black leather thing. To say that it didn't go with her 'outfit' was an understatement. She closed her door behind her and the evening air, surprisingly warm for September, hit her. The effect of the vodka on an empty stomach made her slightly unsteady for a few seconds.

She rang the bell and his wife came to the door. She was a decent sort, not the brightest, but she wouldn't do you a bad turn.

"Hello Kate, is Dermot there? I need a favour," said Pauline.

The woman was slightly startled to see Pauline Duffy at her door and in that instant she knew that that Kate knew about what had happened last year. Pauline detected a flicker of resentment in Kate Murphy's tired face, but it was gone in an instant.

"I'll get him" she said, but there was no invite into the house.

Yeah, she knows, thought Pauline. Fucking hell. He came out to the door and looked simultaneously disorientated, excited and unsettled.

"Ah! Pauline," was all he could muster.

He was even fatter than she had imagined. Pauline realised that she hadn't seen him about the place in months, just his taxi parked up.

"Dermot, I need to get over to Springfield, bit of an emergency."

"Yeah, grand, I'll get me keys," replied a very flustered Dermot.

After he had acknowledged that he had the correct address on the other side of Tallaght, Dermot didn't say a word to her on the way over to Siobhán's Ma's house, which was weird in itself. She was convinced that his wife now knew what had happened. OK, it was just that once, but don't shit where you eat.

It seemed to take an age to cross Tallaght in uncomfortable silence. He wouldn't take anything for the fare and the taxi was gone as soon as she closed the door outside Mrs Delaney's front door. Just before she rang the bell she was convinced she could hear his raucous laugh. Mary Delaney answered the door, a sixty year old bundle of energy in constant organising mode.

"Pauline! Come in girl," she said and walked into the kitchen, which was clean as an army barracks with nothing out of place.

Before she could ask questions Pauline Duffy was hit with Mary' Delaney's interrogatives.

"You heard from our Siobhán today?"

In that moment the anxiety circuits inside Pauline Duffy's head started to short in a blizzard of guilty sparks.

"I saw her this morning at Smithfield, Mary."

The sound of an explosion coming the living room made Pauline jump. Mary Delaney raised her voice to a decibel level that her visitor didn't think the woman of the house could muster.

"KEVIN!" shouted Mary.

"Sorry Granny," said the little voice from the living room.

"That feckin' X-Box. Glued to it he is. Jaysus. Sure I haven't had the telly on all day because of it. Still, it's good to have a break from it. In any case that Jeremy Kyle is an awful bollox so he is," observed Mary.

It was then that Pauline Duffy realised that this happy tubby Tallaght granny had no idea what had happened in town that day. When she had woken up this morning Pauline had been stressed about going to court, but at least she'd had some idea of what to say. Now she knew stuff that she had to tell this warm, welcoming woman, but she had no idea of how to do that. No idea at all.

"Where did you see our Siobhán?" asked Mary as she organised a pot of tea.

She didn't even ask Pauline if she wanted a cuppa. Tae was non-negotiable in Mary Delaney's abode.

"She's a law unto herself that one. Different generation. Would she not meet some nice fella? That's what I'm always sayin' to her," burbled Mary as the tea was conjured up.

Pauline was OK about letting her go on. It gave her time to think about how she was going to share this information that might send her off the worry scale too.

"Mary…"

"Oh she's had plenty interested in her. There was a nice Donegal lad, living down here, school teacher and all. Oh no, not good enough for her. Then there was this bucko from Clondalkin. Now I DIDN'T like the look of that character. You know…"

Pauline had to stop this and cut across her. She stepped off one of the stools at the breakfast bar and moved towards Siobhán's mother. Kevin had forgotten his Grannie's rebuke. The sound of digital carnage was getting louder from the living room.

"Mary, did you not…"

"Lovely Donegal fella, gentleman he was. Then a right skanger from Clondalkin. Tattoos on him."

"Mary, sorry…"

"What is it pet? Is that tea strong enough?"

"You haven't heard the news from town today?"

"News? Ah sure I'm up to me eyes here. The state of this house, you'll have to avert your eyes."

"Mary, there's been bombs in the town. On the Luas," blurted out Pauline, knowing that there was no way she could have done this any better.

"Jaysus!" Mary Delaney stepped back unsteadily. The news had hit her like a shock wave from one of the bombs had finally reached her pleasant little home in Springfield, Tallaght.

"Mother of God…"

Then she moved with a speed and purpose that gave Pauline Duffy a start.

In an instant Mary Delaney was across to the far end of the kitchen where a cordless phone was sitting it its charging dock. Pauline felt powerless and prescient as she knew that Siobhán's mother was going to try what she had tried herself just before she had rang the doorbell.

"She's not answering her phone," said Mary with the unmistakable sense of maternal dread that her child was missing.

"I saw her at Smithfield this morning Mary. She's got my Pádraig with her, she was giving me a break. She said she'd bring him here to play X…" Pauline Duffy's composure left her as she heard herself sketch out the facts and collapse into tears.

Mrs Delaney's response was as assured as when she had dashed for the phone. Pauline found herself enveloped in a big hug by the mother of her bestie. The embrace worked and Pauline was able to start to piece things together.

"She should have been home by now. Here. Long ago."

Mary Delaney nodded in agreement. Pauline brought her iPhone from the deep pocket of her grubby grey hoodie. There was a signal and she had some data left from the last top-up. Twitter soon told her that there was an information line.

"Mary, there's a number we can call."

She dialled in the numbers as Pauline called them out. And then Mary Bernadette Delaney, mother of Kevin and Siobhán, listened to the automated voice and offered a prayer to the Sacred Heart for the safe return of her daughter and the child of the young woman handing her a cup of tea.

Gareth Scully was in make up at RTE and enjoying the close proximity of the young woman applying the industrial grade slap to his large forehead. The make-up room was very narrow with mirrors on both walls and seats for the victims virtually back to back. The girls had to weave and slither as they applied the face paint.

The breathless researcher girly had told him before he had entered the room that he would be interviewed on the events of the day and that he was scheduled to appear later in a special discussion on the bombings. Scully was fully aware that he was the most important voice of the government on a day like today, and that fool in the Taoiseach's chair knew it too!

No one had ever had the top job in the Republic of Ireland who wasn't from one of the big two parties. In normal times there was no chance of the leader of a minor party leading the country, but these weren't normal times. This nation needed a new direction, thought Scully, and history had given him the task.

"There, all done Minister," said the pretty little thing. Scully gave her his best smile.

The interview went as planned and Scully avoided anything that suggested that these outrages made the passage of his controversial bill through the Dáil a foregone conclusion now. It was his best performance so far. He was statesmanlike, yes, very much so. That cretin from Kerry must be curled up in a ball. There were only two reasons that he was Taoiseach and everyone knew it. One, the McCarthy brand was Fianna Fáil royalty in Kerry. The Taoiseach's grandfather, Con McCarthy, had died in a particularly grisly Civil War atrocity in that county. This meant that his line was henceforth anointed with the miraculous powers of Republican martyrdom.

Secondly, Jimmy McCarthy had been very good at Gaelic football in his youth. When his father dropped dead at the age of 56 his young son, clutching several All Ireland medals, was presented to the people of South Kerry for their approval. It was a coronation not a by-election. Since then Jimmy McCarthy had risen without trace.

The Justice Minister was being ushered out to his car when one of his mobile phones went off. It was his office.

"Yes, yes, I'm on my way. Tell the Taoiseach's office I'll be there as quickly as An Garda Síochána can carve a way through the traffic," said a dismissive Scully.

"Yes, Minister," said Niamh Murphy.

Scully's car was accompanied by two motorcycle outriders and he was surprised at how well they did in getting them swiftly to government buildings on Upper Merrion Street. This wasn't a full cabinet meeting so there was no need for all of those cumbersome formalities. When Gareth Scully came into the office, he could see that An Taoiseach Jimmy McCarthy TD looked utterly ashen. Here, thought Scully, was a man finally realising that he was totally out of his depth.

Brady the Defence Minister was also there, and Scully knew all about this rather dull plodder from Carlow.

"Good afternoon Taoiseach, Minister Brady." It was Scully at his polite dismissive best.

"Why were you at RTE? You should've been here!" blurted out McCarthy in his thick Kerry accent.

"I considered it important to get a calming statement out to the country, Taoiseach," soothed Scully.

"That's my feckin' job Scully! I'm the whoreing Taoiseach. Not you!" shouted McCarthy as he slammed the table.

Scully inwardly punched the air. He had this clown rattled already. This would be easy. Brady seemed to cower and make himself smaller as these two Alphas went at it.

"It was a rapidly developing situation Taoiseach; that called for a ministerial decision from my department, especially with the new legislation going through the Oireachtas."

The privately educated Minister for Justice was the epitome of professional calm and objective detachment. He knew that this made McCarthy feel even more insecure about his abilities and therefore more likely to explode. Brady looked terrified.

The phone lit up on the Taoiseach's desk and he picked it up.

"Ah course send him in! Jaysus!" said McCarthy.

The door opened and in came Commissioner Keegan. Eamonn Keegan was a tall man in his fifties from Donegal. He was famed in the force for his fitness addiction and it showed and he strode into the Taoiseach's office. He had spent most of his Garda career in the

Bad Lands of Limerick and consequently he hadn't been damaged by the corruption scandal in his home county. He had led a rather unorthodox crew of detectives against that city's notorious drug gangs and this had made his stock soar.

Magill magazine had done an interview with him in 2002 and the photographer had caught one image that would define him. The photograph was of Keegan leaning back against the bonnet of an unmarked police car on a piece of waste ground with the infamous Moyross estate in the background. He was briefing a crew of detectives before an early morning raid. The sun was rising behind him and the detectives had their back to camera. Keegan, the tallest of the ensemble, was emphasising a point and stabbing forward an index finger towards his crew. His battered leather jacket was unzipped at the shoulder holster and the butt of his pistol was clearly visible. Irish cops just weren't meant to look this cool.

The interview itself, which had been authorised by the Garda press office, was uneventful enough, but it was this photo that captured the mood. The Guards were getting tough with the scumbags who were ruining the lives of the people of Limerick and that took some tough guys. Eamonn Keegan was a tough guy. His harsh Letterkenny twang made him sound like a tough, no-nonsense cop to the denizens of Leinster House. Back then he was just an Inspector, but he wasn't that for long.

He didn't want to leave the streets, but he knew that the upper echelons of the force were top heavy with desk bound politicians who had hardly ever made an arrest. If the force was going to be turned around then his sort would need to take over. However, this was the toughest day of his career. His stellar rise had been due to the fact that he was always the guy with solutions. Today he didn't have any and he knew that was why he was in the Taoiseach's office.

"Commissioner Keegan. Welcome. You have the floor," said Jimmy McCarthy.

Keegan moved to the side of the large office and put his slim leather document folder on a round table that didn't have any chairs around it. Perhaps it was there for decoration, but Keegan used it as an ad hoc lectern as the others were all seated. There was a seat there for him, but Keegan wasn't the type for sitting all day.

"Thank you, Taoiseach."

He quickly glanced down at the loose A4 sheets, typed double spaced as he had requested. The Commissioner's eyes scanned the first page then he began. Keegan started to go through the facts methodically.

"Four explosions. Three on Luas trains and one on the concourse of Connolly Mainline Station. The three in the Luas trains appear to have been suicide attacks. The death toll hasn't' been officially confirmed, still many seriously injured and some of them won't make it."

"No group has so far claimed responsibility. However, as these were suicide attacks, multiple no warning bombs on a mass transit system, it strongly suggests that Islamic extremists are the likely authors of this atrocity."

"Durty basturds," seethed Jimmy McCarthy.

"We don't have forensics yet on the devices, but the scale of the damage and the casualties suggests that this was high grade explosives. We'll know more later today about the precise nature of the devices; tomorrow at the latest. The technical bureau are working flat out and the PSNI have offered their help through the normal channels," concluded Keegan.

Then Scully made his move.

"If I may Taoiseach; Commissioner Keegan, what intelligence do we have on the profile and intentions of Islamic radicals currently resident in the state?" asked the Justice Minister.

Keegan was thrown by the question and didn't really know why. After all, it was fair enough under the circumstances However, from the first time he met the new justice minister he had a feeling about Gareth Scully. A bad feeling. The big Donegal man was no politician. His family had all voted for Fianna Fáil, but politics were never around the kitchen table when he grew up. It wasn't that type of house. He looked through the other papers and he could feel three pairs of eyes on him.

Keegan looked up and gave the room what he had.

"Special Branch report is sketchy, I asked Assistant Commissioner Gaffney for an update for this meeting, but…"

Scully pounced on the hesitation.

"Commissioner Keegan. This isn't the time for 'sketchy'. The country is under attack. I would wager that the attackers did not arrive here this morning. Consequently, I think that An Garda Síochána should be across this."

This was Gareth Scully at his predatory best. He had Keegan on the ropes and he knew it. Before going into politics he had skewered many a fumbling Guard in his courtroom career. The Taoiseach looked on in silence as Scully speared the Commissioner. He couldn't fathom why, but for the first time ever he was frightened of Gareth Scully.

Doctor Karim Bessaoud had driven into Beaumont Hospital that morning with a smile that even he could not have surgically removed. His long weekend on the Wicklow Way had ended perfectly when Noreen had decided not to drive home to Portlaoise as she had originally planned. They had found a lovely little place in Glendalough. As they had booked into the B&B it was clear that they were not married and the lady of the establishment clearly did not care. Noreen was gleefully enthusiastic about having Karim in bed and this he had not expected. She was not fearful nor ashamed and as they parted that morning, she made it clear that she wanted to do this thing again. At breakfast the Irish lady, about the age of Karim's mother, was cheerful and fussed over them, asking them if they had enough toast. This was a long way from mores of life in his home village of Al-Hoceima.

As he manoeuvred his Volkswagen Golf through the early morning traffic he experienced, for the first time in his life, the exhilaration of anonymity, autonomy and yes…freedom. He had just spent the night with a woman who was not his wife. She did so willingly and no one cared because it was just between the two of them. This, thought Karim, was how he wanted to live.

As he turned into the staff car park he knew in an instant that something was wrong. Very wrong. He spotted one of his Irish colleagues who he was sure was on annual leave running from his car into reception. He recognised that run. It was the run of a medic trying to get somewhere in to save a life. When he saw Doctor Liam Kavanagh pushing his tubby body to its limit across the tarmac, the wonderful feelings of Noreen and Glendalough drained from him in an instant.

Doctor Karim sprinted from his car, his long legs easily consuming the ground in powerful strides. In doing so he easily beat his puffing colleague to the door of Beaumont Hospital. As the Moroccan pushed into the building he could feel the urgency in the air and the cacophony of noise bouncing down the corridors. Something huge was happening.

Mary Bernadette Delaney's constantly referencing the mercy of God had completely freaked Pauline. At this stage no amount of tea was settling her and she just wanted to hear that her son was OK.

Jack had given up on getting through to anyone on his mobile. The service was down and Dempsey was experiencing a thoroughly modern form of digital bereavement. He stepped out onto the street and flagged down a taxi.

"Tallaght," he said to the driver as he slid into the back seat.

"Some fucking shite this," said the driver.

There was no other subject of conversation acceptable for the day that was in it, but Jack wasn't in the mood to talk.

"Get to the shopping centre and I'll give you directions from there."

Paddy Keenan from Finglas glanced at the big fella in the suit behind him and got the vibe that he wasn't in the mood for small talk.

"Grand so," said the driver and he started to manoeuvre his taxi through the worst traffic chaos in the history of modern Dublin.

Jack fingered the empty hip flask in his pocket and wished that there was some of the magic liquid inside. The Gobshite whispered that for the day that was in it no one would begrudge him a couple of swift ones.

It seemed to take an age for the taxi to fight its way out of the town. When they were passing the Liffey Valley Shopping Centre Jack saw fire engines and ambulances heading in the opposite direction into Dublin. What a fucking day, he thought.

"Where in Tallaght boss?" asked Paddy Keenan.

"Killinarden. Know it?"

"Do surely."

"Grand. Kilkenny Avenue."

Jack suddenly thought that he might not have enough cash for the fare. That was all he needed. When he looked inside his wallet there were several crisp €50 notes. So he was sorted. As they passed by Clondalkin there were two more ambulances sirens screaming racing in the other direction. He rummaged into the wallet and found a key ring fob that was broken. It couldn't be attached to a key ring anymore, but there was no way he was getting rid of it because it had a picture of the little guy encased in it. He was about a year old and it had been snapped in Tallaght shopping centre. The guy had done a great trade that day. On the other side it read "I love Dad." The world was shot to shit, Dublin was in flames and all he wanted was to see his son. When it came down to it thought Jack, there were only the people you loved. Nothing else mattered. He cupped the little picture in his big meaty hand like he was cradling the wee fella that first time in the Coombe.

"What number?" asked Paddy Keenan.

Jack was suddenly back in the taxi and in the worst day of his life since he got the news on the Isle of Wight about poor Dermot.

"What?"

"We're in Kilkenny Avenue boss. What number?"

"A hundred and six. One. Oh. Six."

"Got it."

Tom O'Shea had led a life of rules and routine. When Mairéad died he was determined that the place would not go to shite. She wouldn't have approved of that. He was no longer in the Gardaí and the widower lived alone, but he would maintain standards in this Terenure home; even if there was no one waiting to inspect them.

He presented himself band-box smart every morning at Saint Joseph's Church on Terenure Road to pray for the soul of his departed wife. He reckoned he was one of the younger ones at ten o'clock mass. The new generation had lost their faith as well as so many other things.

On the way back to the house he stopped into a shop run by

a local man for milk and bread. The routine suited him. It kept him in order. Order, O'Shea thought, was all that kept a man from becoming a lazy useless gobshite. The old Kerryman missed the woman of his life every day. She had only been gone from him a year and her presence was everywhere in their home where they had reared their family. A daughter in Australia and a son in England. Mary in Sydney did her best to keep in touch. Tomás had to be hunted down like a suspect. Daughters were different, thought O'Shea. Women were different, there no question about that, concluded the ex-policeman.

He was back through the door he put the sturdy old steel kettle on the gas stove. O'Shea got eggs and rashers from the fridge and started to busy himself with the stuff of breakfast. The kettle squealed and the tea leaves were already in the small brown teapot. It was all in order. He had been reared in the Kingdom of Kerry with the importance of the tea ceremony. This tea bag in the cup thing wasn't civilised.

He sat at the small Formica table in the kitchen. Mairéad had always sat across from him for their final years together. The children up and gone and it had just been the two of them. Him, quiet and stoic, her chirpy and chatty. Her laugh lit him up; it always had, ever since the first time he heard it when he had met her at a dance in Sneem in 1964. God had been good to him all of these years to have this woman at his side. Now there was only an empty chair and silence across from him.

The noise from the radio was a poor substitute, but it was better than the silence that normally followed him about the house. As usual RTE was utter shite, although Seán O'Rourke wasn't the worst. Thank God he was at Mass when that smarmy little gobshite Turbridy was on. Yer man O'Rourke was chatting about what Scully the Justice Minister wanted to do. He was probably a gobshite, thought O'Shea, but he wanted to get things done.

The toast popped up just in time to join the poached eggs. Most important meal of the day.

O'Rourke was playing a clip from yer man Scully the day before in the Dáil. On the face of it the measures seemed sound enough, though O'Shea. If he got it through then it might put manners on some of the skangers. Something had to be done, that was for sure. This country was going to shite.

Then the show moved onto something from Britain. A town called Luton – a lot of Irish there, thought O'Shea – the local council wanted to ban the sale of alcohol during Ramadan. What in the name of Jaysus was going on with them? Different days sure enough. His father had worked in England in the 1950s, sending money home. He saw the signs, "no Blacks no dogs, no Irish!" Now these fellas were getting everything their way. Different days for sure.

The journalist fella from England was telling O'Rourke that 'Moslem patrols' were stopping men coming out of Off Licenses and giving out to them. O'Shea immediately thought that the English police must be on feckin' blue flu. That place was going to shite, thought the retired detective. Going to shite for sure. Then there was some foreign fella was ranting on about Allah and alcohol. Gobshite. If they bump into a Paddy outside one of those off licenses those Moslem lads better be ready for trouble, thought O'Shea, chuckling to himself.

It was probably the first bit of mirth that had been in his head since he had lowered Mairéad into the ground at her home Parish of St Michael's in Sneem. There was no way she was for going to her rest eternal in that Glasnevin place. She was a Kerry woman and she had followed O'Shea around Ireland on the job. She had always been at his side. Now there was that empty chair.

Still, he had his standards and his faith. A man needed something. If he had nothing then he would just go to shite altogether.

"We interrupt this segment to bring you a newsflash" said yer man O'Rourke, "There are reports of multiple explosions in Dublin."

O'Shea froze with a piece of toast in his hand. The day that had started like any other in the past year was suddenly changed, changed utterly. Tom O'Shea didn't go for all that gobshitery about Pee Tee Ess Gee or whatever they called it, but the old Kerryman was wrong. The newsflash on RTE was still giving out the sparse details, but O'Shea had stopped listening. He was somewhere else.

He was standing at the door of Jervis Street hospital as the wounded were being carried in. He was twenty-eight. It was 1974. The screams of one man remained in his long term memory. Down the corridor, he never saw that man and didn't know what had happened to him. In truth he didn't really care, he just wanted him to shut up for the love of Christ! The noise he was making! Those screams. Anyone making that racket had to be in a state of pain that he never wanted to be in. It went right into the marrow of his Kerry bones. That screaming. The RTE breaking news alert had turned that sound on again. It was always there; those screams. That noise. That desperate fucking noise.

He hadn't moved. He was still holding the toast. And that poor bastard was still screaming in Jervis Street hospital. Tom O'Shea hated his good memory. He had marvelled at the efficiency of the hip replacement that had given him the ability to walk again. He prayed that the man upstairs would one day give the doctors the ability to dig out memories.

"Wait here," said Jack.

The taxi driver wasn't for arguing. Other men tended not to argue with Jack Dempsey. Strange that…

He rang the bell and waited. Nothing. Again. Nothing. Fuck it, she could be anywhere and this was probably just him worrying about nothing. Anyways, she would probably just call the Guards. That barring order shite. That was all he needed. He tried her phone again. Straight to voicemail.

He stomped back into the taxi.

"Where to boss?" asked the driver.

Jack had no idea. He hated that. You always have to have a plan, even if it wasn't a very good one, thought Jack. The Gobshite had an idea. He always did. Just find a decent spot and gargle some down you Jack. That was the Gobshite's plan.

"Town," ordered Jack. He couldn't think of anything else.

"The traffic will be murder," said Keenan.

It was an unfortunate choice of words for the day that was in it, thought the driver as soon as he said it.

"Drive." Jack wasn't in the mood for a debate.

The taxi man obeyed in silence. Jack Dempsey could have that kind of effect on people.

The taxi driver wasn't lying. The traffic was horrendous. The Gobshite started to whisper his plan to Jack when the phone started yelping in his pocket. He fumbled underneath the feckin' seatbelt to get it out of his pocket before it rang off. He glanced at the screen. It was her.

"Where are you?" She sounded panicked and tearful and that hit Jack in the gut. Something must have been wrong or she wouldn't be calling him.

"In a taxi, coming into town from Tallaght."

"Jesus…" She couldn't get the words out and Jack, in that moment, was frightened to ask her.

After a long silence she said, "I'm at Beaumont. It's the wee fella."

Jack Dempsey's world started to disintegrate as he sat in traffic beside a man who had no fucking idea what was going on inside his head. For some reason Jack hated him for that.

"On my way," said Jack.

"Thanks."

It was strange hearing a grateful word from her. Things had to be bad, thought Jack, but he was too frightened to ask as he hit the red button on the screen.

"Beaumont," said Jack to the driver.

"The hospital?" said the driver, slightly wrong footed at the change of plan.

"No, the fucking lap dancing club! Yeah, the hospital. Move it!" Jack had an outlet for his rage.

"In this traffic boss?" pleaded Keenan.

"Just get me there. My kid's in there." Jack almost whispered it. That was what happened to Dempsey's voice when he moved beyond shouting and growling. It was a dangerous whisper. The taxi driver didn't need a translation service. It was time for extreme measures, thought Keenan. His taxi driver circuits kicked in.

"I'll get us there sharpish! Here we go!"

He did a handbrake turn and went back the wrong way down the hard shoulder beside the Liffey Valley Shopping Centre. In seconds the blaring of horns was all that remained of the crazy thing he had done. He was in the country lanes beside the exclusive King's Hospital private school. This guy knew the back roads, thought Jack. Dempsey nudged his upper arm.

"Good driving buddy."

"Emergency situation boss."

"Sound."

They hit the N4 and they were on the M50 very quickly.

A few traffic regulations had been fractured, but they were on the right road to the hospital. Keenan was good as his word and he wasn't finished with the law breaking. He weaved in and out of the traffic like he was a blue light driver. At one point Jack felt like telling him to slow down or they would finish the journey in an ambulance, but he decided against it. This was a decent sort doing his best and, in fairness, he could move this thing. They whizzed past Blanchardstown and Ballymun like they were a hundred yards apart. He hit the anchors as they got to the big roundabout that sent them south again on the M50. He was going a slightly less mental speed when Jack recognised Coolock Lane Park on his left. They were nearly there.

"Owe you buddy," said Jack.

"Ah away with ye."

"How's yer kid?" asked the driver.

"Don't know yet. The mother's there with him."

"Jaysus."

By the time they got near to Beaumont there was another traffic jam. Of ambulances. Keenan and Jack looked at each other. The decision was clear.

"I'll get out here."

"Best of luck boss."

Jack started to fumble in his pocket.

"Put your money in your fucking pocket." Keenan was very serious.

"Ah now…" Jack was the one protesting.

"I'm fucking serious. Get in there to your kid, big fella. Good luck and God bless." And with that Keenan gave him a nod and the Toyota wheeled around in the road and was gone.

Dempsey said under his breath, "Dubs. Best fucking people in the world."

Jack started walking to the hospital, it was a good four hundred yards to the main entrance but every fucking ambulance in Ireland seemed to be waiting to get there. He hit the call button and her phone rang. This time she answered.

"I'm here. Outside. Where are ya?" asked Jack.

"In reception," said Pauline. Her voice was trembling.

When he walked into the hospital the place was chaotic. There were people everywhere. It was like the AVIVA or Croke Park just before the start of a match with everyone milling about. Paramedics in those yellow vests and relatives. Lots and lots of relatives. This was mental, thought Jack. She spotted him before he saw her. The height of him made him stand out in a crowd. She tugged at his sleeve and he turned round. Dempsey noticed that she wasn't in her court rig out and her face was pale white and tear stained.

Jack had been sitting beside the mother of his child for over an hour without a word between them. There wasn't anything to say. He detested her, and she probably felt the same way about him. However, they both loved a wee child more than life and at that moment they didn't know if he had much of that left in him. He stared at his shoes for an age, like the cracks in the leather might yield up some enlightenment or comfort about what the future might bring.

It made him think about his Granny sitting beside an open fire chatting to her neighbour Peggy Doyle about what the old woman could see in the tea leaves. A five year old Seán Dempsey was fascinated that HIS Granny had such magical powers. Peggy Doyle hunched forward eagerly awaiting the next prescient observation from her neighbour who had the gift. Jack Dempsey had lots of great memories of when he was a small child. He always considered himself lucky that he could go there when he needed to. When he was in solitary on the Isle of Wight the crews were baffled at how he emerged from that situation with a smile on his face. He had a safe place inside his head, formed when wee Seán Dempsey was surrounded by love and fun. Whenever they put him in solitary they were packing his bags back to a happy childhood in North Inner City Dublin in the 1960's.

Then one day he cheerily emerged from that concrete coffin and they told him about Dermot. After that it had been different. When he was put in solitary after that it was a place of grieving. He sobbed inside, but he would never let the screws see it. He had abandoned his son. What kind of man did that make him? As he looked at the stitched welt of the Clark's shoes he wrestled with thoughts of poor Dermot.

Herself beside him remained silent. Jack was grateful for that. He had no idea what he would say to her. The mobile phones seemed to be working again and she was fidgeting with her little glass screen, her little thumb moving at humming bird speed across the iPhone.

RTE at Donnybrook was a hive of activity and the flagship debate show Frontline was having an unscheduled special tonight. Occasionally there was a programme devoted to one special subject. It was a no brainer that the Luas bombings would have a Q&A devoted especially to them.

Gareth Scully came in with his Garda detective. He demanded attention.

"Coffee please, black."

On the first couch facing the glass and aluminium door that Scully had entered was a large man, taller than Scully, probably either heavily built or obese; it was hard to tell under his flowing robes. The huge beard and skullcap added to the dramatic effect. This was Abu Musa of the Inchichore Mosque. The production team were delighted that he had agreed to come on the show. He had refused a few times to come onto various RTE programmes about religion. Abu Musa immediately stood up to establish his ownership of the space. He extended a hand of friendship, but he really was looking for a Godfather "kiss the ring" show of respect from the infidel.

"Salaam a alakam," said the cleric, taking Scully by surprise.

"Delighted. Hello, Gareth Scully, Minister for…"

"Yes of course you are a very famous man…in Ireland." The last part of the sentence had been left hanging for effect. Scully winced, but tried not to show it. At this point Scully wanted to say something to his detective, who was from Kerry and was a native Irish speaker apparently. He wished he could speak Irish, but they weren't terribly keen on Irish at King's Hospital the exclusive English public school he had attended on the outskirts of Dublin. There had been a couple of Arab boys at "King's Hos." They had been tormented by the boys in Scully's dorm and by Scully himself. The Arab boys desperately wanted to fit in, but they were denied this by Scully and the other rugger buggers. There wasn't any chance that this maniac been to a rugby and hockey school. A cave in Afghanistan perhaps!

The little production girl fussed around them.

"No need for introductions then," she simpered. Scully knew the rest of the panel. The usual suspects, His opposite number from Fine Gael, a member of the Labour Party and a leftie journalist from the Irish Times who Scully thought was fuckable. She was in high heels and a skirt. Scully approved, although he was sure that the camel driver would rather have her in a beekeeper's suit.

The last to arrive was the Sinn Féin chick. Another of the production line of Sinn Féin PR girls. Squeaky clean, presentable and robotic. They would say what the non-existent Army Council would deem that they should say. This one was Caoimhe Ni Chuireain, a Donegal girl being groomed by the godfathers. She was also highly fuckable, thought the Justice Minister.

The Shinner, in the interests of multi-cultural political correctness, went over the Imam and offered her hand.

"Hello. I'm Caoimhe Ni Chuireann of Sinn Féin." The cleric glowered at this uncovered woman who clearly had no shame. He simply turned away avoiding all physical contact with her. The Sinn Féin girl didn't know what do to. Scully saw his chance.

"I don't think he approves of your policies," he chuckled. The production girl was starting to stress out.

Also there was Anas Iqbal. For the RTE crowd he was the media Moslem of choice in contemporary Ireland. He ran a successful criminal law practice in the North Inner City, but his main talent was in front of the camera rather than in the court room. Scully was sure he was there to skewer the Minister about the government's closeness to USA foreign policy in the Middle East. Iqbal had been born in Liverpool England, but had moved to Dublin as an eight year-old with his Pakistani parents.

He had won a famous case against the Guard who had assaulted him during an altercation outside the American Embassy. Fortunately for Iqbal, someone got the incident on their phone and uploaded it to YouTube. For the left he was their legal hero, their Go-To Guy. He was an immigrant to Ireland, an Asian, and a Moslem who was fighting through the courts for the human rights of the oppressed.

It was a strong rumour among the Political Correspondents that

Iqbal had been approached by Sinn Féin to stand in a winnable Dáil seat at the next election. Scully smiled when he saw him looking at him from across the Green Room. The Minister knew much, much more about Iqbal than the lawyer could possibly be aware of, but that was for another day. If only the self-styled 'Human Rights Lawyer' knew that his posturing had made him a person of minor interest to the most powerful state in the world. Scully knew that there was enough on this Pakistani charlatan to unleash the Gardaí on him. However, his transatlantic associates had told the Justice Minister to hold fire for now. They clearly had plans for that strutting narcissist, thought Scully.

Fucking a homeless self-harming kid while he was high on cocaine would not make for an image enhancing story thought the Justice Minister. At the time the object of his affections was just past her seventeenth birthday and he was in his late thirties. He had first offered her Charlie in a nightclub toilet. As he thought of the impact on Iqbal's carefully concocted image, Scully smiled his private smile.

"Can I get people to make-up, please? Minister?"

Scully, having landed a few blows on the Shinner, was delighted to leave the Green Room and walk out on the gangway that connected it to Make-Up. Custom built, the make-up room could deal with ten people at a time being made up for studio. Scully knew the make-up girl. She was usually a chirpy, chatty type, but today she was very subdued as she professionally applied the studio grade make up to the minister's unusually large forehead. She was so much quieter than normal that Scully was moved to speak.

"Busy?"

"Always."

"You're usually chatty."

"Bad day Minister, the Luas, my best friend." Scully was brought back from admiring her small breasts under a tight t-shirt that stretched as she leaned over his head.

"So sorry. Terrible, simply terrible."

"I hope ye catch..." the girl stopped herself. There was no one to catch. The bombers were dead. By now everyone had seen their bye videos on You Tube. Blaming the Irish for being infidels and helping America kill Moslems.

She finished his make up in record time.

"Finished?"

"Yes"

"Thank you."

Scully breezed back toward the green room where he had to negotiate his way around Abu Musa. Big man he was, thought Scully;
definitely suited to the nightshirt look.

Scully, having already dealt with the Shinner, decided to slap about
the Irish Times journalist, just to warm up for the on-camera action.

"I read your column on the Luas bombings."

"Yes?" Scully thought how journalists were always so pathetically
grateful when anyone read their stuff. Yes, pathetic.

"Did you like it?" Was this really meant to be a left-wing firebrand asking him, HIM if he liked this simpering left wing drivel?
Really.

"No." Scully walked off to demand some coffee from the matronly
type looking after the hospitality.

The two opposition TDs were huddled together like they were
trying to stay warm. They were both standing, nursing cups of very
bad RTE coffee. Scully sneered in their direction.

"I trust I, the government, can count on your full support in the Dáil
tomorrow?" It wasn't a question; it was an expectation of obedience.

They looked crushed. Scully liked that.

Jack was eating his dinner in his cell in Belmarsh prison when
the door opened in the waiting room in Beaumont Hospital. He
snapped back to now. Standing in the doorway was a tall slim man.
Almost as tall as himself, thought Dempsey. He was in surgical
scrubs with a theatre cap on. It was clear to the big Dubliner that
there wasn't a drop of Paddy in this fella.

"Hello, are you the parents of Paid Raig Duffee?"

Yer man has no idea how to pronounce an Irish name, thought
Jack. He had no idea why that bothered him so much at that moment.

"I'm his mother," chirped in herself, bouncing up out of the seat
and stepping forward. Jack was side-lined again. Situation normal.

"I operated on your son. And…"

The world stopped in that little room. Dempsey stood up and

he was back in front of the governor's desk as he was told about Dermot. The fact that the screws were decent about it made it somehow even harder to take. It would have been better if they had been cruel about it, but they weren't. It made them harder to hate and back then hate was all that kept Jack going.

Pauline Duffy started to tremble. She couldn't get the words out to ask the Moroccan neurosurgeon. When he saw this trembling woman in front of him he hesitated, and then Dempsey felt the temper rising in him.

"What's the story with him?" It was an order to respond, not a respectful question.

"Yes. The operation was a success."

Pauline Duffy's legs buckled and she almost fell back into the plastic chair. Without her heels on she looked seriously tiny, thought Jack. Almost childlike. He still wanted to break her neck though. Pauline looked up at this man who had saved her son and started to speak.

"Doctor Bessy, Bess…"

"Please call me Karim. My family name is difficult for Irish people," smiled the Moroccan.

This invitation to be familiar seemed too kind to Pauline Duffy. She couldn't take it.

"Doctor… how is he?"

The neurosurgeon was back in clinical mode immediately.

"The operation was a success. However…."

Fuck, thought Jack, I didn't want to hear a "however." I hate that fucking word when doctors and lawyers use it.

"What do you mean?" Jack was in challenging mood now. This fecker was at it!

"Mr…"

"Dempsey."

"Mr Dempsey, the operation was a success, but he is still very ill. He will need a lot of care. He is in the ICU now and we will know in time if there is any permanent damage to his cognitive functioning. But he is alive."

This medial reasoning flattened Jack. There was no point in rearing up at this fella, thought the big Dubliner.

"There are some papers to sign. The next of kin. They're at the desk." Karim was addressing Jack, who was still standing and filling the room.

Pauline stood up and stepped past the father of her child to be in front of him and spoke to the doctor.

"I'm his next of kin. That's for me to do."

The Moroccan was puzzled and looked at Jack. Dempsey felt the need to explain to the man, but he didn't know really what to say.

"She'll sign them," was the best he could come up with.

Karim was still baffled by this interaction. Something didn't seem right to him. This was a strange land, he thought. Very strange.

"Can I see him, Doctor?" asked Pauline.

"Yes of course, you can both go in. He is still sedated and will not awaken for many hours, but you can see him."

Pauline Duffy shot Jack a look. Legally he didn't exist and she knew that only too well after the court appearance today, but she wasn't stupid. She knew he would kick off if he wasn't allowed in.

"Thank you doctor," said Pauline.

He led them out of the room and they weaved between trolleys, paramedics and frazzled nurses. A lot of the walking wounded had been patched up and sent home. Neither of the two parents following Doctor Karim Bessaoud had any idea how long they had been waiting in that little room. They only cared that they were going to see their son and that he was alive.

He looked tiny in the bed. Like a doll. A huge tube was taped into his mouth and there were monitors and wires everywhere. Hugging him seemed out of the question. Pauline crumpled in tears when she saw him. Jack looked at the Doctor for some response that would give hope.

"He will be fine. He just needs time."

"But you said about his, his brain?" asked Jack.

"Yes, the fragments were removed and we avoided any major complications during the operation. Is the brain functioning normally for a child of his age? Only time will tell. That is in the hands of God."

Dempsey didn't want to hear any mention of this fella's fucking God. He felt the temper rising in him, but he pushed it down. He had a word with himself. Catch yourself on Jack. For fuck's sake. This fella is doing his best and nothing to do with those cunts on the Luas. What are ye like?

"Thanks doctor."

"I think it would be best if you both went home. We will call you if there is any change. You both need rest," said the Moroccan.

"Call me. I'm his next of kin," said Pauline.

Jack didn't respond to it and he looked at Karim, trying to send him a message that this wasn't happy families. Then he had a thought.

"Here doctor. Thanks for everything. Here's my card. If there's anything I can do for you call me," said Jack, holding out a business card which he had quickly extracted from his wallet.

The doctor was slightly taken aback, but accepted it and quickly glanced down.

"Ah thank you sir. Ah you are a security person. Many thanks. Mar salaam."

In that moment Dempsey had a hold of himself. This man had saved his son's life. He didn't know yet what kind of life that would be, or what he would be like when he came to, but he had life. And that life was down to this man's skill and goodness.

"Go raibh maith agat!" said Jack.

"Tá fáilte romhat," said Karim easily, pronunciation perfect.

Jack was taken aback.

"My girlfriend is teaching me Irish. A beautiful language. Now I have to go and prepare for another patient. Follow the signs to the exit please when you are ready," said the Moroccan Doctor.

Tuesday

When Alison Fraser disembarked at Terminal 2 of Dublin airport it was her first time in Ireland, despite having been born and reared in nearby Scotland. As she stood in the passport queue beside him she thought to herself that they had been traveling in a strange direction for some years. What she initially thought had been a journey unplanned, a product of the chaos of the universe, had actually been a carefully planned expedition that she had no say in.

The leader of that odyssey was standing beside her and she smiled a reassuring smile at him. He was always checking for any flicker of a problem with her. Alison was now an expert at reading Peter Woolnough. That was a very useful skill to have in her situation.

Alison had attended St George's Independent school for girls in Edinburgh. Her parents were comfortably off. She had four brothers, and she was the late arrival of the brood. Her second eldest brother Malcolm was in the RAF and was a Tornado pilot. The oldest sibling Roddy was very senior in a foreign insurance firm that had a sumptuous office in the New Town part of Edinburgh. Her father worked with RBS and had taken a package some years ago just before the collapse of 2008. Alison's mother had taught piano for years from their home in Aberlour on the other side of the Forth.

The Scottish work ethic had been instilled into her from the earliest age. Alison wasn't the top of the class at St George's, but she was certainly the most driven. When she realised that she might not get the exam results for Medicine, she decided on Pharmacy. She was delighted to be accepted to read for a degree in Pharmacy at University College London, Brunswick Square. The anonymity and bustle of London excited the ambitious girl from Aberlour.

She was attending a department event towards the end of the first year when she met him. It was a thinly disguised marketing exercise for a big pharmaceutical firm. One of the speakers was from the company, and he stood up to make the pitch. That was why they were there funding the research. As he spoke, she was aware of him checking her out. In the mingling afterwards, he made sure that they came to close quarters.

Peter Woolnough was over fifty, but could have passed for his early forties. His dress sense indicated a man of style and substantial means. Alison had just turned twenty, and it was like a moth to a flame. He knew that night that he had a real chance of snaring her. Peter Woolnough was good at this, becoming more practised which each 'recruitment'.

He left the event with her number, and she had his embossed business card. She received a call from him the very next day. The first date was just lunch, but Peter staged it perfectly. Then a series of sumptuous dinner dates ensued.

At the end of one evening, he asked if she had a current passport as they would have to travel outside the UK for the next date. She thought she was joking, but he wasn't. He sent a car for her and brought her to Farnborough airport. Peter was already there with the company Lear jet. It was Bond movie glamour. She was disarmed as he already knew her so well. He did not tell her where she was going until then.

They had dinner in Cannes. He suggested to her that she could travel back that night to London on the plane or she could stay with him. Alison quipped that as she hadn't had a chance to pack, she would at least have to return for some clothes. Peter told her that there were many high-class clothes shops in Cannes and that he was buying. The deal was sealed and that night Alison Fraser became Peter Woolnough's lover. It was just as he planned it.

And Peter Woolnough loved to plan things.

What she couldn't have imagined were the long-term designs he had for this young long legged Scottish undergraduate. Peter Woolnough love bombed her, and she responded just as he knew she would. He told her everything that she wanted to hear.

Alison couldn't believe her luck when he handed her own key to his Docklands apartment that overlooked the Millennium Dome.

This was a world away from the flat she was sharing with a nice couple in Bromley. She didn't need to be convinced of his bona fides of his offer. She moved in, and they were an item.

Yes, he was older than her, much older, and divorced, but none of that bothered her. Suddenly she was at elegant dinner parties in the West End where people from politics and the media were sitting across from her. Her boat had come in. Peter Woolnough excited her, but she was also intoxicated by the lifestyle he could show her. Ah yes, 'Lifestyle'.

They were together about six months when he floated the idea of having another "playmate," in their bed occasionally. At first, she thought he was thinking about another woman in the bed as well as her. However, it was another male that was part of Peter's plans. She said she wasn't sure and for the first time across the breakfast table she sensed a flicker of something in Peter Woolnough that she had not seen before: Anger. He smiled and said it was no big deal, but she knew that it was.

The subject would be broached every so often and was never far away from their post-coital chats. Finally, she agreed to try it out once. Peter smiled a superior delighted smile and in the days that followed the big love was turned up, and she received several well-judged gifts. Alison asked him who the other person would be as she didn't want it to be someone they knew as a couple. She booked into to a mid-range totally anonymous hotel in North London and waited for the guy.

Then, at the eleventh hour, she backed out and said she couldn't go through with it. Woolnough snapped. She had never seen him so incensed to his bones, and in that moment she was frightened of him. He told her that she could be out on the street that night with the bags that she had arrived with. It was a line in the sand for him.

She caved.

The guy turned up, and he introduced her as Annabel. He looked incredibly normal, five foot ten, well-spoken and in reasonably good shape. They shared a glass of wine in idle and somewhat awkward chit chat. And then Peter took the wine glass from her hand and said, "Let's get started." At that moment, she didn't feel that she had any choice.

Peter was incredibly excited and mainly watched, giving the man instructions as to what to do. When it was over the man dressed and left. Peter Woolnough was over the moon and incredibly grateful. He showered her with compliments as they drove back to the apartment. It was still early enough, so he told her to change and he would take her to their favourite restaurant. She was being rewarded, and she knew it. Alison loved Peter Woolnough, for her he was in many ways the perfect man. She thought that if her participation in this lifestyle made him love her more then so be it. "This makes us stronger as a couple," was one of his phrases as they discussed afterwards what had taken place in the nondescript hotel room. When Alison heard that, she believed him.

She was told that they would never meet that man again and that he had no idea who 'Annabel' was. Condoms had been used throughout. It was all safe and no one had been hurt. Alison did not know and didn't ask where the man had been sourced; she thought that it might have been a business associate of Peter's. She was wrong. Woolnough had accessed him through a website for 'swingers'.

She had no idea that a few hours after the first event 'Annabel' had her first review from 'Dark John', the username of the City chap who was something in offshore trusts. Woolnough smiled as he saw an avalanche of men wanting to get a look at the new meat. This would have to be done gently, but Phase One of his plan had been completed. It was no longer a theory; he had managed to get her cross that all-important line. The next time would be easier, and so it proved.

The men were picked with care. All the sort of chaps who Alison might consider dating on her own terms. They were always gracious, polite and no rough stuff. Looking back years afterwards it was clear that Woolnough had an outside agenda. It worked so well because she had no idea that there was a plan. She thought they were exploring things together as a couple. He controlled the entire process and, for a long time, he completely controlled her.

The next step in the lifestyle would be introduced gently. The porn they would watch would depict a scenario that had never happened in reality for them. Then it would be brought up in a later conversation. The idea would be suggested that she was turned on watching something. It was deftly done with flattery and always just at the right moment over dinner or after sex just between the two of them. He would then wait until SHE brought up the issue, the idea, the fetish and then say he would try and make it happen for her. And it usually did. Peter was very accommodating and helpful for his lady.

The next step along the road was moving from one man to two. Again, it was a gradual raising of the temperature of the water she was in as her self-worth was being slowly boiled away by Peter Woolnough. She was his pretty, long-legged frog, and she had no idea that he was drawing huge gratification from her being moulded into what he wanted her to be.

At first, she found these events somewhat awkward, sometimes ridiculous but never disturbing or frightening. Peter made sure that everything was OK, and she trusted him when he told her that the men had been vetted by him; and indeed they had. At some point being in a hotel room and being introduced as 'Annabel' to a man she had never seen before knowing that in a few minutes they would both be in bed became no biggie.

Then she met 'Joe'. It was a game changer. Woolnough had greeted the man like they were long lost friends. Alison was taken with how physically striking he was. He was tall, around six four thought Alison, shaven headed and very well built. She wasn't particularly attracted to black men, but Joe's rich deep African accent drew her in. For a couple of months before she was introduced to Joe, the porn Peter was ordering up for them to watch in bed had been increasingly colour coded. Suddenly, the men in the films were all black. It was done without any fanfare, it just happened like it was coincidence, but it wasn't.

Until then the men she had met through Peter had all been white, British and well-spoken. Joe was none of these things. Originally from Nigeria, he was an outsider to her world in every sense. After the usual hotel room pleasantries, he adopted a different persona. He called her a "fuck slut" as he looked down at her on the bed. She was captivated. Standing in the corner of the room, Peter Woolnough was delighted. He had been searching a while for such an assistant in this project.

Unlike before, Annabel met Joe again and again. In time Annabel found out that Joe's real name was Patrick. She was surprised to learn that he travelled over from Ireland to attend these events in London. He told her that he had citizenship there and that he liked it. By the time that he shared this information with her, Patrick already knew he was meeting up with Peter and Alison not Jonathan and Annabel. An important line within the swinging lifestyle had been crossed. The protection of anonymity had gone.

The first house party Peter took her to was held at the country abode of a leading London QC. As ever there was lots of glamour to sugar the pill. It was also the first time that another female was part of one of the events. When the woman spoke to her in the warm up chit chat, she sounded privately educated. Her husband stood diffidently in the background; he was there only to observe. Some of the rougher chaps, including Joe, had been bussed in. There appeared to be a network of these men and they were all in agreement on the website that Annabel was a star. After that evening the idea that she would object to the meeting, say, two new guys in a hotel room was a nonstarter. It had become workaday and she got competent at it. Peter Woolnough was delighted.

However, there were warning signs that he didn't heed. As her academic training was coming to an end his ability to control her would be weakened. She had allowed herself to become financially dependent on him. The standard of living she was enjoying was only possible through his largesse. As the possibility of a career as a pharmacist loomed, her own earning power meant that she could be a self-financing adult.

Peter was never happy to leave the Lifestyle where it was. He always wanted more from it. "We have to push the boundaries" was his constant refrain. This meant more guys, more rough stuff. Although she put up objections, in the end, she always related, especially if Patrick was part of the event. She was on a journey that she wasn't in control of. It had all been Peter's idea from the start.

When she looked back, she marvelled at how her dabbling in the Lifestyle had started with a very mild liaison with a very pleasant chap from the City in a hotel room to her 25th birthday party.

On one particular occasion, he had promised something rather special and they had travelled to Dublin. She knew that Patrick would be part of the event and that made Alison feel a little better about it. Moreover, Peter Woolnough was well aware of those feelings.

They had picked up a hire car at the airport and booked into a nearby hotel that served the bustling transport hub. It was comfortably soulless, thought Alison. Woolnough said he was waiting for the address, then they would drive there. He told her perfunctorily to go shower and get into her Annabel outfit. She started to get ready.

Then something went off in her head. She had never said no to any of these events. Ever. This was despite the fact that she felt so conflicted about the Annabel part of her.

While she was in the shower Woolnough received a text message from Patrick. He knew the venue for the event would be outside Dublin. The Englishman keyed the details into Google Maps on his phone and it told him that the distance of 57.4 km via the M3 would take 42 minutes.

"We have to make a move Annabel!" Woolnough shouted into the toilet.

His voice was full of light hearted confidence.

As soon as Alison came out of the shower with a towel wrapped round her, hair soaking wet, no make-up on, he knew there was a problem. She sat on the corner of the bed and looked at him. The expression on her face was a picture of dejectedness.

"What's the matter?" asked Woolnough.

"I don't know."

"Not really an answer, my darling."

"I don't feel like dong this tonight," whispered Alison.

It was the first time she had ever said anything like this to Woolnough, although had she thought it often enough and that feeling had been growing.

"WHAT?!"

Woolnough exploded and for a moment Alison thought that he was going to become physical. However, she didn't want to do this stuff anymore and that was it.

The row had made Peter and Alison quite late and she knew the event that had been planned. When they arrived at Patrick's flat,

Alison could see that he was utterly furious. She realised later the huge loss of face he would have suffered if she had not turned up.

The satnav had taken them to the address via the Páirc Tailteann GAA ground. Woolnough was glad he didn't have to stop and ask the way to that particular stadium as he would have had no clue how to pronounce it. He always thought his Oxbridge accent made him sound fairly ridiculous when trying to properly annunciate places names from the Celtic Fringe to a native.

By the time they got out of the car in the cul-de sac in County Meath they were over an hour late. Patrick answered the door and didn't say a word. He simply turned and walked up the hall towards a door. It was an order to follow and Woolnough gently pushed Alison in the direction of the tall African. Patrick walked into the bedroom and she could hear men speaking in the living room.

It was a four bedroom detached house, built in the Celtic Tiger years. It was clear that the builders hadn't splashed out on the sound proofing. Once the three of them were in the bedroom, Patrick slapped her fully across the face.

"You're late!" he growled.

Alison felt the sting in her face and said "sorry."

Peter was standing behind her and didn't intervene. This sort of interaction would have been unheard of at the start of her foray into the Lifestyle.

"Those are my friends in there. Now you put a good show on for them!" said Patrick.

Peter was taking off the little fitted black jacket that was part of the Annabel outfit. Patrick reached for the hem of her little black dress – a central part of the ensemble. He wanted to lift it over her head, but Alison temporarily resurfaced and asserted herself. She held the dress down with both hands. When he realised she was resisting he looked into her eyes and smirked.

"Don't be foolish" said Patrick with a sardonic smile.

He was no longer angry with Alison and she could tell that from the tone of his voice. The Nigerian knew that there was no need for his anger as he was confident she would be back under back under his control easily. Something in her realised that this was futile and Annabel was clawing to get out. Alison relented and lifted her arms up – surrender style. The dress was off in an instant. Patrick allowed himself a small smile. Alison had caved in and she knew there was no going back.

Almost immediately, but without any fumbling rush, he fastened a black leather collar around her neck. It had a light chain. Annabel had reasserted herself over Alison with help from Patrick, and by now the former was trembling with excitement at what was about to happen.

Then Patrick produced a contraption from a bedside drawer. It appeared to be comprised of a series of straps, buckles and small yellow plastic ball with holes in it. This was new for her and at first she didn't know what it was for. The small harness was arranged around her head, and she was told to open her mouth and duly obeyed. Alison found that she could breathe easily through the ball gag and the practicality of the Annabel ponytail hair arrangement once more asserted itself.

Patrick tugged at the leash, and she instinctively knew what was now expected of her. She went down on all fours and started to follow him out of the bedroom across the hall and into the living room. Then she heard the cheer. Years later she could still hear those cheering men in her head.

There was a blue coloured double airbed in the middle of the floor. This was all for Annabel and they had been waiting for her. She was scanning the room as the introductions were made by Patrick. Peter shook the hands of the three men on the sofa nearest the door. They were all unknown to Annabel.

There was another man in the room. White and middle aged. He was sitting in the corner on his own. This man was wearing a bathrobe. He looked simultaneously highly excited and very uncomfortable. When she looked up at him, the man in the robe put his head down.

"Sorry for being late," said Peter, "it was the bitch's fault." The men on the sofa laughed.

The tallest one of the three who clearly seemed the most dominant of the trio asked him:

"Did you train her yourself?"

"Yes" said Woolnough proudly, like he was at a dog show.

That was it, thought Alison, when she recalled that interaction, although not at that moment as Annabel was in full control. She loved the conversation. In those moments before the action started Annabel had never felt so excited or so alive. Prissy little Alison was silent. She was merely a spectator, just like the man in the corner of the room.

Peter Woolnough had indeed trained her; he had spotted the possibility that she was trainable. That was why she had been courted so assiduously by him. She was a Peter Woolnough project five years in the making.

Patrick led Alison by the lead to the dominant man in the trio and handed her over. They all had African sounding accents like Patrick. The big man looked down at her. He was tall and well-built with a shaven head.

"Now I know what you REALLY want in your mouth girl!" he said.

He fumbled to release the ball gag and so it began. At one point early on in the proceedings, Alison looked up from the airbed to see the two spectators sitting at the small dining table. Peter was so excited he couldn't sit still and he was literally fidgeting, beside himself with glee. Patrick was fascinated. Yes, he was turned on, but there was an expression on his face that stayed with Alison years later. It was a look of self-satisfaction mixed with hatred. He hated her, as he hated all females.

Several times she could see the man in the corner. He had not altered his stance since she had been led into the room.

When the three men were finished, they sang Happy Birthday to her. It seemed to cap off the humiliation. Annabel enjoyed being treated as worthless, but in the hours after an event Alison would re-emerge and the self-loathing cycle would begin anew.

After the four men in the room had left the property Patrick and Peter then took their turn on her in the bedroom. Patrick in particular was frenzied, as if he was trying to outdo the previous efforts of his three friends. As she left the house in Navan, she felt as if, somehow, she had achieved something. It was the Annabel part of her. On the drive back to the airport hotel Peter was giddy with excitement and gratitude, constantly wanting her to re-run over what had happened and what part she had enjoyed most.

When they had argued in the hotel room Woolnough had made it very explicit that he would expose her secret life as Annabel. He said that people would soon know that she was a whore and a black man's whore! The way in which he spoke to her was crude and racist, the exact opposite of what she had thought this man to be. Woolnough had told her that he would tell her parents and that he had plenty of incontrovertible evidence. She didn't know if she was bluffing, but she didn't want to find out.

Alison had once stopped and called a halt to proceedings when one of the guys she had met in London had taken out a smartphone from his jacket that was draped over a chair. She thought he was about to photograph the ensemble on the bed; even worse, video it. In fact, he had been startled by a message as his wife had her own text alert. She could still remember the fear and then the relief that this guy wasn't about to break the Lifestyle rules. No pictures and no video. She had forgotten about that day in London as she left the house in Navan with Peter Woolnough.

What she could not have known was that thousands of miles away in Maryland Chuck Gretz had watched the whole event. From the time Patrick opened the door until Peter and Alison left the NSA analyst in Fort Meade was watching in real time. Although the 42 year old bachelor from Harrisburg, Pennsylvania enjoyed the floor show and admired the young woman from all angles, it was the little white guy in the corner who was his target. When the guy in the blue bathrobe finally got out of the chair and took part Gretz knew that the guys at Langley would put this to good use. Those spooks loved a sex tape. This one would go into Chuck's private collection, a secret stash that his supervisors didn't know about. Gretz was no Edward Snowden, but what he had just watched was too good to let go. As a misogynist voyeur, he was in the perfect job.

Jack's head hit the pillow like a depth charge. He took the kindly Doctor at his word that he would be contacted if anything changed. That authorised him to go home and sleep. He had stumbled up the iron stairs to his apartment. When the taxi dropped him off in Dame Street he had looked down the lane where the entrance to his apartment was. It was usually buzzing, but Temple bar was eerily quiet. People were staying off the streets tonight. Dublin was in shock.

When he awoke he grabbed his mobile, which had been on loud all night. No matter the time, if it had gone off he wanted to hear it. Exhaustion could wait. The voice mail icon was on the top of the screen. Shite, he had missed a call! He dialled 171.

"You have one new message…"

He hit the button and it was from Dicey in the office wanting to know if everything was OK. Then he noticed the time. Fuck, it was half ten in the morning. He called her quickly.

"Howya girleen?" said Jack.

"Jaysus. I was worried about ye!" said the little Cabra woman.

"I'm grand Dicey. Just bollixed."

"How is…"

"He's grand. They operated on him. He's still out for the count. But the doctor there reckons... well…we still have him."

"Thanks be to God."

"You can sing that."

"Is there anything I can…?"

"You're grand. Anything jumping there?"

"Stan was in earlier. That gobshite he was minding was on a plane this morning. He wanted to know what he was doing next."

"Grand lad that. I'll be in a bit later. I might go up to Beaumont first."

"OK boss. I'm holding the fort here."

"No better woman for it!"

"You mind yourself."

There was genuine concern and affection in her voice. Jack registered that, but didn't respond in kind.

"Grand so," said Jack and he hung up.

Then he had to do something that he didn't want to do, but first he needed a piss. The luxury jacks was a long way from the stainless steel shitter in Belmarsh, thought Dempsey, but it was still solitary. Perhaps it suited him. He padded out of the toilet in his crumpled shirt from yesterday and nothing else.

He picked up the phone and thumbed the screen. She answered the phone immediately and he was ready for her snarling response. Instead she was reasonable. It threw him.

"I haven't heard anything different. I called this morning and the nurse said he was still under sedation and not to worry. The consultant will see him later today and I can call then," said Pauline.

Jack hesitated at this open sharing of information.

"Ah grand. I'll talk to you so."

"Bye," said Pauline and the line went dead.

He didn't know what to make of that. She had been civil. He hadn't expected that. For the first time since he had woken up yesterday with the court appearance looming he started to relax slightly. Sure, his kid was unconscious in hospital and Dublin was bombed to fuck, but things would work out. He was sure of that. He reached into the shelving unit inside the walk in wardrobe and found a pair of grey training bottoms. He pulled them on and walked into the kitchen.

He would step downstairs in an hour or so and get a lunch in Niko's. They would look after him. The coffee was ready and he poured the orange juice into a tall glass. He even put the biscuits onto a plate. That was as homely as it got around here, thought Jack. He walked up the three stairs into the living room area at the front door. The conservatory type Perspex roof brought in the light. Without that this place really would be like solitary, thought Jack. The low table accommodated the plate and the coffee. He went back down for the glass of OJ, but it didn't survive the journey back as he simply necked the contents He walked back to the seating area empty handed and sat down and picked up the cup of black coffee. Jack didn't mind it that way, which was just as well as there was no feckin' milk in the place!

It seemed at least a week since he had picked up the remote control that activated the huge flat screen TV on the wall across from where he was sitting. He hit the button and the TV started to go through the start-up rigmarole. He selected Sky News. It was full of the Dublin bombings. Although he had been part of it, he'd had no idea of the scale of the thing. There had been pretty much simultaneous suicide attacks across the mass transit system. The Luas and the concourse at Connolly Station had been hit.

The presenter said that a statement had been issued to the news network Al Jazeera which included a video. Jack was slurping his coffee when a young man in traditional Arab headscarf holding an

AK 47 rifle looked directly at the camera and addressed the infidels of the world. In particular he spoke to the Irish people. In that moment Jack Dempsey stopped listening to his ideological rant and just studied the face. That face. He reached for the remote control without looking away from the screen. He found the mute button first time and the young man was silent even as he continued to talk. Dempsey just looked at that face. Yesterday, an age ago, he'd felt what the breath smelt like coming out of that mouth.

Jack Dempsey, who stepped aside for no man, started to shake. He encountered a very unfamiliar sensation. Fear. Gut churning fear. The lad on the video and two of his mates had blown themselves to bits yesterday to take as many as they could with them. How many were on that mini bus? Ten? Twelve? Volunteer Seán Patrick Dempsey had sceál, and he couldn't sit on it.

He walked out of the living room down the three steps into the kitchen and was in the bedroom quicker than a man of such bulk should have been able to move. He grabbed a large leather jacket that had once been destined for the German Polizei until Frau Merkel decided to change the livery. Jack had bought it in Omagh when he was up visiting an old comrade. There was a garden centre army surplus place that seemed to have all manner of strange product lines. The jacket had been brand new when Dempsey had bought it. The garment had plenty of pockets and it served as a walking office when he was out and about checking jobs. The shirt was dropped onto the floor, where it would remain until he got round to picking it up, which could be quite a while. He pulled on a plain black t-shirt and boxers from Dunne's Stores. The Levis were ancient, but they fitted him like a second skin. His runners were newish. He put the leather jacket on and went through the pockets. The wallet was retrieved from the suit jacket that was on the chair in the bed room.

He was good to go and he knew where he had to go. There was a man who was always in a suit that he had to chat to. Yet there had been a time when that man was far from wearing suits. Changed days… However, in that moment he couldn't think of anyone else to give this to and he certainly wasn't going to the Staters. The suits in Sinn Féin might have "moved on," but he wasn't there with them.

He closed the door behind him and emerged onto the metal

work landing. Sky News was still telling his empty gaff what had happened in Dublin the day before. Rolling news for an empty apartment. In seconds he was down on the cobbles of Temple Bar. The aroma from the kitchens in Niko's smelled great, but food could come later.

He was operational. There were more of those fuckers out here and someone in authority had to know. A reasonable person would have gone straight to the police, but there wasn't anything remotely reasonable about Seán Patrick Dempsey in these matters.

He walked out onto Dame Street and flagged down a cab. He bounded into the passenger seat.

"Parnell Square."

"Jaysus boss. I'll take the fare, but O'Connell Street is still a nightmare. You'd be better…" the driver trailed off.

"Grand, I'll walk." And with that, Jack was gone.

He lengthened his stride and felt his heart start to hammer. There was no way he would get on the phone about this. He had to see this man face to face. It must have been, jeez, three years since he had last seen him at a commemoration. He was all friendly and gregarious, but uneasy at the same time. Jack was like a poor relation turning up as reminder to the Lottery winners that they had come from nothing. He was quite the politician these days, but there was another time that they both knew about. That seemed so long ago, but yesterday had brought it all back and not in a good way.

The Austin princess had been bought for cash from a rude man in York. He got a good price for the car and sniffed. Jack drove it back over the A64 to Leeds listening to Thatcher laying into poor Michael Foot. No contest. The lock up garage was in Beeston in south Leeds. The area was rundown; no one would notice a shabby second hand car. The trick was to be invisible. To be so ordinary that no one would pay you a second glance. The Austin Princess is a broad car and the drive into the lock up was tight enough.

There was a small work bench in the top corner of the lock-up. The front bumper of the car was almost touching it, but there was room to squeeze around. There was a brand new black Adidas bag on the bench. A pair of household rubber gloves and the makings of a bomb. The makings of a bomb, but not a bomb. This was all meant to be done! He closed up the lock up and went to check where yer man had got to.

It was his job to rig the bomb, Jack was just the driver. He jumped on a bus into the city centre and got out on the Head Row, Leeds' main thoroughfare. He walked the two miles up to Bellevue where the two of them had a flat. In the year and a half they had been there he hadn't spoken to any of the neighbours and, consequently, the neighbours didn't know him or the Liam fella. Like the garage, it was perfect. They had lived in an old terraced house when they had first set up the unit. Jack had rented it from a pair of postgraduate students – an agency found it for him. They were Israelis with Yank accents. Jack had nearly fainted, but they were nice young couple. He did the blarney on them and he told them that his girlfriend would be joining him soon.

The housing association flats in Bellevue were perfect. Much, much better for their purposes. Far more anonymous. He had found them by accident. It was a break. There was no great key security, just a Yale lock. Jack turned the key and was immediately in the tiny entrance facing the toilet bathroom. To his left was his Bedsit and to the right yer man's tip. It took 30 seconds to find the place empty. The plan was to be over at the lock-up waiting for the car.

He wasn't there, the useless bollix! Where was he? A thought came into his head that he hoped was totally wrong, but he decided to check it out. If Dublin knew about this he would have his arse kicked for a month. He swapped jackets, putting on a brown leather bomber and roll hat. It wasn't much but he might not look like the same fella coming out of the building. Keep sharp Jack.

Gerry had got in touch to say that the thing was brought for-ward. There was no way that the car should have been bought and the Op done on the same day. This was tight. Anyway they were there. [I think this should go earlier in the section, to explain why Jack needs Liam so urgently]

He wandered down the road towards Kirkstall and he could see the lights of Armley prison. There were a couple of POWs in there he knew that. Leeds had a big Irish community and plenty of pub republicans. They were under orders to steer clear of these watering holes. He wouldn't be that fucking daft, would he?

Better to check it out. Jack hated needing other people to do a job, but this useless Belfast bastard was the gear man. He went up to a local taxi office, which was beside a bookshop that seemed to deal solely in witchcraft books. Inside the Asian drivers were sitting on a rough bench seat next to a hatch were the control was.

"Taxi?" asked the controller.

Jack nodded.

"Where to?"

"The White stag, Sheepscar." The controller said something rapid in Urdu and a large taxi driver, almost as tall as Jack, got up and walked out to a green three year old Ford Granada.

Jack sat in the back seat. This gave him two options to get out of the car if he needed to. Keep sharp Jack. The journey didn't take long the driver knew the way and the lights.

"Wait here," Jack said. The driver fidgeted around, in the universally understood swivel of a taxi driver who thinks his fare is about to bolt without paying. Jack was way ahead of him. He handed a tenner over – more than enough for the journey and back to Bellevue.

"Wait. Two minutes." The driver nodded silently and relaxed back into his seat.

The White Stag was the last building standing in Sheepscar. It had been a densely populated Irish area of Leeds back into the 19th century. The pub had been spared the wrecking ball and it stood in an oasis on a car park surrounded by a dual carriageway a slip road. Over the road, signs told you what lane to get into if you were heading for the A61 or the A58.

Before Jack approached the big double doors of the White Stag he could hear the session in full flow.

It was Reb night and all the pub republicans were on active service as usual.

Wankers.

Jack would be in and out of that place in two minutes, check the snug, the bar and the toilet.

He hadn't got five feet inside the door when he saw him. Jack felt the temper rising in him. He was hammered, that much was clear,

86

would he even be able to work? He was standing up at an angle, his right arm leaning on the wall. He was drooling over a woman on a stool. She had short dyed blonde hair and, in her jeans not a bad figure by the look of her. Liam looked up and saw Jack. He gave Jack that "Ah fuck it, I'm on the lash!" look.

Jack's temper was nearly over the edge.

He approached him and whispered as loudly as possible into the Belfast man's ear.

"We've got work to do."

Liam looked at the ceiling like Jack was the party pooper.

The woman turned and looked Jack up and down. She was a looker. Blue eyes, slightly turned up nose and big wide smile like a yank.

"Hello, what's your name?" she said.

"Paddy. Pleased to meet you." He didn't want to appear rude. She would remember that.

How, thought Jack, do I get him out of here without many people noticing? Anyway, is he any use? Can he work?

Then Jack got a break. Liam needed to get rid of some of the beer. He lurched towards the gents. Jack followed gratefully fully focussed on what needed to be done. There was one guy standing having a piss when Jack and Liam went through the narrow door almost together.

Jack acted all friendly to Liam.

"You OK mate?" he asked.

Liam, his brain fogged with drink, was surprised at Jack's concern and conciliatory tone.

"Grand."

The guy having the piss finished off and left. Jack wasted no time. He buried a right upper cut deep into Liam's solar plexus. He buckled like a rolled up carpet. Jack pushed him into the cubicle and shut the door. This, thought Jack, had better work. Liam was gasping for breath. He couldn't get a word out. Jack heaved him up off the toilet seat and buried another in his gut. Liam was now a total dead weight, but he was conscious, just totally winded and in severe agony. Jack leaned over and whispered in his ear.

"Sober up you useless Belfast cunt or I'll break your fucking neck right here and leave you in this fucking jacks!" He pounded Liam's exposed kidneys. Liam started to yelp. Jack, in that moment despised him and the man in Belfast who had picked this cretin for England work.

Was this the best the Army had? Jack was lathered in a sweat. He lifted Liam up and, finally got an eye contact that wasn't glazed over.

"Work!" snarled Jack, "It has to be tonight." Liam slowly nodded.

"We're goin', OK?" Liam gave a nod. They backed out of the cubicle as two lads came in for a piss, both of whom put their heads down and went straight to the urinals. Jack wanted to explain that it wasn't what they might have thought that they weren't, well, you know, but there was no time and they might remember the incident more the next day. None of this was meant to be happening. Cold water battered onto Liam's face from the tap. At last he started to rub the water into his face and nodded to Jack. The nod said 'OK, I'm OK. I fucked up, but I can work.' Well, that was what Jack really wanted the nod to mean.

"What about Alison?"

"Who?"

"Herself."

"Fuck, one minute. Sixty fuckin' seconds. We have to go to work. What did you tell her you did?"

"Worked in a warehouse in Kirkstall, industrial estate."

"OK. Now."

They pushed out into the narrow bar and herself was chatting to another fella. Result. Jack dragged Liam out of the side door. Thank Christ she was that easy!

The taxi was still there, but the tenner might have been wearing a bit thin.

"You long time." Jack handed him another fiver. Questions over.

"Head Row!" They would change taxis in the town centre and walk a few hundred yards Liam would need to be compos mentis when they got to Beeston and he didn't want the three places joined up. Bellevue-White Stag-Beeston.

The Head Row was quite busy for a Monday night, but no harm in that. They got out and the taxi was gone. They turned and walked towards Leeds Train Station. Liam hadn't said a word. He was struggling to get his head around the situation.

As they were passing the Midland bank on the right, which had a sort of square seat outside of the entrance, Liam veered towards it. He wanted a sit down.

"Two minutes." His tone sounded like an order to Jack. He was the senior guy so Jack went with it. Maybe he was trying to re-establish the chain of command. Jack needed to know.

"Liam you…"

"Grand, we'll get this done!" good, thought Jack, his brain was working. It had to be tonight. The scéal had come through. It was meant to be next week but they had moved it forward. It was tonight and they could do it. They still had time. This one was too good to miss. This one would be right up there.

In fairness, once he was standing over the gear with Jack holding a mechanic's lantern over his head he set to work. He was good. The man in the model aircraft hobby shop in London had been very helpful. Now the gizmo that should have been guiding a plane in the air by radio signal was going to be put to a more deadly purpose. With the server arms cut off, the switch had been modified to complete an electrical circuit when it received the radio signal from the control pad. They would only be a few hundred yards away.

"OK. The car," said Liam. He was sober and back in charge. It was like two different people, thought Jack.

The spare wheel was taken out and the well packed with commercial gelignite. The other fella had sourced that from a quarry in Southern Scotland. In all probability it would have been blamed by the police on Ulster Loyalists. Liam used a double detonator; insurance. This one had to go off. They wouldn't be able to back and retrieve the car. The carpet went back over where the spare wheel had been. It wasn't a big bomb in size, but the quality of the explosives meant that the Austin Princess would be turned into shrapnel in a millisecond, killing anyone near it.

Jack had some last minute things to do to the car. A back window sticker for the Parachute regiment. The other lad thought of everything. Belfast hadn't lied about this kid. He was good, very good. Anyone looking at this car in the car park of a TA barracks with the Parachute regiment sticker wouldn't give it a second thought.

It was time. They drove slowly to where the second car was

stashed in a side street near Radio Aire on Burley Road. When they reached the Mini Cooper, Jack stopped the Princess. He turned to Liam.

"You OK to drive?"

"Fuck off!"

"That a 'yes'?" Liam got out of the car. He was happy that Liam wouldn't be driving the bomb. Jack wasn't sure what would happen if the Princess and he were involved in a smash. Would it go off? The Op would be fucked anyway that's for sure.

It didn't take long to get "on target" it was dual carriageway almost all the way to Pudsey is a nondescript little place on the edge of Bradford.

They pulled into a side street with high hedges that were sorely in need of a trim. The extra bit of luck was that there was a streetlight out. Jack, for the first time that day had started to feel a bit better about things. Liam got out of the Mini and walked to the princess. Jack noticed that he pulled at the door handle with his sleeve. Jack was pleased. He was sharp now.

"Out." It was an order. Jack didn't argue.

In fairness, he looked less conspicuous than Jack. Even from a distance there wasn't anything that Jack Dempsey looked like other than a big red-faced Mick.

Jack squeezed into the Mini. Not comfortable, but this little thing could shift.

The Princess swished past the Mini and crossed the road over into the unguarded car park of the TA barracks. These fellas were asking for trouble. In the back seat of the mini was the Adidas bag. That was Liam's job. He didn't look in it or touch it.

He was back in a couple of minutes.

"This OK to do it, from here?"

"Perfect" Liam was focussed. He was stinking of stale drink, but he was sober.

Jack moved in the tiny bucket seats and the Browning hi-power 9mm automatic dug into his beefy side. It reminded him. Liam wasn't carrying.

He reached into the pocket of his leather jacket and handed him a 38 special snub-nosed Colt Cobra.

"Just in case," explained Jack.

"Grand." They weren't exactly equipped for the gunfight at the OK Corral, but it might get them out of a roadblock or help them hi-Jack a car if they were being chased.

Liam put the snub nosed revolver in his pocket and reached back for the Adidas bag.

He reached inside. There was the sound of fixing something, switching. Jack started to be slightly concerned.

"Everything OK?" Liam shot him a glance. He was on this.

"Sound," said Jack. This wasn't the drunk he had beat sober in the White Stag a few hours ago. Gerry was spot on. Timing prefect. Two Bedford army trucks pulled into the car park of the barracks. The lead driver even thoughtfully pulling up just parallel to the bomb. Liam put the Adidas bag at his feet and brought out a small black box with a small antenna out of one side and two control levers on the top. He flicked a switch and a small light said that there was power. Liam glanced at Jack and gave a slight smile.

"Give our fella a minute. He might be on board," said Jack. Liam smiled.

Cool bastard. Suddenly Jack was scared that they were too near and he was about to ask Liam if they were parked too close. BOOM! The mini shook with the tremor.

Car alarms went off with the vibration. Other than that there was nothing for a very long sixty seconds; then the screaming and shouting started.

Jack listened to it and felt sick.

"Drive," said Liam. Jack was startled out of it. Fucks sake! He almost took a left to avoid the scene but he had to take a right to get straight onto the main road to Leeds. It seemed like an hour, but in less than a minute they were driving on a perfect road surface towards Leeds.

Jack gunned the engine and thought, "Job done." This car would be abandoned outside the Serbian club in Chapeltown. They would split up; Jack would dump the gear. Liam got out and walked down to the bottom of Chapeltown road to the curry houses and late night Rasta shebeens where a drunk Paddy wouldn't be too out of place. Moreover, he was among people who had no time for Her Majesty's forces.

Jack flagged down a taxi and gave the lad a great fare. He was dropped outside a pub in Yeadon to the north of the city of Leeds.

Near there was a set of lock-up garages where this Active Service Unit of the Irish Republican Army had its equipment. He walked back onto the main road into Leeds and waved down another cab.

"Guisley," he said, trying not to sound too Irish.

The driver was Asian, a Pakistani, so he didn't really give a fuck. The other fella didn't have that problem, he thought, but the risks he was taking were no one's business.

He gave the driver the address and he was pleased that the light was one when he got there. He just hoped that Beth didn't have company; that would be awkward. She was a top girl. She worked like a Trojan in a local pram factory. She said she was the fastest girl in the pace. She was certainly the fastest girl to drop her knickers, thought Jack.

He knocked on the door and she opened it. His luck was in; she was wearing that little silky robe and a smile. She was alone.

"Well look what the cat dragged in!" she said.

"Sorry Beth. I'm empty handed. I'll go around to the off licence…" She shut him up with a kiss.

"This house is full of booze Paddy. So you're in the right place."

"I'm not interrupting anything tonight then?"

She knew what he meant, but she let it go and told him that the kids were at her mother's place.

He knew she had other company at times and he was fine about that.

As long as she didn't tell tales about the big Paddy that came visiting he was delighted to be her bit on the side, just as she was that for someone else. Beth had two children by a failed marriage. The guy had sounded a real piece of work and had died in a road accident. The verdict was that he was pissed out of his head when it happened.

They had already split up, but her eldest the lad remembered him. The little one, a girl, had no memory of her father.

She had been a really good find for Jack. She didn't have a notion that this amiable Dubliner was anything other than a fun loving Paddy out for a good time. Her house was outside of Leeds and it wasn't in an identifiably Irish area. The pubs were all local and he visited her to drop out of sight. She was happy to have him there, but not all of the time.

Afterwards she moved across the pillow to whisper in an impeccable Yorkshire brogue:

"Ay up! That were fuckin' marvellous that were."

And with that the petite little blonde bounced out of the room and slipped on her robe. Downstairs he heard the fridge opening and the kettle being put on. Jack stretched and smiled.

He could get used to this. No one. Not even his own knew where he was. It was just Beth and that suited him. There would be a lot of scoops in the West Yorkshire area over the next week or so and there were a few loose heads out there.

That was why he was edgy about the whole White Stag thing. If Belfast got to hear about that then yer man was for it. No matter how well connected he was to the Big Fella in Ballymurphy.

As he walked past Trinity College Dublin and the Central Bank, Jack headed for the GPO on O'Connell Street. This was where the Dempsey clan had got their first taste of Republicanism. It was hardly any wonder he ended up where he did, thought Jack.

He hoped yer man would be in 44. That was where he had his office. Fuck, he could be anywhere in that suit. He better be there, thought the big Dubliner, because at that moment he couldn't think of anyone else.

There was a time when having a place to hang your coat in the Kevin Barry Memorial Hall, 44 Parnell Square, marked you out for Special Branch attention and generally being considered filth by daycent society in the Free State. These days it was a smart career move. When Seán Patrick Dempsey had been younger and more dangerous it was a hive of revolutionary activity. He walked in and he didn't recognise the lad on the door. He was mid-twenties and looked as if he could handle himself.

"I'm here to see Liam…. Deputy McMillan."

The lad was no nonsense.

"He doesn't have an office here. He's down at 58 Parnell Square, that's…"

"Yeah. I know where it is. Grand," said Jack, and he was gone.

For years it had been the offices of An Phoblacht, the official organ of the Republican Movement. Selling it around the pubs of Dublin once a week was a rite of passage for young activists in the 1980s. There was always some Free State gobshite with too much drink taken that wanted to have a go. Funnily enough, Jack had never had much trouble in that direction. Then it had been named "Mick Timothy House," after the Irish Mancunian who had been the newspaper's brilliant editor.

Jack walked in and turned left into the book shop on the ground floor. The lad who minded it was an old timer.

"Jaysus Jack!" said old Benny.

"You well Benny boy?"

Dempsey was on a mission, but this oul fella was one that he wouldn't pass. Anyway, he might have sceál himself.

"Is that man in?" asked Jack nodding his head towards the door.

"Ah he, might be, but..." stammered the old man from Finglas.

"Yeah?" asked Jack.

"Ah, feck the meeting, He'll see you, big fella." Benny caught himself.

"I'm here to see JFK. He doesn't know I'm coming though."

"Grand job," said old Benny McCabe.

The movement was all that he had and he would sit minding this shop until freedom was achieved. Some people need something to assure them they're not just wasting their time waiting to be the star at their own funeral.

Most people in the Republican Movement had nicknames. One of the lads had spotted that Liam McMillan bore an uncanny resemblance to Kevin Costner in JFK. It stuck. One Dublin Dáil Deputy was, the lads concluded, a dead ringer for actor David Duchovny in the X-Files. He was always in a sober blue suit, never a hair out of place. And thus he became Sinn Féin's very own 'Agent Mulder'.

Jack walked out of the small book shop and turned left. The door next to Benny's domain had a sign on it which read 'Liam McMillan TD Constituency Office." Jack knocked on the door and tried the handle. It was locked. He gave the white door anther rap, this time a proper one. If there was anyone in a coma inside it would have done the trick.

There was a shuffle of notice behind the door and it opened, a bit hesitantly at first. It was a young woman, perhaps around twenty-two. She had short brown hair and an intelligent face.

"Deputy McMillan please," said Jack.

"He's in a meeting I'm afraid. Do you have an appointment?

"Tell him Peter Simpson from the Beeston Building Society is here about his account. It's very urgent and he'll see me."

Louise Toal didn't know what to make of this large man in the leather jacket and jeans talking all business-like. She had never seen him before, of that she was sure. There had been a time when he was an ever present face around that place. She decided that she better pass the message on.

In an instant Liam came out looking every inch the politician. He smiled, but it was a fixed politician's smile. Dempsey fixed with his gaze and let him know he wasn't there to fuck around.

"Ten minutes of your time, Deputy."

He let the word "deputy" hang there. It wasn't an accolade as far as Jack was concerned, but this man standing in front of him had a line of communication that Seán Patrick Dempsey had lost a decade ago. In that moment he needed Liam McMillan and he hated that. In normal times they probably would never have seen each other again for any reason. However, these weren't normal times.

Liam ushered him into his office with a sweep of the arm. The whole being a Sinn Féin suit thing suited Liam. It was a perfect fit for a smug arsehole like McMillan. Liam pretended to be pleased to see Jack.

"Howya Jack?"

"Not great. My kid. You don't know him. Mother's from Tallaght. He's only four. He was on the Luas yesterday. He got hurt. Bad," said Jack.

"Jesus…" uttered Liam. It was genuine. "Is he…" Liam started to ask THAT question.

"He's…he's. He's OK. Well, still unconscious, he's in Beaumont. The doctors there. A hundred per cent. Did great work."

"Jesus Jack… Look if there's anything I can…"

"There is; something important. I have to put something inside your head."

It was a turn of phrase that meant something very specific to Liam McMillan.

"Not here," said the TD in an instant.

Jack nodded.

"Phone," said McMillan and put out his hand expecting to receive something.

Jack knew that this was normal craic for such a yarn. Liam McMillian took Jack's mobile phone and his own, walked back in top his office and put them in a desk drawer.

"We'll go for a walk. Bit of fresh air," said McMillan.

"Grand job."

They both stepped out into the street and headed north on Parnell Square. It wasn't until they passed by the Teacher's Club that Jack started to speak.

"I was in court yesterday morning. Phoenix House. Down at Smithfield. Family court. Anyways... After that I went for a gargle up to Stoneybatter. The old haunts." Jack could see he was losing the man across from him, so he cut the story shorter than he had intended.

"Look..." said Jack to make sure he had Liam McMillan's attention.

"I bumped into a bunch of lads getting off a mini bus. Not far from the court. Foreign crew. One of them was yer man in the video this morning," said Jack, waiting for a response. It wasn't the one he wanted.

"Video? McMillan's puzzlement was genuine, but it infuriated Dempsey.

"Look, I'll cut it short. You're an important man these days."

"Don't, Jack..."

"I bumped into a bus load of those fuckers near Smithfield yesterday. There's a pile of them. I was standing next to one of those shites who blew himself up on the Luas," growled Dempsey.

"You serious?" McMillan was genuinely shocked.

"No, I'm making it fucking up!" snarled Jack.

"You told anyone about this?"

"Just you. This is Army business and I'm out a long time. But I reckoned that..."

The two men had stopped walking and had come to a halt outside the Irish Writer's Centre on the North Side of Parnell Square. Jack looked over McMillan's shoulder to see the wall of the Garden of Remembrance. He had temporarily stopped listening to the Dáil Deputy when he jumped back into the conversation.

"Say that again Liam?"

"Were you not listening to me Jack?"

"I'm going deaf. Getting old,"

"I said those days are over and it is a matter for the guards."

"We signed an oath!"

"Times change Jack. New realities."

"Not for me," snarled Dempsey.

"I was sorry when you resigned. You've been missed."

"Bollox."

"Look Jack. We're old comrades. Leave this go. The Guards will deal with this."

"Will they?"

"Sure,"

"So I've to go to the Peelers like a tout? Is that what's happened to this movement?" growled Dempsey.

"New realities, Jack. Changed world. We're solely political now."

"Against all enemies foreign and domestic," said Seán Patrick Dempsey as if reciting from a card.

"Jack for fuck's sake."

Dempsey walked out onto Parnell Square. He felt stupid to have even imagined that there could have been any other response from yer one. He walked across the top of the Square and down past the Garden of Remembrance. When he was a kid this place had said it all to him.

Abu Musa was giving the talk after prayers in his mosque. An audience of young men, no more than boys, sat on the floor their bare feet tucked under their legs in the pre-ordained fashion as they listened intently.

"Your brothers are now feasting in Paradise!" He had every one of them in the palm of his hand. He knew it and he loved the power.

He could feel that Allah himself had given him this gift to be a messenger of his divine truth.

"This was the end of days and the path to salvation will be built in the blood of martyrs. We will build a caliphate in Europe and deny this continent to the Great Satan. This little part of Europe would be an important part of God's plan to deliver his final victory over infidels."

He was in full flow and the boys waited eagerly for the next morsel of divine truth from this holy Imam.

"In this Infidel island they will claim to be your friends, but remember that is Satan's plan. His plan is to lead you away from God's truth. You must resist any contact with Infidel. They are not your friends. They can only become your friends if they submit to the will of Allah through the message of the Prophet Muhammad, peace be upon him. Your brothers yesterday did God's work! Soon you will join them in Paradise if you feel God's truth in you. Allah Akbar! Allah Akbar!"

As he chanted "Allah Akbar," the audience of boys joined in. His work was done. He had deliver God's message in God's house. He was satisfied.

Wednesday

Jack just knew that Tom O'Shea, if he was still in the land of the living, would be in that house in Terenure. Sure enough, there he was on this bright Wednesday morning out in garden. Sure, he was much older, but it was still the same oul Branch man. Jack walked up the garden path and Tom O'Shea, struggling with some over-grown briars, didn't hear him. "Enjoying the retirement?"

Old Tom O'Shea jumped and wheeled round as quickly as his seventy-seven year-old frame would allow him. He saw Dempsey and the old man was, for a moment, scared. When he realised that Jack was just standing there the fear subsided and anger overtook him.

"Who the fuck bought you Hush Puppies? I have a bad heart ye know!" growled O'Shea in his Kerry accent.

"First time I've ever been told I was light on me feet. How ye Tom?" joked Dempsey.

"Not too good for seeing your ugly face. How the fuck did you know where I...What de ye want?"

O'Shea was flummoxed as well as pissed off. Jack was enjoying the advantage. It was a first between them, he thought.

"I'm just after a wee yarn with ye Tom."

"I have nothing to chat about with your kind! It's Joe Duffy you want, not this fella! So phone RTE!" harrumphed the old ex-copper.

Jack got serious; he was there for a purpose.

"Tom, I have some sceál for you. Really important info, for ye boys in the Guards."

What Dempsey said blindsided the old Kerryman, he took a moment to process what had been said to him.

"Never thought I'd hear those words out of your mouth, Seán Patrick Dempsey."

"Times change Tom, and it's Jack. Always Jack," he said warmly. "Time waits for no man. Come inside."

They both entered Tom's house by the side door that led into the small tidy kitchen. There were no fitted units, or indeed anything that could be considered remotely up to the minute, in Tom O'Shea's scullery. Jack sat down without being asked at the kitchen table and Tom went silently to the gas cooker. He turned a ring on full blast and filled an ancient whistling kettle. Nothing modern, thought Jack, just like O'Shea himself. He glanced up the wall beside a row of coat hooks and there was a Sacred Heart looking over the souls that lived in this kitchen.

Jack spoke. "I was sorry to hear about your wife, Tom."

O'Shea did not turn around as he rinsed out two cups. Dempsey could see his shoulders sag slightly. This man was heading for eighty and still he had the will to continue, thought Jack. O'Shea didn't respond at first, like it was too raw for him.

He attended to the kettle and it was soon wailing through the spout. An old brown tea pot was placed on small Formica kitchen table. Like the rest of the place the table had seen better days, but it was scrubbed like it was about to accommodate open heart surgery.

"You want something stronger in that?" asked O'Shea.

"No, that's grand Tom. I'm off it, well trying to stay off it."

"Fair play. The ruin of many a good man." There was an understanding tone in his voice and a hint, Jack thought, that the 'good man' comment was directed at him. These were changed times indeed.

Duffy poured the tea and sat down. His body language said that he was intrigued by his visitor, but still wary. This was not the day that O'Shea had been expecting. Retired over twenty years, the old suspicion circuits were still there; they just needed the stimulus to switch them on again. O'Shea felt a strange sensation that he was alive again. Sitting across from a Provo who wanted to give him information. In his time there was no better man at flipping Provos than Tom O'Shea, and those feckers in the Phoenix Park knew it. At first he had been off hand, but his wily Kerry brain was turning over at a speed that he hadn't experienced in years.

"Sure I'm retired Jack, you know that don't you?"

"So am I, Tom."

"Why come here to me then?"

Jack appeared a bit embarrassed at that point, thought the old detective.

"Dunno, I always thought you were a straight arrow, for a peeler."

That caught O'Shea by surprise "Hah!"

The response made Jack a bit pissed off; "It's the truth."

Something in O'Shea made him forget the task at hand. He had something to say to the likes of Dempsey and he probably wouldn't get the chance again.

"Truth? Your lot and truth. Now there's a strange pairing," said the old man.

He was clearly baiting Jack and Dempsey knew it. This wasn't what he had expected from O'Shea. Jack tried to keep a lid on his temper and fought with himself to stay focussed.

"Pot and kettle Tom. Look I have a sick kid in the hospital and I have sceál for you. Useful sceál. This isn't a social call. If I give it can you get it to the top? Get something done?"

O'Shea was thrown by what Dempsey had said to him and by the obvious sincerity in his voice. In that moment he felt that he was behaving like a bit of a bollix.

"Sorry to hear about your kid. Wait. Didn't you have a kid that..."

Jack cut him off, "Yeah. Long time ago."

O'Shea continued, out of genuine concern rather than cruelty, but his questions were opening old wounds for Jack.

"Did you and the kid's mother have another?"

Dempsey was getting seriously irritated by these questions. This wasn't why he was there. "No. Another woman, long story. Tom, listen..."

O'Shea forgot himself and launched into a Catholic Ireland homily for the younger generation.

"Ah now. Different days. Kids everywhere with no fathers. Like farm animals! Different in my day. Marriage was for life. You made your bed!"

Jack was now very close to getting terminally pissed off with this old shite. He reckoned it was probably a mistake coming here. One last chance, he thought. "Come here to me for a minute. My kid was on the Luas. The bomb. He needed brain surgery."

Tom O'Shea was taken aback, he stopped the sermon.

"Fuck. I'm sorry lad. How is the child?"

"He'll be grand, they reckon, but they're not sure. The doctors did great for him, but he might need another operation. We nearly lost him on the night of the…"

O'Shea was angry now:

"Fucking Arabs. They shouldn't fuckin' be here!"

"It was an Arab that saved him, Tom."

"How so?"

"The doctor at Beaumont. Sound fella. He worked for hours on the wee fella. Jesus I owe him. Fuck do I owe him Tom!"

This still wasn't good enough for O'Shea.

"Ah, just doin' his job, they should be grateful we let them in here! Yer Man Scully is the only daycent man in the Dáil. He should be in charge! He would sort this. Another Kevin O'Higgins, he is!"

Jack Dempsey had heard this shite before and it was old then.

"You'll always be a Free Stater, Tom…" observed Jack.

O'Shea wasn't going to take this from the likes of Dempsey.

"I'm a patriot from a line, a fuckin' long line of patriots!"

"Yeah?"

"That's right! My father was mobilised in 1916 and he was out on Bloody Sunday for Mick Collins," said O'Shea.

"Your Daddy? Out with the Squad?" Jack was genuinely interested and impressed.

"Staff Captain Tom O'Shea, Cork No 1 Brigade. He was one of Mick's most trusted men in the Rebel County. In Frongoch with him in Wales. He was out that Sunday in Dublin. He nearly went to the feckin' match at Croker afterwards." A small man, O'Shea pushed out his chest as he put the Dubliner right.

Jack forgot why he was there for a moment and enjoyed the craic.

"Your oul Da was a terrorist killing poor innocent policemen and harmless British spies? Sure if he was there he was soldiering with my lot that day!"

This annoyed the old Kerryman. "Don't start with that Provie shite. Those days were different!"

Jack sighed and said: "It's easy to sleep on another man's wound."

O'Shea was puzzled, "I've heard that. That's a quote. Who said that?"

Jack enjoyed the advantage.

"Ah he was a terrorist Tom. Ernie O'Malley. He was in the Four Courts with my grandfather. Sure he might have known your Daddy down the west."

O'Shea hated this kind of talk.

"Your lot blackened the name of Republicanism!"

Jack was a veteran of these spats with old Free Staters. He was enjoying himself.

"Ah Tom. Just like those feckers from Cork Collins and Barry in THEIR time! The same thing was said to them off the pulpit about the Flying Columns and Mick Collins' squad here in Dublin."

The old man was getting frazzled and a bit tired. Jack reflected that this could become cruel to his host. Tom was what he was and Jack was what he was.

"Giving me the gospel according to Gerry Adams isn't what you're here for…"

"You're right Tom. I have scéal. That's why I'm here."

"You said that already," said O'Shea, annoyed.

Jack got down to business. At this point neither of them had touched their tea. O'Shea took a drink from his cup.

"Those boys on the Luas. I saw them, Tom.

O'Shea was nonplussed at first.

"The whole feckin' world knows about them. They made home movies about it, the bastards! Did you see that shite from Afghanistan? They cut a man's head off and put it on that internet thing. They're animals!" said O'Shea.

O'Shea was off on one as Jack tried to cut across him.

"Tom? Tom…"

O'Shea was furious about the world outside his door in Terenure.

"I'd kill the lotta them, the whole lotta them!" O'Shea fumed. Jack tried again and then old man O'Shea finally drew breath.

"Tom, I saw those two boys before they went on the Luas. The same fuckin' day! They were in Smithfield that morning. The thing is there was a crew of them; at least eight others, maybe ten. I think they came up into town from down the country. The two lads parted and the rest of them headed back on to the van that they had got out of. I wanted them there saying their goodbyes. The thing is, there are more of them Tom. These fuckers could do this again. Eight more time at least, by my counting."

O'Shea was all business.

"You sure about this?"

"Look, I SAW them!"

O'Shea was mulling over what he was hearing.

"Look Tom, I SAW these boys and their pals," said Jack forcefully.

"Tom?" checked Jack, looking for some response.

"It's a long time since I read YOUR file Seán Patrick Dempsey. I never thought I would be sitting listening to you offering information! Anyway the world saw them Jack, they're dead! Them and a hundred odd poor people who never lifted a hand to anyone. Kids and...Oh, sorry."

"Tom, for fuck's sake listen, I saw those two boys and the REST of them."

Jack was now fairly convinced that this was a bad idea. This was a befuddled old man twenty years retired.

"TOM?"

O'Shea was startled out of his thinking.

"OK. OK..." O'Shea was stalling to think what to do next.

"Tom..." said O'Shea. He wanted a response. Anything at this stage.

"I'm thinking," snapped O'Shea.

Jack tried one last time.

"Tom. Please. There are more of these boys, there will be more attacks. This IS sceál. Will you take this inside and put in someone's head? These boys need scooped now before they blow more people up! They're careless. They don't think anyone can't speak their lingo and they don't intend on operating for a while like... One operation for each man. One way tickets..."

The use of the word 'please' by Dempsey had O'Shea taken aback, but he still couldn't let the old days go that easily.

"Murdering bastards. Innocent civilians? Like you lovely fellas in England?"

"I'm fuckin' serious Tom! These cunts need lifted. Or... "

"Or?"

"Just get them lifted! That's what ye are paid for! My kid was on that Luas. My kid!"

O'Shea felt he had made his point. He got up and left the kitchen without a word. Jack didn't know what was happening. O'Shea came back in with a small hard backed note book that had seen better days. He sat back down and started to take notes. Suddenly he was a Guard again.

"What approximate time where you in Seán Heuston Station on the day in question?"

Jack was startled at O'Shea's formality.

"I'm not giving a statement!"

"I can't take a statement, but I need to the information to be sound." O'Shea was assured and in control.

I came out from Phoenix House, the court at Smithfield and I and bumped into them."

"You stupid bollox," observed O'Shea.

"That's how I got a look at them. Up close. Especially the lad I think was their OC. Tall compared to rest of them. I would know him in a crowd, Tom. Hundred per cent."

O'Shea was taking notes. Jack was ransacking his memory. There was something else.

"Fuck it!" said the big Dubliner.

"What?"

"There was a CCTV camera on the wall above those roller shutters!"

"Might be able to see the licence plate on the van if it was parked in view of the camera.'

"They'll get scooped then?"

"Once we know where they got off then that bunch of fucking bastards shouldn't be too difficult to find."

Jack finally relaxed.

"Sound Tom. I appreciate this. I know you'll get this done."

"I will. This very day and I know the fella to take it to. He's well up the tree now. I wiped his nose when he came out of Templemore! Ha!" Tom enjoyed the memory. Then he did something that totally surprised Seán Patrick Dempsey.

The old man leaned forward and patted Jack on the shoulder.

"You did the right thing doing this today. We'll get these fuck-ing gobshites before they can do anything else. There will be plenty looking for them now anyway. I would be surprised if they were in the cells before they have another shite."

Jack looked at the old man. There was still that steel in there he thought.

"Cheers Tom. I knew you were the man to come to. No messing about. I'll be watching the news for developments."

Jack stood up. He towered over O'Shea. The Kerryman must have only just made it into to the Guards on the height thing, but these days he was growing down the way. However it was his brain not his spine that was the important part of him.

Jack left O'Shea's house feeling that at least he had done something about this. Life is strange, he thought. He waved down a taxi and told the driver to take him to Beaumont Hospital.

The place was still in barely controlled chaos, thought Jack, but fuck it they were doing their best. The place had been deluged. Not a bed to be had the number of dead was still going up. People were missing their loved ones. This was fucking awful.

"President Adair was on the line today and asked about you, Garry," Scully almost spluttered his soup.

"Sorry?"

"Indeed so sir! Straight from the Sit Room too!" guffawed Brannigan.

"Sit...?"

"Situation Room. Where it all happens, Garry." Scully was hushed. He desperately wanted to ask what President Adair had said about him.

"The President knows how important you are to the set up here. He reckons you're a 'stand up kinda guy'. In fact he reckons you should be the big cheese here. The top guy!" said Brannigan.

Gareth Scully was in raptures.

"You're main guy though here...no question about that. The President is quite clear on that, Gareth," said the Ambassador.

Brannigan let it run for effect. Scully was all ears.

"The President doesn't think your Prime Minister guy can grow a pair for the shitstorm you guys are facing," observed Brannigan.

"Sorry, Mr Ambassador?"

"Jesus H, Garry, it's 'Chuck'. We're buddies!" Scully didn't think it was the time to correct Brannigan on Scully's first name.

"The President?"

"President Adair doesn't think your guy, what's his name? Maloney?" queried Brannigan.

"McCarthy."

"Yeah, he, the President thinks you're the guy here. Said that himself to me in the Oval Office!" chuckled Brannigan.

"You're the guy, Garry"

"Chuck...."

"Yeah?"

"It's Gareth," said the Justice Minister weakly.

"Sure, no problem. Jack Daniels? Or do you want some of your Scotch? You guys love it."

"More red wine would be fine Mr....Chuck," said Scully.

Jack looked up at the door of Nico's Restaurant and smiled. For the first time in days there was something familiar, something safe. He was perched on his usual chair at Nico's. It was the only place he sat, back to the wall, facing the door. Between Jack and the door was an upright piano pushed into the wall. Sometimes, if he was in later, there was a guy playing it. The place was class, thought Jack. Real class. Some things didn't change. There was little need for formal pleasantries from the staff. He was something of a fixture in this restaurant that itself was a fixture on Dame Street in the heart of Dublin. Jack couldn't remember the first time he'd set foot in Nico's but it must have been thirty years ago. It was at least twenty-five years ago. He couldn't really remember and he didn't care. It was a place that was familiar and where he felt safe. The fact it was now just round the corner from his apartment made his visits there ever more frequent and he had seen young staff there, usually all Italian, come and go. This was a real Italian restaurant, thought Jack. Italians came and ate here and everything about it was well, Italian. As he thought of the little fella in hospital and the days that had passed, he looked up to his right and he was sitting underneath a print of a church.

It read "del Castello dell' Acqua Felice."

The lad brought the menu and the wine list. Jack handed him back the wine list. The kid was new and didn't know the form. Almost absent-mindedly Jack asked about the print that had probably been there all the years that he had sat there. The kid replied in broken English – clearly Italian – said he thought it was a church in Rome. It struck Jack that the Italians had an ancient history and they were the better for it. As he sat waiting for his dinner he knew he was in his beat, in his operational area. His boys kept order in most of the places in Temple Bar. If anything major kicked off there was always a crew there fairly quickly to back up the lads on site. His security boys were mainly lads from Tallaght, but he had a fine bunch from the 'Mun.

When the lad came back he had the answer for the huge shaven headed man who was jammed into the corner and staring at the door.

Enzo Rossi knew that he would not like it if this man was angry.

"Sir, the picture. I ask in kitchen. The chef know. It is the Church of Santa Maria della Vitoria. It is in Rome. Definitely. Very famous. Very beautiful," said the waiter.

"Thanks lad," said Jack. He had just earned himself a better tip. Dempsey believed in looking after people who deserved it.

Jack paid for his meal and left Nico's, turned down onto the cobbled lane where his apartment was, walked past it and headed straight for the other side of Temple Bar where he had an office that no one could find unless they knew where they were going. It was above an internet café run by some Chinese guys. The narrow stairwell would not have been approved by the nice man from the Health and Safety Committee. The office was tiny and dingy but the rent was affordable.

There were two desks pushed beside each other. One was pristine and orderly with everything in its place. That was where Dicey worked. And the other desk was chaotic and cluttered and that was where Jack threw things to get to them later, lost them, then Dicey found them again. She knew he wasn't going to change, and he really needed her there. However, at that time of the evening he was surprised to see her there as he ducked his head to come through the door. These buildings had not been built for people the size of Jack Dempsey, he thought.

"You're pulling a late one," remarked Jack.

"You're grand, with everything that's been happening I thought I'd get on top of the things, and try and work through your mess as well."

"Sure you're grand, what would I do without you?"

"Anyway, the lads'll be turning up for their jobs. There's a few new lads I think. Few more lads coming in from the 'Mun."

"Yeah. They're well-recommended, and we've more work after all this shite on the Luas. An ill wind and all that, Jaysus."

Dicey set about going through some files that were on a shelf behind her. Jack thought that he'd have been in trouble if his secretary wasn't so petite. There would have been no room for a bigger woman jammed into the wall in that tiny office.

Then he thought, "This woman has a kid to get home to, she's probably been in here since early. I'll need to throw her out of this place."

So he said "Look love, you've probably been here all day, and I've just stuck me head in. You get going. Have you got a list there of the jobs for the new lads and let me do it."

"Ah Jack, it's grand, listen, me Ma's got the wee fella. He's having a whale of a time."

"Ah, no arguments now girleen. Give me the list. I'm sure it's all spick and span. You get yourself home. Here's a bit of a bonus. New EU regulations and all that sort of shite," choked Jack, and at that he thrust several fifty-euro notes in the direction of his secretary. She reacted with a start and smiled, embarrassed.

"Ah Jack for Jaysus' sake, I've only been doing..."

Jack cut across her "Look, no arguments girleen. I haven't been here. You been brilliant, and brilliant in other ways, about the wee fella. So listen alright, put that in the Christmas box for the wee fella, or buy yourself something, or go on the lash. Do what you have to do, but thanks."

Dicey Riley quietly took the money, put her head down and put it into her bag, like she didn't want to acknowledge it any more. She was embarrassed, but very grateful. She looked up. "Ah you're some man, Jack Dempsey."

"Ah, I've been called a lot of things," said Jack laughingly.

She got back to business, handed him the list, and said, "It's all there. My mobile will be on. I just need to get on to the Luas..." Dicey caught herself. Just mentioning the Luas seemed to be bad form. Jack picked up on it right away. "Yeah sure, you're heading out on the Daniel Day, right? And don't be worrying about those fuckers, right. Sure they're all blown to bits."

The brutality of Jack's language caught Dicey aback. She knew plenty of Jack's background; everyone did in Dublin; but the matter-of-fact way he was discussing this, and his kid in the hospital, made her think that there was more to Jack Dempsey. She didn't really want to know more than what she already did.

She became a bit flustered and said "Ah grand, I'd better be off now. Thanks Jack."

Jack took the list from her, scanned it down, and said, "Grand so, Dicey."

And at that, the little Cabra woman had her coat on and was gone, down those rickety narrow stairs and out onto Temple Bar. Jack looked through the list of guys and jobs that his secretary had prepared. A single A4 sheet. Everything in order, everything in its place. She was a real gem, thought Jack.

As Jack looked down the list, scanning names and phone numbers, his mind quickly drifted to the little lad in the hospital.

He had been helpless when he had lost his first son, and now, once more, he was helpless, impotent, as his young son lay in a hospital bed. Jack was awakened out of his introspection by the sound of footfalls on the narrow wooden staircase and deep, throaty laughter that he recognised instantly as emanating from his main man, Stan.

Stanislaw Franciszek Sosabowski Kowalczyk didn't enter a room, he exploded into the space. Six foot two, well-built and in excellent condition, the twenty eight year old seemed to have a constant smile on his face as he strode out to meet the world, shake it by the hand or drop it with a left-hook. Just being in his presence brought Jack's spirits up. This lad was a hundred per cent, thought the big Dubliner, and he would always be dependable.

"Thank you, thank you gaffer, for sister, thank you," said Stan.

This was the third or fourth time, thought Dempsey, that his very dependable Polish worker had thanked Jack for getting his young sister work in one of the bars in the area.

"It's grand, it's grand."

"No, no, big help Jack, big help. I tell parents Poland. Big help. Thank you."

"Listen big fella, you've thanked me, it's grand and it's better that it's one of the places we work at. That's why I've put you there for as long as she's there, unless I need to move you."

"Yes, yes, of course. I can check on her. She very young. But good worker!"

"Stan, the day I meet one of your country men or women that's not a good worker, I'll be shitting red, white and blue," said Jack, laughing at his own joke.

"Yes, yes, Pole. Pole work hard."

At that, two other lads, clearly not from Poland, shuffled in to get their orders. Jack looked up, smile gone from his face. "You two fuckers are late," growled Jack.

"It's the traffic out there boss. It's those Arab fuckers," said John Daly, all the way from the outlying satellite of Ballyfermot.

"Yeah, you've had a long way to travel, you poor bollocks," said Jack, very unsympathetically.

"Sorry boss. Anyway, we're here."

"Right, you're going to that place there. New themed bar. Upmarket," and Jack handed him a slip of paper. Dicey had the name of the guy and the name of the place they had to go on slips of paper, easy for Jack to hand out. She had thought of everything, thought Dempsey. What a girl.

Daly looked at the piece of paper and Jack cut across him.

"You can fucking read can't ya? Teach you to read in Ballyfermot don't they?" said Jack, just oozing the milk of human kindness and respect.

"Yeah, yeah, grand. I – I know what it is," stammered Daly.

"Well get yourself there then, don't be standing here costing me fucking money. Fucking move!" said Jack. The tone was insistent but, but nonetheless retained a certain warmth.

"Sure gaffer, sure gaffer, we're gone, we're out of here." And at that, Daly and his buddy Mick Foran, who hadn't even been introduced, but who Jack knew, because again, Dicey had put his name on a piece of paper, were gone to stand on the door of yet another heaving Temple Bar night spot. This was Jack, in his patch, in charge, and for the first time since that awful morning at court and the events afterwards, he felt something that he liked to feel all of the time, and that was being in control, being in charge.

After Daly and Foran left the office, Stan followed them out and there was something of a traffic jam on the narrow, creaky stairway as the other lads started to file in. It didn't pass Jack's attention that the only lad to be there on time, in fact five minutes early, ready to rock and roll, ready to get his job and ready to get it on, was Stan All the Irish lads, every one of them was late. Not much late, but they were late, and that pissed him off. He remembered being told by one of the old fellas who'd been out in the War of Independence that Mick Collins had said that Ireland would be free when he could teach an Irishman to read the clock. Punctuality still seemed to be something foreign to our kind, thought Jack. They shuffled in, he handed them their bits of paper, and they shuffled out. He was in charge, he liked it that way and no one who'd worked for him, either for five minutes or five years, thought anyone other than Jack Dempsey was the boss. That said, he looked after them all like they were family. That's why he had some lads who'd been working with him for years. Punctuality aside, when it came to it, anybody who'd been working for him for any length of time was entirely dependable. There was a simple reason for that; if they weren't dependable, they didn't last long. Jack Dempsey saw to that.

There was a procession of big lads ducking their heads into the office to get their orders. Then there were no more names on the list that hadn't turned up. Jack was pleased.

With all of the office work done, there was no reason for him to stay in that tiny office. There was only one place Jack was going to go, and that was to Beaumont Hospital. And with that, he flicked open the phone and phoned his favourite taxi driver. It was time to be heading up to the North of the city to see how his son was.

Jack walked down the narrow stairs, onto the cobbled lane and out onto the quays and turned right to head up to O'Connell Bridge. He was talking on the phone to Tommy by the time he reached Ballast House straight across from the O'Connell Bridge and looking up O'Connell Street, when as if by some magical radar, Tom's taxi swung left round onto the quay across from the taxi rank and opened the door. Jack smiled. There was nothing in life like reliability and loyalty, he thought. He had a good crew around him in Dublin, people who would always be there for him, and that was worth more than houses in Spain and money in the bank. He jumped into the taxi.

"Where to, gaffer?" asked Tom. He had a big smile on his face and he was obviously glad to see Dempsey.

"Beaumont, buddy. Take me up to Beaumont." The tone of Jack's voice said it all, and Tom picked that up instantly.

"Grand, grand job. How is the wee fella?"

"Aye, he's – he's out the worst of it I think, out the worst of it, Tom. Good man," said Jack, who was clearly in no mood to chat about the situation, or indeed anything.

It didn't take Tom to weave a route up to Beaumont that wouldn't have been advised by any satnav bought from Amazon, but he got Jack there in no time. Jack knew there was no point in trying to offer Tom money. He just waved his hand away. He wanted to do this for Jack, and the big man reciprocated with a gesture that indicated: "Many thanks buddy. I owe you."

The Beaumont Hospital that Jack stepped into was like another world from the last time he had been there. It was evening time, the day staff had gone home, and the hospital had a quiet hum of methodical organisation. There was hardly anyone there as he walked to the wee fella's ward. He was passed by staff who didn't acknowledge him. This felt soothing to Jack. Clearly, the people here were in charge, they knew what they were doing, they weren't fazed or fussed, and if that was the case then chances were his wee fella was gonna be OK. It's at times like this you look for anything, anything at all to give you some hope, thought Jack. He turned into the ward where the wee fella was, and for a moment he lost his bearings. He turned left, and he wasn't in the bed. That bed was empty and Jack panicked. But in fact it was Jack who'd taken the wrong turn. He took a step back and nearly squashed a young nurse who put her hand on his back. Jack turned around and, clumsy as ever apologised.

"Ah sorry, I didn't see you there," said Jack apologetically.

"Can I help you, are you looking for someone?" said Mary Doherty.

"Yeah, I'm – I'm looking for Pádraig…" Jack almost said "Dempsey" instead of "Duffy."

"I'm looking for Pádraig Duffy. He's only a…"

Sister Mary Doherty cut across him.

"Ah sure wee Pádraig, yeah. Yeah, he was in great form a wee while ago."

Jack tried to process what he had just heard. He stopped. He took a breath.

"Great – Great form? He was…he was talking?"

"Yeah, of course, he's a lovely wee fella."

Jack took a deep breath. He was processing what he was hearing and he desperately didn't want this person to be wrong. It might have been another Pádraig Duffy. He scrambled in his head to get his date of birth out. He was shite at remembering birthdays, it was… At that point Mary Doherty said, "He's round here, just follow me."

And in that moment, Jack Dempsey looked, and didn't see all the tubes in the mouth, taped in, an unconscious boy. There was the little fella. He was sleeping, he had lines running into his arm, there were still some monitors there, but he looked like a wee boy that was going to be OK. And at that point, Jack Dempsey, rock-solid, street fighter, ex-IRA commander; a man feared throughout Dublin, just started to gently sob.

Stan looked at his watch again for perhaps the twentieth time in half an hour. His colleague for the evening, Anto, was late, and this wasn't the first time. By this time Stan was getting seriously pissed off as he knew that there had to be two on the door. The crowds were starting to gather in the cobbled lanes of Temple Bar and he could sense that they were in for a busy night. Where the fuck was his colleague?

Then, in that moment, around a corner came Anto, all the way from Ballyfermot. He had a big smile on his face, as he usually did. He was a decent enough lad, and quite well-suited to this type of work. Over six foot, broadly-built, but with some subway blubber around his middle, he certainly wasn't in the same class as Stan

"Howya doin', me big Polish mate? How's the form?" chirped Anto.

Stan glowered back at him and with his right hand pulled back his left sleeve to show the watch.

"You being late again, you being late Anto."

Anto grinned at him, knowing that Stan couldn't do a thing about it.

However, Stan assumed that his co-worker was deriving pleasure from Stan's faltering grasp of the English language.

Stan hated that the fact that he knew that his English was bad, but there was only one way to get good at it, which was to keep speaking English, even poorly. Like everything else in life, Stan attacked objectives and reached them no matter how difficult it was. He had always been dedicated, ever since growing up in the rough end of Krakow.

Anto didn't see what the hassle was. Although he was technically late, nothing seemed to be happening, but he knew Stan had a stick up his ass about being on time. It was probably all that army shite in Poland.

"If Jack here he be angry! He be angry you not here!"

"But I am here, you big stupid Polish bollocks. Anyway, how's she cuttin'?"

"She?"

"How's. The. Form. Stan?" Anto deliberately paused his words like he was speaking to a backward child. Stan picked up on this.

"I am fine. I am here for work on time. You late."

There was not much small talk to be had with this big Polish bollocks, thought Anto. It was like being at work with a fucking guard at times, he thought, no craic at all.

At that the punters, in ones and twos, started to come to the fine establishment they were guarding. Most of them were absolutely no trouble; teenage girls on impossibly high heels and wearing very little clothing, already half-drunk from the half-bottle in their bags, and some clearly out-of-towners, mainly British tourists, wanting to soak up the genuine Irish atmosphere of Temple Bar. Even

Stan knew that this place was pretend and that any self-respecting Dubliner knew that this place was just a tourist trap. However, it was good work, good money, and he liked working for Jack. If he couldn't put two sentences together effectively in English, he had his physical abilities, and that was an international language.

Anto was fiddling with his phone when Stan looked up just as two young men were walking past him into the establishment. Stan moved quickly to block the way in to the nightclub and stood between the two young men and the front door. They were both late teens, early twenties, assessed Stan. One was five foot ten, slimly-built, the other shorter and pudgy. They wore the standard skanger uniform of trainers, tracksuit bottom and hooded top. Jack had been quite explicit when first deploying Stan to this nightclub some months ago that it was a weekend rule of the owners, no trainers, no trackies. Stan, like the good soldier he was, had his orders, and would carry them out to the letter, in any language.

"Is rule. No trainers here. Rule."

The two young men glanced at each other and then the taller one looked back and laughed "Out me way Borat, for fuck's sake."

His smaller, pudgier buddy laughed nervously at the in-your-face attitude of his taller mate. As the leader of the duo moved forward, Stan calmly put his left hand out with the palm resting on the chest of the young Dubliner.

"No trainer in here. Is rule."

The young man from Finglas realised that he would have to put this foreign prick in his place.

"Out me way, Borat," and then he pushed forward.

Stan glanced over the right shoulder of the young man and saw Anto looking on like a spectator. Stan realised that he could deal with this situation, but made a mental note of Anto's un-involvement in the situation. Stan took his right foot back to give himself balance, his left foot forward in a boxer's stance. His left arm stiffened so it became an impenetrable barrier to any further advance by the young Finglas chap.

"No one here with trainers. Go away. Go away, is rule."

The young man swung what seemed to be some attempt at a punch at Stan with his right hand, coming over in a sidewinder motion towards the left side of Stan's head. Stan took his left hand away from the chest and just swung it up, open hand, and blocked the punch easily. Then in one smooth, very practised move that he had been first taught at the airborne school in Poland, Stan kicked with the side of his left foot the heel of the right foot of his opponent. He then let the body fall and jerked back on the bent elbow that he had in a grasp with his left arm. The young man let a scream out of genuine agony. Stan merely let him go; he was no longer an opponent. He moved around the crumpled heap of the screaming Dubliner and faced his pudgy buddy, locked him with eye contact, and said, "Take friend away. No get in. Trainers. Is rule. Is rule from owner."

Stan looked away briefly from the shocked friend of the crumpled, screaming would-be thug on the ground, to look at the expression on Anto's face, which was a mixture of shock and an understanding that there was no way in hell he would ever be able to do anything like that. Anto shook himself and thought he had to somehow 'take part' now that the fight was over. He put his left hand on the right shoulder of the shocked buddy from behind him, pulled him round and said "You heard the man, now take your buddy and fuck off out of here. You're not getting in here, OK."

Anto was now very brave and felt able to reassert himself to any onlooker, but it was Stan who had sorted the problem. Because that's what Stan did. It was clear that the fight was over and all that was now to be done by the would-be clubber was to pick his mate up and to shuffle off. Anto was now like cock of the walk, chest puffed out, putting the queuing clubbers in order.

Anto was a big lad, well built, certainly a physical presence, but he knew he wasn't in Stan's league.

"No one's getting in here with trainers or tracksuit, it's a rule," barked Anto while assessing the assembled womanhood with a predatory eye. He was letting it be known that he was the man in charge. Stan didn't care about any of this. He walked towards Anto and just said into his ear "I need to go down and check sister. You OK here on own for five minutes? Only five minutes." Anto turned around like he was the main in the big picture.

"Sure, no problem Stan, Anto's got this covered."

Stan didn't believe that for a second but he wanted to go down and check on his sister. He pushed through the doors and went down into a cavern of thumping noise and flashing lights. Behind the bar he could see his teenage sister Angiesta. She was whirring around like a Duracell bunny, serving drinks and operating the till. In the noise that was the club any conversation would have been impossible, but she saw her big brother and smiled and waved at him. That said everything was OK. His parents had only agreed to her going to Ireland because Stan was there, and it was his job to make sure she was OK. That was why he was so grateful that Jack had allocated him to this club, and indeed it was the big Dubliner himself that had spoken to the owners to give the young Polish girl a start. And it was something they hadn't regretted, she was a brilliant worker, always on time, always turning up with a smile on her face. Stan turned round and went back up the stairs three at a time because he knew he had to be back at his post. He was at Anto's right hand in a second and said, "OK, Stan back. All good."

Anto looked up at him and smiled. "Sure everything's grand here. Big Anto's on the job."

This did not fill Stan with any great confidence, but he knew that if anything happened he could deal with it himself. There was now a steady stream of young clubbers – and some not so young – passing between the pair of them. For any male, Stan immediately glanced down at the footwear. He had his orders from Jack, and he followed orders. One young lad in particular seemed very appropriately dressed, with polished black shoes, suit trousers and a casual jacket. Stan thought he would be warm when he got down into that heaving sauna, but then that's what the cloakroom was for. He looked at Stan and smiled. Stan nodded. The young man was of Mediterranean appearance, perhaps one of those Spanish students that just loved to come into Temple Bar to soak up the Irish experience. As far as Stan was concerned, they were always nice, chatty, loud kids, never any trouble. With a nod of the head the kid passed through, being followed by two giggling drunk teenagers about the same age as his sister, wearing impossibly high heels and ludicrously short dresses. They only way they could not be freezing would be if they were on something. The young Spanish student smiled as he passed Stan the Man and Anto and walked into the heaving, throbbing darkness of the nightclub.

Upstairs in the street outside the club there was a steady procession of clubbers passing between Stan and Anto, like two pillars, one solidly-fashioned and the other a bit of a put-up job. But whatever his failings in the moment, Anto had enough physical presence to put off all but the most problematic customers. Anto called over the heads of the customers who were passing between them and sought to engage Stan in some conversation.

"Your young sister, then. Enjoying it?"

Stan didn't look at Anto when he spoke, as his eyes and his mind were on work as he scanned the male customers for tracksuits and runners. He had his orders after all. Without looking at Anto he said, "Yes, yes. Agniesta good worker. Enjoy here. My sister I care – I care for. Tell parents, OK." Stan was still at the stage of being very frustrated that anything other than the most basic sentence in English was beyond him. He knew what he wanted to say, but translating from his native Polish in his head and trying to mangle it into something that sounded like English; he was convinced he sounded stupid, and that made him angry, and Stan wasn't a man you wanted to make angry.

Sister Mary Doherty put her little hand on the heaving shoulders of this big man standing at the door of the ICU room where his son lay unconscious. Although the little fella wasn't her patient, she'd checked the charts and knew that he was making a good recovery. The ICU nurse, who was sitting by little Pádraig's bedside, didn't react. She'd seen it all before. Her job there was to keep an eye on the monitors and make sure everything was OK. So Niamh Mooney didn't look up.

Jack felt ashamed inside that he had let go, and Jaysus, even in front of a couple of women. That wasn't how he'd been reared. Men didn't show this stuff, just kept it inside; otherwise you weren't a real man. But his was all too much. He didn't even feel Mary Doherty's hand on his shoulder, but when he heard her voice he wanted to turn round, but he didn't want her to see the tears in his eyes, so he just spoke to the floor.

"Is he going to be grand?" He was desperate to hear the answer, an unequivocal "Yes" from the mouth of this nurse.

"He's doing great, he was conscious today. He's been brilliant. He's a real wee fighter."

Jack didn't know whether to stay or go. He didn't want to be in the way, these people were doing great, but he wanted to be with his son. In fact, he didn't want to be anywhere else but that room. And in his head, fighting for attention; was the thought of Dermot all those years ago, hanging in a garage for the best part of a day while people were out looking for him. But he wasn't out looking for him then because he was in a cell on the Isle of Wight, trying to make Ireland free. He decided to go. He didn't know what to say or what to do.

He turned, and as he turned he looked up and nodded an appreciative communication, feeling to Mary Doherty. As he turned into the corridor he saw herself, who was definitely not who he wanted to see. But of course she was his mother. Pauline Duffy could see that he had been crying and in that moment she didn't know why, so suddenly Jack became her source of information.

"Is he OK? Is he OK?"

Jack just wanted to walk past her, but he was in a situation where he had to communicate and that was something he wasn't good at. He just nodded, but that wasn't good enough for Pauline. She wanted words. She blocked his path.

"Is he OK? Fucking speak to me!"

Jack knew he couldn't get round her.

"Ask the nurse. He's doing grand."

Mary Doherty was suddenly by Jack's side. She smiled.

"Come in here Mum, the wee fella's doing great. He's doing great."

At that point, Pauline Duffy was torn. She wanted to just go in and see her son, but she also wanted to say something to his father. But as usual, that was out of the question. Jack just lengthened his stride, moved and was gone, down a corridor, probably quicker than a man of his bulk should be able to move. On the way out to his right at a Coffee Doc place, he saw Dr Karim. He was at a coffee machine waiting for a plastic cup to fill. Now Jack did want to speak to this person, so he turned promptly right and walked in and said, "Ah it's yourself, Doctor."

Again, the tall slim Moroccan man was in surgical scrubs and Jack thought to himself, "Does this poor bollocks actually live here? Jaysus, the hours these people put in are great."

"Ah, Mr Ah…"

Jack cut across "Dempsey. But Jack. It's Jack. I'm Pádraig's Dad, the wee fella you…"

"Ah yes of course, I'm sorry. So many at the moment. Um, we're very busy."

Jack understood this. He wanted his lad to be the only thing on this doctor's mind but he caught a grip of himself. This whole thing the last few days, this Luas thing, this place must have been mental. Must still be mental.

"Sure I know you're must be mad busy Doctor, but I was speaking to the nurse and…"

"Yes, he was awake today. A great sign. A great sign. The signs are very good. God is smiling on him and he's a strong boy. I think like his father" said Karim with a smile.

Jack didn't want to stare but noticed something around the doctor's left eye and down onto his cheekbone. Now the man was dark-skinned, but Jack knew a smack in the face when he saw one.

"What happened there Doctor?"

And Jack Dempsey was no doctor, but he could spot when someone was uncomfortable or embarrassed or ashamed, and it flickered across the Moroccan's face.

"Ah, a – a problem, a problem here. It's – it's OK."

Jack knew that he wasn't getting the full story and something told him to press it further. Ask. And he tried to pick his words because Jack had an extensive vocabulary for the landing and the receiving of blows.

"Did some fucker – Did someone hit you, Doctor?"

Karim realised there was no point in lying to this man, and anyway, he didn't feel like lying.

"Last night, late, um, I was going to my car in the – at the late-night shops and two young men – It happened very quickly. I'm OK."

Jack replied in the vernacular. "Fucking skanger bastar – Sorry Doctor."

Karim just sighed.

"Because of Luas. Because of bombs. People are angry. People look like me. People on TV make video. You understand. I understand. It's normal. But I am OK."

In that moment, Seán Patrick Dempsey was deeply ashamed of his city. This man was here, working more hours than he probably should have, literally saving lives, and some skanger decided to mete out some justice on him because he looked like the guys on the video. The guys that Jack knew, that Jack had seen.

Down the stairs he went. He passed by the cloakroom which was doing a brisk trade taking jackets and coats, but he had reason not to require their services. He walked into the nightclub itself and he was met with a totally alien environment. He could smell sweat and alcohol. In the middle of the floor the strobe lights momentarily revealed gyrating bodies. There was more bare female flesh on display than he could have ever imagined. He walked round the outside of the room, weaving between women on high heels and young men who were swarming around them. In the corner, there was one table that had been abandoned, so he found a seat. He sat down, looked at the scene and smiled. One young woman, emboldened by alcohol, spotted the foreign-looking young lad and approached him.

"You for dancing?" said the young girl from Galway. The young man just shook his head and smiled.

"Don't know what you're missing, son," she giggled, and turned, deliberately wiggling her bottom as she walked away. It was at that point that Ali Muhammad Al-Badri Al-Samarrai realised the full importance of God's work in this playground of the devil. He was in the wrong place now to do what he needed to do, so he started to walk very purposefully into the centre of the dance floor. The noise all around was deafening, the smell of the bodies almost overwhelming. The air was thick with sweat and alcohol on the breaths of the dancers. The girl who had approached him turned round as she was dancing with two bodies and saw the young lad and she moved towards him in a 'come and get me' dance move.

"Change your mind then, big lad?"

Ali merely smiled at her and gave the hint of a nod, but he was just standing there, the only motionless person in a heave of shaking, moving, gyrating bodies.

Rachel Murphy really liked this shy lad standing in front of her. She liked the foreign-looking ones, definitely. She'd just had a little line in the ladies and she was really up for it. Charlie did that for her. For whatever reason he'd pulled his right hand away, so being the cheeky bitch that she was she stepped forward, gyrating and flicking her pelvis, all Miley Cyrus at him. She took her left hand and her index finger and started to flick it towards her in a beckoning gesture as if to say to the young lad "Come and get it now. It's here if you want it." He just looked at her and smiled. Not a big, huge, grinning smile like "I've scored," but a serene smile that she saw every time the strobe hit the floor and flashed across his face. He was a lovely-looking lad, she thought, and he was hers for the night. She was determined of that.

"Show us your moves then. Show me what you've got," she giggled.

Ali smiled again. He could almost taste paradise. Rachel realised that this one would need a bit of encouragement, but he was a looker, so she reached down and grabbed both his hands in hers. His left hand she could take without any resistance, but he jerked back his right hand. She looked down, and in his hand she saw a coil of wire and something that looked a bit like a doorbell. She looked up at him, not understanding, and he just looked back at her and smiled.

She took the bent index finger and hooked it through the D-Ring of the zip on his casual jacket. He certainly wasn't a snappy dresser, she thought, but she really liked the look of him. She pulled the zip down, making it obvious to a blind man what she wanted. She thought he must be sweating like hell in that jacket in this place. All Rachel Murphy was wearing was the standard LBD, a thong underneath and no bra. Her coat was in the cloakroom, but that was just a short yoke, twenty euro out of Penney's. But she knew she looked the business. As the zip came down on his jacket his smile broadened. "Ah," thought Rachel, "a response. I'll have you my lad." And then she glanced down and didn't understand what she saw at first. She thought it was a t-shirt logo and then she realised. The last thought in Rachel Murphy's twenty-two year-old head was, "Oh Holy Jesus," and then Ali pressed the button in his right hand.

Anto and Stan were checking through the clubbers when, as usual, Anto had to make his excuses. Stan knew what was happening. This always happened, but he tolerated it as he could handle the situation most of the time on his own. Anto looked across to Stan on his right and said "Ah big lad, I have to go down to the jacks. Burstin' I am."

Stan nodded. The nod communicated that "Yes, I know that you are going down to the toilet, but I also know that you'll get a free pint when you're down there, so you're not really doing your bladder much use." It was that sort of nod. Stan couldn't put that together in a coherent English sentence yet, but he knew Anto was at it. But he had the situation under control at the queue, so it was no problem. Having received Stan's nod Anto skipped down, eagerly anticipating the pint and maybe getting a chance to have a quick chat with the new redhead who had started the same day as Stan's sister. With Anto happily going downstairs to get his pint, Stan moved more to a more central position in front of the large double doors to check the crowd going in. It was only a step across, but it made him more of a barrier as opposed to a bystander, and Stan was on duty.

As he was looking along the fairly orderly queue – well, as orderly as it got – outside the Dublin nightclub, he was scanning lower legs for trackies and trainers more than making eye-contact, assessing if there was a problem coming along the line, and thankfully he couldn't see any. And at that moment, a huge lorry hit him from behind and propelled him into the queue, knocking them over like skittles in a bowling alley.

Jack Dempsey was walking out of the main door of Beaumont and rummaging for his phone to get a taxi. It would be probably too late for Tom, so he would use this MyTaxi thing that Dicey had put onto his phone. It seemed to work OK, although he hadn't been sure of it at first. Then he heard a car door slam hurriedly in the staff car park, and a woman, about thirty, running past him. Then there was the sound of more feet running, and then a car screeching in what he didn't know was the staff car park.

Something was happening, thought Jack. Something bad.

Eddie McCarthy had been a paramedic in Dublin for five years, but nothing prepared him for what he saw as he ran down the narrow lane in Temple Bar to the entrance of the nightclub. He had been in Cork visiting an aunt when the Luas bombs had gone off, so this was the first time that Eddie had ever been at a bomb site, and the first thing that hit him as he got close was the smell. He'd never experienced the sensation that was going through his nostrils at any time in his personal or professional life. That, and what he would have expected at a bomb site, which was screams. If he had been asked the day before "What would you expect to hear at a bomb site?" it would be screams. But the screams he was hearing were like nothing he could ever have imagined.

Like all first-responders, Eddie was trained in triage: Ignore the ones that are walking around screaming, because they are conscious, and they can walk. Go to the ones that are lying unconscious, and check for vital signs. He was at this stage so practised in dealing with the unconscious of the Dublin streets that a finely-tuned robot from Japan couldn't have the job as well as he could, if such a thing had even existed. He weaved between dazed and screaming club-bers, some of them just shocked, others suffering from lacerations and head-wounds.

To the onlooker, it looked like this man, with his yellow vest and his green builder's hat and pack on his back, was running past people in need, but what he was doing was trying to get to the people who were really in trouble and they were almost certainly inside the club. The two large, heavy, wooden doors that Anto and Stan had guarded like sentinels were gone, in many thousands of pieces, the moment that the air blast had rushed up the stairway. The splinters and larger pieces had become shrapnel, spraying anyone who happened to be in the way.

Before attempting to go into the club, Eddie did a quick scan as his not-so-fit buddy Jimmy Doyle caught up. There were several people lying in the laneway, motionless. A quick check for vital signs proved to McCarthy and his colleague that they were beyond saving. A two-finger, index and middle finger pressing into the throat felt for a pulse. Then the ear to the mouth, listening for a breath. Then a hand over a midriff, checking for the rising and falling of a breathing person.

McCarthy looked up from the first, a girl who had been wearing a short red dress with dyed blonde hair with glittery fingernails. He looked up and shook his head. She was gone. It was easy to see why, as a large part of what had been the door had impaled her. It had entered just below her ribcage on the left side, and had caused massive internal damage. By the time these Dublin paramedics had got there, she had been dead for several minutes.

The taxi had got as far as Bachelor's Walk. Jack could see the flickering lights of ambulances and other emergency vehicles all the way down Aston Quay. He got out of the cab and did his best to run across O'Connell Bridge. Twitter had said "Bomb in Temple Bar." The hashtag "Pray for Dublin" was trending again. Twice in less than a week. He instinctively headed to where his folk were on duty. The word "nightclub," meant that he immediately ran to where Stan was working. He hoped he was wrong, but the bomb seemed to have gone off in an upmarket venue in Aston Place.

By the time he got there the lane was already taped off, with a young Garda minding the yellow crime scene barrier. Jack had done his best to jog most of the way down Ashton Quay to the barrier, and he was wheezing and fit for not very much. The young guard was assessing whether or not he had a call to the paramedics on his hands as he saw this large, overweight man put his hands on his knees and bend over.

"You OK sir?" said Garda John Brophy, a native of Carlow.

"I'm fucking great. I'm training for the fucking Olympics," said Jack, trying to cope with the buffeting of his heart against his ribs.

As Jack caught his breath, he said, "I have to get through there. I run security for a…"

"Sorry, sir. No one's allowed through at the moment. There's been a…."

"I fucking know what happened!"

Young Garda Brophy was doing his best.

"There's a number you can call if you're worried about anyone. It's…"

"Look kid…" said Jack, starting to boil. At this point, Garda Brophy tried to appear taller and, well, more Garda-like as this large man towered over him. Jack made a calculation: Push through here and get scooped. And what would that achieve? It wasn't a result. Jack turned to walk away, and recognised an older face under a Garda cap coming towards him. Eugene McGuinness was a decent sort. He worked out of Pearse Street these days, and he knew Jack's security operation in the town. Jack spoke to him.

"Howya Eugene?"

"Jack!"

"Fucking gobshites."

"Bastards," replied Eugene. Eugene McGuinness was from Louth, and had relatives in South Armagh. It coloured his view of things. He knew all about Jack, well, what was publicly known about Jack. Privately he had no problem with it, with what had happened in his home county when he was a young boy.

"Any scéal?"

Eugene stopped. "The bomb was in Angela's, that nightclub place."

Jack's heart sank.

"I had lads working there, Eugene."

McGuinness could see the anguish on Dempsey's face.

"Look, it's bad, big fella. That's all I know from this," as he tapped the radio attached to the side of his high-vis Garda vest.

"Can you get me through?" said Jack, almost pleading.

"Not a chance, Jack. Not just now. Sure they're still digging bodi…" Eugene McGuinness stopped himself. He didn't need to be that graphic. Jack was distraught, and McGuinness could see it. The Louth man knew he had to do something for Jack if he possibly could.

"You got my number Jack? My number?"

"No, but you have mine. Here," said Jack as he flicked a business card out from the sleeve pocket of his bomber jacket, where he carried a stash of them. It was Dicey's idea, and a good one at that.

"You hear anything, I'd appreciate it Eugene. That would be a hundred per cent."

Eugene McGuinness took the business card from Jack Dempsey and very deliberately put it into an inside pocket of his Garda tunic.

"I've gotta go now big fella, but I will be in touch if I've got anything for you. Awful sorry Jack."

Jack Dempsey nodded his appreciation. "Sound, Eugene. Sound fella. Mind yourself."

McGuinness and his colleague walked towards the tape and went under it. Jack Dempsey watched them going away. He turned round and walked back towards O'Connell Bridge. The noise of the assembled sirens seemed to get louder, a deafening cacophony of urgency, chaos and grief. Around Ashton Quay and O'Connell Bridge and Westmoreland Street, young people in their "going-out" clothes were wandering around distraught, crying and dazed. Half-way across O'Connell Bridge, Jack reckoned that it was no use for him to stay here, but there was a man he had to have a very serious word with.

Tom O'Shea jumped out of bed as he heard his front door in Terenure almost come off of the hinges. There was mighty, steam-hammer tump after thump on the door. It was a knock that O'Shea himself had given to many a criminal over his long career in An Garda Síochána. It was as the old man stumbled down the stairs that he realised that he didn't have a weapon in the house. He could always have applied for one, but didn't think it necessary. He thought of going into the living room to pick a fireplace poker up, but then just decided to shout through the door to whoever was banging the door in such an angry and deranged manner.

"Who the fuck in the name of Jesus is that?"

"Open the door to me ya old bastard!"

"Is that you, Dempsey?" said the old man.

"No, it's Garret fuckin' Fitzgerald. Open the door."

O'Shea's police judgement told him that the man standing outside his door posed no real threat, but there had better be a damn good explanation for his presence. Dempsey heard the clanking of the chain and the turning of the lock. He didn't ask to be invited in. He walked straight past the old man standing in his pyjamas, much shorter than Dempsey. Dempsey simply entered and walked into where he had been sitting, only a day before, in O'Shea's kitchen.

This enraged O'Shea even more than the fact that he'd been woken up out of his bed in the middle of the night, so he followed Dempsey in, ready to have it out with him. Dempsey turned round, standing in the middle of the kitchen, and let rip.

"I fucking trusted you, you old Free State bastard. Fucking trusted you. Stuck in my craw to come to you, you Peeler bastard."

"Wh-What are you in the name of the mother of Jaysus speaking abou-" Before O'Shea could finish his sentence, Dempsey was in no mood to hear explanations or process caveats. He was just very, very angry.

"I trusted you, I brought you scéal. You said you would get it fixed. And now this happens tonight. You useless old doddering cunt!"

At this O'Shea's temper broke. He knew he was old, he knew he wasn't the man he was, but he wasn't taking this from this skanger.

"Who the fuck are you calling old, you useless piece of…"

At that point Dempsey realised, as his temper started to recede slightly, that old man O'Shea had no idea what had happened in Temple Bar tonight.

"You don't fucking know, do you? You demented old cunt, do you? You doddering, old, piss-stained fucker…"

O'Shea then realised that Dempsey was genuinely angry about something and that he might have had some acceptable reason for his late-night appearance, but that reason was still a mystery to Tom O'Shea. The Kerryman lowered his tone. One of them had to back down in this, and in this case it would be the Kerryman.

"What's happened, Seán?"

The very fact that O'Shea had used his first name, and in a sincere tone, pulled Dempsey back. The tension gone from the confrontation, Dempsey's shoulders sagged under the weight of it all. He sat down, put his head down, looking between his feet at the linoleum floor of this old man's well-scrubbed, well-looked after house. He didn't look up, but merely spoke to the linoleum.

"Another one tonight. Temple Bar. Suicide bomber. I couldn't get through the line. My lads on the door are both dead. They're still counting the bodies…"

It hit O'Shea like a slap in the face.

"Oh Holy Jaysus. Ah son…"

Dempsey was trying to keep a hold of it. "Ah, don't start. One of my lads, he got his sister a job there. I spoke for her. He said she was seventeen but she might have been younger. I don't know if… Ah fuck, it's a mess down there…"

Jack was trying to compose himself so this wouldn't start a row again. He looked up and said, "Now don't rear up at me you old bastard, but you did put this in to your boys, didn't ya?"

O'Shea didn't take anything like it was bait or a gesture. This man had reason to be angry. He'd brought information to O'Shea, and the Kerryman had promised him he would do something with it, and he had, but the man sitting in his kitchen didn't know that.

So O'Shea just steadied himself, took a deep breath and waited for Jack to look up, locked him with eye contact and said "On the soul of my past wife, and those two children of mine, I took it straight into the Park and spoke to a man who would know what to do with it. My word good enough for you, Seán Patrick Dempsey?"

At this point, Dempsey had another focus for his anger, and it wasn't standing in the kitchen in Terenure.

"Fucking useless bastards!"

O'Shea was ransacking his now fully-awake mind to think what could have happened.

"Look, Seán. I – I can only think that some fecker has dropped the ball on the chain of command. I sat down with the man. I went through it with him. They made me a cup of tea, and they came back and they said they'd got the CCTV out of the place where you'd bumped into those boys and it looked like we were suckin' diesel."

Jack was thinking very, very seriously about what he was hearing from inside An Garda Síochána from this old man who used to be his adversary, but at this point seemed to be his only hope. Jack took a breath, looked up.

"OK, OK Tom. So you're saying they accessed the CCTV at that place where I bumped into those feckers and got the plate off the van."

"That's exactly what I'm telling you."

"So why weren't those fuckers scooped?"

O'Shea didn't have a response, but one possible answer was starting to trouble him. Lots of the buried stuff from the 1974 Dublin bombings was starting to gnaw at his gut again, but he wouldn't tell the man in front that. There were things that had to stay in the job, and even all these years after retirement he was still a member of An Garda Síochána in his head.

"I'll go back into the Park tomorrow and see that man if he'll see me. He should, he's way up the tree now but there was a time when I was wiping his arse at Store Street."

Jack laughed at the idea, and that sort of broke the tension that the two men were feeling. He looked up and said "There's something not right about this Tom. I believe you. I believe you took it in. But those boys should have all been scooped."

O'Shea was now being the deductive policeman, the brilliant detective that he had been for decades in the Force.

"Now you don't know it's for sure that it's the same…"

Jack cut across him, anger rising again. "Yeah, there's two lots of suicide bombers in Dublin. Yeah, yeah, sure. For fuck's sake. Cop on Tom!"

"Yeah, the chances of it not being the same bunch of boys are close to zero, in fairness."

"So you're in the Park, give these boys top-class scéal, they get it on a plate. They should get them where they are, or where they've been, with all this surveillance shite they've got now. And hours later, one of their boys walks into a nightclub in Temple Bar and blows himself to fuck. That's more than dropping the ball, Tom."

"Ah, you're ahead of yourself now, Jack."

Tom's use of Dempsey's preferred name help to bridge the gap somewhat between the two men. Jack mulled something over in his head. Should he tell this man? But he did trust him. He looked up and said to Tom, "Tom, there's more of these fuckers. Now, I don't know what your guys in the Guards are doing, but somebody has to find them. If I can get more scéal on these feckers, and I bring it to you, will you make sure that something happens? Will ya?"

There was something close to pleading in Jack's voice, and that disarmed Tom O'Shea. He had never seen Dempsey like this. Not in all the years that he had hunted him, in all the years he had tried to get a set of handcuffs on him for operating in the IRA's Dublin Brigade, knowing that this was a central man in directing men and munitions over to England where terrorist atrocities were happening. Here was this man, all these years later, in his kitchen, begging O'Shea to process information on catching bombers. O'Shea's jaundiced view of the world enticed him to say something cutting about that, but he realised it wasn't the time. He wanted to stop these guys just as much as Dempsey did, and, as he knew, Dempsey had a child in the hospital after the Luas bombings.

"I give you my word. If I'm telling you a lie now it's the first lie I've ever told you, Seán."

With that authorisation, with that promise, Jack now felt that he had a plan of sorts; and as he was taught in his early training in the Republican Army, a bad plan is better than no plan.

Jack looked up.

"OK, I'm gonna get someone to help me on this. And he'll know everything."

O'Shea was confused about what Jack was saying.

"Well, he'd need to be a clever fecker."

"Well, don't they say that God knows everything? I'm going to have to go and speak to God."

O'Shea didn't like this talk. He was a daily communicant.

"Don't be blaspheming in my kitchen."

"No, I'm gonna have to go and speak to God. He'll know what to do."

"And where would the likes of you find God?"

Jack realised he had no idea what he was on about, and smiled. It was one thing that hadn't made it into the files.

"Well, when God isn't at Paradise watching Celtic, he lives in Donegal these days. Last time I heard he had married a Colombian. I'm going to see him tonight."

"Seán Patrick Dempsey, I have no idea what you're on about. But you mind yourself, and if you do get anything more on these boys, come back and tell me. Just don't knock on my door at this time of the fucking night! Nearly ended me with the fright ya big gobshite!"

And at that, the little Kerryman put his hand out.

"Now did you hear me? You mind yourself, son. These are bad, bad hateful fuckers. And I'm sorry about tonight. I'm really sorry about all of it."

Jack stood up, took the handshake and brought his left hand over, clasping little Tom O'Shea in the crook of his arm, looked at him, and nodded. The look and the nod was enough, and at that, the big hulking shaven headed man in the black leather jacket was walking out the door like he'd never been there. He closed the door behind him when Tom O'Shea sat down. The big fella was right, there was something that was stinking about this. But before O'Shea could properly process it, he would have to make a cup of tae, because he was heading into the Park start of business to have a word with that useless bollocks who now sat behind that great big desk.

For the first time since he had been banned from driving, Jack Dempsey cursed the stupidity of getting behind the wheel that night. Then again, it had been the Gobshite's idea. The Gobshite was good at that, always on hand to give him advice when he was at his weakest. He unlocked his iPhone and opened the MyTaxi app, and was told that there was a car in the area. This surprised Jack given the time of night. He walked out of Tom O'Shea's front garden and out onto the road, and very quickly the taxi was there. He climbed in beside the driver and said "Busáras."

The driver glanced to the side and said, "Any buses this time of night?"

"Well, we'll see when we get there," said Jack, who was clearly in no mood to chat.

The driver stayed silent for the rest of the journey, which didn't take long given the lateness of the hour, and before long they were passing Liberty Hall with James Connolly looking across, keeping an eye on the Irish Labour movement. The taxi came to rest between Busáras and the Customs House, where Jack's grandfather had incinerated a lot of the Empire's Irish records back during the War of Independence. Jack went to his wallet absent-mindedly and the driver said

"It's grand. It's in the app. The payment gets processed."

Jack handed him a tenner, said, "That's a tip. For keeping quiet" and gave him a little smile. The driver was delighted. He put his index finger to his eyebrow in a sort of mock salute, tipped it towards Jack and said

"You're a gent, sir, you're a gent. I hope you get that bus!"

Jack often thought that the Busáras Bus Station, as the main bus station in the Republic of Ireland, was an embodiment of how shitty and down-at-heel the Free State could make things. At this time of night it was a gathering point for the homeless and the hopeless, and people like him who just wanted to get a fucking bus.

He wandered into the large, mostly empty concourse, and saw a lad in a yellow high-vis vest and a radio walking across. Jack cut him off at forty-five degrees and the man stopped to await Jack's question.

"I need to get to Letterkenny, when's the next bus?"

The man thought for a second. "Ah, that will be the ..., but I'll just check for you."

"Cheers boss," said Jack.

Jack walked across and sat down on one of the park bench-type wooden chairs. There was a very thin young man who was going around everyone who was sitting asking them if they had any change. He had a polystyrene cup. He was clearly begging, and Jack reckoned that if he got enough money he would be escaping the misery of his existence for the duration of a hit. He came towards Jack. Jack looked up, and the look said, "Fuck off." But the young junkie was desperate, and took a step towards Jack.

"Any change there, mister?"

"No, but I could break your fucking jaw for begging."

The young man, who probably weighed about the same as one of Jack's arms, didn't want to push the issue. He was desperate, but not that desperate, so he shuffled off. To the onlooker, this would have looked like an interaction between a vulnerable person and a very unfeeling man, and in that moment, that would not have been an inaccurate assessment.

But Seán Patrick Dempsey had other things on his mind. As he was waiting for the bus, he thought that it would have been much easier to jump in a car. But that would just cause more problems if he was stopped. And then there was the other point whereby, if there was something not right going on, if someone was following him, then being on a bus would be a good way to find out. As this thought went through Jack's head, he caught himself: Why would anyone be following him?

The conversation in the kitchen with O'Shea was replayed in his head. He did believe the old Kerry bastard had taken the stuff into the Park. He believed everything he had said, but what he couldn't process was why there hadn't been some scoop-up operation. The idea that there were two sets of Islamic suicide bombers in Dublin was just nonsense. It was the same group of boys, no question in Jack's head. And as he was trying to fit the chess pieces inside his head, it washed over him again, standing at the tape, being held back by the guards, and hearing that the two security lads on the door were probably dead. He should have gone to hospital, he should have checked it out, but something had made him in the first instance go to O'Shea's door.

And now he was sitting in Busáras, ready to head north to Donegal, to have a word with God. Jack asked himself the question inside his head: Was he making any sense? His own child was in the hospital, shouldn't he go back there and visit? That, after all, was all that mattered. But something gnawed at Dempsey, that he knew he could change things, he knew he could make a difference. It was the same gnawing in his gut he had felt when he was eighteen years of age, when he'd walked through a door in the flats in Ballymun and sat down with a man and asked him to be allowed into the Irish Republican Army.

The Bus Éireann coach stopped at a garage on the outskirts of Monaghan for a toilet and snack break. The place did a nice little trade selling the usual pit-stop shite that stops you falling asleep at the wheel. There were three single toilets in a row around one side of the building. Jack waited in line and the man who came out of the toilets got a start to see big Jack standing there, so close. Dempsey could have that effect on people. As Jack stumbled back towards the coach, his stomach reminded him that it had been many hours since there had been a delivery there. He turned left and walked into the garage shop, where his fellow passengers and local taxi drivers made up the bulk of the night-time clientele. Two local lads were at the self-service coffee machine, very Monaghan by the sounds of them. They were chatting about the latest Dublin bomb.

Jack questioned the sense of what he was doing going to Donegal several times on his journey. Day was starting to break as the bus entered Sion Mills. It was like someone upstairs was poking a stick in his ribs and laughing at him. The first time he'd heard of the place was in the late '80s at a training camp in Donegal, when he had accompanied a member of the IRA's Engineering Department up to the most northerly county in the Republic to check out a new device. The Drogue bomb was a new invention from the IRA's bomb-makers. Jack was along to assess the efficacy of this weapon, with a view to using it in England. The weapon was deployed to deadly effect in that small Tyrone town in February 1989 when it was dropped from a great height onto an RUC unmarked car. As Jack remembered, local lads and lasses coming out from a nightclub showered the security forces with bottles and glasses and taunts. Yeah, Jack was sure that someone upstairs was poking him with a stick and laughing.

Thursday

Tom O'Shea hadn't slept after Jack had left. He'd sat down and opened a reporter's notebook and started to take notes, working it out in his own head. When he was finished, he ripped out the pages, crumpled them up, opened up the top cover of the old range, and threw them in. His wife had insisted on them having a range, and if it had been down to her, the turf would have come all the way from Kerry. With that, he went upstairs, washed, shaved, and dressed in suitable attire to go in and see an Assistant Commissioner in An Garda Síochána.

As Tom O'Shea was waiting in reception at Garda Headquarters in Phoenix Park, Gareth Scully's ministerial car was taking him to another building in the same expanse of green space in Ireland's capital. The American Ambassador's residence is one of the most impressive buildings on the island of Ireland. It was Pelfrey's idea to have the meeting there, and Scully had readily agreed when he had been messaged.

Ambassador Brannigan loved the gig that President Adair had gifted to him. However, there was one thing he didn't like about his ambassadorial role, and that was early mornings. Most nights, Brannigan and Jack Daniels met for in-depth discussions about the state of the world, and that made the early morning difficult sometimes. He had a 07.00am briefing scheduled with Pelfrey. Brannigan had a private joke about the tight-ass CIA Station chief. Brannigan had mentioned in passing to one of his buddies in DC that this guy probably didn't sleep. Painfully thin and cadaverously pale, Brannigan, never slow with a cutting quip, had dubbed his Company guy "Dracula."

Pelfrey had indeed been up most of the night, as he could perfectly function on three hours sleep without any failing or fumbling in his mental processes.

As far as Brannigan was concerned, he was just another Bonesman, another tight-ass from Yale. Brannigan hated blue-bloods. The path to success and power was laid out for them before they were out of diapers. Guys like Brannigan had to scrap and dig and battle and make it on their own. Guys like Pelfrey, it was handed to them.

Brannigan only knew the headlines of what had happened in Dublin the night before at the nightclub. He sure hoped that Langley and especially this Yaley knew what the fuck they were doing. If this sucker went south, no one would come out of this with a recoverable career, and even Frank Adair wouldn't be able to save his big white Irish ass.

When Brannigan got to the secure room in the base of the embassy, a place that was impenetrable to any electronic eavesdropping, Pelfrey was already sitting at the simple metal table. The objective of this room wasn't to be aesthetically pleasing or comfortable. It was entirely functional in this era of global digital surveillance. Attached to the wall outside the door was a small safe for dropping in cell phones and other electronic devices. Nothing electronic could be allowed in this room. It was pen, paper and spoken word, and nothing else. Brannigan went through, still resentful at the hour of the meeting, and Pelfrey looked up.

"Good morning, Mister Ambassador."

"Kiss my ass."

"I have an initial briefing on what happened last night in the Temple Bar area of…"

"If I'm here to hear all this bullshit that I've already heard on every news network, then you're wasting my friggin' time, Pelfrey!"

Pelfrey continued as if Brannigan had said nothing, and his monotone didn't alter as he went through the things that the Ambassador needed to know.

"Mister Ambassador, we are monitoring all Irish government communications, and of course, the NSA has plugged into what GCHQ in England is monitoring. The initial death toll is eighty-seven, but that's expected to grow, and as yet there has not been a suicide video released by the terrorists. I suggest that we bring in Scully for an informal debrief."

At this, Pelfrey had Brannigan's full attention. It sounded like a problem.

"Why do we need to do that? He's still on the team, yeah?"

Pelfrey again didn't look up, merely shifted through some A4 pages that were resting on an open plastic folder.

"Mister Ambassador, we are monitoring Gareth Scully's devices and NSA have picked up high stress levels in his voice, and Langley's matrixes indicate that…"

Brannigan was getting impatient.

"Don't give me all that Star Wars bullshit. Is this sucker still on the team?"

"I believe an informal briefing of the Irish Minister for Justice would be helpful at this time, Mister Ambassador, and your input is considered to be useful."

Hearing the word "useful" from Pelfrey made Brannigan seethe with resentment. Here was this tight-ass blue-blood from Langley telling HIM, the US Ambassador to Ireland; that he could be of use! What was he around here? The friggin' help?

"Minister Scully has intimated that he will be happy to meet with you at 07.30. As you can imagine He's got a full schedule today Mr Ambassador, so we have 45 minutes to prepare."

"Prepare what?"

"To keep Scully onside. We have to stiffen his resolve Mr Ambassador and Langley thinks that you are best placed to do this."

"This sucker better not go south, Pelfrey. You Langley SOBs will disappear like panties off a prom queen in a frat house!"

"Mr Ambassador I…"

"Yeah. And who will take the fall for this?"

"Langley has…"

"Langley can kiss my big white Irish ass!" thundered Brannigan.

Jerome Pelfrey was a slight man and to say that he lacked physical presence in a room was an understatement. Five foot six, thin and with lifeless black hair, the bespectacled Beltway wonk wouldn't fit anyone's preconceived idea of a James Bond type character. However, his pride lay in the fact that he considered that, almost all of the time, he was the smartest person in any room. That was certainly the case in this strange little electronically pristine space. He waited until Brannigan had punched himself out with his impotent rage and then the CIA man continued.

"Langley believes, and I agree with them, that Scully can be a very important agent of influence. As with many of these operations, he doesn't really know he's an asset right now. He hasn't been flipped in the classic sense. However, today might be the day when we appraise him about just how well we know him."

Brannigan looked puzzled as Pelfrey pushed a plastic folder across the desk to the sweating Ambassador.

The man who represented the United States of America in the Republic of Ireland opened the folder and started to read. He had gone from snorting anger to librarian quiet in a very short space of time. Pelfrey studied Brannigan and the Ambassador read through the briefing notes. This was information that had been collated at Langley in Scully, but, until then, Brannigan hadn't been in the loop.

"Jesus H Christ ..."

Brannigan looked shocked at first and then started to giggle like a teenage boy. Pelfrey hated that he had to work with this boorish drunk from Texas. Hopefully he would soon be back Stateside with a massive operational success on his resume. No one in the Company would then be able to point to a lack of experience in the field.

Tom O'Shea was waiting quietly in a bar in Store Street beside the barracks where the old Kerryman had once been a detective. It was connected to a hotel that used to be called the Isaac Butt. It wasn't called that anymore, noticed O'Shea. Places had a habit of changing their names in Dublin these days. No need for that carry on, thought the ex-policeman.

That was before he had moved up the in the Garda world to Special Branch in Harcourt Street. In the Branch they were convinced that O'Shea had off-books informants because his score rate against the Provos was so good. However, it was just that the man from Kerry had a natural policeman's sixth sense for things that weren't right. In the age before psychological profiling and databases, O'Shea was a massive asset for the Irish State in their fight against the IRA.

He was a street cop with a visceral hatred for the Provos. The Kerryman saw them as desecrating the name of the Army that his father had fought in during the War of Independence. That for O'Shea had been a noble fight, but these terrorists shamed Ireland with their brutality. Especially the bombings in England.

That same gut instinct told him that something wasn't right at the Park. He had taken actionable intelligence to the very top the day after the bombing. That trail was still very hot. He believed Dempsey; he thought he was a decent skin, for a Provo. He also knew that Jack didn't have any reason to lie to him and that among his crowd it was a big thing to go to the Guards with information.

When he followed up after the nightclub bombing he had been left sitting there in reception like he was a salesman cold calling trying to flog them paperclips. That fat arsehole Gaffney wouldn't even see him! He had wiped that bastard's nose when he had been assigned to Special Branch from the Drug Squad.

He was useless at hunting the heroin dealers and he was no better trying to keep on top of the Provos in the city. Now he was the top of the tree in the Special Branch and tipped to be the next in line for the top job. The old gnawing in the gut troubled O'Shea. Then his throat started to play up on the way home. A nervous catarrh type of tick. It was his stress sign.

Gaffney had been all nicey-nicey when he had first called in with the information that he had received from Dempsey. Too fucking nice. Then, after the night club bomb, he was left waiting in reception like he had Ebola. Why the big change? First it was tea and biscuits and "we'll get right on it Tom. Haven't lost your touch. You're a legend here. I tell the youngsters about you all the time. We need to get you down to Templemore." Then nothing. Not right at all.

*Armies, all armies, put their misfits into intelligence. The IRA was no different. The recruiting officer who screened him in the kitchen of a terraced house in Upper Meadow Street in the New Lodge are*a of North Belfast in 1977 knew that he had talent sitting in front of him.

This kid from Glasgow was a cut above.

The OC of the Brigade had put him into this work because he was good at it. He was a good judge of talent and he had a nose for touts.

The kid checked out in Glasgow. He was who he said he was. They had vetted him through the band that his cousin played in. His second cousin Kevin who played in the James Connolly Republican Flute band had known him since they were both primary school kids. They had lived around the corner from each other all their days. Even at nineteen, the kid looked young for his years. He would have passed for fifteen or sixteen. He was stick thin with a shock of wiry hair that seemed to grow out of his head horizontally. The young man from Glasgow was quite clear about why he had travelled over on the ferry. He wanted to join the IRA. Yes, he knew what he was asking, yes, he knew the risks. The recruiter was non-committal, as he had been trained to be. The main man for recruiting in Belfast gave him all the out-of-towners. He had a knack for spotting nutters and plants. This kid was neither. He was a find. A real find. A blind man could see that. That was it. What the recruiting officer took away from the meeting to report back was the kid's eyes. Piercing blue, really blue. The kid was sent away and told that he would be contacted within a few weeks in Glasgow. He was given half a bank note – a Northern bank fiver.

The meeting never took place. The lad sat on his hands for three months. He avoided all known republican haunts in Glasgow, as he had been told. He realised that he would need to go back to Ireland. The thing was, every time he travelled to Belfast he could be spotted. If that happened, his usefulness to the IRA would be greatly reduced.

At nineteen he was already thinking like a revolutionary soldier. A private awkward kid, who had no siblings, he didn't seek out company. He was perfect for operating in England and that was in the front of Paddy Magee's head as he was driven back to his native Lower Falls. The kid was a find. A real find. The man he reported to did not agree. He took some pleasure in reminding Magee that he was the senior man and he took recommendations, not orders, from the man from the 'Murph. Paddy could feel the temper rising up in him as they sat in a sparsely furnished front room in Leeson Street. The old widow woman who owned the house had been told that her parlour was needed for "army business." The British army foot patrol outside slithering its way up onto the Falls Road had, of course, no idea what business was being conducted just a few feet from them. The British Army, probably the best in NATO, was a blind giant trying to stamp on a persistent, annoying insect. As their counter terrorist guru General Kitson had written, "The first problem with the terrorist is to find him."

At this stage of the war the British had very little idea who they were fighting.

The kid went back to his factory job in Glasgow with the words of the army man seared into his memory. "We'll be in touch." He was also told to stay away from anything openly republican in Glasgow. It was like a switch in him had finally been found and this Belfast man in his thirties had the magic touch. In the age of punk rockers and rebellious teenagers, all this kid wanted to do was be a soldier and follow orders.

Gerry O'Donnell was gunning the engine of his Mercedes van over the Droichead Na nDeor when his mobile phone chirped away in the door well. He knew it wasn't herself as she had her own ringtone. Anyone else could wait. Droichead Na nDeor – literally "the bridge of tears"- was where people parted as some walked on to Derry and the boat for America. Many ended up living in the Appalachians Mountains that connect to Muckish. In many ways the local quip about the next parish being America was true even geologically.

He knew the mobile coverage along this road from Falcarragh to Letterkenny like a Bedouin knows the desert. It was a text message, but not from one of his contacts. He tapped on the screen of the Samsung galaxy S5 and he took one in the gut.

"Glad to hear that GOD is in his Donegal. I need help wee lad. BEESTON."

That could only have come from one person. It was a code between the two of them that they had never shared with anyone else. O'Donnell's survival instincts, dormant for twenty years, went into overdrive. He hoped that Jack would be careful enough to use a non-traceable mobile, and he would have to do the same.

He texted back:

"Will contact you in one hour. PUDSEY.

The finely engineered turbo diesel engine in the Mercedes van and O'Donnell's intimate knowledge of this road had him cresting the Mountain Top at Letterkenny in only a few minutes. He dropped into the town and went immediately to a mobile phone store in the shopping centre. The cheapest one came with free credit. He wouldn't be using it for long anyway.

"This is a new number. Safe to call. RIPON."

In an instant the new phone jangled. It was Jack. He smiled when he heard his old buddy.

"I've something to put in your head. I NEED a yarn."

When Gerry heard those words, he knew this was the old stuff, but this was one man he couldn't turn down. He just couldn't.

"OK, big man. Can you get up here?"

"That was my plan. That place is mental down here."

"OK. You should do it in three hours. Let me know on this phone. I'll tell you where to meet me," said Gerry.

"The bus is just pulling out of Lifford, wee lad."

"Fuck! You're nearly here!"

"Yeah. Got a late bus. Long story. See you in a bit."

"That's a hundred percent big man. I'll meet you off the bus."

The moment the call ended he thought of herself. This day was always going to come along, he thought, and cursed the certainty of that. Now that it was here, whatever it was, he just didn't know how to handle it.

Then Carlos Baute started to sing 'Te Regalo' on his Android. She had her own ringtone. In fact, she had everything. He swiped the phone.

"Hey Chiquita…"

"Ola, Chico. You steel in Letterkenneee?"

Oh that voice! It would never stop disarming him.

"I'm still here Chiquita. I got everything on the list, but I'll be longer than I thought. I have a meeting to go to about work and it will be a while. Is that OK?"

"How long is meeting, Chico? I am making dinner for you tonight, special."

There was no point in telling her stupid lies, he had to tell her some smart ones.

"A friend of mine is travelling up from Dublin now. I have to see him, just for a short time," said Gerry.

Her voice was instantly inquisitive. Smart Chica, thought Gerry.

"You deed not tell mee about this in morning Geree…"

He knew he was in trouble when she used his name. At all other times if was just "Chico."

"I know love. He only called me an hour ago. He's in a bit of trouble. He needs some help."

"Geree, is he from old times?"

"No. Oh no love. Nothing like that."

And there was the real fucking lie right there, thought O'Donnell. He didn't know what the Big Man wanted, but it must be something heavy or he wouldn't be using security measures. The ONE thing she had made him promise never to do, he was about to do. That night in Madrid in her sister's apartment, she'd made him pledge that those days were behind him. If they were to have a life together, it was non-negotiable. When he'd agreed he'd done so with all of his heart. One phone call from Jack and that was it fucked. "Husband of the year…" he thought.

Five years earlier Gerry O'Donnell had had no idea where he was going in life. Physically he was travelling in the direction of Santiago de Compostela with the rest of the Peregrinos. Then he met Maria and everything changed. Her father was nonplussed to say the least about the man that his eldest daughter had given her heart to. More than twenty years older than her and a gringo, and worst of all, ateo. Gerry's atheism was non-negotiable and it had been since at the age of eighteen he had kissed the coffin of his mother's mother in a Catholic Church in Glasgow. She had mothered him while his own mother had worked two jobs to support him. The quiet awkward teenager just knew that all of this was a culturally approved charade to make people feel better about someone leaving their life forever. She had soothed him once in a voicemail and he had kept it and backed up the file as an Mp3.

"Gerree you are not gringo. You are Iralandess…"

He loved that voice and the woman who owned it. After a while his father-in-law came to accept his daughter's choice. Especially when the little fella arrived. However, he might not have been so accommodating if he had he known the whole truth about Gerry O'Donnell.

Most people are fairly nervous when they meet their protective in-laws. However, Gerry had more reason than most. When he got off the plane in Bogota it wasn't his first time in Colombia, but old Carlos could never know that. By the time she presented this ginger haired stranger to her family in Altamira in the Antioquia region of northern Colombia, she knew the truth. It was their secret from her family. They were reasonably impressed with Gerry's functional Spanish. They naturally assumed that his Colombian turn of phrase had come from their daughter teaching him and thought no more of it.

However, Gerry' O'Donnell's accent had come from the best part of a year spent in Camp Diamante, deep within the Colombian interior. The IRA man was an esteemed guest of the leadership of Fuerzas Armadas Revolucionarias de Colombia. The world knew them simply as "FARC". He was in Havana having a meeting with senior members of the regime there when three of his comrades... were apprehended. Not for the first time, Gerry O'Donnell was lucky. Everyone in Colombia knew that hombres Irlandéses had been teaching FARC to make better and bigger bombs.

Herself had a very genuine reason to detest FARC and anyone who would help them. The little shop that the family run made them a target for the guerrillas. The day her life changed was the day that men came and took him away. Everything they had they sold to raise the ransom and finally he was set free. He had aged twenty years. He was an old and a broken man. They had taken away his pride and his strength. The look in his eye that made her worship him as the man who would always be there to protect them was gone. He was sick with shame.

Her mother had fairly quickly dissolved into alcoholism. FARC might have claimed to have been about liberating all of Colombia, but they had destroyed her family and made them little more than beggars. The first time she had really thought of Ireland, it had been because of these men in her country teaching these bastardos how to kill more of her people.

Slowly the family got back on their feet with the help of relatives in Medellin. She went to work there, shared a tiny room and sent almost all of her income back to the family. Her younger sister Carmen became old enough to work and then the family had two incomes, both children supporting the parents. This is natural when the parents are very old, but her mother was not yet forty-five.

Her life had improved immeasurably by that day with her little boots off sunning herself on the veranda of Albergue la Faba in Galicia. She had just prayed in the little 12th Century church there of San Andrés. To the blessed virgin she asked that her family would suffer no more pain or trauma. She also asked for something for herself. Could she have someone to walk with her on her Camino – and she wasn't thinking of the remaining kilometres to Santiago. The religious are always vulnerable to interpreting a chance meeting as some kind of a 'sign' that it was meant to happen.

Gerry O'Donnell would reflect in the years that followed that when he bumped into Maria Garcia Jimenez that day in 2010 he'd had God on his side. That day his fair skin had taken a particular beating under the Galician sun. He cursed to himself that this was meant to be the cloudy part of Spain. The furnace in the sky followed him relentlessly that day. The final few hundred meters up to the Albergue was particularly steep up a narrow cobbled path. He had nothing left and had not drunk enough water. A combination of factors that meant that he stumbled into the court yard.

There is a life size statue of the man himself in the court yard and at first Gerry thought it was an actual person. Then he stumbled and was prostrate on the deck with his rucksack coming over his head. It was cartoonish. The little lady sitting on the veranda with her back to the wall showing off the soles of her feet to him laughed at his misfortune and crinkled up her nose. In that moment he could have been sinking into quicksand and all he wanted to know was more about the woman who was laughing at his Tom and Jerry stumble.

By the time he had struggled to his feet and wrestled his rucksack back into place he was already smitten. He had read about this moment in literature and seen it many times in the movies, but he had always dismissed it as a fictional creation to make a story go better. No there wasn't a God, Gerry, but the O'Donnell luck had finally came through in affairs on the heart.

He went and sat down beside her like they had been together

for years and he had just popped over to the village shop for a few minutes. He didn't say a word at first. He just caught his breath and smiled at her. He introduced himself in Spanish and offered his hand which she took.

"Maria…"

"Bueno…"

She had no idea who she was sitting beside, but she didn't want to leave his side until she had found out. His first faux pas was to assume that she was Spanish. Her eyes flared in indignation.

"Colombiana!"

She pronounced it with such a flourish that any defences he might have had to this woman utterly evaporated.

The week before he had packed his bag in Donegal for the Camino he had taken a trip over to Belfast. It was arranged and he thought there would have been more to it. However the Adjutant General of the Irish Republican Army, a household name in Sinn Féin, was happy to see him because he already knew why Gerry O'Donnell was there. The journey that had begun for him in 1977 was over.

All of his adult life had been about this and he had walked out of that house in North Belfast feeling very strange. It was his decision to resign, but he had more than a feeling that it suited the organisation that he was resigning from. His time had passed and he wasn't sure how he felt about that. He had read before that career soldiers in conventional armies felt dislocated when finally the day came at 23.59 hours that they became civilians. No longer subject to military law, but also shorn of the status and respect that often flows to those in uniform from the wider society.

Gerry had a friend in Donegal who was a member of walking club and had been raving about El Camino Santiago for a few years. So he had all of the information on this well-worn path across Northern Spain; the guide book and everything he needed. He was aware that many of the people who embarked up El Camino Santiago did it for religious purposes. It was, after all, a pilgrimage. However, the last thing he could face was all those happy campers for weeks on end. He knew that close proximity to them for any length of time could lead to violence. The Christy ones were particularly cheerful

148

and O'Donnell didn't plan on starting life as a civilian by offing some friend of Baby Jesus on a pilgrimage in Spain.

He wasn't going to do the whole thing, but part of it might just be the job. As magnificent as it was, Errigal and the beach at Machaire Rabhartaigh could get a bit samey. On a complete whim he had clicked onto the Aer Lingus website and a day later he was heading to Dublin airport. The last minute flight could have been cheaper, but it was no biggie. They flew him straight to Bilbao, a city he knew every well indeed.

After years of trying to slip through airports unnoticed, Gerry O'Donnell suddenly realised that he had nothing to be fearful of. He wasn't going to a clandestine meeting with the ETA lads and he wasn't concerned if he was followed. In that moment, for the first time since he had held up his right hand in that house in Upper Meadow Street in the New Lodge Road area in 1977, he felt a strange sensation. He was free. He was free of Army rules. The irony was not lost on him that he had done all of that for something called 'freedom'.

In Bilbao airport he handed over his Irish passport to the Guardia Civil chap.

"Welcome to España," said yer man, doing his bit for the tourist trade.

"Spain? Oh I'm going there tomorrow I will get the bus to Asturga to start El Camino," said Gerry.

The policeman was puzzled.

"But señor, you are IN Spain now."

"This is Euskadi. España tomorrow."

O'Donnell smiled and watched the policeman starting to boil over.

To complete the insult the Glaswegian asked:

"Noiz Euskadi emigratzea duzu Espainiatik?"

The Irish citizen was sure that the policeman had enough Basque to know that he had just been asked when he had emigrated from Spain. Even indulging in that politicised ribbing with the Spanish policeman gave Gerry O'Donnell a juvenile rush.

It was that this off the cuff decision to walk El Camino Santiago that changed Gerry O'Donnell's life forever and for the better. The Gerry O'Donnell that was waiting for Jack at Letterkenny Bus

Station in Donegal was in a very different place to the man that Dempsey had operated with in England decades earlier.

As the Dublin bus pulled into Letterkenny Bus Station, Jack didn't have to look very hard in the crowd waiting for the conveyance to spot his old buddy. The Mera Peak Berghaus jacket was even redder than his old comrade's ginger hair.

As Jack stepped off the bus Gerry causally threw the pay as you go phone, minus the sim, into the litter bin beside the wall of the bus station that he was leaning against. The sim would be disposed of elsewhere shortly.

Tracks covered.

Jack stepped off the bus and headed straight for Gerry. Anyone looking at these two men meeting would not think that they had not set eyes on one another for decades. But for these two it didn't matter: Five minutes, ten years, there was a bond, there was a connection. Gerry O'Donnell stepped forward and it was handshake, then a hug. Jack looked at Gerry and thought, if anything, he was younger-looking than the last time.

Gerry got eye contact with Jack and said, quickly and curtly, "Got the text messages, so I know this isn't exactly a social call."

Before Jack could say anything, Gerry took out his smartphone, waved it with one hand and put his other hand out, palm upwards, in the accepted gesture of "give me yours." Jack complied. He usually complied with Gerry's requests, because they were usually grounded in something fairly smart. Gerry nodded to him, turned, and stepped to walk away from the bus station. Jack simply followed. They crossed the small access road with its speed bumps, over into the car park that served Letterkenny Shopping Centre. Gerry walked towards a green Mercedes van, unlocked a door, put the two phones in the door-well, and closed it. He turned and stepped forward to Jack and said, "Now we're definitely alone, darling, what can I do for you?"

"I could do with something to eat to start with."

Gerry nodded past Jack over towards a bank of shops on the other side of the main road from Letterkenny Bus Station and said, "We can get something in there."

"Grand," said Jack.

They walked over to a place called the Coffee Factory. At that time of the morning there were a few taxis waiting for business that buses usually brought them in. They went into the modern café that did what it said on the front. One of the staff behind the counter, a pleasant-looking girl in her twenties with blonde hair, looked up, saw Gerry and nodded. O'Donnell was obviously a regular in this place. Gerry walked toward the back of the café and commandeered the corner, which was two small leather sofas with a coffee-table arrangement at knee-height. It was as quiet and as private as they could manage in the place. Most of the other customers were in the tables nearer to the door, perhaps some of them waiting for buses coming in. Gerry ordered a cappuccino and said that Jack could get a toastie, or some such.

As if the pleasantries and the formalities were too much for Jack, he blurted out, "I need your help."

The unvarnished plea and emotionality in his voice caught Gerry O'Donnell unawares, and that was something that rarely happened.

"Anything, big fella, anything."

"Where to fuckin' start?" said Jack out of the side of his mouth, trying to process what he was about to try and boil into some understandable communique for the man sitting across from him, who he knew had a brain like a computer.

Gerry realised that Jack possibly needed some help to put this together.

"Well, just start at the beginning. I'm gonna go and get you a… ham and cheese toastie?"

Jack nodded.

"Yeah, that's grand."

Gerry went up and ordered, came back, sat down and said, "Just take your time. Whatever it is, maybe the beginning's the best place."

"What is it?"

"OK, the Luas bombs in Dublin…"

"Aye, cunts, nutters."

"Let me…" Jack started to get angry. He wanted time to tell the tale, he didn't want a dialogue. Gerry acknowledged with a wave.

"Go ahead big man."

"The Luas bombs. My kid was on one of them. He took one in the head. The girl who was minding him killed," said Jack flatly.

Gerry stiffened and his face went white.

"Fucking Hell, Jack. I mean, fuck's sake mate. Sorry."

"You can sing that, O'Donnell."

"How's the wee lad? How's your son?" asked Gerry, his voice lowered, one father to another.

"He's gonna be fine. The doctors were fucking great. It was touch and go."

"That's the main thing, that's the main thing. What age is the wee fella?"

"He's four, five next birthday. Great wee man. Great wee fella."

"He's going to be OK then?" asked Gerry.

"Yeah he's fine. Well. He's in hospital still in Intensive Care. He got hurt the wee fella, hurt bad, his head, but he'll be fine. Well, I hope he'll be fine. He's through the worst of it. The doctors were brilliant. "

At this point, Gerry didn't know what Jack wanted, so the next question seemed appropriate.

"How can I help, big fella? How can I help?"

"I wouldn't be here if I wasn't stuck, you know that?"

Jack knew what he was about to ask Gerry was a big ask, but then again he knew he had a big favour to call in from this man, a man that he trusted totally.

"Go ahead big fella. All ears here," said Gerry O'Donnell.

Gerry was totally focussed on what Jack was saying. When Gerry O'Donnell listened, he listened. Jack realised this and had the confidence to continue.

"The morning of the Luas bomb I was going to court to try for the guardianship to see the wee fella. Before that I saw these two boyos getting out of a mini bus. Inside the minibus was a pile of lads. And in the passenger seat was this mental looking fucker with a beard."

"Was it Adams?" asked the Glaswegian.

The humour hit Jack like a punch in the gut and he bent double laughing. Gerry, the genius, had pierced the tension. Jack knew that he needed this guy on his side, now more than ever. Jack's reaction created an equal reaction in Gerry and all the crap they had about the movement spewed out in one along fraternal belly laugh. Gerry had a laugh that made you laugh so it was a chain reaction. The baton was passed from laugher to laugher. When one stopped for breath the other would start again as they both thought of the ridiculousness of what they had been through to serve the Republic or further a few personal careers. On second thought, forget the stuff about the Republic; it was all about personal careers and that this stage it was just plain stupid to think it was anything else. Jack was laughed out as was Gerry.

"You're the business, big man. The best I ever served with, comrade. Now finish the sceál."

Jack smiled and nodded then refocused. He took himself back to Dublin on the day of the Luas bombings. His head was full of images, but he shuffled through them until he had eye contact again with that fucker in the minibus.

"I sees these two lads head off with backpacks," said Jack, "The next day those two boys were on every TV in the world doing their goodbye videos. It was them Gerry!"

"You a hundred percent on that?"

"Totally!"

"How long did you see them for?" asked Gerry, leaning forward.

"Look, Gerry…"

"How long?"

"A minute."

"Long time, a minute," said Gerry as he rotated the bezel on his diver's watch.

"OK starting…now…" announced the Glaswegian.

Jack took the point and got angered.

"OK, thirty seconds," said a relaxed Gerry. He knew that the point had been made.

"You're going to the court to fight for your kid and what a pair of strangers look like is the last thing on your mind."

"Aye. So?"

"It hasn't happened." Jack realised what he was about to say Gerry might not take well. They had both sworn an oath to the Republic. They didn't recognise the 'Free State.'

"Look, I went to the Peelers." Gerry was quiet. Processing what he had heard.

"Gerry….." asked Jack, looking for a reaction.

"Sound, sound, it's your kid."

"Don't fuckin' make excuses for me; I'm no tout!" Jack was raging at how this was playing out. Now Gerry was thinking had Jack always talked to Peelers? At least that was what Jack thought Gerry might be thinking and it wasn't true, but he might now think it was true. Oh fuck this, thought Jack. Gerry was quite calm. It was all being processed.

"OK, you went to the Peelers." He left it there hanging in the air. It was stated for the record. Jack Dempsey went to the Peelers. Jack took a breath and tried to stop himself losing it.

"Look, I went to our lot first."

"Who?"

"Who do you think? Mr Movement."

"Gerry A?"

"No, our old buddy."

"Who?"

"Who do you think? Mr Dáil Deputy from the old days," said Jack.

"McMillan?"

"Liam McMillan TD, if you don't mind," said Jack harshly.

"No? You're fucking joking? That piece of shit?"

Yeah, put people in suits give them free dinners and they forget who they are." Jack was no longer angry, he wanted to set the record straight with Gerry. He had to do this for several reasons the most pressing of which being that if he was to get Gerry's help he would need to totally level with him. He was one man who could spot a lie like no other he had ever operated with.

"What did McMillan say?" Gerry was fascinated to hear.

"He just told me to either let it go or take it to the Peelers," said Jack.

Gerry gently shook his head.

"I didn't go into the barracks. I went to an old Peeler that scooped me years ago. I always thought he was fair."

Gerry was dumfounded at what he was hearing and let Jack continue. He needed to hear it all.

"You remember the old branch man O'Shea? Tom O'Shea?" asked Jack.

"I know of him. Never met him thankfully."

"OK. A straight enough boyo."

"For a Peeler," said Gerry, and Jack acknowledged the caveat with a weary nod.

"OK, decent skin for a Branch man then," Gerry continued. Jack conceded this with a wave of the hand.

Jack seemed to take a breath and nod, and he laid it all out for Gerry, the court appearance, trying to see his kid, the collision with the young lads, the Luas bomb, and the suicide video. He tried to keep it in order as much as he could without deviating, and Gerry sat listening and taking it in. O'Donnell remained silent for about thirty seconds after Jack had clearly indicated that he'd told him as much as he thought he needed to at that point.

"I know that those fuckers aren't going to stop. There was a van full of them, and they're not all fucking blown to bits yet. The Peelers don't seem to want to move on this, and I'm still working that out in my head, but I know that I have to, and that…"

Gerry cut across Jack with some alarm.

"YOU need to do something?"

At this point Gerry was feeling uneasy about where this conversation was going.

Jack realised he'd hit a bump in the road with Gerry.

"Look, I bumped into these fuckers the day they blew themselves up on the Luas. There's a van-load of them. One more's gone in Temple Bar, and I lost boys there. On the door. My workers. One lad, hundred per cent lad. Polish kid. Look…"

"Jack, your kid's in hospital and…I'm not following you, big fella."

Jack started to feel a combination of anxiety and anger. He had travelled through the night on a bus to Donegal to meet this man, because he knew he could help. If anybody could help, it was him. And he was suddenly getting dragged into some sort of debate about what should happen. This hadn't been part of whatever plan Jack had had when he was sitting in Busáras in the early hours of the morning.

Jack made his pitch.

"Gerry, we need to find the rest of these fuckers and make sure that when they go to fucking Heaven, they don't take anyone else with them."

Gerry O'Donnell, who had been leaning forward in the standard conspiratorial way that he'd used in meetings for over thirty years with comrades, sat back, putting distance between him and Jack. It was like a wall had come down. He looked at Dempsey straight in the eyes.

"Are you fucking serious? In case you hadn't noticed, I'm retired. And so are you."

"I took it to our lot and…" said Jack.

"They're not my lot any more, and haven't been for a while. Thank fuck for that."

"Gerry, you know what I mean…"

"And then you went to the Peelers? Jesus Christ!"

Jack could feel his blood starting to boil.

"I had no fucking choice!"

Gerry O'Donnell owed this man a huge amount, which was the only reason he didn't get up and walk out. Thirty miles away on the Donegal coast, he had a life, and it was a life he had built since he had last seen Jack Dempsey. Gerry took a breath.

"Let me get this straight, big fella. You want ME to help you find these boyos?"

Before Jack could answer, Gerry continued.

"Have I got that right?"

As he said it to Jack, even Jack realised that what he had travelled to Donegal to ask for sounded preposterous. Gerry continued.

"Jack, you've a kid in hospital, and you jumped on a bus to speak to me. Not for me to tell you your business, but you really should be there. But instead you're here, asking me to help you on some sort of half-arsed jihadi hunt in Dublin?"

Jack, at this stage, didn't have an answer. As usual, Gerry O'Donnell had taken Jack's plans and with his forensic intelligence had demolished them the way an angry toddler would knock over a set of building blocks. It was not Gerry O'Donnell's objective to lay into his old friend, but a best friend will always tell you what you need to hear. The worst type of enemy will tell you what you want to hear.

"You look fucked, big fella, utterly fucked. And there's no surprise in that. I have to pick some things up for Maria. That's why I'm here in Letterkenny. I was halfway here when I got your texts.

Come out the road with me. Stay the night. Back down to Dublin the next day, see the wee fella in hospital. Now, Maria's grand, but no military chat in front of her. Nothing. And I'll tell you why on the way there."

"Oh, and thanks for the invite to the wedding," Jack half-joked. Gerry smiled.

"It was in Colombia, ya big bollocks."

Jack was happy to have a break from the intense discussion that hadn't got anywhere.

"We used to be close, O'Donnell."

"We ARE close, so don't start, you big bollocks, I love ya."

Within the man-banter, as Gerry O'Donnell let slip the "L" word, Jack knew he meant it. There was a time when this man sitting across from him would've happily taken a bullet for Jack, and the feeling was mutual. Then Jack pounced.

"I'm really glad you didn't get scooped that time, you know…"

"Here we fucking go. OK Gerry, pack your bags, you're going on a guilt-trip."

"Ah, you could move quicker anyway. I wasn't built really for going on the run. I would've just went to jail tired. Jaysus, you're still built like a fucking whippet," joked Jack. It was a joke, but the point was made.

"You know I'll always owe you for that. But this?"

Jack pushed the advantage. The door was half-open.

"Well?"

"Look big fella, by the time you're back Dublin, these fellas will be scooped!"

"You sure about that, O'Donnell?"

Gerry took a breath and assembled the facts in his head to present to Jack, mindful that he didn't want to say anything that was hurtful, given what the man had suffered in the last few days.

"Jack, those boyos must have stuck out like a PhD student on a Rangers Supporters bus. Now, they had the element of surprise on the Luas…"

Jack cut across him: "And the nightclub?"

Gerry nodded, but tried to continue.

"Yeah? And? The fucking nightclub?" pressed Jack.

Gerry wasn't pushed off course.

"Jack, anyone looking like they're from the Middle East, or any of those countries, the Peelers are going to be all over them now. You can only imagine that this is a massive top priority for the Free State now."

Jack wasn't satisfied with this reasoning.

"Gerry, mate, for fuck's sake. I gave them top-class sceál. Before the nightclub bomb. What I gave them would have got them a plate for that van…"

"But that van might have been ditched," countered Gerry.

Jack wasn't buying.

"Even at that, it was a lead. A good one. Fuck, you remember that Austin Princess in Leeds?" said Jack, reminiscing.

Suddenly, the pair of them were in an apartment in Yorkshire in the early 1980's, trying to stay at liberty and trying to stay alive. There was a bond between these two, the type of bond that only exists between men who face danger together, and have to rely on each other.

"Oh, don't fucking start Dempsey. Yeah…" laughed Gerry.

Jack reached his hand across the coffee table palm down on the surface fingers outstretch. A huge meaty implement that was designed for punching and grabbing.

He was, in every sense, reaching out.

O'Donnell closed his eyes and valued the solemn promise he had made to the woman who had brought in the happiness of his life.

He opened his eyes and looked at Dempsey.

"I made a promise to Maria."

"You swore an oath!"

"I was nineteen."

"It wasn't a temporary thing, O'Donnell."

"Actually it was, Jack. Look at the suits at Stormont. They took an oath too."

"Wankers."

"I went for a dander in Spain and I met my life. Our lads must be about the same age. That wee fella in hospital. He's your Republic now. Serve him and his mother."

"I'm not with her, it was… ah…. Ah a fucking mess."

"Sorry mate."

Jack wanted a break from this. His head was bursting with all of it.

"You're doing grand?" he asked Gerry.

"Yeah…" O'Donnell savoured the word. He never thought things could land for him the way that they had done.

Jack didn't know what his next play was with Gerry. The man across from him had always been the psychologist of the two. Gerry could read Jack like no one he had ever met. It was like how some people were born with music in them and never really need formal lessons. Gerry was like that with people; he took things in, thought Jack. Things that others missed, others like him.

"I should be getting back. To Dublin."

Gerry knew that Jack wanted some objection from him, some signal that Gerry was entertaining his request.

He wasn't.

"Yeah. Good call buddy. We'll go and get your phone out of the van. There a bus back in about forty minutes."

Jack was crestfallen. This trip had been for nothing, it had been a bonkers 'plan'. Then again Jack had never been one for the plans; that was O'Donnell's department.

"Yeah. Cheers buddy."

"They'll drop you at the airport. Handy for a taxi to Beaumont."

"Yeah. Good shout."

Gerry got up; there was no point in prolonging this, he thought. He knew it was the correct thing. Jack wasn't thinking straight and there was no surprise in that. His 'plan' was a grief reaction to the impotence that any victim felt.

The two old friends walked out of the Coffee Factory and across to the car park beside the bus station. They passed the busiest roundabout in Letterkenny. The very idea that this could be a traffic hub would have been laughable to any Dubliner, but this was as busy as it got on Donegal's roads. In Gerry's boyhood visiting from Glasgow he remembered relatives discussing the introduction of traffic lights as the wonder of the age.

Gerry opened the van door and handed Jack his iPhone.

"Piece o' shit, those things, big fella. First of all, integrated battery. Gerry no likee."

Jack looked at him quizzically.

159

"What the fuck are you on about?"

"Integral battery means you can't really switch it off. Fuckers can track you anywhere. Now, your old buddy here is on Team Android," said Gerry, lifting up a leather-covered Samsung Galaxy S5 and waving it the way leftist Zealots in the seventies would wave the Little Red Book.

"Detachable battery, which means I can carry spare power packs. Never out of juice. But very importantly, when I disconnect this fucker, it goes dark on the world. Mr Snooper in Fort Meade in Maryland doing his NSA thing doesn't know where Little Gerry's going or what he's saying..."

Jack tried to process the level of information that had just been thrown at him as an afterthought by Gerry.

"Head like a computer. Always a head like a computer."

Jack paused, quietly took a breath, and gave this one last go.

"I really could use your help on this, son. I really could."

"Jack, I gave you my answer. I don't think you're making sense, and that's no disrespect. Jesus, what you've been through. Back down town. Go see your little fella. When he gets out, when he's better, if you want, there's a place for you and him to take some time together, up here with Maria and the little fella and me. The two of them are about the same age. Now there's a plan!"

"I want to put the old crew together. Deal with these cunts. But I need your brains on this Gerry. Please."

"Let me get this straight. You want to assemble a group of near pensioners to attack this ISIS lot in Dublin?"

"Fuck off!" Jack growled. This was not how he imagined this was going to go on the journey up to Letterkenny.

"Just askin', Jack. I mean. I just wanted to get it straight. I didn't want to think it was anything daft like, "said Gerry.

Jack wasn't for hearing any of these nice, forward-looking ideas. He'd travelled overnight on the bus to Letterkenny for a reason, a very good reason. And he hadn't been able to get his ideas across to Gerry, and that stung.

"I have work to do before I can even think about that. There's more of those fuckers around, and no one seems to want to stop them. Not even you, Gerry."

And at that, Jack turned and walked towards Letterkenny Bus Station. Something dropped in Gerry: an emotion, an impulse, an instinct. He turned and purposely strode towards Jack, caught him with the cup of his right hand in the crook of Jack's arm as he was walking forward and spun him round, and then put the palm of his right hand slap bang in Jack's sternum, like he was going to push him over, just to stop him.

"Don't fucking speak to me like that!"

Jack stiffened. His natural reaction was to send that right hand, fisted, straight into Gerry's face.

"I came here because I needed you. There isn't anyone else here who can help me the way you can. And I need you now!"

Gerry had quite naturally assumed the stance where his left foot came behind his right foot, his knee slightly bent, and his right hand across the front of his body at a forty-five degree angle. His left hand dangled by his side. If Jack was going to throw a punch, Gerry O'Donnell was ready for him.

"I know what you need Jack, and it's not what you're asking for. What you need is to go back down, see your lad; be with your son. And when the time's right, me and my family are there for you. That's what you need, not some half-arsed Jihad-fucking-hunt in Dublin that's going to get you precisely no-fucking-where, except back to fucking prison. And you were in prison the last time that your..."

Gerry trailed off. He had almost stepped over the line in reminding Jack about Dermot. That would have been completely out-of-order. But the half-sentence was enough. For a very long millisecond, Jack Dempsey didn't know whether to collapse in tears, or launch himself at Gerry O'Donnell and beat him to death.

"Call me when you get back to Dublin, big fella. If there's anything that you really need, I'll be there for you. Remember, a real friend will tell you everything that you need to hear, not what you want to hear. The worst type of enemy will tell you what you want to hear. Your plan, for the avoidance of doubt, big fella, is utter shite, and in a couple of days you'll look back and know it was shite. But even if you came up here on a shite plan, it was good to see you."

The tension in Jack subsided. He couldn't do harm to this man.

He knew that Gerry believed what he was telling him to be in Jack's best interests. This was still Gerry O'Donnell, the man who would've taken a bullet for him, and the man who got him out of quite a few scrapes back in the day. Jack didn't want to say goodbye and part, so he stood there and fiddled with the iPhone. Gerry realised that the confrontation, such as it was, was over, and he didn't want to part on terms of anger and enmity with Jack. As Dempsey clumsily switched on the iPhone, Gerry raised the mood.

"Total piece of shite, that."

"Oh, Dicey got it for me. She knows all about this craic."

"Dicey?"

"Girl that runs the office for me. She's a genius, a fucking gem. Lost without her, I would be. Me. Paperwork. Jaysus."

Jack punched in the PIN code into the iPhone. It took a few seconds for it to become aware of itself in the digital space, and draw down a signal from a nearby tower. Then the phone went mental, beeping and vibrating, as a series of emails, text messages, WhatsApps and voicemails clamoured for Jack's attention like a bunch of Senior Infants kids jumping up and down with their hands in the air, hoping Miss would ask them the question that they knew the answer to. Gerry looked and said, "Someone's popular."

Jack was old-school when it came to the device in his hand, and he still thought of it as a phone as opposed to a powerful hand-held computer and, if properly used, the remote control for his life. He went to the voicemail icon, hit it, and put it to his ear. The nice lady from Meteor said that he had eight unheard messages. The blood started to drain from Jack. He dreaded that one would either be from Beaumont Hospital or the mother of the wee fella.

He heard the first message, and immediately hit the button to call the sender. It was Dicey.

"Howya Dicey?"

"Where the fuck have you been? I've been demented with worry. Are you OK?" said Mary Riley, immediately awake and alert in Jack's office. She had been in there since the early hours, trying to collate what had happened in the chaos of the Angela's nightclub, where they had staff on the door and downstairs.

"I've been calling -I've left loads of messages on your phone.

Didn't you get them? Anyway, when are you coming in? There's, there's loads to do and…" said Mary Riley.

"I was for heading straight to Beaumont, see the wee fella first."

"Oh Mother of Jesus, is the wee fella, is he, is he OK?"

Mary Riley was blindsided, as in the whole carnage of the night before she had forgotten that Jack's wee boy was still very serious in hospital, and perhaps there had been some sort of relapse.

"No, I'm just gonna get dropped off at the Airport when I leave Donegal, and…"

"DONEGAL?!"

Mary Riley was incredulous.

"Bit of a long story. Came up overnight…"

"Must be some fucking story. You're in Donegal?"

"Letterkenny, to be precise. Seeing an old buddy."

"You took some time to see an old buddy?" The annoyance in Mary Riley's voice would have been clear to hear for any onlooker in the office or in some far-off listening station.

"'I'll tell you when I see ya, and I'm sorry for leaving you with all of this. I wasn't thinking straight. I – I was down at the – Tried to get to Angela's after the – after the bomb."

"Were you there?"

"I got down Ashton Quay, got as far as the tape, and this young fucking bollocks of a Garda wouldn't let me through the tape and, then I saw a head from Pearse Street, a good skin, you don't know him, he's from Louth, and he said he'd let me know but they said… ah, they were dragging bodies out. He didn't seem to think there were any survivors among…"

"I was at the hospital this morning for an hour, asking about Stan."

"I know; it's shite. Only a young fella."

"Jack, Stan isn't…"

Jack was totally rocked by this. He had processed in his head on the bus to Letterkenny that Stan had fared no better than those poor bastards on the Luas days earlier.

"Jack, Anto's…Anto, he's – He's on the list. He's dead. But Stan must've got…Well, he's badly knocked over, but he's – He was lucky." Mary Riley knew she was breaking news to Jack.

"Ah for fuck's sake. Am, I thought that – What ward is he in?"

Mary Riley reassessed the situation on the phone. "You get to Beaumont and see your boy. Stan's in the same place. I'll find out the ward. They're saying that it's only family can visit, but Stan doesn't have any family here, Jack, just his siste…"

"Oh Jaysus, that kid. She was working in Angela's…"

Jack was frightened to ask.

"She's on the list too, Jack. The bomb went off down where she was working, they think. They're still working out how many died. She's on the missing list" said Mary Riley as the emotion started to build up in her voice.

"Holy Mother of Jaysus," said Jack, "The bus takes me out of here in about half an hour, Dicey. I'll phone you when I get to Beaumont. OK love."

"Yeah Jack, that's grand, I'll – I'm holding the fort here, OK. See you."

When Jack stepped on the Number 32 bus to Dublin an hour later he felt utterly foolish.

Worse than that, he had no idea what to do next.

On the drive back home, Gerry needed to process a very disconcerting meet with his old buddy. As he passed the Mountaintop at Letterkenny he hit the button his mobile on the seat beside him and, with the earphones in, waited for herself to pick up.

"Hey, Chico!"

Everything that was weighing on him in that moment was gone. That voice!

"Hey, Chiquita! Look I got all of your list and I'm leaving Letterkenny, but I want to take a walk before I come home. Is that OK?"

"Sure, Chico. Where you going?"

"Ah, the usual stroll love. I just need to stretch the legs."

"Oh, you go Muckeesh! Nice for you Chico, be careful. I got hake from fish man; I cook it good for you. But I feed our hombre now. He's a hungry Toro!"

"Bueno!" laughed Gerry.

The phone clicked off at her end and as he drove along the N56 towards the turn off at Termon he knew that if there was a luckier man alive he hadn't heard of him.

He felt a pang of guilt about sending Jack away. He wanted to help him, but not in the way he was asking. That was mental. His kid in the hospital, all the shit with court and the mother, then losing his guy at the nightclub within the space of two fucking days. He wouldn't be human if he wasn't all over the place and he knew that Jack Dempsey was a thoroughly human man. He wanted to have something for Jack. A solution. He had to think about it.

Whenever Gerry O'Donnell was processing where to go next in life, he walked the mountains of Donegal. Preferably alone. Muckish was Gerry's very own mountain. He was on it most weeks. Sometimes day after day. Since he had settled in Donegal in 1994, the same year as the first IRA cessation, Muckish Mountain had dominated his skyline, his consciousness and his understanding of the place where his son was now growing.

The home place was his uncle's on his father's side, but old Micheál was settled in Glasgow. He had never intended to do that when he had first travelled to Scotland at the end of the Second World War to work alongside his brothers digging the great Hydro schemes in the Highlands. However, life had gotten in the way and he had made the Gorbals his home. When Gerry was itching to get back to where he had spent his childhood summer holidays, his uncle was happy for someone in the family to take over the house and live in it. As the era of the Celtic Tiger was about to pounce on Middle Ireland, Gerry O'Donnell was enjoying a mortgage free existence.

Every morning the sun shone over Muckish and right into the bedroom. In summer time it was like a laser beam alarm call. All he needed to do to keep the demons at bay was to keep wandering the hills.

He was nervous in the passenger seat of the Ford Transit van on his first real day of work. He knew the man sitting beside him would teach him his trade. Everybody said that yer man really knew his stuff. He had been told to keep his nose clean, do what he was told and he'd be fine.

Liam McHugh sat in the driver's seat with a newspaper resting on the steering wheel. He read the Daily Mirror from the back to the front losing interest about halfway though. Scanning the tabloid for any news that Steve Coppell's injury had cleared up did not do anything to lighten his mood. He was convinced, unlike some of the lads in the pub, that Jimmy Greenhoff could not carry the whole campaign on his shoulders. This season was going from bad to worse, he thought, and that Sexton would have to go. "It's always good to get an early start on a job like this. In an hour this yard will be heavin'. This way is better. We get what we need and we're off. Go you check them tools again." It wasn't a polite request and the young fella's opinion wasn't being asked for. A flash of resistance started to kindle in the lad's eyes and then he remembered himself.

"Aye, no bother Liam." Stepping out of the van, creaking in his brand new overalls he opened the doors and started to check the tidy rows of plumber's tools. He knew everyone and what everyone did. Big Liam had seen to that. Even before he picked up a Kangol hammer and switched it on he knew what it was for and how to use it. Very thorough was big Liam, in fairness. He was getting a good teaching from him. Not many would be this way with a new lad. That was being fair about it, but how many times did tools need to be checked over? He was still making sure the tools were where they should be when a light green Mercedes swung into the parking space beside the plumber's van.

"Morning, gentlemen! You're the early birds today!" said Ian Baxter.

"Mornin'," said Liam, getting out of the driver's seat and standing up. He spoke across the roof of the van towards the other man.

"We're here to do a wee job in town here and we just need some Yorkshire fittings off ye."

"Aye, I have all them in stock. Nobody beats me for price in this town."

"You're well recommended right enough," said Liam with a hint of a smile.

"What's the job you gentlemen are doing?"

"A central heating overhaul in a house and a new ensuite. We just need the Yorkshire fittings and we're pushed for time." Ian Baxter caught himself.

"No bother, just let me open up here," he said as he fumbled with a gaoler's bunch of keys. He opened the door and turned an alarm key that stopped the place sending an alert to the local RUC barracks. He flicked on the strip lights that illuminated the rows and rows of products. If Aladdin had been a plumber this is what his place would have looked like. The two men stepped inside adjusting their eyes from the dull early morning to the fluorescent daytime inside.

"Some amount of stuff!" said the young man. Ian Baxter beamed a smile at the boy's impressed face.

"You're not from around here with that accent, young fella. You're far travelled I'd say. You up from the Free State?" said Baxter, cheerfully.

Liam McHugh shot the teenager an angry glance. The message in his eyes was clear: focus on the job and keep your mouth shut. The youngster's face registered the rebuke and he put his head down. Silence and obedience was all that was required of the youngster and he had better remember it.

"Those Yorkshire fittings…" said Liam McHugh, bringing back the conversation to business and preventing the youngster from having to answer.

"Aye Yorkshire fittings! Just the job!"

Ian walked down the aisle with the men following; he turned and said:

"Did you gentlemen say that you were doing a new ensuite as well?"

"Aye," affirmed Liam.

"Well I've just got some lovely new shower cabinets in from England. The very best quality. I'm the sole supplier around here. You'd have to go up to Belfast to get these, but I have them here. Top quality they are," Ian enthused.

"Look mister we just need the…Aye OK, we'll have a wee look at them," relented McHugh.

"Good to see two working men hard at it. Terrible all these strikes in England. The dead not getting buried now. What's the country coming to?"

"Now just wait to you see these cabinets," Ian was delighted; he would sell to this man, he knew he would. He'd show Hannah she hadn't married a failure. He approached the standing rows of cabinets. Ian had opened some of them for display the night before. Now he was glad he had put in those late hours last night. He reached the first cabinet and drew open the sliding door with a flourish. Before he could turn around to greet impressed faces most of his lower brain spewed out of the gaping hole where his face had been. The second round from the three fifty-seven magnum shot into his slumped body was totally superfluous. The young man stood looking down, disbelieving at what the Ruger pistol in his right hand had just done to the part-time soldier. Liam took the weapon out of his limp hand and roughly shook his slim upper arm.

"OK, job done. Go you and wipe down the counter with your sleeve. You put your palm on it when you came in." The big tall youngster looked down at Liam McHugh for some answer, some understanding.

"MOVE!" Liam made almost as much sound as the Ruger through his ringing ears.

Hannah Baxter was on the school run. She was distracted by wee Elizabeth singing a nursery song for all she was worth in the child seat behind her. The playgroup was her 'school' and she was a big girl now, she told everyone. When Hannah saw the little Ford transit Van pull out of Ian's yard she allowed herself a smile. A customer this early would put Ian in a good mood. Once her majesty was dropped off she would go to Knox's dairy in Portadown and get something nice for a cup of tea. Stop by on Ian and surprise him! 'Why was I like that to him this morning?' she wondered. 'Maybe it was because I'm late. Two weeks! He is a good man, one of the best, doing his best.' The thought of making up with him in the back shop over a cuppa made the day seem better than it had been an hour ago.

In a terraced house in Auburn Terrace in Phibsborough, two men at a kitchen table together. They had made sure that they were far from any electronic device. The property did not have Wi-Fi or cable TV. As much as possible this little corner of North Dublin was off the grid.

The pair of them had known each other for many years. A Saudi and a Pakistani, they had met as young men in the city of Peshawar.

By that time they had already signed up for Jihad. They had both been on a long road as Holy Warriors. Sometimes side by side and on other occasions serving the Prophet on different continents. The leader of their organisation had made a good choice when putting them together. Although the Saudi was senior in the chain of command he knew he would delegate and defer to his Pakistani brother when it was operationally expedient.

"Our martyrs have done God's work here."

"We have more to do, my brother."

"You are sure that the special equipment we need will arrive?"

"It has been promised from the most high among us."

"Things will be more difficult for us now. The Irish police will now be on guard. We have been lucky."

"No. God has been protecting us as we do his work. God will protect us until his will is obeyed by these infidels or they are in hell."

"They are disgusting slaves of America, my brother."

"They are all destined for hell and our martyrs will feast in Paradise."

They stood up as one and embraced as brothers. If this mission was a success then they would go on to inflict more damage on the infidels, and if they failed then they would be rewarded for their sacrifice in Paradise. They were both experiencing a feeling that they knew the infidels could feel only through alcohol and indulging in the pleasures put in front of them by Shay⊠ān.

The feeling that ran through both of the men was that of pure joy.

All the guys in the platoon were all watching the title fight. All the guys except Meadloe. He was in his bunk submerged in the Bible. Like he always was. Always the fucking Bible. Still, he was one of his guys.

"You aint watching the fight Meadloe?"

"No Gunny."

"OK. When you next on guard?"

"Zero Six Thirty Gunny."

"OK you get enough sack time. Copy?"

"Roger that Gunny."

A roar went up. Something had happened in New York. The fight was on every TV and on every laptop screen in the barracks. He walked past a room with some of his guys in front of a large plasma TV that they had bought here on base. It turned the grunt's room into a small cinema. Most of his guys were shouting for Garcia the Venezuelan. The Hispanic was relentless. He wouldn't give O'Brien a second's respite. This one was only going one way. O'Brien was the bigger guy, more reach, but the South American had him for moves. Always slipping inside and throwing bombs. Upper cuts, hooks. O'Brien wanted him out in the centre of the ring where he could use his reach and height. Even the crowd in the Garden couldn't get their homeboy off the ropes. Garcia's gloves never stopped swiping and moving. O'Brien's head moved and twisted like he was trying to avoid a wasp. One more shot from the little Venezuelan and it would probably be all over.

This was only going one way.

He'd seen enough; anyway he had a date with the boss.

He walked down the long corridor. It could have been the administration building of a college back home. The floors shone as two little Filipino men worked floor bumpers. Bagram airbase had an invisible army of brown workers and they did everything. They cooked, cleaned and did your laundry. When he had deployed from Paris Island back in the day the mark one Marine did everything like that for himself and everything else for the Corps. He and his buddies were the cleaners and workers. Not now. This was war with a cappuccino and it was all going on the card. Uncle Sam was picking up the tab for this whole circus. Anytime the Afghan National Army guys were brought in here for a briefing they just stared at the opulence of the place. For them it must have been like visiting the alien mother ship at least we didn't do experiments on them, he thought; well, only on their heads.

Tom "Scooter" Robinson passed him in the corridor talking in a rapid Arkansas accent to a satellite phone. Pashtu sounded better, thought Powell. He was probably calling home on the most expensive way possible. Another tab for Uncle Sam. Scooter gestured to him with the other hand. The gesture sorta said: "Yeah I see ya, I'll catcha later buddy." He smiled in reply. Scooter was a good guy.

Ex-Recon. Most of the good guys here were ex-Recon. There just weren't enough of them to fix this clusterfuck of a unit.

Tom was the senior Non-com in the company's "Rotimi" platoon. The brass went ape over this new nickname for any sniper platoon since the Kenyan got whacked. As soon as it happened everyone had known it was an ex-military guy. No fat ass redneck with a civilian Remington could have pulled off that shot. No way. Scooter said that there was no chance that he was Army, only a Marine could take that shot. Scooter was a sniper and he was right.

The shooter was top class sniper and a loser from Lawrence Kansas. He had been in Fallujah with the 1st battalion of the 23rd Marines and had been sent back for a psych evaluation after he lost it when he was told that his unit's rotation was being put on hold. Aaron Walker just couldn't handle another week in Iraq. He went to pieces so they shipped him out.

Back in the world he went AWOL from Walter Reed. Somewhere along the line he got himself into some old time militia white supremacist religion and a Cheytac Intervention.

One shot.

Even if President Jonathan Rotimi had been wearing body armour, the custom built .408 round would have penetrated it. As it was, Rotimi was in a t-shirt walking through the area of Chico California where he grew up.

One shot.

The CheyTac cartridge was developed to fill the gap between the 338 Lapua and the fifty cal, yet the downrange characteristics outperformed the best fifty cal projectiles. It was a better system than Walker had used in the Marine Corps. Great weapon, great round. The lathe turned projectiles of a copper/nickel alloy. The 419 grain projectile that left Walker's rifle had a supersonic range of up to 2200 yards in standard air conditions. The retard used the CheyTac Advanced Ballistic Computer to calculate the trajectory and bullet drop over a mile and half to the target. A small gizmo the size of a cell phone. Helluva weapon, helluva round. We can still make things in America.

Suddenly everyone knew about the ballistic qualities of the four oh eight round. The country boys in the unit called it the "Jim

Crow round." Even with the four oh eight it was still a helluva shot. Not bad for a retard loser. That's what the US Marine Corps does for ya!

Yeah.

One shot.

The first lady got splattered with bits of the President and the whole world saw his head explode.

One shot.

Away from a sniper rifle a retard, though, is still a retard. The FBI weren't long in picking him up. In a few hours Aaron Walker was the world's most famous loser. There were, of course, the usual conspiracy theories about the organization that Walker was really working for. It was Dealy Plaza for the Twitter age. Everyone tweeted their theory. The truth was that Walker was just a loser who could, thanks to the Corps, shoot a moving target over that kind of range.

He got the needle in Terre Haute, Indiana on the same Gurney that they strapped Timothy McVeigh onto in 2001. President Adair didn't hang around on this one. He wanted this asshole processed through the courts. Walker obliged the Irishman from Scranton by waiving any right to appeal. He had done his duty to the American people, he told the court. Rotimi was a Kenyan and a Muslim. If that loser hadn't been well trained then he probably wouldn't be going to see the boss now. How good was that shot to take Rotimi? What if there had been a little more crosswind? Just at the last minute a slight change in wind direction, but there hadn't.

Now President Adair wanted out of the AFPAK region like yesterday. All around this place looked like somewhere Uncle Sam didn't want them to be. The unit rotation was stopped. No new units coming in, units getting ready to ship out. President Adair didn't want them to be here because President Adair wanted to remain President Adair.

The Pentagon was pouring out industrial levels of BS on how the Afghan National Army was good to go. We knew the truth, thought Powell. The guys on the ground can always call it real. They had pulled back the Corps from most of Helmand. The Brits were already gone. The French were a joke and the Germans in the north wouldn't patrol after dark. There was a joke that their shoulder flashes "ISAF" (the International Security and Assistance Force) really stood for "I Saw Americans Fight."

However, he thought, the US wasn't really fighting much either. The Taliban controlled the countryside the same way – whisper it – the Vietcong had controlled the rural areas in Vietnam. Only Recon was still out there with the Navy Seals and the Army guys from Bragg. Hell, they were still up in Tora Bora and – whisper it – over in Pakistan. And what was he doing? Babysitting retards like Meadloe.

He went into the office adjoining the Major's. The PFC looked up and then straightened up in this chair from the slouch he was in.

"Morning Gunny!"

"It is. Tell Major McLean I'm here, he's expecting…"

"Yes Gunny!" the PFC wasn't hanging around.

The door closed and he looked around the well-ordered office. Some people were born to live in offices. He wasn't. The PFC was well suited to it. He could tell. The "Don't ask don't tell" policy seemed ridiculously redundant for that paper clip queen. How the fuck did THAT get into my Corps, he wondered.

The faggot came out looking slightly upset, ashamed.

"The Major wants you to wait, he's on the phone to Division. He will be at least thirty minutes Gunny."

"Then I'll be back in thirty minutes."

"But Gunny, the Major…."

He fixed the office boy with a stare that immediately silenced him.

"Back in thirty. Copy?"

"Yes Gunny."

The PFC prayed that the Major wouldn't call for the Gunny in twenty minutes.

A five-minute march from the office was a Starbucks with Internet. Yeah, war with a cappuccino. He would have time to check his mail. He found an empty terminal and shouted up a large Americano. He logged onto his Gmail: "jumpinjarhead1981", Password: beruit83. The usual garbage that had evaded his spam filter was there, but some stuff was useful, one of them gold dust. It was from his princess.

"Hi Daddy. This is just a quick mail to tell you that everything is cool here. Mommy has a new job and my new sitter is really cool. She's from Mexico, she's called Carmen and she's really nice. School sucks and I really miss you. When you coming to see me? I know you told me, but I deleted a lot of my mail by accident – DUH! LOL!

Aunt Molly was here last night and she got us take-out. Sushi! She's sooooo totally cool. When I'm big I'm gonna be a newspaper reporter like her.

She was asking if you were OK.

I gotta go – I'm doing this on Mom's laptop ;) I will speak to her about when I can see you again. Leave it to me Dad. I can handle Mom. She'll give in to me ;) Love you Dad. You're the best. My bestest friend Kathryn at school – she sooooo looks like Ariana Grande – she told me that Marines ROCK! OK, really gotta go. Love you. Annie x"

He didn't know what to write back to his daughter. He would try later. He was no writer. She was all he had back in the world and the last three access trips hadn't happened because Paula was checking out how easy it was for her to pull rank on him. She had won in court; she now controlled the battle space. He needed a plan.

He flipped open his wallet and looked at a picture of Annie when she was seven. Only five years ago. Now she was Miss Attitude and she knew stuff – you know – stuff! Twelve! Anyway her mom had a new life and he wasn't in it. The only thing left was Recon and he wasn't there either. He logged out and looked at his coffee. War wasn't meant to be this comfortable, he thought.

He still had time. He reached inside the right leg pocket of his desert combat trousers and took out a small E-reader. This was clever technology. He had hundreds of books in here, none that Meadloe would ever read. He had just finished Roth's "The Human Stain." It had convinced him of two things.ONE, that Roth was the finest American writer alive and that TWO, that the US Marine Corps Non-Comms in a war zone should not have this much time on their hands. If he was reading Roth the enemy was having a day off. Unacceptable.

Now he was back to Hemingway. Like Meadlow looking for inspiration in the passage of the Bible, he found this in a Hemingway short story published in 1927. "In the fall the war was always there, but we did not go to it anymore." Yeah.

War was seasonal in Afghanistan. The enemy expected that. They would sit out the winter, rest up, replenish; then go for it again when the snows melted. We had to stop playing their game and start making them play ours. That was exactly what Recon were part of now. Not letting those backward bastards rest. Finding them in their caves. Changing the game.

Here this marine infantry unit pulled guard duty and watched a fight in the Garden. The nearest he got to action was separating bored grunts squaring up to each other over the ownership of an X-Box game or a computer disc with pornography on it. This unit wasn't going to the war anymore, but he was going to Recon. Whether Major Paperclips wanted it or not.

He checked the time on E-reading device. It squared with his watch. Eight minutes. He switched off the Kindle and headed back to the nice office. The PFC faggot looked pathetically grateful when he showed up twenty-seven minutes after he had seen him last.

"Gunny!"

"Yeah, is the Major still on the phone?"

"I'll see."

"You do that."

He was in and out of the boss's office in seconds.

"The Major will see you now, Gunny."

He marched in and came to attention whipping up a salute. This guy was a wuss, but he was an officer in the Corps. Officer on the Bridge! End of.

Before he could say a word, Major McLean threw a buff USMC personnel folder across the well-ordered desk in his direction.

"What the fuck is this?"

"Sir? It's a request for…"

"I know what the fuck it is gunny, what I wanna know is what the fuck IS this? Am I being clear?"

"Sir…"

"A request for transfer? We're shipping out in weeks and one my non-comms wants to up sticks and get outta MY unit!!!"

"I'm recon sir."

"You're a US FUCKING MARINE MISTER!!!!!! Request FUCKING Denied."

"Sir. Yes. Sir! With your permission sir I'll avail of my right to contact Division Sir. Under section…."

"I know the fucking section!"

The Major was furious. He knew he was only delaying the inevitable. This SOB ticked all the boxes and Recon would want him back. The Major sank back in his chair. He didn't understand this man in front of him. He didn't understand the type. He knew they existed but he didn't get them. Fucking Recon!

"Request approved. Now outta my fucking sight."

"Roger that sir." His right hand whipped up to his right eyebrow with rattlesnake speed. He looked straight ahead. Just like he had on the island at nineteen years old.

He went to pivot and march out of the office with the news he had wanted when the Major stopped him. The major softened; maybe this would work, he thought.

"Powell, you could be home in weeks with this unit."

"Yes sir."

"I could pull you some R&R now. You're due that and then some. You could be in Ramstein tonight. Stateside tomorrow."

"Appreciated sir. All due respect sir I…"

"OK, OK. Recon then? You asked for 7th Marines who just happen to be up in Tora Bora?"

"Roger that, sir!"

The Major flipped one the folder and leafed to the back of it, to the beginning.

"You're a corps brat?"

"Roger that, sir."

"Your father…"

"Sir?" Powell faltered.

"He was in Beirut? In eighty three? What age were you then? Two? Tough break Powell; that must have…"

"You have it there sir." Powell's tone was one of controlled anger. Just sign the fucking papers, he thought.

"You want one more crack at those ragheads. Don't you?"

"Sir?"

"Listen war hero, you can't get the one that offed your old man because that crazy fucker died that night. That's why they're called suicide bombers."

Powell fixed his stare on the wall behind McLean's desk. Standard anti-interrogation procedure. No eye contact. Betray nothing. No emotion. No weakness. Inside he was shaking. McLean was warming to the task.

"Yeah. Big revenge mission. We're shipping out but big fucking gung-ho Recon are still whacking ragheads. Hooah!"

"Is that all, sir?"

"No. Your platoon will be A1 for handover to your replacement. You got that, Powell?"

"Roger that, sir!"

"Well, Recon hotshot the Corps says where you go, not you! You hearing me Marine?"

"Sir! Yes sir!"

McLean savoured the moment and sat back in his chair and smiled.

"So I calls in a favour from a guy up the line. He owes me big. I did him a solid on the Island when he fucked up with some recruits. Want to know where you going?"

"Sir! Yes Sir!" barked Powell.

"I'm sending your sorry ass to MARFOREUR. You're gonna do your Recon thing when you're guarding a mother fuckin' Embassy somewhere!" laughed McLean. Powell felt the blow like he had taken a good one in the unarmed combat pit.

"They can work out what to do with you. Don't be expecting a glowing report either. You've been a pain in my butt with this transfer grief! Dismissed!"

"Sir, yes Sir!"

Powell would do nothing for McLean to write him up. Another perfect salute and he was gone. McLean was a vengeful man and a bad Marine, thought Powell, but the chain of command had decided and there was no arguing with it. In the Corps it was a case of 'FIGMO': Fuck It; Got My Orders…

His stride along the corridor lengthened. He was already mentally packing – even though it would take a few weeks. An hour ago he thought that would be in Recon before this shambles of a unit was back stateside. Now? He was being sent to some Embassy for Guard duty. To a Recon guy it sounded like the Stockade. In the bargaining part of grief he just hoped that it would be somewhere that the Embassy actually required protection.

As he was turning into the part of the building where the Starbucks was, he came across two young, marines, both privates, both African Americans, dressed in half uniform, half civilian clothes. They both sounded like they were from Chicago, and they looked untidy even by those standards. They were shambling along, staggering and giggling.

Powell detonated. He covered the twenty or so feet to them in an instant. The two young blacks were totally taken unawares. Something that should never happen to a Marine. Never.

"What the fuck do you two think you're doing?"

"Gunny?"

"Are in uniform or are you out of uniform?"

"Ah Gunny... I..."

"Names? Units? You two sorry ass holes are on a charge."

The taller of the two young men thought he might have the measure of the Non Comm. The crack cocaine he had just smoked had given him a false sense of his own importance.

"C'mon Gunny. It's all cool! We're all brothers. You're coming at us like a cracker!"

"You two are under arrest. NOW!"

Powell's right hand—in a millisecond- started to engage the muscle memory of a thousand unarmed combat sessions. The big one would go down first. A palm strike in an upward direction from five foot nine Powell on this six foot four shit head would put him down. It would be instant lights out.

"Jones! Ellis! What the fuck, you two..."

It was Scooter. These two must have belonged to him. Scooter was also a retard herd for the Corps. Powell stepped back. One blow from Powell would have given McLean his "out" of Powell's transfer. The thought of that scared John Powell. An emotion he was always trying to keep in check. Fear. Always the fear.

Powell launched into Gunny to Gunny speak.

"Gunny Robinson, these two marines are improperly dressed, that's just for starters. We also got insubordination, we also got, maybe…"

Scooter needed no more prompting.

"These two realize they're under arrest, Gunny Powell?"

"I was just informing them of that reality, Gunny Robinson."

The two grunts were deflated. Even the crack cocaine couldn't cloud the reality that they were in shit and had better shut the fuck up. Powell left the two brothers in the capable care of Scooter.

He got back to his unit's quarters and the little Venezuelan and a battered New Yorker were waiting on the result. Well whaddya know – it went the distance. Respect to O'Brien. The Brooklyn guy must have made it off the ropes after all. The first two scores came in, split decision so far. The third judge would be the casting vote. "Garcia 142, O'Brien 149 and the new middle weight cha…" The Garden erupted in cheering and flash photography as O'Brien was hoisted up onto shoulders. Most of his guys couldn't believe it.

Corporal Ramirez, one of the best in this unit, went into a rant in Spanish. Powell hardly had a sentence of Spanish, but could tell that the little Hispanic wasn't happy. It started to become physical around a few screens, as the country boys – who had backed O'Brien wanted their cash from the other grunts. A bet was a bet. Powell should've intervened. The grunts had seen Powell in the corridor.

He turned and walked back to his quarters as he heard the sound of what was probably a large plasma TV being smashed on the floor by a disappointed grunt. Shit gets like that when you back the wrong horse. It would be the only action this lot would see before they shipped out, thought Powell. He had work to do for the new guy.

Powell wanted back to Recon, back to where the war was. His Dad would have understood.

Friday

The Deerfield Residence in Phoenix Park was once the Chief Secretary's Lodge back in the days of British rule. In many ways it was now the abode of the new colonial overlords, although the twenty-six counties of the Republic of Ireland were nominally independent. The bank bailout of 2010 had proved that, just like the Greeks, the Irish were a small part of the United States of Europe and they would do as they were told on major matters. When it came to the geo-political stage the Irish state was firmly under the control of Uncle Sam, they just had to play the game that the Dublin Government was fully sovereign. It wasn't and if this Operation was successful then a lot of the pretence could be jettisoned.

Despite Rotimi's posturing on the campaign trail, he never did manage to shut GTO on Cuba. Now that Vice President Adair had been elected by sniper rifle any mention of human rights abuses was off the agenda. Langley and the Pentagon wanted something more permanent at Shannon.

It was Pelfrey's idea that they meet with Brannigan at the residence and not at the Ballsbridge Chancery. They had just arrived only twenty minutes before the Justice Minister was ushered in. It was a rare enough occasion, thought Pelfrey; that the Ambassador had taken the brief on board and was on the same page as the CIA Station Chief. Given what the Company man had told Brannigan, he was looking forward to how Scully would react.

"Well this is nice," said Brannigan as Scully was ushered into the large palatial sitting room. "Pretty nice, huh?"

"Yes, exquisite, Mr Ambassador," said Scully, not really knowing what to expect. Part of his unease was caused by the thin man sitting beside Brannigan.

"How's it going inside the Irish Government? We there yet?" asked Brannigan, cutting to the chase.

Scully was unsettled by this man who was sitting silently fingering an iPad. He hadn't spoken and Brannigan hadn't introduced him. Scully looked at Pelfrey and Brannigan rather nonchalantly took the cue.

"Oh, yeah. This is one of my guys. He's sitting in on this to help things along Garry."

Scully tried to assert himself and stood up from the two-seater couch across from the Ambassador and the Company guy. He walked over and extended his hand.

"Gareth Scully, Justice Minister, although I suppose you know that." He said with a diffident laugh that contained arrogance too.

Pelfrey glanced at Brannigan. The CIA Station Chief had official diplomatic cover so this wasn't a problem.

"Jerome Pelfrey. Pleased to meet you Minister. Cultural attaché. Just here to assist the Ambassador," said the bespectacled spook.

"Cultural Attaché?" Scully was blindsided. He didn't know why someone in that department would be in a meeting like this.

"Oh let's cut the horse shit" blustered Brannigan. Pelfrey shot Brannigan a look that communicated disdain, but not anger.

"He's Company, but you probably guessed that. Didn't ya?" said Brannigan.

Scully looked puzzled and Brannigan spoke in mock stage whispers like a ham actor.

"Cee Aye Ay!"

Scully was chilled, his comfort zone was now in another constellation on the edge of the known universe. Brannigan nodded to Pelfrey and he took his cue from the Ambassador. He stood up and his finger swept the iPad. The CIA man touched a folder and it opened an audio file. The sound quality of the device was surprisingly good and it filled the room.

"Hello Mr Mugabe. How are you?"

It was Scully's voice.

The Justice Minister could feel a pressure on his bladder and he was convinced he was about to uncontrollably urinate in fear.

"Ah yes Mr Murphy! Are you on your way, we will not start the party without you!"

The man's voice sounded very African, but it probably wasn't the leader of Zimbabwe.

"Oh I wouldn't miss it for the world. I will be there in about thirty minutes."

Pelfrey realised that he had made his point and stopped the file. He didn't look up from the iPad. It was delivered in his trademark monotone style. Androids put more heart into their presentations than Jerome Pelfrey. It was just how he was.

"Minister Scully; the house in Navan where you have attended some… social gatherings… four months ago a man called Suleiman Òréotitololuwa was there. He stayed there for three weeks. He is from Nigeria, a Yoruba man from Ogbomosho in Osun State. He is a cousin of your friend Mr Patrick Adebayo who we just heard speaking. As well as being a relative of Mr Adebayo, Suleiman Òréotitololuwa is also a senior officer in Boko Haram."

Scully started to tremble. He was convinced that he would wet himself right there. It was animal reflex of fear and submission and he had been a bed wetter at boarding school.

Pelfrey did not halt or look up.

"When he returned to Lagos on a false passport our people alerted the Nigerian authorities and they arrested him. He and his family were immediately flown to Abuja for further inter-rogation. He was in Ireland scouting out resources for opera-tions. Now, were all of this to come out Minister I'm sure you can appreciate…"

"Oh God…" pleaded Scully.

"Listen, Garret…" said Brannigan.

"Gareth!" implored Scully. They were casually outlining the death of his career, the death of everything and this fat stupid American couldn't even get his name right!

"Yeah. Sure. Look you're a good guy Gareth. Hell, I like you and we'll protect you. We take care of our own. Pelfrey here can make all sorts of shit go away like it was never there."

Scully looked up with pleading and hope in his eyes, he was utterly dependent on the two men sitting across from him.

"And Hell, you got a world a shit floating up around your pecker, buddy," chortled Brannigan.

"You'll be working with Pelfrey now, so best that I don't know stuff. All that plausible deniability horse shit. But here's the rub buddy. You need to deliver for us. I know you got your troubles in that penny-ante congress thing of yours. But we need that deal that you signed up to. Capisce?"

"Yes, yes of course."

"Good, we're done here. Uncle Sam has a world to run. Hooah!"

Gareth Scully looked utterly crushed and on the verge of tears. Pelfrey had used his iPad and his monotone delivery to outline the inescapable reality that the Americans knew every single thing about the Irish Justice Minister: things that he thought he had worked so hard to keep hidden, from his wife, from his party, and from the world. Brannigan could see that sitting across from him in the Ambassadorial residence was an utterly defeated man.

"Look Gareth, you work with James Bond here. He's your contact now, and you two gonna get real close. Hey, but no tongue!"

Brannigan laughed at his own joke, as was his habit.

The Irish Justice Minister rose unsteadily to his feet, nodded, and left the room silently. There didn't seem to be any words appropriate for what was going through his head at that moment. Pelfrey, standing to the left-hand side of Brannigan at the rather magnificent fireplace, looked up from his iPad, and Brannigan said, "Well, we got that fucker by the balls, that's for sure, but I think we need to give him something as well."

"Mr Ambassador?" said Pelfrey.

The CIA man glanced down at his iPad, looked back up and said "Yes, I concur, Mr Ambassador."

"Woah, hit me with such enthusiasm, Pelfrey," jibed Brannigan.

"We'll need to raise his stock inside the Irish government. He's the Justice Minister, so I suggest that we deliver to him some major security coup that makes him the man of the hour."

"Way to go, James Bond. We're on the same page here. We gotta give this guy some good. Something he can take home. Something he can cash in with his government buddies. 'Cause we need this hound to hunt."

Pelfrey was looking down at his iPad, going through files. Then he looked up.

"I think I may have something here that fits the bill, Mister Ambassador."

"Well, don't fucking tell me! We're moving into this plausible deniability shit. You work it out with Scully. Leave me out of it. I've gotta go and meet some visiting kiss-asses from Stateside."

"Very good, Mister Ambassador. Leave it with me."

Pelfrey's last statement sounded pretty dismissive to Brannigan. Of course he could handle it, and actually he would have preferred if the Ambassador had never been involved in this operation at all. But Langley had sanctioned that the best person to bring Scully in initially was the Ambassador, and Brannigan had enjoyed playing at being James Bond for a while. However, Brannigan now realised that, as they said back home in Philly, shit was about to get real. And although he would never admit it to Pelfrey, he knew that what was going on in Ireland was way above his pay grade. He just didn't like to be reminded of it by that tight-ass Yaley.

The Company Man didn't care to loiter around the residence. He wanted to get back to his work station where he had everything that he needed to function. As he was going out of the front door he noticed a new addition to the Marine Guard; a very striking African American about the same height as Pelfrey. The medal ribbons on this Marine's uniform indicated that this was someone who had seen a lot of action. Pelfrey felt the need to nod in gratitude when this man crisply saluted as he passed him on the way out to his official diplomatic car.

Jack walked into the office like a husband coming back from a quiet pint that had turned into an all-nighter who hadn't called Herself. There was a clear unspoken understanding between the two of them that the ostensible boss was accepting a subservient role in that moment so that Mary Riley could give out to him for sending her off the roof with worry after the bomb at the night club.

"Well. He's here. Alive and well," said Mary Riley.

"Look Dicey…"

"Doney fucking gall?"

"Long story…"

"Long fucking road Jack!"

"It is."

"I was DEMENTED with worry you big cunt!" tears started to well up in Mary Reilly's eyes and although calling the boss the C word probably wasn't such a good idea she was going for it now.

Jack accepted his going over with the contriteness of that husband returning from the all-nighter. He perched himself on the edge of Dicey's desk as she stood up and went for it.

"Your phone was off. They were digging bodies out of that place and one of them could have been you!"

"I was at the hospital. They've discharged Stan," said Jack trying to buy back into the conversation in another way. His current role of "target of female ire" was one he had performed many times. Mary Reilly ignored his attempt to divert the conversation.

"How is he?" asked Jack.

Mary Reilly took a breath and sighed that she was having no effect on this big useless bollox who she worked for.

"He was really lucky. The Guards reckoned that what blew upstairs Anto took the full force of whatever blew upstairs and Stan was mostly shielded from it. The bomber was downstairs. Everyone on the dance floor, the bar staff...." Mary Reilly couldn't bring herself to say the word 'dead'.

"The people in the toilets were mainly OK. Some injured. A girl in my street has a brother who is a paramedic. He said that the mad cunt had ball bearings in his pockets. So they flew all over..."

"Yeah." Jack knew all about ad hoc shrapnel in a device, but he didn't want to talk about that right now.

El Tiburón was a trawler operating out of Cadiz. As it headed for the west coast of Ireland the Captain knew that although they hadn't caught a fish yet, they already had precious cargo. The cocaine made landfall in Spain coming across the Atlantic in a Panamanian freighter flying under a flag of convenience granted by the Bahamas Maritime Authority.

The trawler was perfect because it was no stranger in Irish waters and Pablo Rodriguez was known to the Irish customs officials. Pablo Rodriguez had facilitated Colombians before, but now it was the Sinaloa Cartel. The Mexicans were expanding into Europe. They already were the main supplier of the white powder to the addicted gringos in El Norte. Now they wanted access to the European market.

The Satellite phone on the bridge beeped and Rodriguez picked it up. It was his amigo Irlandés. The code had been prearranged when he had met this man's boss in a villa outside of Marbella the week before.

Another reason that Rodriguez had made himself employable for this Irish gig was that he spoke very passable English.

"Hello my friend! How is the fishing in your waters?"

"Very calm no bad weather. I hope to catch something."

The west of Ireland was poorly policed at the best of times. The Irish Naval service only had five ocean-going patrol craft. With the humanitarian mission in the Mediterranean diverting scarce resources this was a good time to deliver the cargo. The Dublin docks could still be a problem, so it was easier to deliver to the west coast via a trawler that was well known in the area as a working fishing vessel. So well-known that the navy boys would wave to them.

El Tiburón was a good move.

The Irish Naval Service, even at full strength, was looking for needles in a sea of needles. It was a largely futile task unless someone told them where to look. The Sinaloa Cartel had been on the CIA's radar for some time. The potential for political trouble in Mexico had made them a target for infiltration. The Drug Enforcement Agency already had several deep penetration agents within the Mexican drug outfit, but Langley had pulled rank and the assets were now with the CIA. The guys at the DEA were pissed, but they had seen this movie before. If the Company stepped in they had clout within the Beltway that the DEA simply couldn't match.

All Langley had to do was suggest the possibility of the Sinaloa Cartel facilitating ISIS operatives through their smuggling route and Homeland Security rowed in behind them. The DEA were beaten before it started on the Hill. Fuck, even the FBI weighed in on the side of the Company. Someone somewhere was calling in major favours and that somewhere was 1000 Colonial Farm Rd, McLean, VA 22101, USA.

Therefore it was no problem for Pelfrey to order up a headline grabbing drug bust. It was like ordering take out. The power thrilled him. Although he had no field experience Jerome Pelfrey was an expert at manoeuvring his way through the labyrinthine world of the US 'Intelligence Community'. For many outsiders the system of sixteen separate United States government agencies that work both separately and together to conduct intelligence activities considered necessary for the conduct of foreign relations and national security of the United States seems hopelessly over complicated. The danger of duplication of effort was almost built into the US intelligence structures.

What newbies soon realised was that they were as much up against other American spooks as they were against the 'enemy'. Pelfrey was a natural at this and he knew that being CIA Director was his destiny. Under him the Company would have no rivals within the Beltway. All he needed was for Operation Rushmore to be a success.

They were nearly there, very close. Giving Scully a political victory would help him push the changes through the Irish Government.

As Pablo Rodriguez spoke to Tommy Rooney on his Satellite phone, the forty-one year-old native of Moyross had no idea that their carefully choreographed chat was being recorded and digitally analysed in Fort Meade, Maryland on the other side of the Atlantic. The NSA was pulled in by Langley to provide their smarts on this. No one asked why but this drug boat suddenly had gone to the top of a lot of piles in the US Intelligence Community.

No one asked, because that was part of their professional thing. You were told what you needed to know when you needed to know it. Nothing more.

Since the meeting at the Ambassadorial residence, Scully had felt like he was on political death row. He and his wife Emily had agreed to separate beds years ago because she was a very light sleeper and he moved around a lot, but now it was him who lay awake at night. When he did drop off, usually about two hours before he was due to be up, his dreams were never enjoyable.

He met Pelfrey in a small apartment in Ardilaun Court, on Patrick St. The Company had purchased it through a property company as a buy-to-let opportunity. The purchaser was a shell company in the Channel Islands. Pelfrey had been given a substantial budget of black money. This was an off books operation. It was a fatal flaw in the system of checks and balances. Congress could only carry out their constitutional duty of oversight if they were the ones pushing money across the table on the Hill.

Scully had been told to cover his tracks. Of course, he had learned to do this during his trips to Naas. For example, he would never travel by Ministerial Car. The CIA man had given him a 101 in counter surveillance when they had first met there. Scully had taken in every word as this man was clearly a professional. In fact, the brief had been prepared for him by an experienced field operative who was currently heading up a new unit at Langley.

It would not have helped the Justice Minister to know that the man sitting across the small dining table from him was a complete novice at tradecraft and was in Ireland to burnish his resume with an operational success in the field.

Tom O'Shea was early for the agreed meeting. He knew that Joe Byrne was a good skin, and dependable, and would probably be on time. O'Shea had picked a bar that he knew well, right next door to the Store Street Garda Station. Le Monde bar was just across from the Busáras main bus station. Consequently, it was well-frequented by commuters grabbing a coffee or a lunch before their bus. It was one of those places that didn't have a regular clientele, therefore no one noticed a stranger in the corner. It also meant that Byrne could nip out from the barracks, only a few yards away and meet O'Shea. O'Shea had thought long and hard over who to approach within the force: someone he knew, someone he trusted, and someone who owed him.

Joe Byrne ticked all of those boxes. A decent street copper, originally from Kildare, who had put most of his service in on the rough streets of the north inner city of the capital. He had a good nose for the job and, as O'Shea remembered, he was not allergic to a bit of knuckle when required. Of average height and in his early forties, Byrne came from a family of hurling fanatics due to his father hailing originally from Kilkenny. He still played with his local club, and this gave him a physique that was better than the average guard in his forties.

Although O'Shea didn't fully realise it, the old Kerryman was back in the job himself and he was unwittingly recruiting an asset. When Byrne came into the long bar, O'Shea looked up and made sure they had eye contact. He walked across, extending his hand. O'Shea didn't get up, but shook it and gestured to him to sit down. Byrne had his back to the door and O'Shea could see all around him. That was how he preferred it.

Before Byrne could say any more, O'Shea leaned forward across the table and put something into Byrne's hand. It was two A4 sheets of paper folded several times so that they fitted into the palm of a man's hand. O'Shea looked directly into Byrne's eyes.

"Here's a briefing. Go downstairs into the jacks, read it in there, rip the fucker up and put it down the pan. Make sure everything flushes away. Then when you come upstairs we'll have a pint and you'll know what I'm chatting about. OK?"

Byrne assessed for a second what O'Shea had just said and nodded.

"Away with ya then, what'll it be- Pint?" asked O'Shea.

"Coffee will be grand. Sure they would smell the drink off me in there."

"Away with ya then," ordered O'Shea, as the little Kerryman stood up to go to the bar to get Byrne his coffee.

When Byrne came back up from the toilet he didn't have the paper that O'Shea had squeezed into his hand, but he had a lot more information in his head. He sat down to see that there was a white coffee sitting in front of him.

"Is that what you wanted, or did you want one of those fucking cappuccino-things?"

Byrne smiled.

"No, you're grand Tom, you're grand."

O'Shea leaned forward over the table and Byrne reciprocated.

"Did you get all of that?" asked O'Shea.

Byrne nodded and lowered his voice. "Some story, Tom."

"Indeed it is, young fella. Indeed it is, Joe."

"I – I don't see how I can help you with this," said Byrne rather hesitantly.

"I think you can. I think you can Joe. In fairness, I think you can."

"This is well up the chain of command, Tom. Things are different from your day."

"Some things don't change," said O'Shea, quietly but emphatically.

Byrne could feel the little Kerryman's eyes piercing into him and was acutely aware that he had a debt to pay the man across from him. O'Shea didn't mention it. O'Shea didn't need to mention it. They both acknowledged that Byrne was in the job still only because O'Shea had covered for him when he was a rookie.

"I wouldn't ask you to do anything that would put yourself in a bad position Joe," said O'Shea.

Byrne nodded, but before he could speak, O'Shea continued,

"Sure, I didn't save your ass all those years ago to get you canned now."

And there it was. O'Shea had mentioned it, and Byrne knew there was no going back. This wasn't blackmail, it was just one man reminding another man that he was indebted to him and that he expected Byrne to return the favour. Byrne sighed, his shoulders sagged slightly and he looked up from the table and said, "OK Tom, how can I help?"

"I'm glad you said that Joe."

"Sure I owe you Tom. Owe you plenty. I'll do anything, but don't ask me if ye boys can grow hurlers in Kerry. No one hurls in the Kingdom!" chirped Byrne.

"Hah! You're still a Kat Byrne. Feckin' hurling mad ye all are!" laughed Tom O'Shea. Through the darkness of life, thought the old Kerryman, there was always the Gah.

Some things in life just don't mix well. They are combustible and dangerous when brought into close proximity. That was certainly the case with an angry Gerry O'Donnell and the three litre V6 CDI diesel engine that lurked beneath the bonnet of his Mercedes Benz Vito van as he sped out of Letterkenny. As the van speeded up, O'Donnell seemed to get angrier. He was still processing the confrontation in the car park at the bus station with a man he considered to be a lifelong friend. No matter how long they had been out of touch, there was still that connection. But the combination of Jack turning up largely unannounced, the proposition he had put to him, and then the allegation that Gerry wasn't there for him; it was all too much.

He took the left turn onto the Errigal Road just past Termon far quicker than he should have. The van was, at times, on these narrow roads under O'Donnell's control, more sports car than commercial vehicle. However, there was a limit. Thankfully there was no one coming in the opposite direction. He was replaying the conversation that he'd had with Jack over and over again, and with each play in his head he seemed to become angrier. He was several hundred yards past the turn for Muckish when he realised that he had failed to notice it, and this gave him cause to pause and try and put his anger in a box.

He knew he needed to stretch his legs: Walking was his therapy. Walking in wild places. Walking alone. Maria wasn't expecting him any time soon, and he had a good reason to put that allowance, that approval, to good use. He could see from his vantage point as he passed with the Aghlas on his right-hand side that there was a succession of brightly-coloured jackets making their way up Errigal. He didn't want company. He was after solitude, not altitude. So he pulled into a small, dark road that he knew very well, several hundred yards before the Errigal car park. He was pleased that there was no one else parked there. This was the road to Altan House.

Gerry knew the story well, had been told by a friend of one of his uncles. It was a happy story because it involved a lawyer losing money. Better still, it was a lawyer from Portadown, a loyalist spot that Gerry O'Donnell knew only too well. The legal chap in the nineteenth century had wanted to build a country pile in Donegal that would rival the majesty of Gleanveagh Castle, and he had established a substantial amount of money to carry out this project. However, the materials to build his folly had to be transported down to Altan Lough. An approach road had to be built down to the Lough over several kilometres of boggy ground, first going up over a small redoubt and then snaking down to a small stream that ran into the Lough. This approach road, which was built by local men including relatives of O'Donnell, had cost so much money that when it was finished there was very, very little left in the pot to build anything that looked like a castle. Consequently, all that was built on the site – and it was a magnificent site – was a square, two-storey house with a flat roof that kind of looked like a castle. As legend goes, it was never ever lived in, and these days it was just a shell inside, constantly covered in a fine carpet of sheep shit.

However, it was a stunning situation, and one of Gerry O'Donnell's favourite spots in the whole of the Derryveagh Mountains. Although he had known the place since he was a boy, he remembered specifically the first time he saw it through Maria's eyes, as he brought her down that summer night. Just at the right moment as the path was snaking down towards the lough, the setting sun over at Goath Dobhair was shining through the top window. It made it look like Altan House was on fire, hit by a large, orange napalm bomb. It was a stunning sight that an artist or a photographer couldn't have truly captured. You had to be there. He remembered looking at her face, and she was captivated by the beauty of the place, and he was captivated by her.

He had led various visitors down to this place over the years, and the most impressed and the most appreciative that he could remember was when he had taken the Japanese Ambassador and her personal cook down to see the place. The Japanese love water, and there were stepping stones over to where Altan House was, and beyond there, there was a small waterfall. As the Ambassador looked at the beauty of the pool beneath the waterfall, Gerry O'Donnell stood silently beside her, also in contemplation.

Without much forethought, he simply said, "Zanshin."

The Ambassador, a woman in her sixties, who had been one of the first economists to be employed by the Japanese government in the immediate post-war era, broke into a huge smile of mutual understanding. What she could not know was that her mountain guide had been a very determined JudoKi and was fully conscious that this concept, a state of awareness or relaxed alerted-ness within Judo, was often explained as the quality of water. Being very still and tranquil, but if disturbed, could be an unstoppable force. The literal translation of "zanshin" is "remaining mind," and Gerry O'Donnell had always found this very useful in the fight against his own inherited short fuse.

He took off the small day-sack that lived in the van that

contained everything he needed for his safety on the hill, threw it down at the start of the small beach at Altan. If anyone had have gone through the contents of the Berghaus Freeflow II 35+8 they could only have concluded one thing. This belonged to a mountain professional.

He sat down and looked out over the Lough, and thought of what had just transpired in Letterkenny with a man who he once trusted with his life. Moreover, he knew he owed his freedom to Jack. O'Donnell knew that he would have been accommodated in a British prison cell for decades if it hadn't been for the big fella that time in Leeds. Jack had never called in a favour until now.

Gerry O'Donnell now had to process how easy he had found it to tell such a friend that he was on his own.

It wasn't a good feeling.

Tom O'Shea was pleased with his morning. When things went to order and on time, it pleased the man who had spent his life serving the state in uniform. He was closing the door to make the short walk to St Joseph's church on Terenure Road when he sensed that he wasn't alone. He spun round as quickly as his old frame would allow, and immediately got a start. There were two men standing there and, worst of all, he recognised both of them. Pat Rooney and Johnny Buckley were now quite senior in the Branch, but O'Shea remembered them when they had first come in, and by the Kerryman's assessment, they were fucking useless then. And he didn't hold out any hopes that their uselessness quotient would have diminished with their years on the Force.

"What the fuck do you two want?" snarled O'Shea with a mixture of alarm and anger.

"Top of the mornin' to ya Tom," said Pat Rooney with a mocking conviviality.

"Out of my way. I'm going to fucking Mass," barked O'Shea.

"That's some tongue in your head for going to church," said Johnny Buckley, trying to assert himself in the conversation.

"You two aren't here for a social call, and you're going to make me late for Mass, so out my way," ordered O'Shea.

At that, the little Kerryman tried to walk between the two Special

Branch officers. It was Rooney who put his hand, open-palmed, fingers stretched, pointed upwards, onto the little Kerryman's sternum. It was a standard police gesture, stating to the target that they weren't going anywhere until the police officers said so.

"Now Tom, we just need a few minutes of your time. We're here on official business," said Pat Rooney.

When he heard that, O'Shea felt a sense of dread and confusion. His top-class mind was still fully-operational, although the wiry little body that had made him a very competent street cop had now passed with the aging process. He was an old man, and certainly no match for these two big men in their forties. If they were physically stopping him, then stopped he would stay.

"Well, try and make it quick, I'm going to Mass," said O'Shea, bargaining with the two men.

"I'm afraid Mass'll have to keep this morning, Tom. We need to have a serious word with you. Just friendly, like, but we're here on orders from the Big Fella."

When O'Shea heard that, he knew they had been sent by Assistant Commissioner Gaffney, and he had an idea of why they were there.

"What is it you want?" said O'Shea, all fight gone from him.

"Just passing on the compliments of the Big Fella. Really, really grateful that you came in that day to the Park to assist with that matter, which obviously for operational reasons we can't discuss with you. But the Big Fella, the Gaffer...Just thinks that you should leave it there. We've got everything in order. No need to be going down any other roads," said Rooney in a friendly way that nonetheless had an undercurrent of menace attached to it.

Any doubts that O'Shea may have had as to why these two men were standing blocking his way from getting out of his garden and going to Mass were gone.

"Tell Assistant Commissioner Gaffney I was asking for him, and if you gentlemen don't mind, I'll be on my way to Mass," said O'Shea with a mixture of diffidence and firmness that hoped that the twin pillars that were blocking his way would open up so he could walk out of his garden. Pat Rooney locked eye-contact with Tom O'Shea.

The big Dubliner's right hand was still on O'Shea's sternum. He brought in down and put the palm of his right hand onto Tom O'Shea's left forearm and gave it a tap.

"I'll tell the Big Fella that you took the message in the correct spirit, as we would expect from a man of your standing, Tom. And, ah, sure you can say a prayer for us all at Mass," said Rooney with a slightly derisive tone.

"I'll say a prayer for ye lot surely," said O'Shea with a slight tinge of anger in his voice.

And with that, he took a step forward and wasn't stopped and moved between the two men. His legs carried him out onto the road, and he kept walking, partly expecting these men to stop him again. But they didn't. By the time that the little Kerryman had got to St Joseph's, the usual crew were filing into morning Mass, and the familiarity of the surroundings and the people was presented a strange juxtaposition to the feelings that O'Shea was feeling at that moment.

He could never remember being in the walls of that church and feeling frightened. That made him angry. It felt like a violation of a place that had been such a comfort to him since his wife had gone to her rest eternal.

As Jack Dempsey walked up the narrow wooden stairs to the office and stooped his head going in, Dicey Riley was at her multi-tasking best. The phone had been going all morning, and she was dealing with the competing demands on her attention like a member of an Olympic plate-spinning team. One of the objectives of asymmetrical warfare (otherwise known as common or garden terrorism) is to damage the economy of the target country. This was the aim of the IRA's campaign in Northern Ireland throughout the 1970s and 1980s, and it was certainly their aim when they were detonating huge bombs in the city centre of London in the early 1990s.

However, it's an ill wind that blows nobody any good. Since the nightclub bomb, it seemed that everyone in central Dublin with any premises that was licensed to sell alcohol and admit the public wanted two big guys on the door. Obviously in the panicked response to the bomb at Angela's Nightclub in Temple Bar, it had been lost to many that the club had sported exactly that type of security on the door. How two 'bouncers' could deal with a suicide bomber hadn't really been thought out. In a quiet second, Mary Riley had thought that having staff on the door was just a sort of comfort blanket for everyone involved, the idea that something was being done, and that somehow, the night would go OK.

When Jack walked in the office, Mary Riley looked up and nodded to him. She was on the phone to a prospective customer. They had called, and it wasn't a hard sell. Essentially, the man on the other end of the phone owned three pubs on the North side, and although he had said that he had never had any trouble, he wanted guys on the door; that day if possible. Mary Riley said she would get back to him and put the phone down. As Jack sat on the edge of the desk, she looked up.

"Jack, it's goin' like a fair here. You would need an army of lads to cope with the demand now, after the…"

She didn't want to say the word "bomb." Jack looked at her, unsure of what to say. This bomb had killed one of his lads along with an awful lot of other innocent folk, young people just trying to have a good time. Only he thought he had done something to prevent that happening, although Dicey didn't know anything about that. And now he was on the cusp of making more money than he'd ever seen in his life. If there was a God up there, thought Jack, he was one sick, cruel bastard. He certainly didn't want to think that the boyo who had pressed the button inside Angela's Nightclub was currently being attended by seventy-two virgins, or used-to-be virgins, or whatever happens when these boyos go to Heaven. He looked up at Mary.

"I'm not minded to makin' a killin' out of this Dicey."

As soon as he had used the "K word," he realised it would sound either incredibly heartless or cleverly ironic, and he hadn't thought about it at all when he'd used it. He looked for Mary Riley's reaction.

"Well, you can take more staff on, 'cause we certainly can't cover the jobs we've been offered just this morning. Seems like every fucker wants two lads on the door."

"Sure I could take plenty more on, but I've always tried to just have reliable lads. Times like this, things can get mental."

Jack and Mary were far too engaged in this conversation about the potential economic benefits of the nightclub bomb to hear someone coming up the stairs. As soon as the door moved they both turned round to see someone that they had thought for a while that they would never ever see again. It was Stan His left arm was in a hospital-issued sling. He had various running repairs to his face, including stiches above his left eye, and there was also bruising to his right cheekbone. Otherwise he looked absolutely fine.

Any time Stan had been in the office before he always stood to get his orders for the next job. He certainly wasn't a slouch, and Dicey hadn't ever remembered him actually wanting to sit down, but now he took the chair that was at Jack's desk, and was grateful to sit there. He lowered himself down on the chair slowly and he was obviously in some pain. Jack jumped up and moved towards Stan, his first inkling to put an arm round him. However, the big Pole pulled back, though not through any hostility.

"Still sore, boss. Still sore," said Stan.

"Fuck's sake. Sorry, big fella. Look, it's – it's great to see ya. Shite, I thought that…"

"Dicey tell me you were there night of bomb, tell me everything when I was in hospital," said Stan, looking up at Mary Riley.

She nodded and smiled. At that point, Jack felt some need to explain why he hadn't been there the following morning, but that would have meant telling him about his fuckwit Odyssey to Donegal, and all of that was way too much explaining. But he felt he needed to say something.

"Sorry I wasn't at the hospital, big fella. It was just that…"

"OK boss, I know you very busy with everything. Bad time. Is OK."

Seán Patrick Dempsey had had a chance of being a professional boxer when he was a youngster, but he certainly wouldn't have made the cut as a poker player, because his face betrayed everything, and right now it was a wide canvas etched in guilt, as his most reliable soldier in his firm was saying it was OK, when Jack knew it was anything but OK.

"What are the doctors saying about you? Are they saying you're gonna be OK?"

"Doctors say shoulder bad. Might need operation. Not sure. I have to wait. I have medical card. Not private. Private is much money."

"Jaysus if it's money! Fuck's sake I didn't know that. We'll get you in and get it sorted now. I'll pay for it," said Jack.

"Not know if need operation yet, gaffer. They have to erm... photograph shoulder."

"You mean an X-ray? A scan?"

"Yes, yes. Those proper words. Photograph, scan. Yes," said Stan again; once more pissed off at his stuttering facility in English.

Jack looked at him, just amazed that this lad, who he had been convinced was dead, was still there. Although he had been told by Dicey that he had survived the blast, just seeing him there filled him with gratitude that he was OK, but also with remorse that he hadn't been there, and instead had been on his way to Letterkenny. Jack wanted to kick at himself for how stupid that was.

Although Stan's ability with English was rudimentary at this stage, he could certainly read a face and read body language. It was one of the things that made him excellent in his current line of work.

"Is OK gaffer. I will be OK. Been blown up before."

"Fuck. Blown up? Before?"

"Yes. Blown up before. I say. In army. In Poland."

"Fuck's sake. Never said that before, big fella."

"Yes, in army. Just a small problem," explained Stan, rather off-handedly.

"What happened?"

"Was training outside Krakow, with, em...hand bombs?" Stan knew he wasn't using the correct word.

"Grenades, hand grenades," corrected Jack.

"Yes, yes. Hand grenades, yes. I was training, and stupid bastard make mistake with a hand grenade, but I was far away. I was OK."

"What the fuck happened?" asked Jack, genuinely engaged with this anecdote in a way he probably shouldn't have been.

"Oh, stupid bastard make mistake with a hand grenade. Stupid bastard dead. Stan OK," explained Stan in his machine-gun, staccato delivery. He was reduced to very simple sentences in this strange language he was struggling with. Had he been speaking to a fellow Pole, then he would have been able to regale him with the full background of the stupid bastard, who had been transferred into Stan's beloved 6th Airborne Brigade only a month earlier from an artillery outfit.

"Fuckin' Hell. Nine lives," said Jack, giving a slight chuckle.

Mary Riley was slightly unnerved by this light-hearted discussion of being very near to explosions and walking away from them. Stan sensed this in a way that Jack didn't. He looked up.

"Is OK Dicey. Stan OK. Stan will be fine. Thank you for being at hospital for me," said Stan.

Stan's expression of gratitude was a further dig of guilt in the solar plexus for Jack. One day there would be a day, he thought, where he wouldn't feel guilty about things. But right now there seemed to be a huge fucking list of things that he had every reason to feel guilty about. And here was another one joining the queue.

Jack was looking down at a young man who had just survived a bomb explosion by the grace of God, or the luck of the Polish, or, something. And he was waiting for the HSE to find time to make sure if he was actually OK or not, when Jack knew exactly what to do. He looked across at Dicey.

"That fella who's the consultant at Blackrock Clinic, Dicey. You remember that bollix?" asked Jack.

"Mr Corrigan?"

"Yeah, I think that was his name."

"What about him?"

"As I remember, Dicey, we did a right good turn for him with that big private party he was having out in Ballymore Eustace. Remember that?"

"Of course I do. That was a saga, wasn't it?"

"Look, get onto his office. Better still, we should have his personal mobile. Get onto that, and tell him we're calling in the favour. We need this boy looked at."

When Stan realised he was being talked about, that Jack was doing something for him, the big Pole interjected.

"Gaffer, is OK. I will see hospital when they are ready. I know private hospital much money. I have medical card. Stan will be OK." Jack knew that the cut-off income levels for getting free healthcare in the banana republic were Draconian. Therefore, a lot of his lads were paid, in part, under the table.

Jack asserted himself. He was the boss, and he knew what to do.

"Listen, young man, you'll do as you're told. We'll have you in a private hospital today or tomorrow, and get that fucking shoulder looked at, and anything else that needs fixed. OK?"

Jack wasn't asking for Stan's approval. Jack was issuing an order, and the Polish ex-paratrooper responded as he had been trained to do in the base at Krakow.

"Of course gaffer. I go if you send me."

And at that point, Jack wished that he had twenty like him, even five like him.

"Good lad. Yer man at Blackrock Clinic will sort you out," assured Jack.

Then Jack turned to Mary Reilly. "Dicey, see if we can get him admitted today. Let that bollix know that I haven't forgotten he owes me," ordered Dempsey to his invaluable office manager.

The immediacy of the possible treatment made Stan become alert and he interjected.

"No. Cannot be today gaffer, "said the Pole.

"Why not pet?" asked Mary Reilly.

"Yeah lad. Get you in, get you fixed," added Jack.

"I have to go to Police. They must test me."

"Test?" Jack was puzzled.

"Yes gaffer. Test to help find my sister. They are not sure who…"

"Oh fuck." Mary Reilly put her hand to her mouth at the awful realisation that this young man in her office had to go to a Garda barracks and get a DNA test done to help identify his sister's remains.

It brought home the utter horror of what they were living through. She looked up at Jack for some support, for some leadership, for something. His look back at her indicated that the penny hadn't dropped with him.

"DNA" said Mary softly.

Jack put his dead down. This was all too fucking real. There wasn't enough of Stan's sister left to identify by simply looking at her. At that moment he didn't want the other two people in the room to know that he was thinking.

The carnage caused at Angela's by that suicide bomber was no different to what he had been the author of in England. Anything about botched warnings or dodgy timers didn't mean a thing to the people who disintegrated in a bomb flash in English bomb that Dempsey had planted.

No one paid any attention to Wojciech Iwanowski on the flight from Warsaw to Dublin. That was exactly how he wanted it, and that was why he had chosen a mid-week commuter flight that landed at Dublin's Terminal Two at 16.00 hours local time. Of course, there was no reason that anyone should pay any attention to this rather nondescript man in his late thirties sitting by the window. He didn't interact with the cabin crew, and again that was entirely intentional on his part.

Anyone giving him a second glance on the flight would have looked at his attire and reckoned he was a working class Polish guy going to Ireland to work or to return to his job there. If clothes maketh the man, then they can also provide a false impression. He was wearing tan cargo pants and a lightweight summer jacket with a hood and a kangaroo pocket. He wouldn't have looked out of place on a building site or in a youth hostel. Transitory and nondescript.

They would have to be serviceable for a few days and nothing more. The clothes had been purchased the previous week in the Zoo Market in Warsaw. This open air bazaar is located along the right bank of the Vistula River, in the historic part of the Praga district and within walking distance from the Old Town. He was wearing Hi-tech Idaho fabric hiking boots on his feet. Given the price he had been charged by the stall holder, he suspected that they were either stolen or counterfeit. Either way, it didn't matter. He paid cash for all of his purchases. There was nothing to connect him to what he was wearing.

His carry-on luggage had also been purchased in that flea market. It was a low quality 30 litre backpack. It had a logo stitched onto it symbolising a mountain range. The Russian had meticulously unpicked the stitching and thrown the badge in the bin of the low rent self-catering apartment he was staying in for that week. Even his luggage was anonymous.

It was important in his line of work to be a grey man, to pass through crowded areas unnoticed and utterly unremarkable. It was the camouflage of the average. Physically he didn't stand out. Five foot nine, in good condition, but not noticeably so. His hair was trimmed short. No earrings or tattoos. The idea was that even the most observant guardian of law and order would walk past this man and not remember him one minute later. Utterly average. In the age of mass surveillance this was how to be invisible, by standing out there in plain sight and advertising averageness.

However, there was nothing about this man that was in any way average at all. He joined the queue of EU passport holders, and his Polish passport, in date and all in order, merited nothing more than a glance from the bored policeman who was guarding entry to the Republic of Ireland. What Garda Liam Rooney could not have known was that the man now passing through into the Irish state was someone who really should not have been allowed access to the country.

His passport was entirely in order because it was genuine, although the real Wojciech Iwanowski had died as a new-born in the maternity hospital at Gdansk in the same year that he saw the light of day in Kaliningrad to proud parents. His upbringing in this Russian enclave in the Baltic made it a no-brainer that when he needed another identity he would pick one from the Polish port on the same Baltic coastline as his birthplace. It was utterly believable and he could easily pass for a Pole from Gdansk.

He was relaxed about landing in Ireland, because he would be making it his business not to interact with the Polish community. In fact, it was his task on this job not to be interacting with anyone unless it was absolutely necessary. He was here to do a job, get his hands dirty, and leave, suitably remunerated.

It had been a long time and a long road since the rubble of Grozny, when the young Russian solider had come face to face with death, terror, and Chechen ferocity. It was in that chaos that a nine-teen year-old Russian grew up very, very quickly and found that he had a certain aptitude for chaos and carnage. He was perfect for the job that he had been selected to carry out.

As he alighted at Dublin he logged on to a computer terminal, put in some coins, and accessed a Hotmail account that had been set up for the purpose of his visit. He wrote an email and saved it to drafts. It simply had the word "maroon" in the subject bar, and no text. He then logged off and left to queue for a bus into the centre of Dublin. Thousands of miles away, in Langley, that draft email was seen by someone who had been waiting for it. And within minutes of that, Jerome Pelfrey had received a secure communication with a designated code-word that told him that his boy had arrived, and that he should proceed to the pre-arranged rendezvous.

The express bus took him from Dublin Airport straight into the heart of Dublin, and he found himself walking across O'Connell Bridge in the direction of Grafton Street. His first task was to pick up a mobile phone, and he did so at the Car Phone Warehouse, paying cash and walking out with an entirely anonymous, untraceable device. He then walked the short distance to the accommodation that had been booked for him in St Augustine Street on the southern bank of the river Liffey, just across from the Four Courts.

For the short amount of time he intended to be in Dublin, he would be in serviced apartments. This was perfect for him in that there were no public areas as there would be in a hotel. There was just a very rudimentary reception area. He picked up his key card, and with that he had access to his own apartment. There was no room service or chambermaid to disturb him. The apartment complex had an entirely transitory population of young travellers and business people, who preferred quiet and privacy over the hubbub of a modern hotel. Apart from being suitable for his discreet work, it was also only a few hundred metres from the address he had been given, where he would meet his local contact the following day.

When he powered up the Huawei Y3, it took a few seconds before it logged on to the service provider and he had a signal. He reached into his wallet and took out a small slip of paper that had an Irish mobile number on it. He tapped the text message icon and sent a simple "Hi" message to the number. Almost immediately, a text message came back stating "Bray Station." He had been told to expect that he would be given some public transport place to meet his contact, so this didn't faze him in any way. He had done his homework on the basic layout of central Dublin, and Google Maps on the mobile phone suggested that he make his way to Tara Street

DART Station to take the forty-minute trip down the coast to the seaside town, where he would get the tools to do the job that he had come to Ireland to do for his client.

By the time Gerry O'Donnell had made most of the climb back from Altan and was looking down across the blanket bog to where his van was parked, just off the R251, he knew in his head that the therapy had worked, as it usually did. He had stopped being troubled by the interaction with his old comrade Jack Dempsey, and he was ready to go home. And as he strode out, digging the trekking poles into the track that had once been a road that had bankrupted a nouveau riche in the 19th century, he thought of how lucky he was to have a home – a real home – to go to. The Mercedes engine, as ever, didn't let him down.

In the age of driverless cars, Gerry O'Donnell's van was almost there on its own. He had driven the back of Errigal road so many times in this fine example of German engineering that he was sure it probably knew the way on its own. As he passed McGeady's Bar in Dunlewey village on the right-hand side, he knew the soft right, the dip in the road and the straight stretch up to the T-Junction where he could take a left to Gweedore and Dungloe, or hang a right to his beloved Cloughaneely.

For every household he drove past before he got to his turn-off, he knew the names and he knew the stories. The Glaswegian was on home turf. On a summer's night like this one of the things he loved was the way that Errigal changed shape depending on what angle of the road he was on. By the time he got to turn for his own road on the left, he was in the townland of Upper Keeldrum. The access road he used had nothing to do with Donegal County Council, but was a very good example of how people in that part of rural Ireland got together and found their own solutions. The road went through a neighbour's land, but several families used it, and all contributed to the financial upkeep of a fine, straight road of about three hundred yards that connected to a rather unkempt borreen that was actually the responsibility of the local authority.

Gerry passed a two-storey house on the right-hand side where a very fine family lived who had been there for generations. Everyone in this townland knew everyone else, which could be a good thing and a bad thing. He was then at another, much less well-maintained T-Junction to the one he'd turned left onto. This one also demanded that he turn left, and he was over a very, very small bridge that couldn't take anything heavy, but his van was fine.

His neighbours were out with their sheep so the gate at the bottom of the road was closed. It was non-negotiable. You opened gates; you closed them in this part of the world. Anything else was seriously bad form. O'Donnell jumped out of the van, opened the gate, moved the vehicle through, jumped out again and closed it. It would never have occurred to him to leave the gate open. The van then went up a very, very narrow mountain borreen, and as it crested, there he saw Errigal in the way that he loved to see his favourite mountain. It looked like a cross between the Matterhorn and a stone-age arrowhead pointing up into the Donegal sky. When he'd got into the van after his Altan walk, he could see what a gentle whaleback Errigal actually was, but from that angle, a hundred yards from his home, it looked bloody magnificent.

Gerry and his family were now the only folk up that road. There had been two old bachelors when he had first renovated the cottage, but they had passed away, so they really did have this little corner to themselves. This drive home would have been treacherous for anyone who didn't know the road, even in a small, manoeuvrable car, let alone a large van, but for O'Donnell this was his day and daily. He turned left off of the narrow, overgrown road and went down a hill, and there was home.

The cottage had been built in 1917, and there were many stories of how the local men had gathered large boulders, with only animal and human muscle power, to lay a foundation. When Gerry had taken the keys from a cousin in 1996, it was pretty much as it had been all of those days. To say the least it was rudimentary. By the time he brought Maria there to show her it, it was almost fit for the princess that he had fallen in love with. With the help of a digger and several sturdy cousins, they had cleared the way out the back and built an extension that made the cottage, from the air, look like a T shape. Then the old, damp, cramped porch at the front was demolished, and, as luck would have it, a neighbour was getting rid of two large windows – teak-framed but single pane. The porch was built around the dimensions of these windows, and a brand-new pitch-slate roof was put on top. It was a community effort, with Gerry paying the lads what he could, when he could. With him supplying the materials, bit by bit, Gerry O'Donnell's little corner of Donegal had been transformed into a very comfortable abode.

As he put the handbrake in the air, Rua immediately started to bark inside the cottage because she could smell him. When he opened the door of the porch, he could hear Herself on the phone, speaking in Spanish. Gerry could tell just from the way she was speaking that she was speaking to her best friend Consuela, a Venezuelan girl that Maria had met when she had first moved to Spain to work. He guessed that she was speaking to her friend about the situation over the last few days in Ireland.

"¡Sí, sí, sí, claro! ¡Hombres, mujeres, y niños, claro!"

It struck Gerry for the first time that Ireland was once again an international talking point because of the slaughter of innocents, and momentarily that made him think of the old days. As he pulled the inside door, Maria was at the kitchen worktop with the cordless phone to her ear, still giving forth to Consuela about her opinion of the Jihadis.

"¡Hijos de puta, sí!"

"I hope you're not talking about me to someone?" said Gerry. Maria spun round, and as ever, her smile lit up Gerry O'Donnell's world.

"Chico!"

At that Gerry knew she was in a good mood. She was in her standard cottage uniform of old slippers, grey leggings and a grey knitted jumper that she had acquired along the way on her Odyssey from El Camino Santiago to a mountain in Donegal with a man that she had met on the pilgrim's route. Her hair was up in a ponytail, but despite her colour scheme, there was nothing grey about this woman at all. She held the cordless phone to him and said, "Chico, speak to Consuela, your Spanish is good."

Before Gerry could take the phone from Maria's hand he was ambushed at thigh level from two directions. Rua leaped out of her basket demanding attention because it was all about her. Her paws came to rest on Gerry's hip as she demanded his full attention. On the other side, he was hit by a loving rugby tackle from a small person who had changed his life utterly. It was his son. Gerry often joked to himself on more than one occasion that, even in diverse, modern Ireland, there could only be one Felipe García O'Donnell on the island. He was pretty sure about that.

"PAPA!" There was the little fella. He had his mother's gorgeous, jet-black hair and, to Maria's delight, Gerry's deep blue eyes. It seemed only ten minutes ago, but it was close on six years, that Maria had been handed this little bundle in Letterkenny Hospital. And all that seemed to matter to her at that moment was that her first-born had his father's eyes. Maria smiled at the pincer movement of affection that had ambushed her husband, and she tilted the phone in her hand in a downward direction, in a beguiling way, because Consuela in her apartment in Northern Madrid wanted to speak to Gerry. When they had come off the Camino together all of those years ago, Consuela had been the first person that Maria had told that this strange man she had met on the pilgrim's path in Galicia was the man that she wanted to marry. Gerry O'Donnell had always thought, rather foolishly, it was his idea. Consuela really liked Gerry, and just loved listening to his Glasgow voice.

Pablo Rodriguez had just taken a cup of coffee from young Carlos Gutierrez and was admiring the mountains of Kerry on the starboard bow. The rendezvous would happen in another couple of hours. The guys were on deck making like fisherman and he could almost taste the money from the Mexicans. He would be able to buy that penthouse apartment in Paseo Maritimo for Carmen.

Rodriguez was still savouring her reaction when she realised that he was the main hombre when at nearly ninety degrees angle on the port bow the LÉ Samuel Beckett (P61) came into view, and it wasn't slow. The ship's namesake would have appreciated the drama of what was about to unfold. Captain Pablo Rodriguez knew that there was no way that his squat trawler, designed for stability in rough seas while dragging nets, could outrun the Irish ship. Propelled by two Wärtsilä diesel engines, the LÉ Samuel Beckett had a top speed of 23 knots. Her Captain, Diarmuid Ó Máille, had demanded every ounce of thrust from those two Finnish engines.

This was no normal patrol. They knew exactly what El Tiburón was carrying and exactly where it was hidden. Someone in the intelligence world had earned their corn.

The Westport man had fallen in love with the sea as a boy out in a rowing boat with his uncle in Clew Bay. He wasn't the first in his father's line to be in the Naval Service, but he was the first to hold the rank of Captain, and today was his day.

As the DART left Shankill Station, the Russian's new Android bleeped with a text message. It was from the only person who had that number. "Citroen Berlingo. White." He knew then that there was a vehicle outside Bray DART Station that would not be difficult to spot. It was a good choice of non-descript vehicle that would not warrant a second glance from anyone walking past it. It was the sort of small commercial van that tradesmen used, and they were ubiquitous in every Irish town.

The Russian walked out of Bray DART Station and immediately saw the vehicle parked next to a small convenience store. He walked across and opened the passenger door of the two-seater vehicle. There was no need for chit-chat. He didn't want to know the man who was sitting in the driver's seat. They were around the same age. The driver was in overalls. The Russian smiled internally. He always was put at his ease when he was working with professionals. The choice of attire was perfect for the vehicle. Once more, no one would ever remember even having seen that van or the occupants.

They spoke in English, and the driver simply said, "Case in the back. It's all there. Do not check it here."

The Russian did not question any of this. He knew the protocols. This was merely a handover. He opened the back door of the van and inside was a holdall that had seen better days but was fully functional. He grabbed it with his left hand and lifted it, and it was substantially heavy, so he separated the two handles and scooped his right arm through it so it hung over his shoulder like a rucksack strap. He closed the van door and turned without saying anything to the driver and walked back to the DART station. Just like on the flight from Warsaw, and on the coach into Dublin City Centre, the Russian was completely anonymous on the journey back to Tara Street.

For the first time since he had been raped by iPad at the US Ambassador's residence by that emaciated librarian, Gareth Scully felt like he was getting his life back. The LÉ Samuel Beckett was the best known Irish ship on the planet by now. The video footage of the boarding party taking down the trawler had gone viral. The very telegenic Captain, a tall chap from Mayo, had been interviewed on the quay in Galway and so had Scully.

The American had arranged everything with a deus ex machina that had unnerved him. If they could pull this off to help him with the Taoiseach and his allies in the Cabinet, Scully shuddered at what they could do to him if they wanted. At his last meeting in the apartment with Pelfrey, he had been further violated with the iPad. Somehow they had been able to film the inside of that bloody house in Naas. They had eyes on every room in the house, by what looked like a camera in the corner at ceiling level.

The last visit to Patrick Adebayo's house was played for him. Scully was in just about every shot and it was unmistakably him. There was no need for Jerome Pelfrey to spell this out. The audio had sent the message to him at the Ambassador's residence that the Americans knew all about his appetites.

Now this…

Scully was sitting in the corner of the room in a large chair. There was a double airbed on the front of the room where a coffee table usually sat. That had been cleared away for the performance art. The Scottish girl was a cut above, that was for sure and she certainly was well trained. Sometimes at these events he wore a rather fetching mask. However, he hadn't on this occasion and he was clearly visible in the video. Damn!

Scully comforted himself that he was their man, comforted himself that they needed him and would protect him. Perhaps this would work out and he would finally oust that imbecile from Kerry and get what was rightfully his. Taoiseach Gareth Scully had a ring to it, he thought.

Niamh Murphy, his PA, came into the office and she looked uncharacteristically flustered. For an awful moment Scully thought that there had been another attack.

"Minister, Garda Commissioner Keegan is here to see you and he said it's urgent."

"He isn't scheduled. I have to go to Cabinet in half an hour."

Before any gatekeeping could be attempted by Niamh Murphy into the office burst Eamonn Keegan like he was taking down a scumbag in Limerick in his prime.

"You're some boy, you!" growled the Letterkenny man.

"I beg your pardon Commissioner?" said Scully in a supercilious, baiting way.

"The first I hear about this operation is when I'm teeing off at a charity event at the fucking K Club!" said Keegan, boiling with outage.

"By the time I get to my office at the Park you're already on the quayside at Galway being interviewed about the great success!" ranted Keegan.

"I think it all went swimmingly, Commissioner," taunted Scully.

The journey on foot from Tara Street to his apartment on Saint Augustine Street was pleasantly uneventful. He walked past some Polish students at Christchurch. He didn't look up in recognition as he heard them chattering excitedly in Polish about their plans for the evening. They were students of the English college a few hundred yards away. He could pass himself off comfortably as a Pole to any Irish person, but to these kids from Kraków and Poznan it might prove problematic.

When the Russian entered the apartment complex he noted that there had been a shift change and that the blonde girl who had given him his key card wasn't there anymore and had been replaced by a tubby young man who hardly looked up from his smartphone. This place was perfect, thought the Russian.

The elevator took him up one floor and then he had to walk out into a court yard area to access the door to his apartment block within the main complex. He then had one flight of stairs to go. His key card was recognised by the microprocessor in the door and it blinked green.

He placed the BXT 65CM Extra Large Heavy Duty sports bag on the bed. The main compartment could be accessed by way of a 'U' shaped double zip. When he undid this he found a towel and a hooded sweat shirt; an extra layer of cover. Once more the Russian gave a smile. The man in the Berlingo van was clearly a professional. If this holdall had been opened then there wouldn't have been anything to be seen to cause suspicion or alarm.

There were various objects encased in bubble wrap secured with gaffer tape. The Russian took the towel from the holdall and spread it out on the bed. The kitchen was well equipped and a small sharp knife proved useful for gently slicing through the gaffer tape without puncturing the precious components inside. Like most skilled professionals, he was very particular about his tools.

He had asked for a VSS Vintorez. Like him, it was Russian. The clients had no problems with facilitating this as anything that had footprints heading in the direction of Russia was good for them. The VSS is a suppressed sniper rifle that uses a heavy subsonic nine by thirty-nine millimetre SP5 cartridge and armour-piercing SP6 cartridge. It was developed in the late 1980s by TsNIITochMash and manufactured by the Tula Arsenal. It was the weapon of choice for the Russian Spetsnaz Special Forces units. It is almost completely silent and consequently ideal for undercover or clandestine operations.

This particular model had left the factory to be stripped down for transport in a specially fitted briefcase. The VSS has an effective range with the fitted optics of four hundred metres. That's a long distance in an urban area.

Also mummified in bubble wrap was a Glock 17. This was almost ubiquitous in law enforcement circles now and much less exotic than the VSS. It had a threaded barrel made by Lone Wolf in the USA and this allowed the Austrian made pistol to take a suppressor. Quietness was important in the Russian's line of work. The suppressor was from the Advanced Armament Corporation in Lawrenceville, Georgia, USA.

It is one of the common misperceptions among the movie going public that there is such a thing as a 'silencer' on a weapon. There isn't. There are three reasons that a firearm makes a noise when it is fired. Firstly, there is the sound of metal smashing into metal at high speed. Secondly, there is the explosion inside the weapon when the cartridge ignites. Thirdly, the bullet leaving the weapon breaks the sound barrier. The VSS deliberately used subsonic ammunition. This was a trade off in power and range for quietness.

Unlike the pistol the Russian rifle had a suppressor built-in it at the factory. This weapon was only ever meant to be used when a lack of noise was crucial. Other performance qualities of the weapon were secondary. With the 'silencer' fitted, the foresight on the Glock automatic pistol was blocked out, but if he needed to use this weapon the Russian would be close enough not to require it.

There was also a rectangle of bubble wrap of about ten inches by six inches and four inches deep. It was the fuel for the mission. Cash. Had the poor manual worker been stopped at the airport it would have looked very out of place to have been carrying a large amount of money.

By his own professional criteria the Russian was taking a job that was atypical for him. He wasn't that nineteen year-old patriot in the rubble of Grozny anymore. This was his chosen profession and he was good at it. As a freelancer, he decided what jobs to accept. The key criterion was calculated based on the odds of completing the mission while staying alive and undetected. So far, his judgement had proved sound. After eleven years in this game Aleksander Mikhail Vasiliev was still alive and at liberty. He was a careful, cautious man and not the personality type that the man in the street would ascribe to an assassin.

He was in this line of work to make money, lots of it. The Russian had acquired a very specific skill set in his twenties that was largely useless in ordinary life. Moreover, the money in his account in Tortola already made him rich beyond the wildest dreams of the people he had grown up with in Kaliningrad on the Baltic. He had a man in Geneva who looked after the financial management side of his business. Payments usually moved through twenty-three shell companies and offshore funds, the Cayman Islands, Dubai, Guernsey and Singapore could all be used. However, the final destination was always the British Virgin Islands.

This job was different as, even at this late stage, there was no specific target. The commission was that he would be briefed in theatre by the client.

Tom O'Shea sat up from a kneeling position as the priest left the Alter. The usual morning Mass crew started to file out to start their day in a state of Grace. By the looks of the other parishioners, the retired Special Branch man could have been one of the younger ones. Morning Mass in Ireland was kept going – for the moment – by a dying demographic.

As was normal for him, Tom O'Shea liked to sit, sometimes for half an hour, sometimes longer, in the Church after Mass. He liked quiet and he liked to ponder. In the frenetically busy Dublin, these were places of quiet, places of sanctuary. One newcomer he did notice as she went up for Communion was a young woman. She could have been no more than twenty, and she was either dressed for running or cycling. Her age and her attire made her stick out a great deal, but Tom O'Shea thought no more about it. She was one of the last to leave, and then he became aware of someone sitting in the pew beside him. And then he realised that he'd closed his eyes for perhaps a few minutes, not to nod off, but to more fully appreciate the silence of the empty church.

He looked up, and it was the young woman sitting beside him. O'Shea got something of a start. She wasn't sitting that close to him – perhaps the width of two or three souls – but close enough. The church was entirely empty beside these two, and she was in the same pew as him, his normal pew, on the right-hand side of the Alter, two-thirds of the way back. He was never one for being down at the front, which he thought should be the preserve of members of the Saint Vincent DePaul and out-and-out craw-thumpers. O'Shea looked at this young woman, and he could now study her face. She had short dark hair, piercing blue eyes and a slightly turned-up nose. She was wearing a lime-green, waist-length waterproof jacket, dark Lycra leggings and training shoes. In her hand she was holding a modern cycling helmet, aerodynamic, ribbed and pink, with a yellow lightning flash along the sides. O'Shea didn't say a word to her, but he really did want to know why she had decided to sit down in the same pew as him in an empty church. And then she spoke.

"Sure they can't grow hurlers in Kerry, can they Tom?" said the young woman.

O'Shea tried to process what she had just said, and it made no sense. Then she spoke again.

"My father said hello, and told me to say thanks for helping him in Harcourt Street that time with the gobshite McLoughin."

O'Shea thought he was having something of a breakdown. This young woman was saying things that were starting to sound very familiar and very precise. The young woman realised she needed to give him more information, as her prepared script hadn't worked.

"Mr O'Shea, my name's Annie. Annie Byrne. I'm Tom Byrne's daughter. He sent me…"

O'Shea wasn't buying this, and he knew in his own head what this was about.

"Look young lady, I told those other two gobshites when they came to my door. Now they send you? A girl?"

Annie Byrne asserted herself.

"Mr O'Shea, I'm Joe Byrne's daughter. Some folks say I'm the spit of him, if you'll look at me. Oh, and he told me the other thing, that you'd definitely know I was from him. He said he was happy to help you out with that job in Finglas that time, near Wellmount Health Centre. And the advice you gave him about that daft one, the schoolteacher in Tralee, sure he was glad he didn't marry her."

It could only have come from Joe Byrne, and O'Shea smiled and felt bad for having given the rough end of his tongue to a young child. He smiled.

"Jaysus girl you nearly gave me a heart attack. What's your father doing, sending you, a strip of a girl here?"

"I'm twenty, Mr O'Shea, and I'm in the next intake for Templemore. I'm joining the job," stated Annie Byrne, quite firmly.

O'Shea considered her words and said, "Ah, y'are the spit of him. Nah, you're grand, you'll do well. What are ya doing here, dressed for the feckin' Tour de France?"

"My Dad can't be seen coming near ya. Those men visited him at work. He took me down the garden to the shed to tell me about this. There were no mobile phones. I don't have a phone on me. Do you have a phone on ya?"

Annie Byrne suddenly became slightly alarmed.

"Oh that yoke? I think I've left it in the house," said Tom O'Shea, patting down his old Harris tweed jacket.

"Mr O'Shea?" said Annie Byrne, trying to get Tom's attention and eye-contact back.

"Yes girleen?"

"My Dad said he's found something for ya, and it's not right, and he said you'd know what I mean. Not right like that fucker Foran. Yeah, Foran, that's what he said. In the Park, all those years ago," said Annie Byrne.

Tom O'Shea processed what this young woman was telling him. She was clearly a bona fide courier from Joe Byrne, and, in fairness, she was the spit of her father. O'Shea thought for a second, and said, "That doesn't sound right girleen. Doesn't sound good. Tell your father to let me know what he's got, and then to forget this happened and tell him keep himself right. And he shouldn't be sending you anyway."

"I'm well able for this Mr O'Shea. I'm no child, and I'm helping my father. And I think he's helping you," affirmed Annie Byrne.

"Did your father tell you anything else to tell me?"

"No, he just told me to come and make sure you knew I was from him. He said that he has some stuff for you, but he's not going to write it down, there's going to be nothing that will trace it back to him. But he told me to tell you that you were right, and there's something that's not proper in the job about these Arab fellas. That's all he told me, Mr O'Shea. But when I go back and tell him that you know I'm from him, I think he's going to be giving me something, or telling me something. Do you come here often?" said Annie Byrne with a smile.

Tom O'Shea took the humour of it.

"Ah sure I'm a regular here, you meet the best people."

"You certainly do Mr O'Shea. You certainly do," smiled Annie Byrne. And with that, she was up out of the pew, and with lithe strides, left the church in seconds. Tom O'Shea once more had the place to himself.

Rose O'Hagan often dreaded a new batch of student nurses coming into her part of the hospital. However, she had really taken to little Mary Murphy. Rose O'Hagan was six foot tall and had had been mercilessly taunted at school as "Beanpole O'Hagan." From Castlebellingham in County Louth, her life at secondary school in Dundalk was an unhappy one. Mary Murphy from Finglas had come up by a different hard route, and at some point in their coffee chats they found out that they both had alcoholic fathers that had made their childhoods constantly chaotic and occasionally terrifying. So although on the face of it they looked very different people, they actually had a huge amount in common.

Mary Murphy at five foot two was never going to be on the Paris catwalk. Throughout adolescence she had struggled with her weight. When it got out of hand she had lost her waist and at the worst she could grab rolls of fat behind her back. By the time she had done her Leaving Cert Mary Murphy didn't rate her chances in the mating game at all. Since she had joined the nursing course she had spent more and more time on her feet and one day she suddenly noticed that she had dropped a size. Given that she was always in a hoodie and jogging bottoms she hadn't really noticed until she had to go to a leaving do for one of her fellow students who was going to Australia. Her black party dress was baggy on her. It wasn't the desired result in that get up, but Mary Murphy was delighted.

Like most young Irish women of her generation Mary Murphy's best friend for a night out was Penney's. The chain store could provide a decent outfit for next to nothing. It worked, and that night in Coppers she was hit on from a nice tall lad from Arklow. He was an architecture student and shared a house with two other lads in Shankill. It was a lovely feeling to be thought of as attractive and she was delighted to take the lad up on his offer of "coffee," at his place.

Mary Murphy had been told that Rose O'Hagan was an absolute monster to work under, but she had found her the complete opposite. Directions were clear and uncluttered, and if you did a good job, Rose O'Hagan liked you. Mary Murphy had learned from an early age to keep things hidden and not open up to anyone. Therefore, she was amazed when she found herself on a staff night out, sitting in the corner of Café en Seine, telling Rose that as a nineteen year-old, Mary had "taken the boat to England," something even her own mother didn't know. Rose didn't judge her, didn't run out the door; didn't berate her. She merely put an arm around her and then got more drink. That, together with the brilliant efficiency of Rose O'Hagan as a nurse in the most demanding of circumstances, had convinced Mary that when she qualified, she wanted to work in an ICU. Therefore, it was probably no surprise that Mary Murphy had no chance in hiding from Rose that something was very much up with her world that morning. Rose took one look at her and took her away from the Coffee Doc, into the corner, and asked her, "What's the matter?"

Mary knew lying was out of the question, because Rose could just look straight through her.

"It's me Da."

"Oh God, what's the matter love? Is he sick?"

"No, worse than that."

"Ah Jaysus, is he back on it? You told me he'd been dry for such a long time, going to his meetings."

"No, it's his job. He's suspended. I – I think he's going to lose it, and I don't know what he'll do if that happens," said Mary softly, looking down at the floor.

"Is it cutbacks or something?"

"No, some fucker… He got reported. A passenger on his bus. He was pulling out of Busáras on the Galway run… Now, don't get me wrong, Rose, I'm not racist, but, anyway, it was one of those Arab fuckers," blurted out Mary.

"What happened?"

"Well, me – me Da said that yer wan didn't have the right ticket and he told her to go and get it sorted at the kiosk, and that she wouldn't do that, and she was holding up the queue, and he said "You don't know the rules. I can't let you on." And then yer one said that me Da gave her racist abuse, and he's suspended. He's in bits, Rose."

"Oh, I hope they get that sorted out."

"Rose, you know me. I'm not racist, but…"

"Oh, don't start me about that. Don't start me about that."

This seemed to be a cue that authorised Mary to say what she really felt to her buddy and mentor.

"Me Da really needs that job, and he's been doing really well in it. Since me Ma left…The Bus Éireann thing… Well, he needs the money, but it keeps him straight. If he's driving that bus he can't drink, and he knows that. That and his meetings. And now that fucker…Probably in the country about two minutes. Did you know me Da was in Busáras the day those bombs went off? He was in the staff canteen," said Mary.

"No, I didn't, love. You didn't mention."

Rose O'Hagan thought for a moment, taking in what Mary had told her, and then she let rip.

"If it was down to me, I'd put a whole load of the fuckers on a boat and get them out of here. They have no place. I'm telling ya, they bring nothing but trouble, and if it was down to me, I tell you I would fucking…"

Rose O'Hagan saw Mary Murphy's face fix a stare over her shoulder and behind, and she turned round and saw Doctor Karim. Rose O'Hagan didn't know how long the medic had been there, but his face seemed to say that he'd heard most of what had gone on.

"Good morning, Staff Nurse O'Hagan. If you will, can you assist me with a patient? Many thanks," said the Moroccan.

And at that, Karim had turned and walked back to the ICU. Rose O'Hagan's face said it all, and there was no need for her to explain anything to her young student. Instead she said, "I'd better be going pet. I'll see you soon, OK?"

"Oh fuck, I hope that's going to be OK…" said Mary Murphy.

"And don't you worry about fucking Abdul Abhaille there," said Rose O'Hagan with a wink indicating that she knew Doctor Karim had overheard her.

And with that Mary Murphy burst out laughing. She was happy that someone like Rose O'Hagan understood and was looking out for her.

Jack Dempsey was led through to the ward that his son was in. He had remembered himself before asking, and given the child's proper name. There were times when it bothered him that his only living son wasn't a Dempsey, but now it seemed like so much bother about nothing. The nurse led him through, and as he manoeuvred round the edges of beds, he came to the end of the small ward. And there on his right was a sight that made all of the pain and confusion and anguish of the last few days disappear in an instant. The monitors and the tubes had not completely gone, but there was his son, little Pádraig, sitting up in bed doing some colouring-in. He looked up, and a massive smile broke across his little freckled face, and he shouted, "DA!!"

His first instinct was to rush over and give the wee fella a hug. But to do so, he would have to delicately sidle past fairly important-looking monitors and tubes. So he reached forward, ruffled his hair, and said, "How you doing, big fella?"

Jack tried to speak without bursting into tears, tears of joy and relief.

"I had ice-cream yesterday," said the child.

And in that, Jack realised that this little person had inherited the Dempsey fighter genes, if not the name on the birth certificate, and he was fine with that.

"Would you like anything, son? Will I get you something? Are you allowed sweets?" asked Jack.

Little Pádraig just beamed a nodding approval. Anyone that was going to deliver sweets to the bed was OK by him. Jack sensed a presence to his right-hand side, and turned, expecting it to be a nurse looking to fulfil some duty around his son. But it was Doctor Karim. He smiled.

"Doctor! You've done mighty work here; look at this fella, colouring in!"

"The operation has been a complete success. I could not say that to you the last time. We were waiting for – perhaps – there could have been numerous complications. But God has been good to us. He has guided us."

If this man had asked anything of Jack at that point, he would have granted it without question if it had been in his power. As far as Dempsey was concerned, the man standing before him had saved his son's life and he couldn't think of anyone he owed a greater debt to.

"I'll never be able to thank you enough doctor, you and your staff here, for – doing everything you've done. Yiz are miracle workers, so ye are."

Karim just smiled without acknowledging the special powers that Jack was conferring on him. Dempsey was no psychologist, but he could read people, and he knew something was bothering the doctor.

"Don't mind me for being nosy, doctor, but – Everything OK since we last spoke? Y'know, those gobshites in the car park?"

Karim felt authorised, looked up, got eye-contact with the big Dubliner and said, "Thank you for asking, Mr Dempsey. Perhaps… I might have…" Karim was trying to find the words in this strange language. Jack cut across.

"Have you had any more trouble? You would tell me?"

Karim realised there was no point in holding this back.

"I live in an apartment in Chapelizod."

"That's a grand spot," said Jack.

"Yes, yes. Is very nice there. I cycle sometimes, in the summer. Through Phoenix Park. Is beautiful. But…" said Karim.

"And you had another problem. A couple of skangers had a go at you because you're an…The look of you."

"Yes, but how did you now?"

"The Good Samaritan that jumped out of his car. A red Toyota…."

"YES!"

"He's about my height, dirty blonde hair, short, dyed, looks awful. An earring in this ear," said Jack, pointing to his left ear. "And he has a, like a scar, over here?" Jack's finger ran across the top of his right eyebrow.

"YES!" said Karim, and then confusion hit the Moroccan doctor: Why would Jack know this person?

"How you know this man?" Karim was fascinated.

"I should have said, but I went ahead. Took the liberty. He's one of mine. Right, he works for me. I just put him on ya to see that everything was OK with all these gobshites after what had happened on the Luas and stuff. Erm, I'll tell him not to get too close to ya, but, eh, that's just a little thank you from me. It's…" Jack tried to explain.

"Ah, of course! I forgot! You are security person," said Karim.

"Security person? Sure I've been called worse," joked Jack.

"Thank you for this kindness, Mr Dempsey. You are a good man.

I now understand why your son is so strong for a child so young. Ma'salaam," said Karim

Jack Dempsey was no stranger to the unmistakable sensation of a punch to the solar plexus: the rapid exhalation of air from the lungs, the crippling pain, and the shutdown of the central nervous system. It is the only body-blow in boxing that can produce a knockout, if delivered in the correct upward direction to hit that junction box of nerves just under the bottom of the sternum. And that was exactly what he felt as he stood looking at this Moroccan man, having said the word "scar."

Jack took a step back, vaguely aware that little Pádraig was clamouring for his father to judge his colouring-in efforts. But all he could find himself doing was to murmur to himself "scar on his forehead." Karim realised that Jack was miles away, and doing something important.

"Is everything alright, Mr Dempsey?"

"Yeah…Grand…" said Jack, absent-mindedly, rapidly processing all of the information he had taken in that morning that had led to him standing in Beaumont Hospital, at the foot of a hospital bed with his son in it.

Jack Dempsey stood there, silent, processing, looked up, got eye contact with Karim and said, "Yeah, yeah, I'm grand. Thanks doctor. Look, thanks for everything you're doing here. If you need anything, you've got my card."

As a sign that the recuperation was progressing apace, little Pádraig wasn't going to be ignored any longer.

"DA!" shouted little Pádraig.

"Da, me drawin'! Me drawin', Da, is it good?"

His father turned to his left, looked down at him, and did his best impersonation of an art critic.

"Sure that's fuckin' mighty, little fella. Fuckin' mighty!" beamed Seán Patrick Dempsey.

"I'll tell me Ma you said it's fuckin' mighty," yelped the child in unbridled glee.

Karim looked on at these strange people. He may not have understood much about them, but he did understand genuine love, and he was looking at it in that moment.

"I have to be getting going, doctor. I won't keep you any longer. Thank you," said Jack, offering his hand.

Karim shook his hand.

"Mar'salaam, Mr Dempsey. Mar'salaam."

"Tiocfaidh ár lá to you too, sir," said Jack Dempsey, as he strode out of the hospital ward. He knew he had a man to see, and scéal to impart.

Jerome Pelfrey sat in the safe-house by the small, glass, dining room table. He couldn't remember when he had ever been this excited as an adult. He was waiting for the wet boy. This was real fieldwork! Not just that, but a Black Op! This was the type of work that created a real aura around you in Langley. After this, no one would be able to say that he was a desk jockey who was just well-connected in the Company. He knew enough about the wet boy to know that he was very good, that the Company had used him on numerous occasions, and that he had always been success-ful. The very fact that he was still alive and walking around was testament to that, especially considering some of the operations that he had been on were above Pelfrey's security clearance. That meant that this guy was very good, and that Langley was pulling out all of the stops to make sure that this operation was entirely successful. The intercom in the small corridor buzzed and Pelfrey nearly jumped out of his skin. He moved quickly, and lifted the slim plastic intercom phone. He heard a distinctly foreign voice speak in functional English.

"Maintenance for Mr Simpson."

Pelfrey pressed the small button that had the icon of a key beside it. There was a long mirror on the corridor wall beside the intercom phone. Previous occupants had perhaps thought it was a good idea to be able to check one's attire before going out into the street below. Pelfrey reckoned that the previous owner must have been a female. He caught a glimpse of himself and allowed himself a quick smile. He was wearing a black Pepe Jeans, three-quarter length jacket with a zip front and ample pockets, Levi jeans and new Nike trainers. Under-neath the jacket he had a thin, grey sweatshirt without any logo.

He looked like exactly what he wanted the world to see: a

middle-class American tourist. On any given day, there were hundreds of such stereotypes walking around the streets of Christchurch and gawping at the various tourist attractions. There was a knock at the door and Pelfrey's heart leapt like he was an adolescent on his first date. He opened the door and the Russian walked in past him without saying a word.

Pelfrey was slightly taken aback by this, but, then again, he'd never met a wet boy before. He closed the door and followed the Russian into the living room. The Russian was sitting down on one of the chairs at the dining room table. Pelfrey pulled up a seat across from him and studied this man who Uncle Sam paid huge amounts of money to turn living people into corpses to order. Pelfrey didn't know how to start the conversation. The man across from him was simply looking at him and waiting for him to begin.

"I have some information for you, for you to be able to..."

"Yes. I understand," said the Russian.

Of course he understood, thought Pelfrey. Get this together. This man is a top class professional. And so are you. Meeting the wet boy was a threat to Pelfrey's status as an accredited diplomat, and there could have been other ways to do it, but Pelfrey wanted it this way. This looked better on his resume, and for Jerome Pelfrey, this sojourn in Ireland was all about his resume.

Pelfrey reached for a small black zipped folder, opened it up and took out an iPad. He powered it up and with a deft movement of his right index finger, came up with the appropriate file. He then turned the iPad, holding it up to face the Russian. It started to play some covert video of the Russian's target.

The wet boy studied it intently. And as he did so, Pelfrey reached into his pocket and pushed over two pages ripped out of a reporter's notebook. On it was printed a home address and several other details.

"You cannot take that paper with you, but take the information. You understand?" asked the CIA man.

"Of course I understand. Is standard," clipped the Russian.

Pelfrey felt stupid. This man was a veteran of many of these operations and he wasn't going to walk out with anything that was incriminating. The Russian looked up having studied the two pages from the notebook and nodded. This guy was good, thought Pelfrey. You could almost hear the neural pathways operating like a camera shutter. The one modern convenience that the Company had added to this apartment was a shredder in the corner. Pelfrey stood up, walked over, switched on the black box with the Perspex bin at the bottom and fed through the two pieces of paper.

He then went back and sat down, faced the Russian, and said, "For this apartment, downstairs there is a box for mail. You will be contacted on your phone with a message that you have mail. You will come here and find details. Do not come into this apartment unless you are told to."

"Yes, I understand."

"We are meeting this time, and only this time, because I wanted to meet you to make sure you knew all about this mission," said Pelfrey, realising that it didn't sound all that professional as soon as he said it.

"Yes, I understand."

Pelfrey was uncomfortably aware that the Russian knew that the American sitting across from him was a virgin in the field and just wanted to meet the real thing. However, it was no problem for the Russian. He would carry out work for the client, and the client would pay him, and pay him well.

He was already working out in his head how this target could be neutralised when Pelfrey said, "One other thing, and it is very important. This target must be neutralised in a way that the authorities do not think it was anything other than an accident."

The Russian looked up, slightly irked. He had gone to great lengths to have quality bespoke armaments transported to him, and now he couldn't use them for this target.

"I have weapons here. Delivered to Ireland for me," said the Russian, trying to seek some meaning.

"Yes, and you will have reason to use them. But not this target. This target must arouse no suspicion when he is…"

"When he is dead," said the Russian with professional finality.

Pelfrey just nodded. He looked at this man across from him, casually-dressed, about the same height as Pelfrey but much better built. Pelfrey found himself looking down at this foreigner's hands,

hands that undoubtedly had done terrible things, but he obviously had a skill-set that the Company found valuable.

The Russian looked to Pelfrey for any other statement or question. The CIA man understood the look and said, "Good. Our business is finished. It was nice to meet you."

As soon as Pelfrey said this he knew it sounded utterly ridiculous, and he just hoped that the Russian wouldn't burst out into derisive laughter at him.

"Target will be neutralised soon. Do you need message from me?"

"No, we will be monitoring all electronic traffic here, and when the target's gone, we will know, so no to that," said Pelfrey, trying to re-establish some professional credentials with the Russian.

And at that, without any small talk, the Russian stood up, turned round, and left the apartment. Pelfrey heard the door close behind him, and realised that he had just taken part in his first piece of genuine fieldwork. Finally, the well-connected and much maligned policy wonk was a spy.

Taoiseach Jimmy McCarthy liked proving people wrong. When he had first got on the county panel in Kerry decades earlier, people had thought he wasn't up to it. In fact, people often thought that Jimmy McCarthy wasn't up to much. When he finally hung up his boots, he was a Kerry football legend. All of the doubters and naysayers had been proved wrong. He couldn't refute the argument that the only reason he had been one of the youngest TDs in the history of the Dáil was that his father had died tragically young, in his mid-fifties. All of this was again dredged up when he had become Taoiseach and, once more, the naysayers had said that he wasn't up to the job. As he sat in the Taoiseach's office, he put both of his big hands on the desk and thought of the men who had sat behind this desk, and privately knew how he didn't measure up. However, he thought he had done an OK job, and he'd certainly done his best. Jimmy McCarthy could look at himself in the mirror and know that the man looking back at him had always done his best.

However, this situation was one that no Taoiseach had ever had to face. The Dublin-Monaghan bombings in 1974 were one awful day, but they hadn't been the harbinger of a sustained bombing campaign against civilian targets in the State. He knew that the buck stopped with him, and that people would look to their Taoiseach for leadership, guidance and reassurance. However, with politics, the main problem wasn't in front of you; it was always behind your back, smiling and holding a dagger, and he reckoned there was no nastier hoor with a dagger in his hand than that fucker Gareth Scully. He had called the meeting today to find out what precisely was going on in his government. He hadn't risen up the treacherous pole in Fianna Fáil without having his men in the right place at the right time, feeding him back information. Sure, he was no CJ, and definitely no Bertie, but he didn't come down in the last shower either.

He had asked John Brady, Defence Minister, to come into the meeting as well. Partly because it was correct for his portfolio to be represented there, but also because he knew that the Carlow man was trustworthy and loyal, and would be a witness in the room when he went head to head with that devious bastard Scully. The intercom on his desk went, and it was his secretary saying that Minister Scully had arrived. Fuck, that's all I need, thought McCarthy. Scully was seriously early, when he had made it a trademark of being fashionably late, holding up meetings that couldn't start without him. This had the immediate effect of accentuating his importance in the room.

This habitual tardiness was entirely intentional on Scully's part. Yet here he was, seriously early, and no sign of Brady. McCarthy flicked a switch to his secretary and said, "Tell the Minister I'm on a call to a Head of Government and cannot be…"

At that, Scully walked into the office like it was already his.

"Good morning, Taoiseach," said Scully with a smile; his best leering, sneering, despising smile. He sat down on one of the large, comfortable, leather chairs on the other side of the desk. Jimmy McCarthy flicked up the button on the intercom, and just stared a look of hatred at Scully. McCarthy knew what was going on, and Scully knew that McCarthy knew, and Scully was fine with that. The Taoiseach was being disrespected in his own office. Scully was letting the Kerryman know who exactly was really in charge in the Irish government, and Jimmy McCarthy hated him for that.

"Good morning, Gareth. You're early."

"I thought we'd make a brisk start, Taoiseach."

Jimmy McCarthy flicked the button on the desk intercom.

"Please come in, Mrs Doohan, to take minutes. Thank you," said the Taoiseach, lifting his finger off the button. Then he looked up at Gareth Scully and locked eye contact. There were going to be no interactions between the Justice Minister and the Taoiseach that came down to one word against another, Jimmy McCarthy was sure of that.

The door opened and in came Rose Doohan, a very efficient, energetic woman in her forties. She originally hailed from Lough Gowna in Cavan, but she had been in Dublin since she was a young-ster. She sat down in one of the hardback seats next to the wall to the left of the Taoiseach's desk and flicked open a reporter's notepad, pen in hand. There was no need for her to say anything. She was ready to take a shorthand note of anything that was said. Her Pitt-man was excellent, something she had studied at night school, and this made her an excellent note-taker for even the most unruly of governmental meetings. Before either the Taoiseach or Scully could say anything the door opened, and it was a rather flustered Defence Minister.

"Am I late?" said John Brady in his soft Carlow brogue.

"No, you're fine John, you're fine. You're in plenty of time. We haven't started without you."

"Oh grand. I thought the schedule had got messed up again," said a slightly breathless John Brady.

Brady was a Fianna Fáil stalwart, originally from Newtown in County Carlow. His politicking throughout his home county was mainly pub-based, and there wasn't a licenced premises that he couldn't be seen in on the stump, buying pints and sinking them. Only five foot six, a life of easy excess had made him weigh almost the same amount as one of the newly-acquired armoured vehicles for the Defence Forces, so he was always puffing and out of breath, even if he had to walk a short distance. He didn't sit down on the other leather chair across from Gareth Scully, he collapsed into it. He looked up at the Taoiseach and gave a breathless nod that he was ready to begin when they were. Jimmy McCarthy liked John Brady. He was loyal and trustworthy. The Carlow man knew he was never going to be the smartest guy in a room, but if you gave him a job, he did his level best to do it without any second agenda. And at that moment, the man from Kerry thought he could do with a government full of John Bradys.

Jack had not been in the apartment in the Spencer Dock Complex since he had handed the keys over to Stan over a year ago. He knew that the big fella was delighted with the place, as indeed he should have been. It was pretty much brand-new and fully furnished. Jack could have rented it out at a good price, but had decided instead to give it to the big fella to get him on his feet. One thing Jack Dempsey was; was a fine judge of talent, and he wanted to keep the big Pole on his team. True to form, it was a kindness that Stan didn't forget. It was a two-bedroom apartment, one double and with a spacious box-room so it was ideal when Stan's little sister Agniesta arrived. At the time Stan had told Jack that his family in Poland were very happy about this. The offer had been on the table, quite literally, for Jack to come up any time he wanted, as Stan's little sister wanted to cook him a traditional Polish meal. He was always saying that he would, but he never ever quite got round to it.

These thoughts were swirling in Jack's head as he headed up through the apartment complex to the controlled entry. Jack still had a set of keys, as he had another two properties in the complex. The black key fob bleeped and did the business and opened the heavy, metal gate. He walked into an open area courtyard that had trimmed gardens and floodlights that would illuminate the place at night. Jack was fumbling for the key to the apartment entrance, when someone opened it and let him in as they were on their way out. He nodded, but the young, upwardly-mobile person was already gone and heading out to the Spencer Dock Luas stop. It was that sort of place, thought Jack. He got in the elevator and pressed number five. The door opened and there were only two apartments there.

He knocked on the door. He didn't want to barge in, but before he could knock again, the door turned and opened and there was the big fella. Even in a sling, the one-armed Stan could still get through a fair bit of work, thought Jack. He followed Stan into the living room, where there was a nice brown leather couch that would comfortably seat three people, facing a large flat-screen TV. In the corner there was a three-quarter standing mirror, and he spotted some of Stan's weights – dumbbells – at the bottom there. Stan sat down on the sofa, cradled his injured arm and gave Jack a look that was searching for answers.

Jack looked down and said, "Look, big fella, you know that anything I can do for you and your folks back in Poland, with your – with your sister. Don't be worrying about a thing. You know things cost, but don't be worrying about a thing, you hear me?"

Stan merely nodded. It was a grateful nod, but the words were difficult – probably even in his own fluent Polish – and in this strange English language that he had been struggling with he just didn't have the words. They were impossible to find.

"Thank you, Gaffer. Thank you, thank you for everything. You're a good man."

"It's a while since I've been called that, big fella. Am, you called me? What do you need? What can I get you today?"

"I just want to – my mother in Poland wants all sister things sent to her, and I don't know…"

"We can get all that stuff couriered over to your mother, anywhere in Poland. We've got an account with DHL. It's just money. Easy. No hassle. Anything else?"

Stan was deep in thought and looked up at Jack again. The combination of the emotional train that had hit him that night outside Angela's, and then coming to and then realising that his sister was gone, and gone forever, the sister he had meant to protect in this strange land; it was all just too much.

"Look, big fella, anything you want, just ask me. Is there anything I can do here now?"

"My sister's things – I don't want to touch, gaffer," said Stan with a vulnerability in his voice that Jack Dempsey had never heard before.

"Ah sure, you sit there. I'll – I'll do me best. Just leave it with me."

Jack then walked down the wood-floored corridor, trying to recollect what door meant what. He opened the first door to his left and realised as the light popped on that it was the toilet and shower, and then headed, fairly convinced of where he was going, to the door at the head of the corridor. This was the small room, but it was clearly Stan's. There were very few signs of human habitation. It was band-box smart. There was a made-up three-quarters bed, a couple of football posters from Poland, and that was it. Jack looked and smiled and thought this place would pass inspection by the most stringent sergeant major. It was clear that big Stan was still in the army in spirit. Straight in front of Jack, with his back to the door and looking across the bed, a window looked out onto the courtyard. To his right, there was a glass door that opened out onto a small balcony with decking flooring.

This was clearly not the sister's room, so Jack turned and opened the door just as Stan was coming down the corridor. He gestured to a door on his right. This was, as Jack recalled it, the large "master bedroom" as they liked to call it in auctioneer speak, the one with the ensuite shower. It was almost like there was a force-field around the place that repelled Stan from entering. Jack just nodded and gestured towards the living room so the big fella could go back there and sit down on the couch. Jack opened the door. To some extent he had internalised Stan's trepidation. Dempsey knew that he was going into a room that had been, up until only a few days ago, the private living space of a young, vivacious woman, the sister of the most dependable man he had known in twenty years, and that this young thing with so much to offer in life had died in a millisecond of heat and blast as she was earning a living and making her way in the world in a Dublin nightclub.

Jack closed the door behind him and looked down at the floor. The first thing he saw was a single purple stiletto. If Stan's room was, ready for military inspection in the barracks of six airborne, then this room was a prime example of the "untidy teenager's room." There were clothes strewn everywhere and, although Jack Dempsey had two functioning hands, very large and capable hands, he was uneasy about going through a young woman's things. But it was a different unease to the one that Stan had. This had been his sister's room. Jack snapped himself out of it. Fuck, this had to be done, and the quicker he got it done, the better it would be for his lad. Jack stepped back out of the room, put a stride on, and came up into the living room. Stan looked up from the couch with a question mark expression on his face.

"Any bin-bags in this place, young fella? Right, and have you got any cases or anything? Luggage?" said Jack in a commanding officer fashion. Dempsey was in charge, and he was giving his big Polish lieutenant his orders. For the first time since Jack had come into the apartment, Stan felt comfortable, in the way that soldiers always feel comfortable when they have direction. He gestured with his good arm to the small kitchen that was a recess off the living area.

"In there in – in units – in cupboard. Cupboard!" Stan seemed satisfied that he had found the correct word in English.

"No problem, I'll have a rummage," said Jack.

It didn't take Dempsey long to come up with a roll of black bin-bags. He walked past Stan, gestured with his hand, palm flapping down to the floor in a "stay seated, I've got this" gesture, and headed back down the corridor and went back into the young woman's room. The big Dubliner sat down on the bed and surveyed the mess. He looked down at another single high-heeled shoe. It was a shade of blue that no doubt any other human would be able to name right away, thought Jack. He couldn't see the other shoe. The girl had probably left the room in a hurry to make her shift on time. He sat in the silence of the place thinking about this child, for that was all she was.

He had met her once. Stan had brought her up to the office and she had thanked Dempsey for getting her the start in Angela's. She was a petite little thing, looked a bit like Stan. Her cropped blonde hair made her look even younger than she was. You shouldn't have to bury your child, thought Jack. He knew what that felt like.

Slowly he bent down, still sitting on the bed, and picked up the shoe. He placed it on the bed and then started to struggle with the bin bag to get it to open. His big mitts weren't designed with dexterity in mind. Jack heard a noise outside the bedroom door and it was Stan. His arm was out of the sling and he had two pieces of luggage. One was a modern airline approved carry on case and the other was a battered green holdall with Polish writing on it. The young girl's life would be packed into these two yokes.

The big ex-paratrooper looked at Jack. No words were said.

Dempsey just nodded. Stan wanted some meaning in all of this, but there wasn't any. So he turned and headed back along the corridor to the living room.

Dempsey took the two pieces of luggage, one new and the other old, and threw them on the unmade bed. The main wardrobe units were in the corridor, but there were two small bedside units and he thought he would make a start there. The first drawer was an entanglement of bracelets, phone charger cables and hair bands. Dempsey thought that Dicey would have been better at this, but it was way out of her job description. So he battered on.

He placed a bin bag on the bed and smoothed it out and tipped the contents of the drawer on it. Most of this stuff was getting thrown out, but Jack didn't want to risk losing anything of sentimental value for the family. He opened the second drawer of the unit that was closets to the bathroom and he just stared down. There was a bottle of Hennessy Cognac. It had probably been meant for the customers at Angela's, but it had found its way to the bedroom of Stan's sister. The Gobshite gently whispered into his ear that he deserved this. After all, what he was going through now was no-one's business. More importantly no-one would know. Just a quick slug. Lovely stuff that Hennessy Cognac. Real class. The Gobshite was going for it, he knew Jack was at a low ebb. Dempsey reached in and carefully extricated the bottle from the drawer like it contained nitro-glycerine rather than Cognac. The Gobshite had won the argument and Jack was already anticipating the sensation of the smooth fiery liquid slipping down his throat.

As he took the bottle out of the drawer something that had been jammed up into the top of the unit by the bottle fell down inside the drawer with a thud. It wasn't his specialist subject, but Dempsey knew a vibrator when he saw one. His left hand reached in and he was sitting on the edge of the bed with a bottle of booze in one hand and a nuclear-powered Rampant Rabbit in the other.

It was the wrong time to look up and see Stan standing in the doorway.

Jack put the two items into the case beside him, open like a grey plastic clam shell. Stan was hugging a pile of clothes, all on coat hangers. He dumped them on the bed. Dempsey got up and awkwardly walked past the big Pole and tried to be busy at the open wardrobe. Stan knew that Jack couldn't drink and there was no real way of explaining why he was holding his dead sister's vibrator. As per usual when two men are faced with an uncomfortable situation, they ignored it and started working.

It was then that he heard it.

John Brady was still vainly sucking in air to his oxygen depleted lungs when An Taoiseach Jimmy McCarthy, started on Gareth Scully. Rose Doohan's pen didn't falter as the tirade started. She had heard the Kerryman go off on more than few occasions, and this one was right up there.

"Who the fuck do you think you are?" The Defence Minister knew the salvo wasn't aimed at him, but he was taken aback by the aggression that was bouncing off the walls of An Taoiseach's office.

Gareth Scully merely looked up from the sheaf of papers on his lap, cocked his head slightly to the right and crinkled a rather sardonic grin.

"I'm sorry, Taoiseach?"

It was a response designed to bait an already infuriated McCarthy.

"That whole feckin drug boat thing in Galway. Commissioner Keegan didn't know about it. John here didn't know about it. How the fuck did it happen?" McCarthy spluttered.

"Given the sensitivity of the intelligence, Taoiseach, and the time pressure, it became incumbent upon me to, how can I put it…"

"Don't come that smart-ass gobshitery with me, you fucker," roared McCarthy.

"Yes, given the time pressure, Taoiseach, it was necessary to improvise organisationally to reach what I'm sure you will agree was a great success for the country," smarmed Scully.

This was more than McCarthy could stand. He stood up. Jimmy McCarthy was a tall man, six foot four. One of the things that he brought to the GAA pitch as a full-forward for Kerry was that he was always at least as large as the defenders he was playing against, and he could, in the parlance of the field of play, "ragdoll" any man that tried to stop him getting a score for the Kingdom. John Brady, whose lungs had just reached some sort of inhalation/exhalation equilibrium, thought that the Taoiseach was going to come round the table and assault the Justice Minister. He tried to catch Jimmy McCarthy's eye the way a diner tries to catch the waiter's attention, but the Taoiseach was focused in on the preening Minister for Justice.

"You're not fucking listening to me, Scully. I want to know what the fuck was going on with that whole fucking – Wh – What the fuck?" McCarthy was so angry he had lost the ability to put a sentence together, and inwardly, Gareth Scully was utterly delighted.

"Taoiseach, with the greatest of respect for you personally, and, of course, for the Office of State that you hold, I think that the decisions that I took, with, as I said, the extreme time pressure, led to a very, very good conclusion for the country, and, if I may say, for your government," said Scully in his most condescending way, which was very condescending by anyone's standards.

Jimmy McCarthy took a step back. He needed the votes of Scully's party to stay in power, he knew that. He wanted rid of his Justice Minister, but didn't really know how to do it. If he sacked him, then the government would fall. And Scully knew it.

He slumped back into his chair, reached over for an official government folder, and flicked it open. He looked up at Scully.

"And you still think this plan of yours is gonna get passed through the Dáil?"

"Taoiseach, I thought it was the government's plan?"

"You know what the fuck I mean. I went along with the bloody Public Services Cards, but a national DNA database, facial fucking recognition? Jesus Christ, you're gonna turn the place into Russia."

"I think the ordinary citizen in this country, Taoiseach, will be eternally grateful that their government, this government, is doing all that it can to keep them safe from this new type of terrorism, this new threat."

"I think you think I came down with the last shower of fucking rain in Cahersiveen."

"Sorry, Taoiseach?"

"This gobshitery has the yanks written all over it. And don't tell me you're James Bond all of a sudden. How the fuck did you know about that fucking drug boat?"

"Of course, Taoiseach, you'll have my full report. But time was just too pressing. Yes, I do have an excellent personal relationship with the US Ambassador to our country, and it was on that basis that I was given that real-time intelligence. I think if this were to come out into the media, your criticisms would be seen as churlish, and, indeed, perhaps unpatriotic." Scully was really going for it.

"Are you fucking threatening me to leak this? Are you fucking threatening me, you gobshite? I'll rip your fucking…"

John Brady thought he was about to have a seizure. He'd had a mild stroke the year before and the left-hand side of his face was still slightly fallen. He had to diffuse this, for his own sake.

"Taoiseach, if I…"

Jimmy McCarthy was distracted. He had totally forgotten that Brady was in the room, not that that was any disrespect to him.

"What is it, John?" said Jimmy McCarthy, slightly mollified. He couldn't be angry with Brady. There was nothing to be angry about when it came to the decent Defence Minister.

"I think that…I think that…Well…" struggled Brady.

"Ah for fuck's sake John, spit it out," said an exasperated Taoiseach.

"Sorry, Jimmy. I think Minister Scully is right about the whole drug boat thing. What ends well, and all that. I think we all have to push on; we're all in government. Y'know, team spirit and all that."

Jimmy McCarthy knew that the Defence Minister was trying his level best. He was a decent if limited man.

"I hear you, John, and I know that you're a daycent fella trying to do the daycent thing. But I'm the head of this government, and I shouldn't be finding out that the Defence Forces of this country are being deployed in international waters on information given to them by a foreign government, and it's all done up, wrapped up with a big fucking bow on it, before I even hear about it."

"I see your point, Jimmy," relented Brady.

McCarthy then turned back to Scully.

"I know you think you can get this through the Dáil, but this is a minority government, and there's some on my backbenches, in my party, that have said they'll cross the floor of the Dáil before they'll vote for this," said the Taoiseach.

"I think then, perhaps, Taoiseach, and with the greatest of respect, that it is a time for true leadership, true statesmanship. And I am sure you can provide that to your party, but, more importantly, to the country."

McCarthy was quite clear what he was hearing. This gobshite was saying that if he couldn't do what was necessary, he should step aside and let Scully, with all of his eight TDs at his back, step into the breach.

"Whatever needs to be done, I'll do. But this is a free country, a democracy. And if this thing goes through, then it won't be," said McCarthy with as much force as he could muster without shouting.

"We have discussed this several times in Cabinet, Taoiseach, and I would only ask you to consider the following: If these reforms had been in place, would all those people have died on the Luas? In the nightclub in Temple Bar?" said Scully, lowering his voice to a threatening whisper.

"That's fucking shite and you know it, Scully," said McCarthy, his temper coming up again.

"Perhaps the bereaved, grieving, heartbroken relatives of those innocent people, their lives taken away by these Islamic fundamentalists, would think differently, Taoiseach, with the greatest of respect," said Scully.

Jimmy McCarthy silently seethed at Scully. The Justice Minister was goading the Kerryman into losing control. Scully looked at his watch with the unmistakable air of an important man with somewhere else to be. Somewhere MORE important than the Taoiseach's office.

"This meeting isn't fucking over yet!" said the titular Taoiseach.

"Jaysus..." uttered John Brady under his wheezing breath.

"A most productive conclave so far Taoiseach. However, if you will excuse me, I...."

Jimmy McCarthy had struggled with his temper all of his days. He was much better than he had been in his twenties and thirties. However, he couldn't remember anyone testing him like this pudgy little smirking fucker sitting in his office. He knew that if he laid a hand on him he wouldn't stop. Killing the Tánaiste might not be the best way of keeping this coalition together.

As McCarthy seethed, Scully made a show of collecting up his papers as slowly as he could. The Justice Minister was holding all the cards, and he knew it. He smiled a little smile to himself. He'd managed to rattle this thick Kerry bastard with just the bones of the idea. If the fools only knew what was coming…

Just then, Commissioner Eamonn Keegan walked into the Taoiseach's office unannounced. The big Donegal man wasn't standing on ceremonies.

"There's been another one," he said.

Pelfrey closed the screen, very satisfied with how the call to Langley had gone. Everything was going like clockwork. It was exhilarating to be out in the field, making his own connections, being a "real" spy. Even in considering that, though, he was aware that his own brand of white-collar espionage was very much the future. These days, with everyone on social media that traditional way of working had gone out of the window. With the advent of big data, the spying was largely done for you. The question now was how to access and use that information. The new facial recognition scanners in Dublin Airport would provide information invaluable to Langley. Those new Mickey Mouse Social Security cards that the Irish had brought in had been a good start, but once the US government had access to the whole Irish DNA database, Pelfrey would be skyrocketing through the ranks.

He took a sip of black coffee, thoroughly satisfied with himself. His unique mix of traditional blackmail and leveraging data analytics was about to provide the Company with its biggest info scoop in decades. And it hadn't cost a single tax dollar.

Tom O'Shea had been very alert on his return to his modest home in Terenure from morning Mass. It was like he had never been away from the old trade. The old Kerryman had noticed everyone and everything on his regular route back. At least, he hoped he had noticed them. When he closed the door behind him he allowed himself to relax a little and looked down at the small, battered suitcase that he had unearthed from a cluttered press upstairs the night before. The venerable piece of luggage was now full of clothes, testament to the fact that he was going to take up his sister's offer and travel down to Kerry and spend some time with her. However, before he embarked on such an expedition, he would need to put some fuel into the body. So, still wearing his coat, he walked into the kitchen and put the kettle on the cooker and turned on the ring. He conducted a search of the fridge to see what was edible for breakfast. Although normally meticulous about these things, the last few days had thrown his routine out of sorts, and that annoyed Tom O'Shea to no end. There were two eggs left in a box, and enough rashers to pass muster for breakfast.

He could hear the water starting to bubble in the old kettle as the gas ring did its job when he heard the door go. For a moment he didn't want to answer it, and then anger washed over Tom O'Shea that he should feel any fear or alarm in his own home. So he turned and walked with purpose to the large, heavy front door of his home. When he opened it, it wasn't who he was expecting, although he wasn't really sure who he was expecting.

"What do you want?"

"Sure you're a cheerful fucker," said Jack Dempsey, walking past the old Kerryman.

O'Shea, wrong-footed and disarmed by this, closed the door and turned and followed Dempsey into the kitchen, where the big Dubliner was clearly making himself at home.

"Where the fuck do you think you're going? You shouldn't be here. Th – this house might be under surveillance," stammered O'Shea.

"Surveillance? Surveillance? You a terrorist or something?" chuckled Dempsey.

"Enough of your shite. And nobody invited you in."

"Relax, I'm only here for a minute. I have to have a word with you about something."

"And I have to have a word with you about something."

This made Dempsey look up. It wasn't what he was expecting from the grumpy old Kerryman.

"You have?"

"I do, but not here. As I said, this place is probably under surveillance. I've had two of those gobshites from my job here. Gaffney sent them."

"Gaffney?"

"The very gobshite."

"Top man in the Branch? In your old lot?"

"Indeed."

"What the fuck do they want? Were they asking about me?" asked Jack, with the paranoia circuits kicking in.

"In your arse they were asking about you. You're a piece of shit on their shoes. They were after me."

"You say the nicest things to me," chuckled Jack, relaxing slightly that the Branch men weren't asking about him. Just like O'Shea's head-on-a-swivel coming back from Mass, the very mention of Special Branch officers in Dublin was enough to make Jack Dempsey spin round 180 degrees to make sure he wasn't being followed.

"Look, you're here now so I might as well tell ya. You were right about something."

"About what?"

"That stuff you told me about those boys that day: Those Arab fuckers."

"Yeah?" said Jack, listening intently.

"There's something not right in the job. I have a boy looking into it, but it looks like the whole thing was closed down," said O'Shea, not really believing he was saying this to someone like Dempsey, even though it was totally true what he was saying.

Jack Dempsey was sitting on one of the plain kitchen chairs and the little Kerryman was looking down at him.

"You didn't get this from me. You hear me?"

He was looking for some measure of agreement from the big ex-Provo sitting in his kitchen.

"You haven't given me anything, oul fella."

"Less of the "oul fella" shite," said O'Shea, bridling.

"I'm no tout, although it's a bit daft me saying that in your kitchen," said Jack with a sardonic laugh.

O'Shea sat down on the chair, put his left elbow on the table, turned sideways to Jack and looked straight in the eye.

"Now you listen to me. I'm only going to tell you this once. I have nothing written down, nothing that can link you to me. Except you being here, you stupid gobshite."

"Sure I'm all ears, you charmin' bastard."

"This all smells like fucking 1974 again. I'm not gonna give you a history lesson, but those bastards from the North came down and did that here, in this city, and I was onto them. And then some fucker in the Dáil decided that Tomás O'Shea was too good at his job," said O'Shea, with a vehemence that took Jack by surprise.

The old man trailed off, looking at the floor.

"Sure Tom, sure. My head's wasted with all this, and now that thing in Spencer Dock."

"That was the last straw for me," snarled O'Shea.

"If that sceál was as good as I think it was, then those boys should have been scooped by now."

"They should have, surely. And instead you get the nightclub, and then you get that thing at that restaurant."

"Sure we were around the corner from it, heard the fucking thing go off."

O'Shea looked up, startled.

"You were?"

"I was, surely. We were up at his flat."

"His?"

"Yeah, the lad outside," said Jack, trying to explain.

"What lad?" said O'Shea, slightly unsettled that there was someone else in the vicinity that Dempsey hadn't even thought to mention.

Dempsey realised it sounded bad.

He sighed slightly and said, "Lad that works for me, Polish lad, Super fella. Good dependable lad. He lost his sister in the nightclub. She was only a kid, and they were staying in one of my flats in Spencer Dock. And I was up giving him a hand with her things. Stuff to be sent back to Poland. Ah, it's desperate shite. And sure we heard the fucker go off."

"You ever think that God's trying to send you a message, Dempsey?"

"Don't fucking start, Tom. I'm not in the fucking mood. Now, if you don't mind, you can say your piece, and I'm going," said Jack as he got up to leave the kitchen and then O'Shea's home.

"Wait a minute, wait a minute!" said O'Shea, putting his hand up as a barrier to Jack.

"What?" said Jack impatiently.

"This is what I was told. I'll make this quick, OK?

"OK, go ahead?" said Jack, now all business.

"Gaffney's in charge of the investigation. That's fair enough. It's a Branch matter. Terrorism. But my guy on the inside knows that stuff hasn't been going straight to Keegan. It's been going straight to that fucker – that fucker in the Department of Justice."

"What fucker?" asked Jack, entirely focused on what O'Shea was saying now.

"That cunt Scully."

"Is that normal practice?"

"Of course it's not proper practice. There's a line of command in the guards, and Keegan's at the top of it, and the Department of Justice should have the square root of fuck all to do with it. But we've the head of the Special Branch reporting directly to fucking Scully."

"Doesn't sound right?"

"Of course it's not right. Smells like fuck. Smells like a pile of shite."

"So that's it? That's the whole scéal?"

O'Shea took a breath. He knew what he was about to say. He never thought he would be saying this to anyone, let alone an ex-Provo bomber that he had hunted.

"There's more than that," said O'Shea, trying to find the words.

"I'm all ears, Tom," said Dempsey softly.

"I have a man inside. Look, you don't know him. I don't want you to know him. He's in Store Street. Sound fella. He's convinced – now he's not telling me everything – but he's convinced that Gaffney's shutting down this investigation into these fuckers. He's put the most incompetent bastards on the job. Anybody showing a bit of energy, a bit of cop-on, has been moved to other duties. It just smells," said O'Shea, who looked up and got eye-contact with Dempsey. Jack read it as the look of a man who was asking to be believed, not to be written off as some tin-foil hat-wearing conspiracy theorist.

"Well, between the two of us, honey, you're the one that knows the Peelers. And if there's something inside smelling, I'd trust your nose."

"And at this stage I have no idea what to do about this."

"Well, that makes two of us."

"I had half thought that…" laughed O'Shea slightly.

"What?"

"Ah, just an old man's stupid foolishness," said O'Shea, dismissing his own thoughts as nonsense.

"Go ahead. You're with friends."

O'Shea looked up at him and reciprocated the smile, and said, "I thought your old crew of gobshites might have sorted these fuckers."

"Funnily enough, I had the same idea myself before I came to you."

"Hmm, thought you might."

"Nothing doing. Suits, photo opportunities, free dinners and by-elections."

"I never thought I'd say this but I'm actually sorry to hear that."

"You know what this means, don't ya Tom?"

"What?"

"Neither your old lot nor my old lot are any use!"

"Jaysus, you're right there boy."

"I've left that boy outside long enough, and I have to get going, but if you get anything more then get it to me somehow."

"I will. But you can't come here again, and anyway I might be going down the country to the sister's."

"You're serious that this place might be getting watched?"

"Those two yokes that Gaffney sent, they're the ones that do his messy stuff for him. Pair of useless gobshites now both of them, so I wouldn't put it beyond him. Gaffney's a cunt."

Jack thought for a second, reached into his leather jacket pocket and pulled out a small notebook.

"Sure that looks like a policeman's notebook," said O'Shea with a smirk.

"Well, you should know."

Jack wrote down his office number and passed it over.

"You can get me at that number. That's my office. The girl that will answer it is smart and sound. Tell her you're Mr Watson who is opening the new nightclub. Leave a number. I'll call you back."

Then the ex-policeman got up walked out of the kitchen without saying anything. Dempsey watched him and before he could say anything the little Kerryman was back carrying a reporter's notebook and pen. Jack watched as the ex-policeman sat back down on the kitchen chair and wrote in the pad. He then ripped out a page and handed it over to Dempsey.

"Read that and then throw it in the range there. Don't take it out of this house."

Jack read the page. It was two addresses.

O'Shea interjected.

"Those are two places that the Branch had under surveillance. They both looked likely spots. Just young men staying there. No families. Lots of them travelling to a Mosque in Drimnagh. Then Gaffney ordered the operations shut down. No warning no explanation."

Jack was studying the piece of paper and listening intently to what the man beside him was saying.

"Then my man told me yesterday that they had spotted a vehicle at the Phibsborough address and I thought of you."

Jack looked up.

"Minibus yoke. New Kildare registration."

"Fuckers!" exclaimed Dempsey.

"You're sure your old crew aren't on the panel for this?"

"A hundred percent, Tom."

"That's a damn shame and I never thought I'd say that."

"But that lad out there is up for anything. His sister in that nightclub. I nearly lost my son."

"That's two of you."

"You would be surprised what I did in England with not much more."

O'Shea didn't say anything, but simply stood up. It was the signal that the conflab was over.

Dempsey reciprocated and stood up, towering over the old Kerryman.

"It sounds like we need to talk again soon. Now I have to get going, but you mind yourself, young man," smiled Jack.

O' Shea put his hand out. He looked straight up at the big

Dubliner. Jack took his hand, squeezed it firmly and nodded with a smile.

"Wherever you're going, you mind yourself, you big bollocks. You might just be one of the few people in this country I can trust at the moment."

"Bet you never thought you'd say that, did ya?"

"Away with ya." And as Jack passed him, the little Kerryman slapped him a couple of times on his big, broad back.

As Jack was heading to the door he noticed a small book case against one of the hallway walls. One title in particular caught his eye.

"Ha! That's funny," said Dempsey.

"What?"

"Tim Pat Coogan's book," said Jack, picking out the well-thumbed paperback edition entitled, The IRA. "Same edition that I used. That's gas!"

"Used?" asked a bemused O'Shea. It wasn't a verb that made any sense to him in that context.

Jack realised that this was all ancient history now, but he wanted to let O'Shea know that he didn't know everything.

"My lot in England; we used this book as a code."

"How?"

"Page number, line number, word number. Unless you know the book you can't crack it."

"Crafty fuckers!"

"Ha!" chuckled Dempsey, smiling down at the old Kerryman and slapping him on the back.

"That's enough loose talk from me for one day."

"Away with ya," said O'Shea warmly.

"Grand so."

"Those addresses?"

"What about them?"

"Are they in your head?"

"A hundred percent. I know that street in Phibsborough. I used to fuck a nurse there. Grand girl," said Jack matter-of-factly.

"Jaysus. The farmyard."

"I was without women for a long time, Tom."

"You won't be needing that paper then."

Dempsey understood immediately and handed over the page of the notebook to the ex-policeman.

"I wouldn't be heartbroken if someone paid those shites a visit. That's all I'm saying," said O'Shea.

"Jaysus, we're on the same side you and me," laughed Jack.

"God moves in mysterious ways."

"Yeah. He does surely. He's got a Mercedes van now. Turbo diesel. Customised. Cracker."

"Away with ya," said O'Shea, slapping the big Dubliner between the shoulder blades. It felt like the gesture of a manager sending a substitute off the bench to save the game.

As Seán Patrick Dempsey walked out of the door and saw Stan across the road in the hired car, for some reason that he couldn't quite fathom, at that moment he felt better than he had since he had got up that morning to go to court.

Emily Scully was in the conservatory looking out over Killiney Bay when her other phone, her special phone, vibrated in her bag. Her heart leapt because only one person had that number. It had been bought specially for him. She looked round to make sure the coast was clear, and then immediately felt foolish. She did, after all, have the house to herself. She got the phone out of her bag and saw that there was a WhatsApp message. She touched the icon and, of course, it was from him.

"Are you free tonight?"

She wanted to be free that night. Indeed, she wanted to be free every night for him, but since the new security regime had come in almost every aspect of Emily Scully's life had come under an Orwellian level of surveillance. The Gardaí were convinced that several members of the Irish government would be prime targets for the Islamic terrorists currently operating in the country, and her husband, the Justice Minister, had very much become the face and voice of the Irish state in facing down this new fanatical threat to the security of the Irish people.

Her thumb hovered over the screen for a second. She thought of how to say no without communicating in any way that she wasn't interested or that she was cutting ties with him. As she searched for the appropriate form of words she was suddenly engulfed by the hopelessness of her situation. It seemed a very long time since she had been in the front row at The Hist in Trinity looking at the forty-year old rising star in the Dáil, Gareth Scully. At that point he still had his own TV show where he discussed the moral and legal issues of the day with a selected panel of worthies and celebrities. That was the time when everyone was saying that if the body politic in Kildare St had a central nervous system, let alone a brain, it would make Gareth Scully the Taoiseach tomorrow.

Therefore, Emily Piggott of Ballymore Eustace couldn't believe her luck when the highly eligible Gareth Scully T.D. had weaved his way through autograph hunters and fans at the end of the debate to extend his hand and introduce himself. But that was then, that was twenty years ago. And now all she wanted to do was to get away to that little rented apartment in Monkstown and be with him. She looked down at the phone and remembered how he had laughed when she had produced it with a flourish and said that this would be how he would communicate with her. She had bought it from the Carphone Warehouse with cash, and therefore it hadn't come out of the household bills, credit card accounts, anything that could be traceable. It was an HTC Desire. He thought the name of the phone was funny, because that's exactly why she had bought it, and that was why he would always answer: Desire. Now it seemed like a bad joke. Since this trouble on the Luas with these madmen, she had a Garda bodyguard anytime she left the house. She was increasingly becoming a prisoner in her own home. Gareth said that it wouldn't last for long, and he could see that it was really killing her inside to lose her freedom in this way, but she couldn't tell him the real reason.

She thought of the carefree way that she had first met him. She was visiting a friend in Dalkey, down in the cottages across from the quarry where the climbers go. It was a gorgeous late summer night and it was still daylight, and there was a real hubbub of activity around the rocks. She still didn't know why she had been drawn to walk across there that night. She had an excuse; Biscuit, her West Highland terrier, was accompanying her, so he was having a good sniff at rucksacks and ropes piled in the central area when he came along to introduce himself. He was wearing black climber's trousers that really did leave nothing to the imagination (the idea was obviously for ease of movement), and a climbing harness with various bits of metal dangling from each side. He had a ragged black t-shirt that had seen better days and his hands were white with chalk. He smiled, extended his hand in a handshake and then thought better of it and just said hello. She was smitten. He was everything that Gareth wasn't, and everything that she needed. Usually the chatterbox, the one that held forth when she and her lady friends would luncheon, she could hardly speak. Even that moment in The Hist more than twenty years ago seemed pale by comparison.

It was hard not to be impressed by the memorial to the Irish famine, thought John Powell as he sat here under the grey Philadelphia sky waiting for his sister-in-law Molly. For sure those folks had it tough. He was no history guy, but that much he knew. Still, there was no monument to black folks in the US of A. He had read that some congressman wanted a national slave memorial, but it had never got beyond a speech on Capitol Hill. If he recollected correctly, that was back in 2002 or 2003. As far as Uncle Sam was concerned, some just didn't merit being remembered. Still, his kid had Irish blood, so this monument was part of her roots too. His mind started to wander on what he was about to do, and the consequences it might have for him and his family, but he was brought out of that quickly.

He looked up and there she was, bright and bouncy as always. Molly O'Reilly, thought Powell, was a hell of a sister-in-law. Her flame-red hair was tied back in a ponytail. She was wearing slim-fitting jeans, green running shoes and some green zipper sports jacket with a badge on it that John Powell didn't recognise. It was clear that for their morning meeting she was going full Irish. He had no trouble believing that she was a kickass reporter. She hadn't got those awards for just being pretty. Moreover, he had complete trust in her, which was something in short supply in John Powell's world since he had been posted to the Embassy in Dublin. He had to tell someone about this, someone who could do something with it.

"Hey big guy!" said Molly O'Reilly, planting a kiss on the cheek of John Powell before he could stand up and tower over her. She sat down beside him and nudged him playfully with a big smile on her face.

"How's my sister?" asked Molly.

"She's awesome," said John Powell.

"Well, we O'Reillys are an awesome family," said Molly with a smile, as indeed are you, Mr Powell. I'm so glad you guys have decided to give it another shot."

"Molly, this is big stuff," said John Powell with a sigh.

"I get that, big guy. You're in safe hands here."

Then John Powell straightened up to signify that a thought had startled him.

"Where's your cell phone?"

"In my bag. Chill."

"Where's your bag?"

"Behind the bar."

"What bar?" asked a bemused and slightly annoyed Powell.

"In the bar where I'm going to buy you breakfast in exactly ten minutes' time."

"Where's that?"

"Well, I can't give you fire co-ordinates, Marine. But it's about a hundred yards from here, just behind us. The Plough and the Stars. You'll love it."

"An Irish bar?"

"I will take you to my people," said Molly with a giggle.

"Wonderful…"

"Don't be like that, my big brother-in-law. Anyway…" Molly stood up and unzipped her green Irish football tracksuit top and opened it like a flasher on the subway to reveal what she was wearing underneath.

"Because we're going to see the…CELTIC!" announced Molly.

"Soccer? Ah, bullshit," said Powell with an air of defeat about him.

"Hey big guy, you'll love it," said Molly reassuringly.

"Hey Molls, y'know, I'm a street-ball guy from the Projects. Soccer's a cracker thing."

Molly O'Reilly looked at him slightly askance, and then Powell realised that he probably had been over the line. This, after all, was his daughter's aunt, his wife's sister, and this was their culture, even if it wasn't his. He put his hands up.

"Yeah, yeah, all good. Let's go and watch this soccerball. You can tell me what's happening."

"Hey, you'll love it John, and there's a really good crew in there. They all know me."

"Oh, I'm sure they know you in there, Molly," laughed John, and his sister-in-law joined in the mirth.

"Anyway, we're playing Sevco. It's gonna be awesome."

"What the fuck are Sevco?"

Molly O'Reilly broke into giggles, realising that she was introducing her brother-in-law to a culture that he knew nothing about, something she found massively amusing.

"Are they Russians?" asked Powell as his sister-in-law continued to be silenced by convulsive giggling.

"No, honey, no," said Molly between the giggles.

"Not Russians then?" said Powell, just wanting to know what the hell was going on.

"They're from Scotland, but their fans are the Klan, yeah? They sing about a guy who was in the Klan, and they like him," said Molly, emphasising the word "Klan."

She suddenly had her brother-in-law's full attention.

"Like, the Klan? Like, the Good Old Boys? Like the KK fucking K?" asked Powell, now giving his sister-in-law his undivided attention.

"The very same, my beautiful brother-in-law."

"Well let's go and kick their ass!"

John Powell stood up, now towering over his sister-in-law, who'd been standing in front of him, and he looked down at her.

"Before we go into this crazy Irish shebeen of yours, I'm totally trusting you with this stuff Molls," said Powell quietly.

"Before you ship out I'll set you up with a super encrypted email. I've got a guy that helps with this stuff. He's worked inside the Beltway, he's worked for Uncle Sam, so you'll have no worries there," said Molly, and then she looked up at John Powell, into his eyes.

"I just want to know why you're doing this?"

"Ah, that's easy, Molls. I swore an oath."

"Huh?"

"Against enemies foreign AND domestic."

He received a text message from the usual number, using the recognised phrase.

"Sorry, I can't make our pre-arranged meeting. Circumstances prevailed, I'm afraid."

He then called the number that was in his head; a number that he would never write down or need to look up in a notebook. The person at the other end immediately answered. It was a voice he recognised, and he said:

"Jury's. Christchurch. Now. I'll meet you in the foyer."

And with that, he set off. It had to be something important as this was not one of the regular meetings, but had been activated for him to immediately comply.

When he got into the foyer of the hotel he saw his guy sitting on one of the sofas. He immediately got up and walked to the elevator. The signal was clear; he had to follow him. Anyone looking on would not have registered that the two men knew each other and had been meeting regularly for the last seven years. Once they were in the elevator together there was not a word between them. Elevators were covered by CCTV. It was important to keep the tradecraft spot on. The elevator doors opened and he followed the man out. He didn't say a word until the door closed behind him and they were in the room together.

The room had a double bed and all the usual fixtures and fittings associated with a high-end hotel, including two soft chairs and a small round table. The man who had opened the door gestured with his hand him to sit down, which he did.

"It's a bit different today. I'm not doing the briefing. There'll be someone here in a few minutes who wants to talk to you."

"Who's that?" said the man.

"You'll see. Just take it easy."

It was an order, not a suggestion.

The Russian closed the door behind him and locked himself in to the apartment that would be his base for the duration of this job.

There was always a bit of tension on how an operation would go in an area that he wasn't familiar with. However, it had been textbook and he was pleased at his precision. He went into the bathroom, put the plug in and turned the hot water on. It was the start of a post-operation ritual that he liked to do whenever it was practical. He had everything he needed to carry out a cleansing process that he had become very attached to. As the bath started to fill up with water he put the back of his hand under the tap and recoiled at the high temperature. This was exactly what he wanted. He picked up the plastic bottle of Dettol that he had brought in a local convenience store the day before, and threw in more capfuls than was advised on the back of the bottle. This would be a stinging immersion, thought the Russian, and smiled.

While the bath was filling up, he went into the living room and opened the small backpack that he had placed on the dining room chair next to the table. He fetched some kitchen roll from the galley kitchen beside the living room, ripped off some sheets and put them one on top of the other to fashion a thick, blotting-type paper arrangement. He reached into the backpack and took out a rectangular envelope with a blue dotted line across the top and the image of scissors. It was clear that this was to be cut to reveal the contents. He ripped at it with his fingers and pulled out a fresh pair of surgical gloves. The pair he had worn at the operation had been safely disposed of on the journey back.

He snapped on the gloves and took out the Glock, removed the suppressor, touched the button on the handle to release the magazine, and pulled back the slide, fully locking it. The weapon was clear and safe, and he quickly, with a pressure of the thumb on the slide-catch release, dismantled the weapon to its main working parts with the practised ease of the consummate professional. He went into the bedroom and fetched a small can of Three-in-One oil from the large holdall that was at the corner of the room. All the while he could hear the splashing of hot water into the bath. The gun would be oiled and reassembled after he had lowered himself into the stinging disinfectant. He was pleased with his precision.

There was a knock on the hotel door and the Special Branch officer, who had been sitting on the bed, stood up, walked over, and opened the door. The man in the seat felt a shockwave through his entire body when he saw the identity of the man who entered the room. The new arrival sat on the chair opposite the man, the small circular table between the pair of them. He placed a slim leather folder on the surface, unzipped it and opened it out.

"Firstly, let me assure you that your continued good health and safety are of paramount importance to this State. Your co-operation in security matters going back to the 1980s is well recorded here, and certainly I appreciate your efforts over this prolonged period of time. I'm not here from the British government, but they were particularly grateful for some assistance in a successful operation back in the nineteen eighties in the city of..." The man studied the file in front of him. "Yes, Leeds. Which brings me to this Dempsey fellow."

Gareth Scully looked up from the file and smiled and then said:

"Now, Deputy McMillan. This Dempsey character. Where is he?"

It is a sociological fact that the more expensive one's property is; the less likely one is to have any interaction with one's neighbours. Consequently, the property in Foxrock was perfect for Abdullah Muhammad. The lady from the letting agency didn't think twice when the tall, well-spoken English doctor asked to rent the property for a year. Which, he explained, was the duration of his contract with the HSE. A four-bedroom bungalow built in the 1970's, the L-shaped property was shielded at the back by mature woodland. It had a long driveway and consequently any activity at the back of the bungalow would be shielded from view. The property had been empty for some time, mostly because of the rent that the owner was asking for.

Penny Chambers apologised that there was no phone line or broadband into the house, and said that she could take care of that for Mr Muhammad if he so wished, but the new tenant was fully understanding and said that he would take care of it himself in due course. The reality was that Abdullah Muhammad wanted nothing electronic on this property whatsoever. It was vital that it remained off-grid in this age of mass digital surveillance and big data.

Anyone who was even mildly inquisitive about the new neighbours in this affluent avenue in a rich area of Dublin would not have paid any attention to the sight of a Transit van coming and going to the property. There could be numerous reasons for such a vehicle, full of workmen, to be going to the bungalow. As it was, no-one noticed, because no-one cared. Abdullah Muhammad had been told, by courier, to be there by ten in the morning, and then to wait.

The property was unfurnished and he had taken his prayer mat out of his backpack and unrolled it onto the pristine hardwood floors and prayed at the appointed time. He had not been finished that long when he heard the crunch of heavy wheels on the gravel driveway. He opened the kitchen door and walked out into what was effectively a courtyard created by the L-shape of the bungalow, and saw his old comrade Muhammad Bokhari at the wheel. Bohkari, from Leeds, bounced out of the driver's seat, tall and agile, and embraced his brother. It had been too long.

Three other men emerged from the vehicle; one from the passenger seat and two from inside as the sliding door opened. He did the introductions, although Abdullah Muhammad knew of the exploits of these men, doing God's work in Aleppo. Akbar Choudry from Liverpool, Muhammad Tirmizi who was originally from Swat Valley in Pakistan, and Hussein Iqbal, who had been born in Islamabad but brought up in Bradford, were the men that Abdullah had been waiting for, because they could deliver a blow that the infidels here would never recover from.

Gerry O'Donnell had enjoyed a lazy morning. Herself and the wee man were down in the village, so it was just him and Rua in the cottage. He was glancing through his book collection but the lady with the nose was distracting him any chance she got. In the end he relented. He grabbed the lead off the hook on the wall next to the front door and she went mental. Even at twelve years old she could still dance about like a puppy when she knew it was hill time. He clicked the lead on, picked up his trekking pole, and headed out onto the Donegal hillside. He had promised that he would meet Herself down in the village for lunch, so it would have to be the short walk today. He turned left and headed up to where the well was that supplied the cottage with water. He got to the gate and went through it, and, as ever, closed it.

Gerry O'Donnell liked to think that he was a good neighbour. He walked past the small water tank that took run-off from an old neighbour's well and provided the cottage with its supply. He could hear the dribbling and tinkling coming out of the hillside. Then he headed left up a very rough bog road, and it was time to let herself run. He clicked off the lead and she bounded away as she always did, explored some smells, and then came prancing back to him with the tongue hanging out the side of the mouth, ears up, delighted. The destination of this short walk was nothing new for either of them.

From the time he had taken over the cottage and renovated it, he had always enjoyed walking up to Lough Agrougha. From end to end the lough was perhaps no more than two hundred metres, but it had once supplied the mine workings at the bottom of his road; hence the locals called it the 'Wheel Lough'. The water wheel had gone, the mining works had gone more than a century and a half ago, but the hill and the lough were still there. The trekking pole was useful even on a gentle decline, giving him a third leg.

For North Donegal, it had been reasonably dry the previous few weeks so the water level was down, exposing some of the lough bed. So his 'Loughside Rock', which was his seat, was set back about ten metres. He sat down in this hidden little area as Rua explored the lough side, smelling for anything interesting. In the twenty-five years he'd been there, Gerry O'Donnell could only remember twice that neighbours and their dogs, trying to collect sheep, had been there at the same time he was. When he first dropped Maria here had she thought it was a little piece of heaven on earth, and she was right.

The walk back down from the Lough was always a pleasant one if it was in any way a clear day. To his right was Mount Errigal, the Aghlas and Muckish, and straight in front of him the day was clear enough for him to see the horizon and the edge of Tory Island. The place was well-named: 'Oilean Thoraigh', 'The Island of Towers'. Gerry made a mental note that he hadn't yet been out to the island this summer, and that was remiss of him. He loved the people there and their attitude to life. There was a time, he thought, when all of Ireland must have been like Tory Island. That was before the strangers came.

He got to the water tank and had to shout Rua over to him. She obeyed reluctantly as she knew that the lead was going back on her. He walked down the boreen, went in behind the back of the cottage under the solitary tree on the property, where herself had a kennel. She whimpered slightly because she knew what this meant. There was a long metal chain fixed round the tree, and he clicked it onto her collar and took the lead off her. This meant she could go into the kennel quite easily if the weather came down, and she had a fair radius to go around sniffing, but she couldn't go leaping after the neighbours' sheep. In fairness, all she wanted to do with the livestock was play with them. But the sheep didn't know that, and in the years he'd had the girl there had never been a cross word between him and the neighbours about his dog, and they appreciated that. Although the sheep had the run of the place around the cottage, they steered clear of Rua, and she strained at the wire lead with her tail wagging, wondering why they wouldn't come down and play with her. He ruffled her head and she jumped up on him, missing him already.

He checked in the pockets of his fleece for phone and keys; that was all he needed, and jumped into the van, which, of course, was unlocked. When the German diesel engine pulled the van up onto the boreen, it would have been a precarious operation for someone who didn't know the road. But that wasn't Gerry O'Donnell. He'd been up and down that boreen, narrow and winding as it was, in various types of vehicle, for over a quarter of a century. Probably longer. He pulled out onto the N56 and headed down into Gortahork village. The sun was shining and there was no reason for him not to smile.

Liam MacMillan knew that the worst thing he could do in this situation would be to withhold information. He had no way of knowing if what he was withholding was already known to his handlers. As he studied the carpet of the hotel room floor, the smiling face of Denis Donaldson was in his mind's eye. So much so that he tuned out what Scully was saying to him; but he snapped up, getting eye contact with the Justice Minister, trying to retrieve the situation like a daydreaming child being shouted back into the classroom environment by an angry teacher.

"Sorry?"

"I really do appreciate you being here, Deputy Macmillan."

"No problem," said Macmillan sheepishly.

"As I was saying…When did you last see Mr Dempsey?"

Macmillan hesitated. He realised he would have to tell Scully the truth just in case the Branch already knew.

"Might have been the day after the Luas bombings. Or the day after that. Can't be certain. He came to my office, it wasn't an appointment…"

"What did you discuss?" said Scully, closing in for the kill.

Liam Macmillan was silent for a second. His Branch handlers had always dealt with him in a professional and neutral manner. They never judged him. He never felt he was being judged, at any rate. He was an asset. It was their job to handle him as an asset. But he was looking across at this Free State bastard who Macmillan had skewered on numerous occasions in the Dáil. He now knew that he would probably never again be able to clash with Scully on the floor of the Dáil and put his heart into it. He felt humiliated. But the smiling face of wee Denis came back into his head. He had no choice.

"He told me…He said…"

"Yes?"

"It was up at Springfield. He was in court for his kid and…"

"YES?"

"He told me he'd bumped into a bunch of foreign-looking lads and that he'd got a good look at them and that they were definitely the lads who did the videos after the bombs."

"Point of order, Deputy. I rather think that they did the videos before the bombs," chortled Scully, laughing at his own joke.

"You know what I mean."

"Indeed, Deputy. Indeed," smiled Scully, who was thoroughly enjoying this.

"Anyway, he said that there was a minibus full of these lads, and he reckoned that they were gonna do other things. Turns out he was right."

"Indeed, indeed."

"So that's it, that's all he told me," said Macmillan, desperately wanting this ordeal, this humiliation, to be over.

"And that was it? He just told you as a point of information?"

"He wanted to talk about it."

"Please, please, please, Deputy. Please," said Scully in his most condescending manner.

"What?"

"He came to you with this information. Yes, you've told me that. Yes, I believe you. But you expect me to believe that there was nothing else? What was the basis for him coming to you? Please think carefully before you give your answer, Deputy."

"Yeah, well... I think he wanted to check out some possibilities," said Macmillan, starting to fidget in the seat.

"I have a meeting in ten minutes in the Taoiseach's office, and I'm not satisfied with this. Obviously this is a Garda matter. Do I have to paint a picture for you, Deputy Macmillan? What's the word that your people like to use for such helpful chaps as yourself? Ah, yes. Tout," said Scully, who imagined he was starting to squeeze Macmillan like he was a satsuma.

Liam Macmillan's shoulders sagged. He didn't know why; he just couldn't bring himself to say out loud what they probably knew anyway. And his mind raced about how to say this without it appearing that it had been prised out of him, or that he had been trying to conceal it in the first place. Words wouldn't come and then he said, "It was a nonsense yarn. He's still stuck back in the old days."

"Mr Dempsey?"

"Yeah, yeah. Jack," said Macmillan without thinking.

"Jack? I've seen his file, it's Sean Patrick Dempsey."

"It's a nickname. He was a good boxer when he was a kid. That's it. You know? Jack Dempsey, the boxer."

"How very droll."

"Well, it's just a nickname."

"What did you discuss? I have approximately six minutes, Deputy Macmillan."

"He wanted to know if anything could be done about these guys," said Macmillan, finally getting it out.

"Done by whom?" asked Scully, obviously already knowing the answer.

"The Movement," said Macmillan, looking down at the carpet again.

"Ah, yes. The organisation that doesn't exist anymore."

"It doesn't, and I told him that," said Macmillan, trying to retrieve some of his dignity from the situation.

"And that's what you told him?"

"Abso-fucking-lutely. Guys like Jack are living in the past. Can't let it go. Some of them are Dissers. Most of them, like Jack, just walked away," said Macmillan, stridently sure of his facts, and confident because he was telling the truth.

"Dissers?"

"Yeah, yeah, dissidents. Y'know, Real IRA, this IRA, that IRA. You know them?"

"Such a rich lexicon you chaps have."

"Well, that's what he wanted. He wanted the lads to do something about these boys. And I told him those days are gone, and that he should go to the guards."

"Ah, such a rich irony in that, coming from you, Deputy Macmillan," said Scully, smiling.

Gerry O'Donnell pulled his van into the main car park of Gortahork, straight across from Óstán Lough Altan. If there was a bustling centre of the village, this was it. In his earphones he had Mairéad Ní Mhaonaigh of Altan singing An Mhaighdean Mhara. He got out of the van, closed the door without even thinking of locking it, and walked over the road into Gortahork's one and only hotel. He went through the two sets of glass-frosted doors and walked straight through to the reception to speak to Sinead, who was a distant cousin. Smiling, she nodded past him before he could say a word. He became disorientated as he saw a reflection in the large mirror on the wall behind her. He spun round. It was Jack.

"What the fuck, big man?" said an astonished O'Donnell.

"Howya wee lad?"

"Jack!"

"I know, I know, I should have called. But, well, you said about phones and…"

Gerry looked past Jack at the young, well-built man sitting on the two-seater sofa that was facing reception, just inside the main door. He nodded in Stan's direction.

"Is he with you?"

"Yeah, he's with me surely. I want you to meet him."

"Sound."

"Yeah, I want you to meet him, he's a good lad."

"Yeah, grand. Listen, I'm glad you thought better about it. A few days up here, that's what you need."

"What?"

"Our romantic rendezvous in Letterkenny, you daft fecker" laughed Gerry.

"Ah, that. Um, yeah."

"Stay with us for a few days. Spare room's a bit basic. But then, so are you." Gerry laughed again.

"No, wee lad. I'm afraid this is just another wee flying visit, but I need to have a serious yarn with you again," said Jack solemnly.

"Ah for fuck's sake, big man, not that again."

"I came a long way. Ten minutes of your time. Listen to this boy of mine. Stan's his name. He's Polish."

"Ten minutes. It'll need to be ten minutes. Herself'll be over soon enough."

"Your wife?"

"Yeah, she's across the road there," said Gerry, nodding in the direction of the community college that was one of the main facilities in the small village.

"Yeah?"

"Herself's teaching watercolour and painting over there. Mainly for local women, they love it. And the wee fella's at the crèche, wrecking the place, so… They do a good lunch here, which is why I'm here."

"You got life kinda sussed here, haven't you wee fella?" asked Jack, rather enviously.

"Ah well, you could say that."

"Here, wee fella, sit down. Have the craic," said Jack, smiling and gesturing towards the couch and two chairs where Stan was.

"Gerry, this is Stan. Stan, this is Gerry," said Jack with mock-formality.

"Pleased to meet you, Stan," said Gerry, extending his hand.

Stan stood up, clearly significantly taller than the wiry, red-headed man in front of him. It was a firm handshake.

"Gaffer said you good man."

"I wouldn't listen to what he said."

"Tell him, Stan. Take your time, son," ordered Jack as he sat down in one of the chairs facing the two-seater couch. Stan took up the two-seater couch by himself, and Gerry sat on the other chair so he could keep an eye on the door and through the glass see Maria and the little fella coming across the road, which he expected to happen in the next ten minutes. So this wasn't going to be a long conflab.

"Stan drove me up here. No bus this time," laughed Jack, nodding in Stan's direction as an acknowledgement.

"I good driver."

"Yeah, you should do bus runs for those Arab bastards. They want to die anyway," chuckled Jack. Gerry burst out laughing.

"It was other cunt's fault in North, gaffer. Other cunt, not me," said Stan in mitigation.

"Yeah, cheek of that bastard. Thinking he could come through a green light, fucker," chuckled Jack. Gerry knotted in laughter, remembering several driving incidents back in the day in England.

"Can I get you lads anything? Lunch is OK here."

"Nah, we're grand. I'm buying anyway. You stay there. Do you want anything from the bar?"

"Nah, I'm grand, I'll wait for herself. Three of us are having lunch here."

Jack seemed to take that as a cue to get to the business end of this unplanned meeting.

"Remember that nightclub? The bomb?" asked Jack, looking at Gerry. O'Donnell simply nodded. Jack gestured with a nod of his own head towards the young man sitting across from him.

"He was working there that night. On the door."

"Fuck's sake," said Gerry, getting eye contact with Stan.

"Yeah, he was on the door. He was lucky. Made of strong stuff, he is. I lost another lad," said Jack quietly.

"Fucking hell," was all that Gerry O'Donnell could manage.

"Stan's sister. Just a kid. She wasn't so lucky. She was working down in the bar."

"Oh, for fuck's sake. Fuck's sake," said Gerry O'Donnell, putting his head down.

"Yeah, you can sing that."

Gerry O'Donnell didn't know what to say about what he had just been told, but he thought his next question wasn't inappropriate.

"How's your wee fella, Jack? Is he still in hospital?"

"He is, but he's loads better. Loads better."

"Then there was that one in Spencer Dock."

"Yeah, yeah. Fucking mental. When's this gonna end?"

"When they run out of guys or somebody puts a stop to them."

"Ah, not that again, big fella," said Gerry, sighing.

"Well?"

"Look, there's three of us here. Rules," said Gerry, looking at Jack.

"He's a hundred per cent, that fella across there. Shite driver, though," said Jack with a smile.

"Phones?"

"They're in the car. Couldn't get a signal up here anyway. Place is dead."

"Yeah, it's patchy around here," said Gerry defensively. Any criticism of Donegal by someone from Dublin tended to get his ethnic hackles up.

"Patchy? It's fuckin' dead. Fuckin' Twilight Zone," said Jack, ribbing the Glasgow-Donegalie.

"Phone fucked here," said Stan affirmatively.

"Cheers," said Gerry sardonically, "there's Wi-Fi in the hotel here. You can use a messaging app if you want to."

"Oh don't start all that internet shite with me," laughed Jack.

"Anyway, big fella. Herself will be over here in a couple of minutes. You two are welcome to stay with us for a couple of days, show you around the place. Might be a good move."

"Nah, we need to be heading back down to the Smoke. Could do with picking your brains, though."

The hotel door opened, and as Gerry turned to his left to see who it was, he was hit with a five year-old bundle of love.

"PAPA," shouted Gerry's son as he launched at his father with a mighty hug. Gerry pulled him up onto his lap and started to snuggle him and tickle him. His son howled with laughter and delight. Stan and Jack looked at this happy moment and then looked up at the person who'd followed in behind the child. Five foot four and a half, in her trainers and tight-fitting jeans and a pale blue fleece with a small backpack slung over her left shoulder. Her jet black hair was pulled back into a ponytail. Maria smiled as she saw Gerry. Her husband looked up, and as usual, his heart skipped a beat. Jack Dempsey instantly understood why his old army comrade was so settled in his life. She was breathtakingly beautiful and her smile lit up the entire hotel foyer.

"Hey, Chiquita," said Gerry, standing up. With his son attached to his hip like a limpet mine, he put his right arm round Maria and gave her a kiss. And then turned backwards, gesturing with his right hand to the two men seated.

"Maria, this is a very, very old friend of mine, Jack. Jack Dempsey, from Dublin. And this is Stan as well, he's a good driver."

Jack laughed, standing up and extending his hand.

"Pleasure to meet you pet, the name's Jack."

"I've already told her that," said Gerry, smiling.

"You're very welcome," said Maria, smiling back.

"The lads are just passing through on a bit of a holiday, and I said they could stay with us for a couple of days. I'll show them around. The back room's OK?"

"It's OK, Chico. We'll be OK," said Maria, smiling. Gerry took an inward breath that she hadn't connected Jack to the old days. That was a stroke of luck.

"Yeah, brilliant. Um, do we need anything else for dinner or anything?" asked Gerry, looking at Maria.

"No, plenty in house, Chico. We still having lunch here?"

"Yeah, sure."

Jack realised he was being boxed in.

"It's a very kind offer, but we're probably going to be pushing on. But, ah, we'll stay for lunch, for sure," he said in as cheerful a way as he could muster, given the circumstances; he knew his old friend was trying to corral him into doing something he didn't want to do.

"Ah, go on, big fella. Couple of days. Do you good," said Gerry, smiling.

"Ah, I forgot something. I need to check the phone. It's in the car."

"I thought you said the phone wasn't working?" said Gerry mischievously. Jack shot him a look.

"This Chico is hungry, Gerree."

"He's always hungry," laughed Gerry.

"I order lunch for us, baby," said Maria, taking charge of the situation. Her son needed lunch and she was starving.

Jack got up to walk to the hotel door and Gerry looked back at Maria and said, "I'll be two minutes, baby."

"Dos minutos, Chico."

Stan got up in silence and followed the two men out onto the tranquil main street of Gortahork.

"Look, wee lad, I can't stay. But I did need that yarn," said Jack, firmly.

"Big fella, if my missus smells Army off you, it's me that'll be looking for a place to stay," said Gerry, very firmly indeed.

"No loose talk here, but I need to pick your brains."

"Come home with us. Stay the night. We can go for a couple of beers tonight, and we'll have a chat then. But not in the house, not anywhere near Maria."

"That's grand. It's a long drive back anyway."

"Done deal," said Gerry, rather relieved.

"Lunch in there good, is it?"

"Yeah, it's grand. Give me a minute," said Gerry, walking across the road to his van. For some reason, Jack felt the need to follow him, and walked across. Gerry realised Jack was behind him and turned to look back.

"I appreciate this, wee lad, really do," said Jack.

"Grand, no hassle."

Gerry opened the van door and pulled his mobile phone out of the door well.

"You don't lock things up round here?"

"No need."

"Different way of life up here," said Jack admiringly.

"You can sing that, sunshine. You can sing that," said Gerry proudly.

Gerry flicked the phone on and started to walk back to the hotel with Jack by his side.

"I meant to say, wee fella, about you and your missus and everything…"

"OH FUCK," exclaimed Gerry, stopping dead in his tracks.

"What is it, wee fella?" asked Jack, sensing the alarm in Gerry's voice.

"You're all over Twitter."

"What the fuck do you mean?"

"Guards are looking for you. For a murder."

Debbie Thompson had told Alison Frazer to be outside the Russell Square tube at midday to wait for a message. It did all seem a bit like a bad spy movie to Alison, but she knew that Debbie was very good at her job, and, after all, it was she who had approached her journalist gym buddy for a meeting about something that Alison had told her was very, very important.

At four minutes past midday Alison Frazer's iPhone wobbled and the WhatsApp icon told her she had a message. She touched the screen with her thumb and it was from Debbie. It said:

"Tavistock Hotel. I'm in the foyer. Switch your phone off NOW!"

In that moment Alison felt that she was being directed by someone who knew more about things than she did. This reminded her of Woolnough, and that wasn't a good feeling. She switched her phone off, put it in her shoulder bag and walked in the direction of Tavistock Square.

Alison knew the area well as it was close to her old college. She walked out and turned right onto Woburn Place and walked towards Tavistock Square. She became aware that on her right-hand side she was passing a little Greek Restaurant that she used to like back in her student days, before she met Peter. It wasn't long until she was turning left into Tavistock Square, and saw Debbie sitting on her own on a two-seater couch facing the window, scanning the street for Alison.

Debbie saw Alison and gave her a wave through the window. Alison came up the few stairs, through the double glass doors and turned to her left, where Debbie was sitting.

"Hi there," said Debbie.

"Thanks for meeting me," said Alison.

"Hey, no bother. This is what I do, honey," said Debbie with a smile.

Alison noticed that Debbie was, as ever, a gym bunny. She

probably didn't need to have much of a dress code at her work, thought Alison. She was in a light, zip-up purple fleece, grey jogging pants and trainers. Her short auburn hair was pulled back into a bun, and it looked newly showered. At her feet sat a Nike gym bag and a small laptop rucksack. Debbie Thompson was efficiency on the move. Debbie didn't get up as Alison sat down, but asked, "Have you switched your phone off?"

"Yes, ma'am," said Alison, putting two fingers up in a mock salute.

"This stuff is important, Al," said Debbie in a sombre tone.

Alison nodded, taking the mild rebuke. Debbie stood up, which rather unsettled Alison as she had just sat down, expecting to have a conflab there in the foyer of the hotel.

"It's a nice day, we'll go out into the Square," said Debbie, gesturing across the road to Tavistock Square.

"OK."

"OK, let's go,"

Within a few minutes they were sitting down at a park bench that had been unoccupied.

"Give me your phone," ordered Debbie.

"Sorry?"

"Your phone. Give me it."

"Oh, OK."

Alison rummaged into her bag and handed over the iPhone to her journalist buddy.

Debbie looked at it and said, nonplussed, "Huh, an iPhone, OK."

"What's the matter with an iPhone?"

"You obviously haven't heard of Vault 7."

"Should I?"

"Oh, it's only the way that the US government can hack into anyone's iPhone and spy on them" said Debbie sarcastically.

"Jesus!"

Debbie took the iPhone, rummaged into her laptop bag and found an old metal pencil case. She prised it open, put the iPhone in, and closed it, putting it at the bottom of her laptop bag. She zipped it up and pushed it under the park bench. Then she stood up, walked behind the park bench onto the grass about fifteen feet and gestured towards Alison to follow her.

"Is there really a need for all this Secret Squirrel stuff?" said a slightly annoyed Alison.

"YES!" affirmed Debbie.

"OK, it's just me that's listening now. Go ahead."

Alison took a deep breath and tried to gather her thoughts as she considered where she should start this story and how much she should tell Debbie.

"This is definitely just between you and me, isn't it?"

"Of course. I'm a journalist. This is what I do. If you're a source for a story, I protect you. To the point where I tell a Judge in the High Court that he can go and fuck himself. I get sent to prison, but you're protected. In my bag's my purse, and in my purse is an NUJ Press Card. That means that I've signed up to a code of ethics. And one of those is that I protect sources. Non-negotiable, honey," said Debbie.

This seemed to have a calming effect on Alison and she said, "OK, I don't really know where to start on this, but I have to give you some background."

"Go ahead, Al, I've got time," said Debbie in a reassuring tone.

"You know that guy I was going with? The guy I broke up with?"

"Yeah. Peter? The Creep? You broke up with him? That guy?"

"Yeah, yeah. The creep. You can sing that."

"Is he hassling you?"

"No, no, nothing like that. I've heard nothing from him."

"Go ahead then."

"The thing you need to understand, Debbie, is that he and I were into some strange stuff. And that's not what I'm speaking to you about now, but that's how I got to know the stuff I'm gonna tell you."

"Go ahead."

"OK, there's no way of dancing around this. Peter and I were swingers. He got me into it," said Alison. As she said it she looked at Debbie's face for a flicker of judgement, any hint of disapproval. Debbie just looked back to her, impassive.

"Yeah, go ahead," she said in a neutral tone.

Alison was relieved that she hadn't seen any initial hint of anything judgemental. She then looked to the right, to the park bench, which was still unoccupied with their bags underneath it. She looked back at Debbie.

"OK, so we're both swingers. We've been doing this stuff for years. And there's one guy we met on a regular basis. I knew him as Patrick. Black guy from Nigeria," said Alison matter-of-factly, surprising herself that she could say this stuff to Debbie in a purely factual way, and that there were with no emotions jumping out and mugging her.

"OK, go ahead," said Debbie, encouragingly.

"We would usually meet him at a Travelodge up in Enfield, but after a while I knew he didn't live in London. In fact, he didn't live in the UK. He was based in Ireland. And that's where you come in."

"Yeah?" asked Debbie, realising that Alison was probably getting to the point.

"I knew for a while that Patrick lived over in Ireland. He didn't have residency or something in the UK but he travelled here. Anyway, he lived in Ireland and, as part of a birthday treat, Peter was taking me over to Ireland. And he said we could meet Patrick at his place and have…some fun."

"OK. Yeah?"

"Well, it was outside Dublin. We got there in a hire car. Patrick was there, with three of his buddies who I'd never met before, but that was quite normal."

"Normal?" asked Debbie. Alison sensed she was being judged and started to bristle.

"Look, it's swinging, you meet people sometimes just for one time. It's – It's – It's part of the lifestyle," said Alison, feeling she needed to justify herself.

Debbie picked up the resentment in her voice, and attempted to reassure her.

"Yeah, sure. Yeah, go ahead."

"So there were these guys who were Patrick's pals, three of them. But there was this other guy who clearly wasn't sort of with them, but he was – he was part of the thing there."

"Yeah?"

"Look, I don't want to give you all the grizzly details. I don't think you need them."

"Of course. Just tell me what you think the story is," reassured Debbie.

"Well, the other guy that I mentioned, an old white guy. The other three guys were black, like Patrick. All African accents. Well, he just sat in the corner for most of the time. Then, towards the end, he came over and did his thing."

"Yeah?"

"Well, you can imagine what the other guys were doing and there's no point in going into that. And then the old guy came over and…There's not any way of putting this gently…" said Alison, her voice trailing off.

"Hey Al, it is what it is. It's consenting adults. You're saying you've got a story for me. You know; there's no judge and jury here."

"I remember you saying to me in the gym that you didn't do the tabloid thing, you didn't think people's private lives were the stuff for the newspapers. You said that, didn't you?"

"Yeah, of course. Only when there's a public interest defence."

"Public interest defence?" asked Alison, "What's that?"

"OK, here's an example. A politician. I'm just making someone up, right? Politician John Smith MP has made a big thing about being a Christian guy: family values, perfect family, 2.5 children, all go to church on a Sunday, and he really hates gays, OK? Yeah?"

"Yeah, yeah."

"Well, if a journalist finds out and can establish it that he's secretly a gay and he's visiting gay hookers, then there's a public interest defence because he's a public hypocrite. You get me?"

"Yeah, yeah, of course. Yeah, I get that," said Alison, smiling.

"However, if John Smith MP has never uttered anything homophobic, but he is a married guy, but he's had a gay affair or he's into the gay scene, and journalists find out then then journalists really shouldn't tell anyone because it's not in the public interest. You follow?"

"Well I'm sure the public would be interested in that."

"Yeah, what the public is interested in is not always in the public interest. Yeah? You get me?"

This seemed to be a releaser cue for Alison. She took a deep breath. She felt that what Debbie had just said to her was authorising and empowering her to go to the next place in this story.

"OK, yeah. I get you. OK, so this guy, the older guy. They had an airbed for me on the floor and the other guys were, well, y'know. He comes over and well, he comes in my mouth. Fine. Nothing new in that. But then he grabs me by the throat and hits me really hard in the face," said Alison matter-of-factly.

"Jesus!" said Debbie, taken by surprise at what she was being told.

"Yeah," said Alison, in grim acknowledgement.

"And what did the other guys do?" said Debbie, shocked for the first time.

"Well, it was all part of that scene," said Alison matter-of-factly.

"Fucking hell." Debbie was genuinely shocked.

"Anyway, thing is, through the site this guy contacted me afterwards. He gave me a really great write-up, but he wanted me to take a selfie every day for as long as it lasted and send it to him."

"What lasted?"

"Oh. Oh sorry. Um, the bruise. The bruise on my face."

"Oh for fuck's sake, that's fucking awful," said Debbie, genuinely shocked.

"Yeah, yeah. He was a real dreamboat, that guy."

"I'm really sorry, Al," said Debbie, genuinely affected by what she was hearing.

"This bruise? Was it really bad? When was it?"

"You saw it, when I was at the gym."

"Oh, the Tae Kwon Do thing? That's what you said?"

"Yeah, yeah, yeah. The Tae Kwon Do. It seemed a reasonable excuse at the time. I was scared people would think Peter had been hitting me."

"No, he was just getting other people to hit you," said Debbie drily.

"Yeah. Look that was then and I'm out of it, thank God. Thing is, I saw him only a few days ago."

"Here in London?"

"No, on Sky News."

"He was on Sky?"

"Yeah, it was definitely him."

"Totally sure?"

"Debbie, I think I would know him, given that I saw him rather close up and personal and I had the bruise to prove it," snapped Alison.

"What's his name?"

"Gareth Scully. He's in the Irish government. He's the Justice Minister," said Alison matter-of-factly.

"FUCK! THE JUSTICE MINISTER?"

"I've got some stuff in my bag. I think you should read it," said Alison, gesturing towards the park bench that was still uninhabited.

"What is it?"

"The email that I sent the pictures to. My bruise. We got into a bit of a, well, correspondence about what got him off and what he liked. Well, I printed all that out for you. You can have it."

"Wow. Well, yeah, sure. Let's read it," said Debbie, heading towards the park bench.

The two of them sat down and Alison reached into her bag and produced a clear plastic document wallet with a stud fastening, A3 in size. And Debbie could see that there was a substantial number of A4 sheets there. She reckoned maybe fifty to seventy sheets. She was like a kid at Christmas as Alison handed it over to her.

"Mind if I have a quick look at this here?"

"No, go ahead," said Alison. Debbie Thompson scanned through the first few pages then jumped to the middle of the bundle, her eyes scanning down the pages, looking for anything substantial, anything newsworthy, anything incriminating.

"So you're Annabel?" asked Debbie.

Alison Frazer simply nodded.

"And he's…" Alison cut in.

"Yeah, he's Dark John. Very appropriate, I thought."

Debbie looked back into the pages and one paragraph jumped out at her. It was from Scully, telling Annabel what the picture of her fresh bruise did for him.

"Fucking sick bastard," whispered Debbie, to herself, but it was audible enough for Alison to hear.

"You can sing that, love," said Alison, bitterly.

"This is dynamite stuff, Al. I promise you your name doesn't come near this, but I've got a really, really good buddy in Dublin. We met at the NUJ conference last year in Southport. She's top class, and, with your permission, without mentioning your name or how I got this stuff, I'm gonna tell her the stuff she needs to know and we can start looking into this scumbag," said Debbie. She looked up to get eye-contact with Alison, and saw that her gym buddy was slowly nodding her approval.

"Are you OK with this?"

"Yeah, yeah. I trust you Debs. But I don't want my name out in this. I really don't. Peter threatened me for years to out me as "Annabel" to my family any time I felt like packing my bags, so…""

"Another scumbag," snarled Debbie.

"OK for you love, you play for the other team," smiled Alison, trying to lighten the mood.

"Hey, honey, there's some psycho dykes out there too," laughed Debbie as she leaned forward and gave Alison a big-sisterly hug.

"You've done the right thing giving me this. I give you my word I'll use it well, and hopefully we can out this bastard. Justice Minister? Fucking hell," said Debbie.

"Thanks Debbie, I feel good about this," said Alison with a smile.

Something in the surroundings now made Debbie aware of past glories. As she looked round the greenery of Tavistock Square, she said, "Remember the 7/7 Bombings?"

"Yeah, of course. Yeah, it was terrible."

"The bus blew up just over there," said Debbie, nodding directionally.

"Fucking hell."

"I was on placement at ITN. I was in second year of my postgrad. It was great."

"Great?"

"Yeah, great – a great story."

"Nothing great about that," said Alison, seriously unimpressed.

"It's journalism, honey. And you know the old saying, 'If it bleeds, it leads'."

"Is that what this is to you? A story?"

"Ah look, Al. This can be a great story because he's a scumbag and we can take him down. This is what I do. This is much better that what stupid airhead celebrity's sleeping with another stupid airhead celebrity, yeah?" said Debbie, looking for indications of approval from Alison.

"Yeah, yeah, I suppose, if you put it like that."

Every person has something that allows them to maintain their self-respect throughout the trials of life. A belief that reassures them that, through it all, they're a decent person. For Mary Riley, that thing was honesty with money. Quite literally, she would never steal a penny. Which was just as well, because over the years she had perfected Sean Patrick Dempsey's signature to the point where she could do it better than he could. This was a vital skill, especially when he was wasted and couldn't sign his own name. Consequently, any official documents or cheques that required his signature were processed by the Dicey machine. Not for the first time, she was running the place entirely on her own. His mobile had been off all day, and her Cabra woman's intuition told her that he might well be on the lash. For sure, he had plenty to cope with recently, so she wasn't too judgemental about that.

However, Stan wasn't available either, and that was puzzling. Perhaps it was something to do with the arrangements for his wee sister, thought Mary Riley. Then there was a pang of anxiety and guilt. Had she forgotten to do anything about that for him? That was a question in Mary Riley's head, and she ransacked her memory, but couldn't think of anything that he'd asked her to do. She'd left a message on both their phones to get in touch, and that was a good while ago. At least the regular lads were about, and they were getting sent to where they were meant to be. The business was going like a fair. Everyone in Dublin wanted security. God forgive me, thought Mary Riley, but those head-cases blowing themselves up had been great for business.

The usual pile of mail was on her desk to sort through. She had a radar for sniffing out cheques, and went to them first. You could tell a lot about a letter by the envelope, thought Mary. Perhaps it was Jack's reputation, or the business them were in, or maybe a bit of both, but they very, very rarely had problems with late payers. Around Dublin, nobody wanted to be getting a red letter from Big Jack Dempsey. Then there was one envelope that stood out: a short, white envelope, the kind that a Mass card would come in. The stamp had a Dublin postmark. The handwriting was a bit spidery, and it was addressed to "Sean Patrick Dempsey" at the office address. That in itself was strange, thought Mary Riley. She opened it up, and inside there was a single page from a reporter's notebook. She looked at it twice to try and make sense of it. Each line had a series of numbers separated by commas. What the fuck did this mean, wondered Mary.

She was still studying the page when the door opened, and there were two men in their early forties. They were well-dressed, and invisible signs seemed to hang above their heads saying, "We're in the guards."

Scully sat down at the small dining room table across from Pelfrey. His mobile phone was off and resting on the cistern of the toilet where the CIA man had told him to put it. Consequently, the phone, though traceable and able to be listened to, was insulated from their conversation by two doors and twenty feet of distance.

"It was good that you could make it. Who knows you are here?" asked Pelfrey.

"My driver, Garda – Police. He's in the car across the road," said Scully.

"Isn't he meant to tail you?"

"Oh, he thinks I'm seeing a lady in this apartment complex, and he knows that gives him a cheque to cash. I've told him he's fast-tracked for promotion. He's a fairly brainless sergeant, and he probably shouldn't have made that rank, but he knows he's going to be an inspector fairly soon, so he's happy to keep a discreet distance while I get it on with my mystery lady."

"Excellent tradecraft, minister. You missed your vocation."

The praise from the CIA man drew Gareth Scully in like a moth to a flame. Then it was down to business.

"Brannigan wants to know if you have the numbers in Congress yet?"

"We're nearly there. As you know, we're in a minority administration, but…"

"And?" said Pelfrey, cutting him off.

"There are a couple of independents who sit on the opposition benches. Real leftie firebrand types. Pain in the arse. If we could get those two then we'd be there."

"And?" said Pelfrey, wanting to hear more.

"Well, I have my guy in the Special Branch leaving no stone

unturned, and something dropped in our lap, if you'll pardon the pun, about one of them in particular."

"Yeah?"

"He seems to have a predilection for underage sex. Young girls. He's been a very busy chap."

"Does he know that you know this?"

"Oh, he will soon enough. He will soon enough. And a promise of discretion should guarantee his undying gratitude and loyalty when it comes to voting through the new national security legislation."

"That's good to hear. You've got a sight of the big picture, and that's what leaders can do, Gareth."

The praise from the CIA man washed over Scully like a warm wave. He was loving this. It also reassured him that his own minor indiscretions were never going to come to light; he was too valuable to the Americans. That gave him another reason to smile. Scully felt relaxed enough now to open up to the CIA man.

"Yes, thank you. This has been a terrible business, but the country – my country will be safer. We'll all be safer in the long run."

"Can't argue with any of that, Gareth."

"I mean, what I'm trying to say, Jerome…"

Pelfrey looked up from his notes and smiled at the Irishman. He felt that Scully might be ready to spill something and didn't want to interrupt.

"I mean, what I'm trying to say is that all this loss of life has been awful. Don't think it hasn't given me sleepless nights, and…Obviously I don't know the full story, and I know you Intelligence chaps are, well, highly intelligent, but, what I'm trying to say is that…I'm just glad it's over."

"You've been a great help, Gareth. The War on Terror is global, and the United States leads that fight. We don't forget our friends, and your country is lucky to have a leader like you."

The CIA man smiled as he re-ordered his papers and closed the leather document wallet with a gesture that signalled to Scully that their conspiratorial conclave was over. As he did so, Pelfrey further understood the essential necessity of the "Need to Know" rule. This venal clown sitting across from him had no idea about what was to happen, but Pelfrey knew that it was absolutely essential to close this deal in Ireland.

Gerry O'Donnell turned the smartphone towards Jack and said solemnly, "Shit like this all over Twitter, big guy."

Jack squinted to see what it was saying; not wanting to admit that his eyesight wasn't what it used to be. Gerry turned the phone back to himself, turned it to landscape, opened his thumb and forefinger across the screen to enlarge the print and then handed it back. It was a Tweet from breakingnews.ie. Jack could now read it clearly.

"Fucking dissident Republican?!"

"I think there might have been an old lady in Gweedore didn't hear you, pal," said Gerry, aware that someone was just getting out of his car to go across the road to Óstán Lough Altan. As with everyone in Gortahork, Gerry O'Donnell knew the man well.

"Howya Manus?" said Gerry, in a tone a tone that indicated that, while he was acknowledging the man's presence, he didn't really want him to come over and be introduced. The man from Killult nodded to Gerry O'Donnell and went on his way. Such polite discretion was actually quite rare in Cloughaneely, thought Gerry.

"Your old pal O'Shea. Somebody stiffed him," said Gerry O'Donnell in a business-like way.

"He wasn't my fucking pal."

"We go see this man. Gaffer and me," said Stan. Gerry O'Donnell looked at the young Pole and then shot a look at Jack. The message from O'Donnell's eyes was quite clear. He wanted to know if there was any truth in what the media was saying.

"He was as right as rain when we left him," said Jack, with his nostrils flaring in anger at the very thought that he might have had anything to do with this.

"OK, OK. This is a game-changer. The guards here are in a coma, but you two stick out like a bulldog's bollocks, so we need a plan," said Gerry, looking up at Jack.

"What then?" said Jack, with more than a hint of pleading in his voice.

"I need to go in and see herself. Then we need to stash your car. OK. A minute," said Gerry, thinking on his feet. He walked around the van and slid open the side door. He walked back round to the front of the vehicle and said to the two men, "Right, lads, jump in here just now, OK? Gets you out of sight. And give me the keys to your car," he said, holding out his hand.

"Grand," said Jack, moving round the van. When he looked inside, he took in a breath.

"Fucking hell, the Batmobile."

"Yeah, I've got it fitted out," said Gerry, in no mood to discuss how well-equipped his vehicle was.

He still had his hand extended, and Stan rummaged in the pockets of his leather jacket, produced the key to the hired Volkswagen, and slapped it into Gerry O'Donnell's palm.

"In you get, lads. What have you got in that car?"

"My jacket. Himself has a small hold-all. Fuck knows why he needed it. Oh, where did you put your phone, Stan?"

"In the door place, gaffer."

"OK, I'll get that stuff. But I have to go and see herself first," said Gerry, with a touch of trepidation in his voice.

"Thanks buddy," said Jack, with genuine gratitude.

"Fuck it, you'd do the same for me," nodded Gerry, "Now get in."

Stan got into the van gritting his teeth from his shoulder injury. Jack stumbled in, stooping his head and cursing his creaking knees. Gerry had taken a car-seat and fitted it into the back of the van so that it was facing out the way the lads had gone in. It was secured by bolts to the floor and the back wall of the vehicle. When seated, the person's right hand was at the back of the driver's seat, although that was screened off with plywood. The wall to the passenger's left hand-side was covered with a metal netting that allowed various bits of equipment to be clipped on or strapped. There were two rucksacks, various bits of climbing gear, lamps, and a secure box attached to the floor of the vehicle.

Maria and her son had already sat down and ordered lunch, and she wanted to know where her husband was. She looked across at the five year-old who was the centre of her world. He was almost certainly the only Felipe Patrick O'Donnell Garcia in Donegal. Probably anywhere. He spoke Spanish to his mother and English to his father, and Irish at school. For Maria, her trilingual son proved the wisdom of her grandmother so many years earlier, in her kitchen in Alta Mira in the north of Colombia. She would say to her favourite granddaughter, "Tu vida será un camino, Chiquita. Nunca tengas miedo seguirte adelante en tu corazón."

Although the little man had her jet black hair and Colombian complexion, he had Gerry's deep blue eyes. Those were the eyes she had fallen in love with on El Camino Santiago that day, when that strange man with red hair stumbled in front of her, and she laughed at him. Lunch arrived, and the little fella's eyes danced across the plate of turkey and ham. It was a full portion, but it wouldn't last long, thought Maria. He could eat for Ireland. He looked up at his mother and smiled. Those eyes would break hearts when he was older. She was once more starting to wonder where her husband had got to, when he walked round into the bar. He looked flustered.

"What is the matter, Chico?" asked Maria.

"Bit of a situation, love," stammered Gerry.

"Your friends? They are staying with us?" said Maria, sensing that something was seriously wrong. She had never seen Gerry this agitated.

"Yeah, yeah, it's, am, it's, am, well, it's a family thing and, um… Well, my mate Jack, he, um…" said Gerry, trying to find words.

Maria's alarm bells all went off at once. She had learned back in her own country to trust the instincts that Mother Nature had given her. There was one time that she could never forget, when she had ignored those warning signals, and it would never happen again. It was the day that those two men came into the shop in Alta Mira. They just didn't fit in. They were Colombian, but they just didn't look like they fitted in right.

It turned out, and she only realised this later, that this was the advance party of FARC operatives who were making sure that her father was in the shop. Later that day, a group of heavily armed men turned up, taking him away as a kidnap victim and destroying her family. She was getting the same feeling now. She knew her family was being threatened. Although she couldn't put it into words, Mother Nature was knocking on the door again, and shouting "¡Cuidado!"

Gerry sat down, smiled, and ruffled the little fella's hair.

"PAPA!" he yelled with a mouthful of turkey.

"Yeah, love, it's just that I might have to go away with the lads just to sort this out…Might be a day, y'know, like, just one of these things that…" said Gerry, trying to explain.

Maria looked straight into his eyes.

"Chico, you are lying to me." She let that hang in the air.

Gerry looked back at her and then looked away. She reached over and touched his hand. He looked up.

"Chico, don't ever lie to me," said Maria. Her tone of voice left no doubt that she was in no mood for joking. She wanted the truth, and she wanted it now.

"Of course not, of course not. I'd never lie to you, love," said Gerry with a weakness in his voice that was making his alarm bells go off louder than they had ever done before.

Gerry O'Donnell, ex-intelligence officer and skilled manipulator, couldn't tell this woman a lie. In their life together through the past almost seven years, he had never been dishonest with her and he had never known happiness like it. Perhaps he was out of practise, or perhaps he simply couldn't lie to her; but she was looking right through him. And in that moment, the quickest thinker that the IRA's England department ever deployed against the enemy didn't know what to say. Gerry was still trying to come up with something she would believe, when the RTE lunchtime news came onto the TV in the corner of the bar, and solved the problem for him. There was Jack's face, large as life, and Maria's head jerked up to look. It was a fairly recent picture of Jack, looked like an ID picture. Something official. Any attempt at a pretence was over. The man she had just met in the foyer, and who had shaken her hand, was on the TV, and the police were looking for him.

Maria García Jimenez's life was falling apart as her son was munching through a man's portion of turkey and ham, with spuds and broccoli on the side. In that moment she could see his life and his happiness being broken the way FARC broke hers. And although she tried to fight the emotions bubbling up inside her like an earthquake, she couldn't ignore the fact that she was starting to hate the man across the table from her. She was so angry she could hardly find words, in any language. She took some breaths through her nose, her nostrils flaring. There had been times in the past when Gerry had found an angry Maria quite arousing, as she flared her nostrils, breathing through her nose to try and control her temper. But there was nothing fun about this, thought Gerry.

There was a family in the far corner, five adults and a baby in a high chair. Their accents were like Gerry's. People from Scotland visiting, probably relatives. And they were all fussing over the infant. It didn't seem that long since her little man had been the chap in the high chair. She felt tears welling up into her eyes. She felt like screaming at Gerry, and certainly didn't want the people in the corner to know what was being said, so she spoke to him in Spanish.

"¿Ese hombre es de tu pasado, no?" asked Maria.

Gerry was so flummoxed that he couldn't find the words in Spanish, so he replied in English with a sigh.

"Yeah, yeah. Yeah, yeah. That's him, that's him. Look, but it's not what it seems, love."

"Si ayudas ese hombre, mi hijo y yo estaremos en Colombia antes de que te vuelvas. Esa es una promesa," said Maria, trying to control the decibel level.

"Look, it's – it's just a big misunderstanding. He needs my help to sort it out. Don't be packing cases or anything. Please, love."

The little fella had polished off his lunch, and was looking up at his mother and father, sensing the tension. But he was processing the information as a five year-old.

"¿Piensas que bromeo? ¿Piensas que no estoy seria? Me has mentido. Quédate aquí, con tu familia, o tu familia estará en Colombia, y no será tu familia. No pienses que yo bromea, Chico. Hagas una decisión. ¿Quién es tu familia: Chico y yo, o ese hombre?"

"Of course you're my family. He's a friend. Just needs my help. Please, love. I'll probably be back tonight, OK?"

"If you go anywhere with that man, the trouble he's in, we are over."

That Maria said the final sentence in English further burned it into Gerry O'Donnell's head that the day that had started so wonderfully was now a category five disaster in his life, and he had no idea what to do next.

Jack and Stan were sitting in the back of the van, looking out on the tranquillity that was Gortahork, and Stan said.

"Gaffer, we should go. We should go now."

"No, not yet. We stay here."

"Why we wait?"

"Because we're waiting for Gerry."

"He going with us?"

"He told us to wait here, so we'll wait," said Jack, not wanting to be part of a debate.

Stan stayed silent. Jack was looking at the other end of the car park at a fine establishment called Teach Maggie Dan's. He thought it highly incongruous that somewhere like Gortahork would have a pizza parlour, but then again, why shouldn't they? He felt bad about disrupting Gerry's clearly tranquil way of life, but he really didn't have anyone else to turn to. He was aware of a flash of colour to his right, and turned and looked through the open back door of the van and saw Gerry break into a jog across the road.

"Right lads, out." It wasn't an offer. It was an order. Stan got out immediately, and Jack eased himself out. He was easily the least agile of the trio. The side door of the van opened and there was Gerry, and he climbed in. Jack was sitting on the chair and Stan was on the floor. Gerry sat down and said, "OK, we got to get going."

"We?" asked Jack.

"Yeah, we," sighed Gerry with a smile.

"OK, big fella, you get in the front passenger seat. I'm driving," ordered Gerry. He looked at Jack and said, "You stay in the back here. Your face is all over the fucking telly. Famous, y'are."

"Ah Jaysus," said Jack, trying to take on board the gravity of the situation.

"We've got some supplies to take on at Letterkenny. We can have a yarn then. Right, OK, let's go," said Gerry, as he followed Stan out of the side door.

The door slammed shut and Jack felt like he was in prison again in the back of that van. No windows, with only Gerry's outdoor gear for company. He couldn't even speak to them in the front of the van. He felt a vibration and heard the noise of the engine starting, and they were moving. He suppressed the stupid thought that he hoped he wouldn't be carsick in the back of the van. That was the least of his troubles. In the back of the van, Jack only had his own company to keep him occupied. However, he had become accustomed to solitude through all those years in prison.

If timing was everything in life, then the Gobshite was perfect at it. As he sat in the back of that van on his own, the Gobshite told him that, with the situation he was going through at the moment, no one would blame him if he tried to take a bit of medication: A couple of Jameson's would do him no harm. After all, said the Gobshite, he didn't even know when he would see his son again, or if he would see his son again. Jack made fists, two huge fists, and squeezed hard and looked at the plywood floor of the van in an effort to make the Gobshite fuck off.

Jack had no idea where he was, and how could he? There were no windows. But he knew that the vehicle was shifting. He could hear the engine whine and whirr as Gerry moved through the gearbox. The journey gave him time to think about the whole situation he was in. Before the Luas craic on the day of the court case, his life had been a manageable mess. Hardly ideal, but if he could keep in touch with the wee fella, he could envisage some point in the future when he'd be able to say to his mum – not as a toddler, but as a kid growing up – that he wanted to see his father. Then it would be two against one. But now?

The whole thing was a mess. Then he thought that if there was any way out of this, then the man driving the van would find it. Out of nowhere, a tsunami of fatigue washed over Jack, and his big head started to slump down as the van continued to move. He closed his eyes and it was all gone. When the door slid back open with a mighty thump, his head jerked back. They were stationary, and standing in front of him was Gerry, with Stan just behind. It was only then he realised he'd been asleep.

"Welcome to the thriving cultural centre of Letterkenny, sir," said Gerry with a smile.

"Where?"

"Also known as the Tesco car park. About as cultural as this place gets," laughed Gerry. He stepped aside and put his arm out around

Stan's back to usher him into the back of the van. The big Pole skipped in and sat down on the floor next to Jack with his legs crossed. Gerry leaned in, the doors half closed now.

"You two wait here. Keep out of sight. I've got to get some supplies and I'll be back, OK?"

"What's the plan, wee fella?" asked a groggy Jack.

"There's a plan forming, son. There's a plan forming. That's why I need some supplies. Now wait here and don't talk to any strange men, OK?" laughed Gerry as he slammed the door shut.

Stan looked up at Jack.

"What we do now, gaffer?" asked the big Pole.

"To be honest son, I've no fucking idea. But the man who was driving the van's got a plan. I'm pretty sure of that."

"You, him: Good friends long time, yes?"

"Yeah, you could say that. Long time. And the pair of us were a lot younger," said Jack, thinking back to the days when the two of them had shared a deadly serious purpose.

The side door swung open as abruptly as it had when it had woken Jack from his leaden sleep. It was Gerry. He stooped his head and stepped into the van.

"Move over, big fella. Make room," said Gerry with a smile. He had a small black rucksack over one shoulder, and he was carrying Stan's leather jacket in the other one. He handed the garment over to Stan, closed the door behind him and sat down on the plywood floor.

"Your mobile phones are in there, aren't they?"

"Yes, yes," said Stan.

"Give me them. Give me them out."

"What's the plan here, wee fella?" asked Jack, not sure what was going on.

"Give me a sec, big fella," said Gerry. It was an order for Jack to shut up as the O'Donnell brain was working on a problem.

"When was the last time you switched these phones on, the pair of ye?"

"Would have been here, when we stopped for a cuppa. Before we headed out over the fucking wild mountains to see you."

"OK."

"Why, what's the problem?"

"Well, that was the last time you'd have been on the grid, so no harm done there," said Gerry, almost absent-mindedly.

Stan reached into the pocket of his leather jacket to take out his iPhone, and Gerry snapped, "Leave that, big fella. Not now."

Stan knew an order when he heard one. He pulled his hand back and nodded. Gerry opened the backpack and out came three identical boxes. Jack looked at him, clearly puzzled. Gerry, as he was opening one of the boxes, looked up at Jack and said with a smile, "No comms, no op!"

"We'll each have one of these phones. This is how we'll communicate. No voice, text only. Got that?" said Gerry, getting eye contact firstly with Jack, then Stan He wanted a nod of acquiescence from each of them.

"Got that, guys, OK? The guards are all over this looking for you, and probably you as well," he said, looking first to Jack and then to Stan.

"Which means they'll be able to voice print you. Text from these clean phones. They're not gonna pick that up, OK? We got that?"

Both Jack and Stan nodded to the man who was clearly in charge. Gerry unpacked the three phones and switched them on. They were white clamshell Doro 6520s, newly purchased from the Carphone Warehouse. The girl who had served him was delighted with the business.

"I told her I had three buddies coming from the States today, and their cell-phones don't work here, and I just wanted something cheap, not smartphones, for them to keep in touch while they're here. I doubt she'll remember me. I doubt she'll remember the transaction after today. Sorted," said Gerry, as much to himself as the other two occupants of the van. As he was saying this, both thumbs were working frantically, first on one phone, then another. He picked up the first phone again; then went to the third phone. He then closed both of the phones, handing one to Jack and one to Stan.

"This is Phone One," he said, waving his phone in his right hand.

"You have Phone Two, and you have Phone Three," he said, pointing first to Jack, then to Stan.

"Each phone has the other two phone numbers down in the contacts as Phone Two, Three, or One. You got me, no names?" said

Gerry, looking for the pair of them to nod that they understood. They both nodded.

"Thank fuck for that."

"Now. We have to trash your two phones."

As soon as he said this, Stan bridled, alarm and aggression going through his weight-trained body. He sat up from the slouch.

"No, no. My phone stay. Have pictures of sister in phone, no," said Stan, ready to fight about this one.

"Look, big fella. I'm sorry about your sister, but this is serious. They can track you with these phones. These phones have to go. We have to kill them now," explained Gerry.

Perhaps the use of the word "kill" made it even worse for Stan, but he was ready to fight on this one, and Jack looked on, not knowing how this was going to play out.

"Stan, this man knows what he's doing. We need to listen to him," he interjected.

"No, gaffer. Pictures of Agniesta."

"Non-negotiable, big guy," said Gerry, trying to communicate some understanding of the emotion Stan must be feeling.

"Only pictures in phone. Phone of – Pictures of my sister," tried to explain Stan, then trying to establish whether he had to fight, whether he had to hit this man.

Then Gerry had a brainwave and got annoyed with himself.

"I'm not fucking thinking straight."

"What do you mean, wee fella?" asked Jack, surprised that Gerry wouldn't have everything thought out in advance.

"Here, give me this phone. I can fix it for you," he said, looking at Stan and putting his hand out.

Stan tentatively handed over the phone, not completely sure what was happening. As he did that, Gerry reached into his backpack and pulled out a laptop. He opened it up and pressed a button.

He then rummaged for a cable and slid the USB connector into the side of the laptop. He handed the iPhone back to Stan and said, "Switch it on, big fella."

The Polish ex-para-trooper complied with the order, and handed back a switched-on iPhone that could now be tracked by GCHQ in the UK, and the NSA in Fort Meade, Maryland. As it blinked to life, Gerry put his left index finger across the centre of his mouth in the international symbol for "No one make any noise at all, please, thank you."

Gerry looked at the screen of the laptop and nodded his approval as the machine went to work. Stan tried to move round to get a proper look, but there was no room in the van and Gerry had the laptop balanced between his knees as he sat cross-legged. Gerry lifted his right hand slightly to communicate to Stan that everything was in order.

Stan looked up at Jack, who nodded that Stan should heed his old comrade, who clearly knew what he was doing. It didn't take long for the CPU on the laptop to hoover out all of the data from the iPhone. When it was finished, Gerry hit the touchpad, and the laptop told him it was safe to disconnect the external device. He did this and quickly switched off the iPhone. He rummaged in the front pouch of his rucksack and slid a 128GB pen drive into one of the USB slots; then he turned the laptop round so that Stan could see. He hit the keypad and a folder opened. It contained all of Stan's photos, including some selfies of him and his sister.

Stan smiled and said, "Thank you."

"No problem, big fella. Give me a second," said Gerry in a business-like fashion. He turned the laptop back round to face him, and started the process of transferring that data onto the pen drive, with the intention of handing it to Stan.

"I've even saved all your contacts. I mean, how good is that?" said Gerry. Stan was nodding his appreciation when a lightbulb went off in Gerry's head.

"Stan, your sister, is her number saved to your contacts? Would her number be in here?"

"Yes, yes. Of course. Her name is Agniesta."

Gerry stopped the data transfer, went into Stan's contacts, and found what he thought was the sister's phone number. He turned the laptop round.

"Is that her number?"

"Yes, yes," said Stan, puzzled.

"Leave this to your Uncle Gerry, son," said Gerry, with real purpose.

He switched on the Wi-Fi capability of the laptop and scanned what was available.

"Ah," he said, "Here's the secure Tesco staff Wi-Fi. Ah, well, every little helps."

"What the fuck's happening?" asked Jack.

"Would you give a man a minute, would ya?"

And then another light bulb moment. Gerry had totally forgotten that when he'd been in for phones, he'd nipped into Tesco as well.

"You lads must be famished." It was an assertion, not a question.

"Yes, yes. Hungry," said Stan.

Gerry reached into the backpack and produced a chicken Caesar wrap for each of them. He handed one to Stan beside him, and threw the other, arching through the air for Jack to catch.

"Here, it'll keep belly from backbone. Let me get back to work," said Gerry with a smile.

Stan broke open the Perspex case that held the food and literally rammed it into his face, munching like a man who hadn't eaten in days. He looked up and smiled as he was stuffing the second half of the wrap into his mouth. Gerry was slightly taken aback.

"He's close to nature, isn't he?" said Gerry, grinning.

Jack broke into a silent giggle as he was eating and tried not to choke himself. Even in situations like this, O'Donnell's humour was never far from the surface.

"Password protected? Ooh, aren't you clever fuckers?" sneered Gerry. His fingers played a concerto on the keyboard as he called up a piece of decryption software and bingo, he was in. Sitting in a van in the car park, several hundred yards from their office, he was picking up the signal from their router. He was in. The laptop was now live and connected to the worldwide web. He looked again at the contact and typed in the number very precisely. He looked up and asked Stan, "What kind of phone did your sister have, son?"

"Mobile phone," said Stan, still munching.

"An iPhone or an Android?" asked Gerry, slightly exasperated.

"Not iPhone. Other phone."

"You mean like a Samsung or something like that?"

"I think so," said Stan rather unhelpfully, finally finishing the chicken Caesar wrap.

"OK, we'll try Google Photos then, if she was on Planet Android," said Gerry, pretty much to himself. His fingers once more danced around the keyboard. He waited for something to happen and then his eyes lit up. He looked up over the top of the laptop screen, locked eyes with Stan, and said, "I think I've got something for you, big fella."

And he turned round the laptop. Stan's eyes opened wide, and then produced an emotional response that Gerry hadn't fully factored in, as the big Polish ex-para-trooper started to quietly sob. Gerry O'Donnell had accessed Agniesta's photographs from the cloud, and the last one that had been taken was of her happy, smiling face, with two of her barista colleagues squeezed in behind her. It was a work selfie, and as the shutter did its job, she only had maybe a few minutes to live. Gerry reached out his right hand, put it on the young man's left deltoid and gave him a squeeze.

"Let it out, big fella. Let it out," said Gerry gently.

Jack sat silently looking at the situation, and was envious that Stan could show that emotion in front of men, because Jack always tried to supress those impulses himself. Stan looked up, tears making his vision blurred, and said to Gerry, "Dziękuję, dziękuję."

"Dobrze," said Gerry, smiling.

Watching Gerry fiddle with his phone gave Jack an idea.

"I have to call Dicey," said Jack to Gerry.

"Who?"

"The girl that runs my office."

"No chance. Fucking suicide."

"She'll be wondering what's happened to me."

"No way, big fella. 'Til we get this sorted, you go dark. They're saying you offed an old copper. So anybody you've been in contact with, anyone, they're gonna be all over. You get that?"

Jack looked down and nodded. It was just starting to hit him, the extent of the mess that he was in.

Gerry closed the laptop, put it back into his rucksack, looked up and said, "Right lads, we've got a long drive. Stan, you can sit in the front with me. Your Majesty, you're in the throne back here."

"Where are we going?" asked Jack, genuinely bemused.

"The scene of the crime, big fella. The scene of the crime. We're going to the Big Smoke. Your home town."

"Three hours should do it."

"Not the way we're going."

"I'm gonna avoid the North. Just a feeling. Given that the Free Staters are saying you're a Dissident Republican."

"Yeah."

"So, next stop Sligo, and then we'll head through Leitrim into Monaghan, Cavan, Monaghan. The long way round."

"Jaysus."

"Yeah, long drive. We will stop on the way and grab something to eat. But you stay in the van, OK?" said Gerry, looking at Jack.

Jack nodded in acknowledgement.

"Oh, and we need to stop by an old buddy of mine in Cavan."

"What for?"

"Well, let's just say that my old mate never did take up General John de Chastelain on his generous decommissioning offer."

"Gear? Ah you're a crafty bollix, O'Donnell!"

"I'll have you know that I resent that remark, Mr Dempsey," said Gerry in a fake D4 accent.

Jack paused before saying:

"Look wee fella. I would be in some fix without your help."

"You're still in a fix and anyway, I swore an oath. Enemies foreign and domestic," said Gerry with a smile.

"Fuckin' right."

"OK, let's get going." With that, Gerry reached behind him, pulled back the sliding door of the van and stepped back out into the open.

The van door slid open again. This time Jack was awake. Gerry was stepping into the van, followed by Stan.

"Where the fuck are we?"

"Where no one in their right mind would be looking for us."

"Where?"

"Well, if you must know, we're in the car park of a theatre in Carrick-on-Shannon."

"WHAT?"

"I told you we're taking a long road round. I know this place, and I'm sure they won't mind me leeching into their Wi-Fi. I have some work to do," said Gerry, getting the laptop out of his backpack and positioning it on his lap, sat in a sort of a lotus position, just as he had been in Letterkenny.

"Would you mind telling me what the fuck's going on?" snarled Jack.

"No," smiled Gerry; looking up.

"Ah, for fuck's sake wee fella."

"Need to know rule, you big ignorant gobshite. Look, O'Donnell's got this, OK?"

"Yeah, yeah, yeah, OK. Fuck's sake, I'll just sit in this chair then," said Jack, surrendering.

"You clever man," said Stan towards Gerry.

"It's been said before, sunshine. It's been said before," smiled Gerry, clearly relishing what he was about to do.

"OK, that's done," said Gerry, with some satisfaction.

"What's done?" asked an exasperated Jack.

"Never mind," said Gerry, closing the laptop, looking up and smiling. He rummaged in his rucksack and brought out a reporter's notebook and a pen. He flipped open the notebook and placed in on the laptop, using it as a desk. He looked up at Jack.

"OK. You and O'Shea. Tell me everything. Don't leave anything out."

"But I told you everything the last time I was in Letterkenny."

"Tell me all that again, and tell me everything that happened after that. Everything. Until I saw you in Gortahork. Tell me everything. Don't leave out a single fucking detail. Got that?"

"Yeah, yeah, grand. Fuck's sake, wee man."

Gerry looked at Stan and said, "Big fella, end of this street. Not the way the van's pointing. There's a Centra. About two hundred yards. Go and get some rations."

"OK, no problem," said Stan, happy to have something to do. As the big Pole reached behind and opened the van's sliding door, Gerry had another thought. He put his hand on his arm and said "Wait." It was an order. Gerry reached into his backpack and came out with a plain black baseball cap made by Beechwood.

He offered it to Stan and said, "Here. Here, big fella. Put this on your head. Don't take it off. Just in case there's CCTV in the Centra. To be sure, to be sure. And don't look up. The Free Staters have invested in facial recognition software recently and it might be live now."

"No problem."

"Now, there's a good soldier," smiled Gerry. And then he looked up at Jack. Across the big Dubliner's face was a relief that he wasn't in charge of this, and for the first time since all this had started the morning of the court case, he didn't feel totally alone.

Gerry listened intently, occasionally looking up at Jack, and scribbling furiously in the notebook.

Jack looked down and said, "What the fuck is that? Some sort of strange fucking language?"

"It's T-Line. I prefer it to Pittman. Now keep fucking talking."

Jack told the whole story, even the bits that Gerry already knew, and then he stopped.

"So he gave you an address in Phibsborough?"

"Yeah, just up from Parnell Square."

"Anything else?"

"That the Branch had been all over it. They reckoned that it was full of likely lads and then the word from the top was that they had to back off. Their guys were raging about it. They were sure that these were the right guys."

"And nothing else?"

"No," said Jack, annoyed.

"OK, OK," said Gerry, absent-mindedly, his brain already working on a plan.

"What happens now?"

"Time for a puppet show," smiled Gerry, opening the laptop again.

"What?" replied a mystified Jack.

"Sock puppets. Very handy things," said Gerry, as he looked down at the laptop, typing away furiously.

"I have no fucking idea what you're on about and this is serious."

"Of course it's serious. That's why we need the puppets," said Gerry, without looking up.

"Please, wee fella," pleaded Jack.

"Not now," said Gerry, annoyed. His fingers on the keyboard if anything sped up as he glanced from the keyboard to the notebook and back again, making sure he was getting all the details correct.

The van door swung open and in came Stan, still wearing the black baseball cap, and carrying a Centra bag. He squeezed in and sat on the floor next to Jack, who was on the chair. Gerry gestured to the door without saying anything, and Stan pulled it shut and then rummaged in the carrier bag. He passed a sandwich in a plastic container and a bottle of Lucozade to Jack.

"Cheers youngster."

"You want something, Gerry?" asked Stan Gerry just shook his head. He was too busy.

"There, there that's it off and running," said Gerry. He closed the laptop and looked up.

"Now can you tell me what the fuck's going on?" asked Jack like an exasperated spouse.

"Well, here's the deal," said Gerry, pausing to make sure Jack was paying attention.

"Yeah?"

"OK, O'Shea's hale and hearty when you leave him, yeah?"

"Sure he was, sure didn't I tell y…"

"Don't fucking interrupt, OK? Just nod." Jack nodded.

"So O'Shea's OK when you leave him. Hale and hearty. By the time you get to Gortahork he's dead and you're all over RTE as the prime fucking suspect."

Jack acknowledged with a nod.

"Based on everything else you've told me, this stinks like fuck. Obviously you didn't off him. The poor old Free State cunt."

"Ah, for fuck's sake," said Jack, not wanting to start that one again with his old comrade.

"Yeah, yeah, yeah. Fine. So you've been set up for this. So I can't see the Guards not being involved. He told you he'd been threatened by two Branch men after you'd been to see him the first time, yeah?"

Jack again nodded.

"So it's important to get your side of the story out there. That'll send them running in a panic. And that's what I was doing," said Gerry with a flourish.

"Yeah?"

"Everything you've told me is with a buddy of mine. He and I are part of a White Hat crew. Been working for the last couple of years."

"What the fuck's that?"

"You've heard of hacking, haven't you?"

"What, computers and stuff?"

"Top of the fucking class."

"Yeah, OK, OK."

"When it comes to the old internet, these boys are the 'Ra, OK. You got that?"

"I think so," said Jack, unconvinced.

"By the time we get to Dublin it'll be all over the internet that you've been set up. That's gonna put some powerful people under powerful pressure. And then we'll see where they run and what they do. I'm working on the theory that you don't know the full picture. But on the basis of what you do know, you've certainly been set up. Now, you might have been the last person to see O'Shea before whoever done him done him. You were in his house, so your dabs and DNA are all over that place. And with your baggage, and some creative journalism, you're the big, bad disser that killed the poor old policeman," said Gerry, by way of explaining it both to himself and to Jack.

"But as long as you're not in custody and my crew can work away, we can put out an alternative narrative. For the moment."

"And?"

"And then we're in a good place to clear your name."

"I don't give a fuck about that! All that stuff in a computer about me! What about these fuckers that are about to do something? There's more of them. That's what I'm bothered about! They nearly killed my kid!" snapped Jack.

"I can't think that those two things aren't connected."

"What do you mean?"

"You were speaking to O'Shea about these boyos, and O'Shea said to you he reckoned someone in his old job was protecting them, yeah?"

"Yeah, yeah."

"Well, if some terrible calamity had to befall these Jihad boys, I think it might flush out the people who done O'Shea and fitted you up, yeah?"

"So you'll help me?"

"What the fuck do you think this is, therapy?"

"Some man, you."

"Now eat your sandwich."

"We get these men?" asked Stan, looking at Gerry.

"Oh this like taking kids to the beach. No, we're not there yet and yes we're having a good time," laughed Gerry.

"What?"

"We're going to the fun park in Cavan to get some bang bangs first."

Jack started to convulse in quiet mirth at O'Donnell's ability to find humour in the direst of circumstances. That man in the New Lodge Road had been dead on about the skinny kid from Glasgow all those years ago. He was a real find. Then Gerry's faced turned grimly serious.

"Cavan for gear then that gaff in Phibsborough. Hit them tonight. No fucking about. A breathing prisoner would be useful, but we'll talk it through in Cavan," said Gerry. It was an order, not an item for discussion.

Jack nodded and Stan said, "dobzah."

Doctor Karim Bessaoud was reading on his Kindle when there was an abrupt knock on the door. He hoped that it was Claire. She had thrown the keys at him, told it was over and hadn't returned his calls. That was two days ago and he had told her that his door was always open to her. So it was with some hope that he opened the door and he was thrown to see a red-haired man in a boiler suit looking at him. What was even more surprising to him was that this man was speaking Arabic to him.

"Salamm alakham," said Gerry O' Donnell.

"Walakam a salaam," replied Karim automatically.

"Mr Dempsey. You operated on his child who was hurt in the bomb. He's hurt. He needs help. Now."

Gerry ascertained that he would remember a man whose child he had operated on after the Luas bombings.

Karim thought later that he probably should not have agreed to let the man into his home, but he was surprised and his medical impulse to help an injured person overridden his concerns about legality. Gerry took a couple of steps down onto the road level and gestured with a 'come hither' motion of his right arm. In no time at all Karim was looking at two other men in identical boiler suits.

One of them he recognised as Mr Dempsey. The other man, much younger than the other two, was holding him up and Karim saw that the man he knew from Beaumont ICU was bleeding onto the hardwood floor in the hall. The medical training kicked in. It was automatic.

"Bring him in here," said Karim, gesturing toward the kitchen.

There was a central unit that the Moroccan really liked. It was a work top with a small sink to one side. There were drawers all around it. However, it made for a decent ad hoc operating table and the kitchen table itself would almost certainly have collapsed under the man's weight.

"Place him face down please," said Karim and the other two men grunted as they lifted Jack onto the worktop.

"Hello Mr Dempsey. You are injured," said the Doctor, stating the stunningly obvious.

"Oh fuck..." was all that Jack could manage. He obviously in a huge amount of pain.

"What happened to him?" asked Karim.

"Work accident" said Gerry.

"Why not take him to the hospital?"

"It's complicated."

Karim opened a drawer and brought out a large pair of scissors, usually used for opening food packaging. He worked through the dark blue fabric on Jack's left leg to expose the area from mid hamstring to lower back. He was wearing boxer shorts that were now a deep shade of red. It was clear to the medic that this man had a wound in his left buttock.

He looked up at Gerry and said, "This is a gunshot wound."

"Fucking tell me about it!" shouted Jack.

"Sorry, Mister Dempsee."

All Jack could muster in reply was a low groan.

"Please. Let me help you," said Karim and he left the kitchen without saying where he was going.

Gerry leaned over and said, "I'll never be able to look at one of these Sunday Supplements about lavish kitchens without thinking about your big arse."

"FUCK YOU!"

"I've always wanted to see you naked."

"I'm in fucking agony here you cunt!"

"Well it wasn't me. It was fucking Action Man here."

Stan looked at the floor.

Karim came back into the kitchen with a medium sized green back pack. He placed it on the work top next to Jack and rapidly opened several of the compartments. The sound of zips being worked and Velcro being ripped apart was the sound of a professional about to get down to work.

Gerry leaned over to Jack and said. "You're doing great honey. One more push. I hope it's a boy."

"Fuck off, you!" snarled Jack.

Gerry smiled and looked over at Stan who was looking very sheepish.

"If I said you had a nice body would you shoot ME in the ass?"

The big Pole didn't know where to look. Karim had a hypodermic syringe in his gloved hands.

"This is a local anaesthetic Mr Dempsee."

"Will it hurt, Doctor?" asked Gerry.

"A little."

"You hear that honey?" said Gerry in a camp voice.

This rather unsettled the Moroccan.

"You are homosexual?" he asked, finally.

"Well that's an intriguing offer, especially as my wife has just left me. What you thinking? Dinner? Something more causal?"

"You fuck off," snarled Jack.

"Jealousy is a terrible thing."

Stan looked up and stifled a smile. Karim decided to tune out this stuff that he neither understood nor wanted to understand and injected the needle into several points around Jack's buttock.

"This will take effect in a small time."

Gerry decided that the time for joking was over and looked up Stan. He made sure he had eye contact.

"Go and make sure that everything is OK in the van, OK? Stay with the equipment. We don't want it getting stolen. Yeah?"

The big Pole nodded and left without a word.

Karim was preparing some medical equipment on the worktop,

ripping open sealed packages and laying them out in a line. It always fascinated Gerry to look at a skilled professional going quietly and methodically about their work.

He leaned over to Jack and said, "You're going to be fine. This man will sort you out."

"Ah…" was all that Jack could manage. It was a mixture of pain, anger and embarrassment. He was in no mood for any of this shite from Gerry. He lay on the cold black marble worktop, feeling a pressure on his arse when he realised that it had stopped hurting.

"Please be still Mr Dempsee."

Gerry looked on as the medic worked at stitching up the wound. It hadn't taken his long to do whatever it was he had done. This guy was good, thought Gerry.

"You were lucky Mr Dempsee. It was a fortunate wound," said Karim.

"That means you have a massive big fat arse that could stop a fucking anti-tank round."

"Cunt," snarled Jack.

"You are Mister Dempsee's friend?"

"We're going steady."

"Your accent. It is different."

"Glasgow. I was born in Glasgow."

"Ah. You are Scottish!" exclaimed Karim as he looked up from Jack's bloodied rump.

"Not really."

"I do not understand."

"It's a long story. I live in Donegal. That's where my people are from."

"I hear it is a lovely place, Donegal."

Gerry smiled at the Arab's pronunciation of his county. The Glaswegian's attention was drawn to the writing on the side of the green medical backpack on the work top. It read "Property of Dr Karim Bessaoud."

"Bessaoud? That's a Berber name, isn't it?" asked Gerry.

"YES!"

"Excuse me if I'm interrupting," said Jack.

"Please Mr Dempsee. Be still."

"Yeah. Be still you," said Gerry, smiling at the situation.

It could have turned out a whole lot worse. He had been reared a glass quarter full guy and anyway, it wasn't his arse that needed the surgical intervention.

"My cousin is in Glasgow. He is a cardiologist at the Royal Infirmary. He is very happy there," said Karim.

"You should visit him and go to see the Celtic," quipped Gerry.

"Ah yes. The football. My cousin does not like sport. We are alike in that way," said Karim as he was finishing off the stitches in Jack's left buttock.

"If you were at Celtic Park on a European night you wouldn't say that again," said Gerry with cool affirmation.

"The place is unique. Celtic is the club of the Irish community in Scotland, but open to all."

Jack harrumphed that he was being ignored.

"Almost finished, Mr Dempsee. The wound is not serious. You were lucky."

"There are Irish people in Scotland?"

"You're talking to one of them."

"Ah, I think I understand."

"If you go to Celtic Park you'll understand. Take your cousin. A cardiologist would be useful there, especially on a European night. You heart can be in your mouth at times."

"Ah, you are making a medical and a football joke."

"Oh, and the supporters call the stadium 'Paradise'."

"I must speak to my cousin about this."

"Am I right there?" asked Jack.

"Almost, Mister Dempsee."

The Moroccan looked across at Gerry and the expression on his face was serious.

"I have to report this matter to the police. A gunshot wound."

"That's a real problem, brother."

The medic was waiting for something more to go on and O'Donnell continued.

"There's a situation here at the moment and, well the police, some of them at least, are part of the problem."

"I do not understand," said Karim. His tone of voice hinted that he had made his mind up to keep himself right on this.

"Can I ask YOU a question doctor?"

"Of course," said Karim, putting the used swabs and syringe into their original wrappings for safe disposal.

"Are there ever any problems in your own country with the police not doing their duty properly?"

Karim blurted out a laugh.

"Of course! It is part of life there."

It was time to make a pitch for this man's trust, thought Gerry. It was now or never. He looked straight into the Moroccan's eyes and said: "Well, I am asking you to trust us on this. We're in the same situation here. This kindness will not come back and hurt you. Mr Dempsey and I swore an oath a long time ago to behave in a certain way. We are not criminals."

"Yes, but…"

"You will read of an event in the media tomorrow," said Gerry, "The men who have been attacking Dublin. We were trying to stop them. We cannot trust the police with this. I cannot tell you anymore."

That was the lot, thought the Glaswegian. If he doesn't buy this we're fucked. Then again, we were probably banjaxed before we started. Karim was silent for a moment and then reached into his green medic back pack.

"These are for pain for Mr Dempsee. They are prescription drugs. Controlled and powerful. But I will not write anything down. I think that is better," said Karim.

Gerry nodded, took the drugs and said, "Shukran jazeeeklan saidi."

"Your Arabic pronunciation is very good."

Gerry leaned over to Jack and said: "I think you're all done here honey. Was the waxing painful? The things you do for me."

"You fuck off!" snarled Jack.

Karim looked on bemused at this interaction.

"We are family," smiled Gerry.

"One thing I must say," said Karim, looking at the Glaswegian. "Yes?"

"One thing you must understand. The men doing these things."

"Yes?" Gerry sensed something of importance was coming.

"They are not true Muslims. They shame the Prophet Mohammed," said the Moroccan with sadness and anger.

"Peace be upon him," interjected Gerry when the Prophet was mentioned.

"Yes. Peace be upon him."

"Mister Dempsee you must rest or these stitches could come out," said Karim, directing his medical advice to Jack who was still laid out on his stomach.

"I will be a good nurse to him."

"Jaysus I'm fucked then," snarled Jack and Gerry laughed instinctively.

Aleksander Mikhail Vasiliev was immediately awakened when his cell phone vibrated on the bedside unit next to him. Only the American had the number. The text message was simple. It was a previously agreed series of numerals. It was the signal to go to the safe house immediately. This meant that something was wrong and needed urgent attention. It was just after two in the morning.

Gerry had the directions from Jack and was in the front of the van by himself. He smiled to himself as he came down Cromwellsfort Road. The history of this island was never far away from you, thought Gerry O'Donnell. He pulled into the industrial units at Walkinstown off Greenhills Road and then he saw a man in his sixties standing by a taxi.

"Where's Jack?" asked Tommy Noonan.

"He's in the back."

"What's he doing in there?" asked Tommy, becoming uneasy.

Gerry jumped out of the cab and moved around to the sliding door. He knocked on the door before opening it. He didn't want the taxi driver to see what was inside the van alongside Jack.

"Out ye come Jack," said Gerry as he opened the van and the big Dubliner eased out of the vehicle, clearly in pain.

Gerry slipped behind him, shot Stan a look and slid the door shut again.

"Jaysus big fella. You're hurt," exclaimed Tommy Noonan.

"Ah it's just me arse Tommy boy."

"Anything I can do?"

"You're doing it now buddy."

"Anything at all big fella. Just say the word. I nearly keeled over when I saw you on the news."

Tommy Noonan clearly wanted the scéal, thought Gerry, and this wasn't the day for standing out in the open air discussing the price of eggs.

"Can we get inside here?"

"Ah. Surely," said Noonan as he fumbled for keys in the pocket of a zipper jacket.

The interior was perfect for what they needed. However, the Glaswegian needed to know more about the place.

"Who else has keys here?"

"No one," said Tommy Noonan firmly.

"You sure?"

"Hundred per cent," said Noonan, getting annoyed.

Tommy had a side-line business in doing up cars and selling them on. It wasn't doing well enough to have anyone working with him and it was more of a hobby. However, he had got a good deal on the unit that he was renting. There was room for two cars, a pit for working underneath a car and a small office with a battered two seater couch. Gerry had a quick look and saw that there was a toilet adjoining the office. The place would be perfect, thought the Glaswegian, if they had exclusive access to it.

"What about the neighbours?"

"Next door is vacant."

"There's two next doors."

"That's a metal polishing outfit. They might be here in the morning. I don't know if they work Saturdays."

"What time?"

"During the week? About eight."

"Grand Job, Tommy boy," said Jack, interjecting.

"Anytime big fella. No loose head here," said the taxi driver.

"Sure I know that," said Jack.

"We need to be getting on here buddy. We'll get the keys to ya" said Jack.

"Grand so. I'll be off then," said Tommy rather deflated to have been given his marching orders.

Gerry looked around the garage. It wasn't exactly the Lubyanka, but it would do the job. For the next few hours they had the place to themselves. That would be more than enough time.

Jack was resting on the two seater couch in the small office and the Glaswegian and the big Pole carried in the two men one at a time. They were both trussed up with silver gaffer tape at the wrists and ankles. They were going nowhere. The tape also covered their mouths.

Gerry checked on Jack in the office.

"Those pills working for you?"

"I'm grand. You get to work in there and don't mind me."

Gerry nodded. The Glaswegian rummaged around the old desk and through the filing cabinet drawers.

"What you looking for?"

"I'll know when I find it."

"Tommy wouldn't have any gear or anything."

"Bingo!" said Gerry as he unearthed a bottle of whiskey from a filing cabinet drawer with a flourish.

Jack stared at the bottle and felt himself go weak. One sight of the booze and the Gobshite was immediately in his head. In fairness, he made a sensible case this time. His inner alcoholic said; "Look, you bollox. You're shot. You've just been operated on. Those pills aren't nearly enough. Taking a few shots wouldn't be boozing, it would be medicine."

Jack shot Gerry a pathetic look. Gerry realised immediately.

"I need this stuff. We can get hammered when this is over."

"You should go to meetings for cunts that drink tea," snarled Jack.

"I'll get you a cuppa shortly."

In the garage area Stan was babysitting the two Arabs. They were still taped to their chairs, and they had been stripped to their t-shirts and boxers.

"Stan, you OK to give me a hand with these two?"

"These ones friends of man killed my sister. We kill them now!"

"No yet Stan. Not yet."

"OK."

"Well he might not sleep through this floor show. Time to get to work."

The taller of the two Arabs stared in hatred at Gerry. The trapped man struggled against the gaffer tape that held his wrists to the wooden arms of the chair. The other smaller one looked broken. His eyes pleaded for mercy. The recruiter, thought Gerry, had made a mistake with this one. Gerry already had a plan and he was pretty sure it would work.

O'Donnell started to calmly and precisely speak to both of the men in slow halting Arabic. It had been a long time since Libya. He wanted to know where their unit was based and what they were planning. Gerry thought carefully before he used a specific word in Arabic. He wanted to make sure they knew what he wanted. He was, of course, asking them to give up their comrades.

The taller man tried ever harder to struggle out of the chair. His eyes were defiant. This one was going all the way. The other Arab's eyes pleaded for some rapprochement. Gerry was reaching into a small sports grip he had with him when he saw Stan out of the corner of his eye. The big Pole moved like lightening for his size. Wham! A big meaty Warsaw fist slammed into the head of the Arab.

Gerry moved in between the Pole and the restrained Arab. Stan brushed Gerry aside like he weighed nothing. Wham! Wham! Like working out on a bag Stan put lefts and rights into the head of the Arab. Gerry had no choice. A swift economical low hook from the side caught the big Pole in the testicles. Stan yelped in pain as Gerry brought his left elbow onto Stan's jaw in a roundhouse action. The left forearm whipped back and up and caught the Pole in the trachea.

The fight was over. Stan lay in a heap on the floor coughing and rasping. Gerry was very precise.

"Stan, don't do that again. I need these two cunts conscious. OK?"

Stan looked up in anger and humiliation, but Gerry was firm.

"No more!"

Stan looked down. It was acceptance.

"Now step back and let me work."

"They will tell nothing." Stan was trying to justify his actions, but in reality he was merely trying to hit back at the men who had killed his sister. He couldn't do much to the remaining bits of a suicide bomber, but these two were mates of the bastard that had taken her life.

"They will talk."

Gerry looked at the tall Arab's bruises. They were bad enough, but Stan was too consumed with rage to be accurate and, fortunately, he hadn't punched his weight. The Arab was conscious. He had to be for this to work.

Gerry went over to the toilet, grabbed a large handful of toilet paper and wetted it. He came back and mopped away the blood dripping out of the left eyebrow. Stan was incredulous, but said nothing. The Warsaw man was now leaning against the breezeblock wall and had no idea of what was about to take place. Gerry reached into the bag and retrieved a Glock and a small green book.

It was a copy of the Koran. They had found it on the taller one when they brought them to the garage. The Glaswegian calmly walked over to the bloodied Jihadi. He put the pistol in his waistband at the small of his back.

Jack hobbled out of the office, clearly in a lot of pain.

"You're wasting your time with those bastards, wee lad. Tommy should have a blow torch in here somewhere."

Gerry wasn't for debating his interrogation methods in front of his captives. He shot Stan a glance and gestured towards the office with a flick of his head. The Pole immediately understood and started walking towards Jack and Gerry followed. Time was against him, but the Glaswegian needed the cooperation of the other two. If this was going to work, it would need to be only Gerry and the two Jihadis in there and no one else. Stan was boiling with rage about his sister and big Jack's main currency was the kinetic energy he could deliver with those big fists.

Gerry had to explain himself, and if he wanted to break one of the men, he had to do it fast.

Stan lowered Jack onto the little couch, then sat down himself. The Glaswegian sat back on the small desk and faced them. He glanced down at his diver's watch and fixed the bezel for 45 minutes. If he couldn't manage it in that time it wasn't going to fly.

"So what're we gonna do with those two cunts in there?" snapped Jack, looking up at Gerry.

"We're not gonna do anything. But I'm gonna talk to them. Nicely," smiled Gerry.

"Fuck off!"

"Gaffer is right. We hurt them."

Gerry paused for a second, looked down at the big ex-paratrooper.

"The hurt has to be on the inside. Hurting them out here," said Gerry, tapping his face with the back of his fingers, "won't do any good. They can take any amount of that, because of this."

He raised a copy of the Koran.

"You think those fuckers'll spill because you speak nice to them?" said Jack.

Gerry took a second.

"Look, big fella. We need what they know, or what they might know. With our luck we probably offed the wrong two, and these two lovelies don't have a scrap of scéal between them."

"Ah, fuck it."

"But we have to try. They're our only chance."

"Well, let's go then!" said Jack, putting a hand on the sofa arm and trying to push himself into an upright position, clearly in pain.

"You just sit on your stitches there," said Gerry.

Jack looked up at him and the Glaswegian continued, "Sure, isn't this a job for God?"

"They're friends of bastard who killed my sister. I make them talk."

The Pole made to rise up out of the sofa.

Gerry eased off the desk that he had been leaning on and put a hand out like a traffic policeman in the Pole's direction.

Stan stopped and Gerry shoved forward with the Koran held in his left hand.

"This here means that physical pain doesn't mean a fucking thing to those boys."

"Bollocks!"

"Big fella, remember that romantic weekend we spent in Moyvane all those years ago? Ah, those were the days. I was single and you had hair. It was the first time we were with the gear. Remember that?"

"I do, but…"

"I remember it well. Old Jimmy Brennan was the teacher. Remember we were all messing and you jumped on me, you big bollocks? Remember that?"

"Yeah, so?"

"The size of you as well, and me barely ten stone. Remember what happened?"

"Fuckin' all our yesteryears," snapped Jack.

"Wanted to remind you. You hit the ground in that byre with a thump," laughed Gerry.

"OK, OK."

"Size of you and me as well. No contest, big lad, but…"

"Fair play. You're handy enough at that Kung Fu shite."

"Judo," explained Gerry.

"What the fuck's that got to do with those cunts in there?"

"Quite a lot, actually."

"Those two bastards in there are laughing at us, and you fancy a bit of reminiscing?"

"Thing is, big fella, I used your weight and force against you. Classic Judo. Look, this is their armour. It protects them against everything. What they believe is in there gives them the courage. Yeah, the courage, to do what they do."

"Fuck that. I'll make the fuckers beg for mercy. Look Stan, give me a hand."

Gerry took a step towards the two men so he was standing directly over them.

"Jack, these fuckers, these suicide bombers? Think they should get the death penalty?"

"What the fuck are you on about?"

"Exactly. Eg-fucking-xactly."

Gerry thought for a second.

"Big fella, you remember getting sworn in? I sure as hell do."

Jack was silent, looking at the floor.

Gerry continued.

"I was in a wee kitchen in a back-to-back on New Lodge Road. Upper Meadow Street. It was 1977. I was sitting at the Formica table. There were chips on the corners. Like everything else in the house that table had seen better days. Then the man I was waiting for came in the back door. Told me to stand up."

Jack looked up and he got eye contact.

"I held up my right hand and I said those words. After that, the wee green book meant everything to me," said Gerry softly.

"Mine was in one of the flats in the 'Mun," said Jack quietly.

"See what I mean?"

Jack looked at him. The expression on his face was demanding further clarification, but he was engaged.

"After you held your right hand up and swore an oath to defend the Republic, there wasn't anything the Brits or the Staters could throw at us. We knew we were right. I learned a few years ago that in the 1980's the Free State Branch went in to Maynooth University to talk to sociologists. They had a simple enough question. They wanted to know how they could beat us."

Jack was now totally focussed on what Gerry was saying.

"The answer the social scientists gave the Peelers was simple enough, and it was this: In order to destroy the IRA, you must destroy their belief system. If you take away someone's motivation it's actually better than stiffing them. The Brits thought they would break us in the Blocks. Instead they got Bobby Sands MP. You getting me? Now, inside this book is their belief system, and I have to get at least one of those fuckers in there to start to doubt it. You and Stan putting in heavy digs isn't gonna shift it."

"What you gonna do then, wee fella?"

"I have to convince at least one of them that they've broken the rules in here," said Gerry, gesturing with the Koran.

Jack was fascinated. He knew there was a brain under that red hair, and he couldn't even imagine the speed that it worked at.

Gerry continued.

"Those boyos and all their mates think they're doing God's work. It's my job to put a doubt in their heads that they're actually doing that."

"Go for it, wee lad."

"Grand. Now you two play nice on the couch. You can hold hands, but no tongue."

"Fuck off!"

"Beir bua!" said Gerry as he turned and walked out of the office.

After that speech, thought Gerry, this had better work. He walked into the garage. They were seated opposite each other, separated by about ten feet. With their mouths taped, they were trying to communicate by eye contact. As Gerry walked towards them, he was ransacking his memory for what his old comrade Mustafa in Libya had taught him about the belief system of the Jihadis, long before the world woke up on the morning of 9/11 to realise that these guys existed. Mustafa had been a high ranking officer in the Mukhabarat El-Jamahiriya, the Libyan national intelligence service under Gaddafi.

Throughout the 1980's, Gerry had been a guest of the Libyan government on several occasions, and had struck up a close working relationship and good friendship with Mustafa, who was a trusted Lieutenant of the legendary Toma Tohami Khaled, the main man in the security agency final years of the Gaddafi regime.

Gerry was immediately transported back to an office in the military base in Benghazi, to a discussion of anti-interrogation techniques that had led Mustafa to explain how he interrogated the religiously-driven enemies of the Libyan revolutionary state.

The two men in the chairs looked at this Infidel holding the Koran, leafing through the pages. Inside Gerry's head, Mustafa was speaking to him in that office in Benghazi.

"You see, Brother Gerry. There are many techniques. The interrogator must try to make the believer realise that he might not go to Jannah, to Paradise. He must try to make him realise that his behaviour has offended the Prophet, Peace be upon Him. This is an important point, Brother Gerry. This is the only way an interrogator can put fear into the hearts of these extremists. If they think they have broken their contract with the Prophet, they will be shaken to their core. It is the only thing that matters to them. Physical pain means nothing to them."

Mustafa had continued, "You must convince the extremists that they have broken their bond with Alllah. In the Koran it states that only Allah is the Judge. You see, Brother Gerry, scholars are not Judges. This is the point to develop during interrogation. You see, extremist scholars inflate their importance to the terrorist pupils.

They are almost divine in the eyes of these gullible young men. If a work is successful, then we will convince the extremist that he has been worshipping a scholar instead of the Prophet, Peace be upon Him. This is a grave sin. It is blasphemy to equate anyone with Allah. We impress upon the extremist that killing innocents in the name of the Prophet is a form of blasphemous worship and would surely block his path to Jannah, to Paradise."

Gerry remembered that Mustafa said that his interrogation team would read relevant holy passages to extremists when they were in a heightened state during interrogation.

Gerry ransacked his memory to try and remember any of the passages of the Koran that Mustafa might have mentioned. In all probability, the Atheist member of the Irish Republican Army and devout Marxist, hadn't been listening at that point. And then Mustafa started again in Gerry's head.

"You see, Brother Gerry, the greatest pain we can inflict upon the extremist comes not from without but from within. The purpose of our interrogation is to awaken that internal pain source. In a higher state of inner conflict, they are much more susceptible to changing their beliefs than most people would believe. They may not tell you everything that day, but that is when the seeds of doubt are sown."

Then Gerry's memory threw up an online conversation he'd had with a blogger in Bangladesh who had told him that the security police in Kurdistan read the Koran to captured Isis fighters to break them. This worked because most of them were ignorant an illiterate and had never read the Koran.

Gerry was standing studying the book. He hadn't moved for a full five minutes. He knew he had one shot at this, and he could only go for one of the men. At that point, however, he didn't know which one. Gerry was no Islamic scholar, but then neither were these two bozos. They key thing he had to get across was that they had been fooled by their scholar into behaving in a blasphemous way. If he could do that with one of them, then he might have a chance.

Hamzah Khan looked across at his brother, Omar Abdullah, trying to find some meaning in the facial expressions of the Arab.

The infidel was standing to Hamzah's left holding the holy book and quietly reading from it. He was directing his comments towards Omar.

Hamzah was amazed that the infidel could read the Koran, and that his Arabic sounded very good. It was clear that Omar was listening intently to what the infidel was preaching to him.

Inside the office, Jack and Stan sat on the small couch with the door open out into the main garage area. They both strained to try and discern some meaning from what Gerry was saying in Arabic. It was, of course, a futile effort, but they tried nonetheless. Stan spoke in a lowered tone.

"Gaffer, you think Gerry will get information this way?"

"The wee lad has some brain on him, Stan son. We let him do it his way, but I'm for burning these bastards."

Although he thought he had made a faltering start, Gerry was now confident that the passages he was quoting from the Koran were having some effect on the Arab, who was taped to the chair and gagged with silver duct tape. Occasionally he would look up from the pages of the holy book, and could see that the Arab was straining to speak or say something. For now, Gerry wanted him gagged so that he had literally no ability to reply. He quoted the passage from Surah al-Ma'ida 5:33-34 about why Hirabah was forbidden, and why to become an agent of Hirabah would prevent a Muslim's passage to Jannah. Most Islamic scholars took Hirabah to mean, in the modern sense, terrorism.

When he was not quoting these passages from the Koran, Gerry was quietly pointing out that Omar had been deceived by his scholar into preforming acts that were blasphemous and that would make God angry with him. Therefore, he would not be granted entry to Paradise when he died in this false Jihad.

On the opposite chair, Hamzah Khan was now definitely detecting the signs of stress, concern, and perhaps even fear on Omar's face. Like the Arab, the young lad had his mouth taped shut and could not intervene or stop this infidel in whatever sorcery he was engaged in. Twenty-one year-old Khan had grown up a few streets from HMP Leeds in Armley.

His parents were devout, hardworking Pakistani immigrants,

and their Jihadi son was the youngest of six. His father had taken Khan, along with his three older brothers, to the Jamia Masjid Ghousia Mosque. However, Muhammad Khan's youngest son had been being secretly schooled on YouTube, and as he had grown into manhood, the message of that Mosque in Brooklyn Terrace had become too tame for his liking. It was not long before he started to frequent an altogether more radical place of worship on the other side of the city.

In the office, Stan and Jack were still indulging in their futile attempt to understand what was being said by their Glaswegian friend, who was speaking quietly and deliberately in Arabic. Jack just hoped that this theological monologue in a foreign language would achieve the objective of getting information out of these men. Jack Dempsey had never been blessed with patience. When the waiting got too much for him, he reached forward from the couch. It had seen better days, and the big Dubliner had sunk into the broken upholstery. He had to reach out, put his hand on Tommy Noonan's cluttered desk and try and pull himself up. On seeing this, Stan put a hand under Jack's armpit, and eased him up to a standing situation. Jack hobbled over to the door of the office and put his head round. He saw Gerry standing with his back to him speaking quietly, and the two men still taped and gagged to the chairs. The man to Gerry's left, the older of the two, was shaking his head from side to side like he didn't want to hear what he was being forced to listen to.

Jack was happy with what he saw, and certainly didn't want to interrupt. He put his hand on the doorway to steady himself, and executed a very clumsy one-eighty degrees. Stan was up out of the sofa and helped him back down onto it.

"Everything OK, gaffer?" said Stan slowly.

"Grand job. The wee fella's in there fucking with their heads, by the looks of it. Some brain on him, you know. Some brain on him."

Gerry was holding the book in front of the Jihadi's face. Then with the other hand he ripped away the tape from the Arab's mouth. Before the man could scream or shout Gerry caught him off guard.

"Salam al akhum saidi."

The Arab replied instinctively.

"Walaykam a salaam."

Gerry held forward al kitab, the only book that good Moslem required to live a good life. Gently, the Arab reached his head forward as if he was trying to smell a fragrant flower. This book was the word of God as revealed to his prophet Mohamed, peace be upon him. This man, thought Omar Abdullah, was showing The Book the respect commanded by Allah and the Prophet.

Perhaps he was not an infidel after all.

Hamzah Khan could only see Gerry's back, but his instinct told him that something was going terribly wrong. He wanted to call out to brother Omar and tell him to resist the sorcery of this non-believer.

"Where are your comrades staying? Where are they now?"

Omar Abdullah bowed his head and quietly whispered what he knew. It was like a prayer to God asking for forgiveness. Gerry didn't ask him to speak up, but gently lowered his head so it was almost touching Omar's face. The Glaswegian had learned that such close contact is considered normal among Arab men and isn't seen as threatening or sexually intimate. Omar wanted to confide in this kind man who was concerned for his salvation. He said he didn't know the house's number, but he knew the street. It sounded believable. Foxrock. Nice area.

"What is the next operation?" whispered Gerry.

The man shook his head and started to weep. The Glaswegian instinctively knew that the individual taped to the chair had been quietly broken without any physical violence. This sobbing came from the fact that he didn't have any more information to give.

"It will be on Sunday."

"Tomorrow?"

"Yes"

"Where?"

"I do not know. I was not selected for this task. Neither was Brother Hamzah," said Omar, gesturing towards the other man in the chair.

In that instant Gerry realised that the worst case scenario had transpired. These men simply didn't have the information to divulge. He had hoped that they both would have valuable scéal. Chances were that the two men that they had killed in Phibsborough had vital information. However, that couldn't be helped now. What was done was done.

Gerry straightened up and stepped aside to give Hamzah Khan a clear view of his comrade.

He gently patted Omar on the shoulder and said, "Shukran Jazilan."

The statement of gratitude was genuine.

In the other chair Hamzah Khan was going berserk. He believed that Omar had betrayed the operation. That he had betrayed God! Gerry walked across to the Jihadi from Leeds and smiled a taunting smile that Omar Abdullah could not see. He needed Hamzah's anger now just as he had needed Omar Abdullah's uncertainty and fear. Gerry ripped the gaffer tape from Hamzah's mouth and he let out an animal scream of rage and frustration.

"What have you done?" he roared at Omar Abdullah.

Gerry stepped in-between them again blocking out Hamzah's view of his Jihadi comrade.

"He is now serving God's purpose. He has turned away from the path of blasphemy. Allah, the compassionate the merciful, will smile on him now."

"Allah's vengeance will fall on the infidels tomorrow!" snarled Hamzah.

Gerry tried to put out of his head that this ISIS tirade was being delivered to him in a Last of the Summer Wine accent. He half expected Nora Batty to emerge in a Burka. He fought to suppress the thought as bursting out laughing might spoil the moment. He wanted to taunt this Jihadi. To smile at him in quiet triumph until he forgot his training and issue threats that would reveal what he knew. He might have heard a fragment of a conversation between more senior operators in the unit here in Dublin. A word, a place, anything. It would be more than they had at the moment, which was very close to fuck all.

"You will not smile tomorrow, infidel, when the judgement of Allah will fall on you from the sky!"

"You should stop serving Shaytan before your soul is lost, my brother," said Gerry in a benign and caring manner.

"I serve Allah and his Prophet Mohammad," snarled Hamzah.

"Brother Omar has travelled back onto God's path. You can do so too, my brother."

"You are not my brother!"

This benign, condescending taunting was too much from the Leeds-born Jihadi. He completely lost it and started to roar and scream, rocking from side to side. Gerry reckoned he had nothing more to divulge.

Jack and Stan emerged from the office, with the younger man helping his injured boss to stay steady on his feet. The interrogator turned around and smiled like a husband showing off a DIY paint job to his wife arriving back from the shops. Gerry nodded to them that it was job done and he appreciated that they had stayed in the office and remained out of the way.

He turned back to the two men. Hamzah was seething with rage and staring at Omar Abdullah. The look was accusatory.

Gerry realised that it was now the law of diminishing returns and that he wouldn't get anything more from these two. He turned and looked at Omar Abdullah, who he thought to be a kindly soul at the end of it all. The Arab smiled back at him.

With the speed of a much younger man, Gerry O'Donnell took the Glock from his waist band and shot both men dead. A round each in the forehead. The sound to the two shots in the confined space of the garage was deafening. Stan was incredulous at what he had just witnessed.

"Are they dead?" he said to Gerry, but it was more a question out loud to himself.

"Dead? Wait and I'll check."

He turned back and put another round into the chest of each man.

"Yeah. They're definitely dead, big lad," said Gerry with a cold determination.

Jack looked down at the dead Arab and could see the UDR man in Portadown slumped inside a brand new shower cabinet.

The nine millimetre jacketed hollow point ammunition made by Federal certainly did what it said on the box.

Jack looked at his old comrade in a new light. This gentle, creative, loving man was capable of this. It made him guilty that he had brought this out in him. This man should be sitting at the table with his wife and child in Donegal laughing and loving.

Instead he was in a lock-up garage in Dublin shooting two men dead.

He was ashamed of himself, and then the Gobshite reminded him that there was a perfectly good portion of the hard stuff going to waste in Tommy's office. The craving started to gnaw at him as he struggled down onto the hard wooden chair, when Gerry snapped him out of it, all business like.

"Result, big man."

"You serious?"

"They have another safe house in Foxrock. I reckon that's where the main ASU is and gear for something major."

"OK. We'll need to check this."

Gerry looked at Jack and said: "Well, we don't have the facilities for prisoners."

"Grand," said Jack softly. If he had been wondering about Gerry's commitment to helping him out of this mess then he was wondering no more.

The feeling of shame washed over him as he looked down at the two corpses. Stan looked at Gerry and received eye contact from the Glaswegian. The big Pole nodded towards him, that acknowledging his leadership.

He had a new gaffer.

"Anything I can do?" asked Jack.

"Naw. Just go back onto that couch, sit there and look pretty."

The Glaswegian looked at Stan.

"We have to get rid of these two."

Stan acknowledged with a nod.

"Where you gonna take them?" asked Jack, looking at down at the two corpses.

"I'm going to give them to the neighbours."

"Jaysus."

The Russian used his key to access the main apartment complex on Patrick Street and made his way up to the door. He gently knocked on the door and it was opened immediately. He thought that the American looked panicked. Pelfrey hardly waited for the door to be closed before he started babbling.

The Russian raised his hand in a gesture that demanded silence, took out his cell phone, walked into the toilet and put it on a shelving unit. Then he made sure it was off before walking past Pelfrey into the living room and sitting at the small dining table. He waited for the CIA man. It was clear to both of them that it wasn't Aleksander Mikhail Vasiliev who was in a panic.

"There is problem?" asked the Russian.

It was the break that Gerry had been looking for and he smiled at his luck. The alarm system to the metal polishing company in the adjoining unit was rudimentary at best and easily bypassed. He opened the door and scanned the facility by the light of his Edelrid head torch.

"OK. This is perfect... let's get the first one."

"What the fuck's happening?" asked Jack with an aggression in his voice when Gerry and Stan went back into Tommy Noonan's garage.

The penny dropped for Gerry immediately. The whiskey.

"Not the ideal time to fall off the wagon, big fella," said Gerry softly.

"What the fuck do you know about it?" snarled Jack.

There might have been about a fifth of a bottle left when Gerry had finished desecrating Islam's holy book with it. However, that had been enough to unleash The Gobshite inside Jack Dempsey's head.

"Have a rest on the couch, big man."

He walked past Jack when there was an explosion on the side of his head. Gerry O' Donnell was sent sprawling.

"Gaffer!" shouted Stan.

"You fucking back off yah Polish retard," snarled Jack.

Gerry O'Donnell had tripped over one of the dead Arabs and had only narrowly avoided falling into the garage pit. He spun around, his survival instincts kicking in, sensing that a second attack could be incoming. Gerry sprung to his feet with agility of a much younger man. His right ear was still ringing and that side of his head was throbbing in pain.

Jack was in full flow.

"I did fucking serious time while you got away, you snivelling little cunt."

Gerry O'Donnell was rattled and furious in equal measure, but he was trying to defuse a potentially calamitous situation.

"Easy, big man," said the Glaswegian, trying to calm him down.

"My son Dermot topped himself while I was on the fucking Isle of Wight. You were fucking around in the Middle East being the big man in the Movement. You and your fucking writing, you snivelling little wanker!"

"Jack…"

"Stick me didn' ya? There was a tout in that unit somewhere," said Jack. He was seething and it was all coming out now. Years of it.

"We've got work to do here," said Gerry.

"You fitted me up in Leeds you Scottish cunt!"

"Rubbish," was all that Gerry could summon up. He wasn't dealing with reasonable here. There was no point in reminding him that he had been in the Army truck in Pudsey and had narrowly missed being shredded by the exploding Austin Princess that night.

"Go into the office and have a sit down buddy" said Gerry as he looked over Jack's shoulder to Stan.

The big Pole gave a look that acknowledged to Gerry what side he was on.

"Don't think I think getting shot was an accident back there. All part of your plan. The pair of you," snarled Jack.

"Fuck sake. It was a struggle in the hallway. Abdul Abhaille there was trying to off you. Stan did great pushing the weapon down." Gerry was trying to reason with Jack.

Jack's alcoholic paranoia went up a notch.

"Ah two of ya! Cunts! Ye were in it together. To get me shot."

Gerry decided to act and moved towards Jack.

The big Dubliner, unsteady on his feet, aimed another crushing right hand at the head of his former IRA comrade. This time it was no contest. Gerry O'Donnell brought his left hand across his face in a palming away motion. It slapped Jack's punch away to Gerry's right side while simultaneously Gerry crouched and brought a low right hook into Dempsey's testicles. Jack howled in pain and keeled over but Stan caught him and held his weight with ease. Gerry looked up and the big Pole acknowledged what had to be done. He dragged Jack back into the office and dropped him onto the old, oil-stained two-seater sofa. Gerry had another quick search of the office. It was important that he made sure the place was empty of booze. Jack curled up on the couch, broken and ashamed. As usual, the Gobshite had fucked off. A bullet in the head and not the arse would have been better to him at that moment, thought Jack.

Gerry realised in a moment of annoyance that he had been sloppy. He hated being sloppy. Sloppy got you caught.

"Fuck it!"

"Is problem?" said Stan.

"It's grand," said Gerry, without time to explain.

He went to the large switch on the wall of the garage and pushed a red button inside a yellow metal housing. There was the noise of machinery kicking into life. Slowly the roller shutter started to lift upwards.

"I should have brought the van inside before," said Gerry.

"OK."

"Better out of sight," said the Glaswegian, as much to himself as to the Pole.

Gerry stooped down under the roller shutter as it slowly inched upwards. He got to his Mercedes van and turned the key. The turbo diesel engine purred to life.

Muhammad Bokhari looked over the weapon and completed his second check on every component. He was pleased that everything had been transported with care. He wanted to use it today, but they had to wait until the infidels gathered in enough numbers. It was almost time for prayer and his thoughts were turning towards that act of worship when he was startled by the knocking at the back door. He opened it and it was young Hassan. He was breathless.

"What is it, brother? Why are you here?" asked Bokhari?

"I was sent for food and when I came back use. Two brothers are dead and two were missing.

"Hamza and Tariq are dead. Shot," said the young man breathlessly.

Muhammad Bokhari tried to process this information as the trembling youth stood beside him.

"Who is missing?"

"Brothers Omar and Hamzah. They were not at the house," said Hassan.

Muhammad Bokhari had been selected by the leaders in al-Raqqah to lead this operation because of his proven ability to improvise under pressure. What he would decide now would establish whether the leaders of ISIS had exercised good judgment.

"This is not the mission I accepted," said the Russian.

"Missions can change," said Pelfrey.

"I am not...bodyguard," said Aleksander Mikhail Vasiliev.

"You are what we pay you to be."

The Russian knew if he walked from away this job then Langley would never hire him again and there might be other repercussions.

"If you check your account in the next few days will see that a new payment has been sent to you. I authorised it two hours ago. Forty percent of your completion fee as an added bonus for your flexibility," said Pelfrey in a superior fashion.

"We appreciate the efforts of our... our...special contractors," said the CIA man, choosing his words carefully.

The Russian was silent for second, calculating the odds; part Special Forces operative, part insurance actuary. Without saying anything more he reached over, dragged the file across the glass dining table towards him and opened it.

Pelfrey supressed a smile. He just wished those field jocks in Langley could see him smashing this one out of the park.

Stan was fully on board. He knew who was in command now and he trusted this man with the red hair and the strange accent. He now understood why his gaffer had approached him for help when all of this business had started.

"OK big fella. We've just got enough time for this."

Stan nodded.

"Just do what I say when I say it. Because this stuff is dangerous," said Gerry as he took two plastic containers from shelving at the corner of the room.

There was various items of equipment around the workshop,

none of which Stan recognised. There were two large metal containers that looked like baths, but at least twice the size, raised up on platforms.

"OK. He goes in there."

This chemical bath was designed for polishing metal, not for the disposal of bodies, but it did the grisly trick. Stan looked at Gerry and the Glaswegian gave him a nod. The big Pole could never have been accused of cowardice, but he hadn't signed up for this.

"OK, you can get next door and check on the big man. I'll be grand here," said Gerry.

Stan didn't need to be told twice and he left the workshop at some speed.

Gerry came back into the little office and Jack looked away in shame. The Glaswegian produced the reporter's notebook from his black backpack.

"This was all the scéal that the old Peeler gave you?" asked Gerry.

"That's it. The address in Phibsborough," said Jack, glad that Gerry didn't want to discuss the previous incident. He knew at that moment that he didn't deserve this man as for a friend or a comrade. Then again, he didn't think he deserved anything that was good or decent in his life.

"OK, well it gave us these two and now we have a street in Foxrock. We've got less than we started with and you got shot in your lovely arse."

Jack started to laugh, it hurt.

"Wait…" Jack was suddenly winded as the realisation hit him with more impact than the dig that Gerry had caught him with two hours earlier.

Gareth Scully was in his study when the front doorbell rang. He knew that anyone at his door would have to get past the security at the gate. That was, of course, if An Garda Síochana were doing their job. He walked up to the corner of the study where there was a small monitor on a table that had originally been designed to hold a fax machine. The man wasn't looking up at the camera, but the stature of the visitor was unmistakable. Then he heard his wife stir, woken by the noise of the bell.

"It's OK Emily. It's work. I will get it," said Scully, shouting across the landing.

"At this time?" shrieked the lady of the house.

Scully didn't even bother to answer as he walked down the stairs and across the large open hallway to the double doors. He opened it and allowed in Assistant Commissioner Gaffney. The policeman was in plain clothes and was sweating profusely. It wasn't a warm night, by anyone built like Gaffney would sweat in the artic.

"In here," said Scully, gesturing to his left. The policeman padded into the large public room just as Scully flicked the light switch.

It was Sunday Supplement stuff. The marble fireplace was like something at Farmleigh, thought the Special Branch man. Gaffney couldn't wait to sit down on one of the luxurious sofas. He turned back towards Scully and said, "There has been an incident in Phibsborough. We had the house under surveillance and you told us to call it off. You said...."

Scully airily waved his hand in the air as if to swat away Gaffney's concerns. The Justice Minister walked towards a very fine piece of inlayed furniture in the corner of the large room. He brought down the front of it to reveal a drinks cabinet.

"Brandy? I have a fine Islay Malt here. So much smoother than what passes for whiskey here, don't you think..."

"Look, you gobshite. This is serious!" roared Gaffney.

Scully turned to face him with a large brandy glass nestling in his little hand.

"Assistant Commissioner, if you decided to withdraw a surveillance operation from a specific address then that is an operational matter and clearly not within my remit."

"But you told me..."

"And you can prove that? I suppose there must a letter from me, a memo even?"

"But you told me in your office. You EXPRESSLY told me. You said the Americans would handle it. That this was a...a...'global issue'..."

Gaffney was beside himself and clearly out of control, thought Scully. He proffered the brandy glass towards the sweating policeman.

"Thomas. Drink this."

Gaffney reached out and gulped it down in a way that reminded Scully that fine things were only meant for the elite.

Back in the bedroom, Emily wasn't complaining. She hopped out of the bed and reached into her bag for her other phone. The wife of the Justice Minister prayed that her man would be awake when she messaged him on WhatsApp. It was too dangerous to speak, but she needed to connect to him like a drug addict needed a fix. The WhatsApp message registered two little blue ticks. His phone was on and he had seen the message. The reply was immediate. An emoji of a throbbing heart. In that moment Emily Scully was happy in a way she hadn't known in years.

With the van inside the garage Gerry decided that it was an asset and not just in the way. Jack would need somewhere to lie down straight. Somewhere that wouldn't aggravate his wound. He opened the sliding door of the van and reached into the mesh grill on the far wall. The Glaswegian unhooked a rucksack and brought out what looked like a blue cylinder. Stan watched with interest. There were many things in that van, and they all had a purpose. It reminded him of the vehicles in the army back home. Gerry unrolled the single airbed and turned to Stan.

"Here, get pumping big lad."

The big Pole moved to obey without a word uttered. Stan started on the foot pump. Gerry's plan was for Jack to have the airbed inside the van. It was a comfy as he could make it for him and the two-seater sofa and front seats in the van would allow himself and Stan to get some shut eye. Tomorrow would be a big day. It was shit or bust and the unit had an injured man. Thankfully, Jack's big arse wasn't the worst place to take a nine millimetre.

The airbed was up and Gerry said to Stan, "Put that back in the van. Jack will sleep there. He needs to lay down flat. Let's get him."

They went into the office and Jack was curled up on the old sofa. Gerry shook his comrade by the shoulder.

"Up you get big fella we have a bed made up for ya."

Jack looked up at him and Gerry could read the shame in his eyes. He didn't need Jack feeling sorry for himself. What had happened was over and there was no booze left. Between Gerry, Stan and the trekking pole they were able to get Jack to the airbed. His legs were weight bearing, but any extended strides could open the stitches. That was what Karim had warned about. They were manoeuvring Jack into the van when Gerry moved a holdall out of the way.

"Here Stan, take your bag."

"That is not my bag."

"Then who the fuck's is it then?"

"I take it from Arab house. I forget," said Stan sheepishly.

Gerry wanted to immediately explore the grip, but they first had to get Jack onto the airbed inside the van. It wasn't an easy manoeuvre, but they got him in. Jack instinctively rolled onto his side and Gerry reached for a stuff sack with a Helly Hansen fleece inside it. It made for an ad hoc pillow.

"There you are big fella. You'll be better inside there," said Gerry in a reassuring voice.

Jack looked up at him and nodded. He was still feeling guilty and didn't trust himself to say anything. Gerry patted him on the upper arm and got back to what he had been thinking about since Stan had dropped his bombshell. He turned round and looked at the Pole.

"Do you know what's inside here?"

"No, gaffer."

"OK. Here we go."

The grip was cheaply made with a single zip. It was purple with a dolphin logo. The Glaswegian took the bag to a work bench against one of the walls. Whoever worked here was seriously tidy, thought Gerry. Some garages were strewn with discarded tools, but not this place. He quietly approved of the man who plied his trade here. Stan stood beside Gerry, towering above the Glaswegian, and awaited the discovery inside. The smaller man undid the zip, which initially stuck only an inch into the journey. Gerry wiggled it a few times and the mechanism worked smoothly.

Inside were some clothes. A couple of t-shirts, boxer shorts. Gerry felt ridiculous for shouting at Stan about this. He could sense the Pole's disappointment too, but then the Glaswegian's hand touched something. Gerry quickly unearthed two boxes. They were mobile phone sims from Vodafone Ireland. The Glaswegian checked the numbers and they were very similar. Gerry looked up at Stan and smiled.

"Is good gaffer?"

"Well these two beauties just might give us more than Stan and Olly did."

"I am Stan," said the big Pole, confused.

"Those two comedians next door. The ones taking the acid bath," explained Gerry, mildly annoyed his joke had fallen flat.

Gerry turned and walked across to the van where Jack was struggling to find a position in which his rear end wouldn't ignite more pain signals. The painkillers that Karim had given him were clearly wearing off.

"Result big lad! Fucking result!" said Gerry, beaming.

"What is it, wee fella?"

Jack's reticence at speaking to Gerry after he had disgraced himself earlier was gone. This was the Gerry O'Donnell the remembered from that crappy gaff in Leeds, bouncing into the flat announcing that he had target information.

"Our Stan here grabbed a holdall when we were leaving that place in Phibsborough. You remember the place where you got shot in the ar...."

"Yeah, Very fucking funny. What've you got?"

"These are part of a batch" said Gerry, waving the two boxes.

"And?"

"Well, the dopey bastards have bought a batch of sims for their phones."

"So?" Jack was puzzled.

"It means that if we can locate the batch then we know the mobile numbers that they're using."

"Then we call them?"

"No big lad. Then we FIND them! Now I have an email to send to a special lady in Bangladesh," smiled Gerry.

"I have no fucking idea what's going on and my arse is in agony."

"Want a massage honey?" said Gerry in a camp voice.

"Oh you fuck off!" said Jack, breaking into a laugh.

"Can I help gaffer?"

"Not for now."

Good soldier. Seriously top grade. This just might work out.

"What about the other thing? You said THAT was a break," shouted Jack from inside the van as Gerry moved back towards the work bench with his small backpack over his shoulder.

"Tomorrow morning is good enough for that one. This one is for now."

Yasmin Mizrah had her Tor Browser opened and was checking out the latest on the leaks from a GCHQ whistle-blower when she checked her Hushmail account. Her telepathy was working well, it seemed, and she smiled. It was a message from the Irishman.

"Hey Yas. I need your help. Pretty urgent. In a scrape here with The Man. Very bad movie. I need a couple of Irish mobile numbers checked. I'm after the batch. I think they were bought in the same store, probably cash. Somewhere in greater Dublin area. REALLY need to find these phones in the same batch as these two.

I will send numbers in separate mail to that Proton addy.

Beir Bua

G"

Yasmin smiled. She had never met Gerry O'Donnell, but she knew him and she trusted him totally. This was the next digital battlespace against the Man. The young Bangladeshi hacker immediately went to her Proton mail account and there was a simple message from an account she recognised. It was just two mobile numbers starting with 00 353...

She got to work on this. Any day that she could do a solid for "Fear le gruaig rua" was a good day. She already owed him. One day she would set foot in Ireland and she knew that there would be people there to help her start a new life.

In the next room her father thought of the three men that he was considering as suitable husband material for his daughter Yasmin. He had no idea that such an event would never take place and that the twenty-one year old, with an IQ off the scale, had already planned her escape route with help from cyber co-conspirators that she had never physically met.

Saturday

Mary Riley actually liked shopping on a Saturday if she could get there early enough. Her youngster was on an overnight at a pal's so she could get into the Cabra Tesco Superstore just after it opened at eight in the morning. The place was almost empty, save for staff, and she whizzed round getting everything on her shopping list, which was balanced on the top of her bag that was hanging from the handles of the trolley.

She was sifting through some oranges at a square stall in the middle of the floor when she noticed a man in a black baseball cap. He had been in the dairy isle as well. She didn't want to look up when he walked up and stood right next to her. The oranges were the same on four sides of this stand, but this man was standing right next to her left arm.

She froze.

"Don't look up Dicey. I'm a friend of Jack's," said the man.

Mary Reilly's first impulse was to run like hell.

She had runners on and jogging bottoms. Although she was no gym bunny, the adrenalin would get her curvy little frame to the check out and help. The man standing beside her sensed the alarm in the woman.

"Here. Read this" he said, handing her a €20 note without looking at her.

She still hadn't turned and looked up at him. Mary Reilly took the bank note and looked down at it. A message was scribbled on it: "Trust him Dicey. He's sound. Jack." She struggled to convince herself that it was Jack's scribble. Something inside her decided it wasn't right and she headed for the check out. The man didn't follow her.

She got to the checkout and realised that she had left her trolley with her bag inside it. Mary Reilly turned round and the man was pushing the trolley like he didn't have a care in the world. He was speaking into a mobile phone.

She looked up and Gerry O'Donnell said: "Here Dicey. He wants to speak to you."

She took the phone.

"He's sound. Trust him for fuck's sake. Don't say my name. Just trust him. OK?" said the gruff voice on the phone.

It was unmistakably the voice of Seán Patrick Dempsey.

"I will surely Jack."

"Jaysus."

"Sorry J…"

Gerry took the phone from her and flipped it closed. The instant the call stopped between Cabra and Tallaght the algorithms within the mainframe at Fort Meade, Maryland were already processing what had happened.

Muhammad Bokhari stood as he spoke to the men under his command.

"The enemies of Allah have struck at the servants of God. Two of our brothers are dead, and two are missing. Young Hassan was saved from this and was God's messenger to us of the new dangers we face here among the infidels. This is a clear sign that our mission must go ahead. It is God's will," said the Saudi, raising his voice at the end.

"Allahu Akbar!" said the men sitting crossed legged on the rug in the middle of the large living room.

Bokhari smiled. This was the response he was after.

"Hassan has been chosen by God to join us in this divine mission. This is an honour indeed," said the Saudi turning towards the young Englishman.

Hassan looked up at Bokhari, utterly convinced that he was destined to implement God's will. In that moment, as he sensed the approval of these men who had helped establish the Caliphate in Syria, he could almost smell Heaven. The lad from Dewsbury knew that soon he would be spoken of in hushed tones of respect in every Mosque in the Ummah.

John Powell sat in the cyber café and looked out of the first floor window onto Grafton Street. Dublin's main shopping street was getting ready for another busy Saturday. Powell looked down into the street and a mime guy dressed as CP30 was setting up for the day.

The Marine was dressed casually in a fleece hoodie and Levis. He reckoned that it was best to be as inconspicuous as possible to be on this operation. Unless he opened his mouth no one would think he was American.

Powell had been struck by just how many Africans, mainly Nigerian, were in Dublin. When he had been posted here he had thought he was coming to the Africa for white folks, but twenty-first century Dublin seemed to be a bit of a melting pot too.

Powell took a breath and went over in his head what Molly had told him in Philly. For a lady reporter she was good at this spook stuff. She had set him up with a Proton mail account. Those guys were in Switzerland. As long as he remembered the passwords (there were two of them) it was cool. Just as she had ordered, he didn't have a thing written down. He wasn't to call her and tell her she had mail or message her in any other way. She would be regularly checking the Proton mail account that she had set up just for this. He knew that what he was about to send her would made Edward Snowden look like the American Boy Scout of the year. Powell looked over what he had typed into the box. It was real-time Intel and Molly would know what to do with it.

This was breaking all kindsa military laws, but it was protecting the Constitution of the United States. If that meant the world fell on him, well then he was a Marine.

Anas Iqbal wasn't usually in his office on a Saturday. However, he wanted peace from the house as he was working on a speech for the Shannon Action Group the following day. His office could have been set up by his publicist. The walls were covered with images that charted his rise as a human rights hero. In a way it was an advertisement. No one promoted the Anas Iqbal brand like he did. Two months ago the Sunday Independent had profiled him. It was glowing stuff. He was delighted with it and had read every sentence over and over. In the corner of the Capel Street office there was a pile of them on the floor, reaching above knee height.

As it was Saturday his secretary Danielle wasn't in. She was a pleasant girl from Blanchardstown. She wouldn't win any beauty contests, but she was just what he wanted. Reliable, hardworking and never likely to distract him with her looks.

He was lost in the text of his speech to such an extent that he jumped when he heard a knocking on the front door of the office. Iqbal was there in an instant, crossing the distance between his chair and through Danielle's office to the door at the end of a small corridor.

"Special Branch," said Pat Rooney as he walked past the lawyer, followed in by Johnny Buckley.

This was a job they were both looking forward to.

A taxi had dropped Gerry off at the SuperValu, where he quickly grabbed some basic supplies. There was nothing to cook with in the garage and eating out was risky. Fuck, this whole mess was risky! However, it was the little things that tripped you up. The baseball cap was handy in the era of CCTV and he paid cash. He gathered up two cooked chickens, milk, bread and things to put in it. There were three men to feed and this was as good as he could do. He also bought enough chocolate to keep a busload of kids happy. Gerry instantly thought of his little fella and pushed the idea out of his head. He had to see this through somehow.

Gerry sent Stan a text message from his unit phone from outside of the supermarket.

"ETA twenty minutes."

He got an "OK" back.

Pauline Scullion came back in from the shops and her husband Benny asked if she wanted tea. She totally ignored him and started to fill the fridge with what she had bought at the village shop. This shite has gone on for a day now, thought Benny Scullion. He snapped.

"What the fuck is it?"

"You think I button up the back, Benny Scullion?"

"Just tell me woman!"

"You said all that shite was done with. Then those feckers turn up in that van. What was that about?"

"That won't happen again," explained her husband.

"Oh you're damn right on that one!" said Pauline Scullion, spitting out the words.

"They won't be back. You won't see them again."

"Will you?"

"Will I what?"

"Fuck... will YOU see them again?" Pauline sounded desperate, worry coming through the anger.

"No. Doubt it."

Pauline Scullion paused, trying to find hope in her husband's words.

"You know what I don't get? What fucking baffles me? Is that these gobshites turn up after years and you jump up like a trained dog!" seethed Pauline.

"It's not like that."

"What is it like then love? Fucking tell me." Pauline was now pleading with her husband. She loved him. He was the father of their two grown-up children. She remembered the days taking the kids, both of them under five, to see their dad in Port Laoise prison.

"They needed help with something. I gave them it. They won't be back."

"But WHY help them?" asked Pauline, pleading for an answer.

"I didn't have a choice really," said Benny reflectively.

"They threatened you?" gasped Pauline, now getting afraid for her husband.

"No."

"What then?" asked Pauline, all anger gone; just wanting to know what had motivated the man of her life to take risks like that on no notice.

"That's easy, kitten. I swore an oath."

He looked at his wife and he was that young Volunteer again explaining to her outside a dance in Castleblayney that he was going away to do a job, he couldn't tell her where and that he loved her. It had been true then, and it was still true now. In that moment Pauline Scullion remembered why she loved this man.

"I'll have that tae now off you mister," she smiled.

"How was she?" asked Jack.

"Not too impressed with the price of their fruit and veg," quipped Gerry.

"Gobshite!"

"The Peelers had been up at your office a couple of times. Turned the place over. Took computers away. The usual craic."

"Cunts."

"Herself was going through the mail. Usual pile. But one made no sense. She held onto it. Didn't tell the cops."

Gerry produced a small brown envelope and inside it there was a page from a reporter's notebook. He handed it over to Jack.

"Is this what I think it is?"

Jack took a second to take it in and felt emotion welling up inside of him.

"You crafty old shite! God bless you!"

"O'Shea?"

"The very man."

"What were you using?"

"Whadya think? The Holy Book from the old days."

"You serious?"

"He had a copy because his old man got a daycent mention in it from the Tan War."

"So, we need to get a copy of Tim Pat Coogan's The IRA: 1970 edition?"

"No hassle. I've one at my gaff in Temple…"

"No chance, sunshine."

"Ah…"

"Off fucking limits."

"But that will be out of print. You need that edition or it doesn't work."

"Not necessarily," said Gerry extracting his laptop from his backpack.

"Come again?"

"I know someone who can find us a perfectly serviceable .pdf."

Across the Atlantic Molly O'Reilly was ordering a drink in the Fado Irish pub in Philadelphia. Red haired and curvy, she always joked with the manager that she should charge them for raising the Irishness cred every time she was in there. She had a point. She looked like she had walked off an Irish Tourist Board poster from 1950. She couldn't see any of the usual crowd in as she scanned up the bar.

The reporter took out her android and disconnected her device from the pub's Wi-Fi. She moved onto data. Simple precautions in the post-Snowden age, she remarked to herself. Molly O'Reilly gasped when she opened her Proton mail account. The big guy had come through and then some! If she could stand this stuff up it was Pulitzer material.

She put the Guinness on the bar and ransacked the Rolodex in her head. There were several candidates that might be able to substantiate some of this. Stephen who worked in State was probably the best option. He didn't have the level of clearance that he boasted about, but he did know people in Langley. She knew that from another source. Once she had asked him he had clammed up. Always a good sign.

They'd had a thing once. A lot of booze, hotel room, no biggie. Married guy, nice family. He had rhapsodised afterwards about the head she had given him. It was probably a fair bet he wasn't getting that in his good catholic home. Molly was certain that he wanted an ongoing arrangement with her. The poor schmuck.

She had a quick professional word with herself. Would she give head for a Pulitzer? It was a silly question. She smiled as she sipped the Guinness and looked at herself in the mirror behind the bar. She looked straight at the redhead with the pint of stout and said, "Well Molly girl, the bold Stephen is about to have his world rocked. Again! Sláinte."

She sent him a WhatsApp message.

"Hey big guy! You in Philly?"

As soon as the two little blue ticks registered he was right back at her. Molly O'Reilly smiled. Guide dogs for the blind were harder to train than men, she thought.

Sunday

Gerry O'Donnell locked himself into the small toilet in the garage. Jack was flat out in the back of the van and Stan was curled up the best he could on the battered old sofa in the office. He sat on the loo and powered up the laptop. There was still nothing from Yasmin, which troubled him. He had asked her to find a .pdf of the Tim Pat Coogan book and work through the numbers. She was usually an instantaneous service. Even allowing for the time difference it was starting to give him a grumble in his gut.

He thought about what he was going to say and then hit the button on the keyboard. It only took him a few minutes. When he was finished he opened up his Hushmail again and sent another email to Yasmin, this time with a link to an encrypted video on the cloud. His hacker comrade on the other side of the world would know what to do with it. That could wait, but he really needed her to get in touch about those mobile phones. She was usually very on the ball with stuff like this. Utterly loved it, she did. However, since yesterday there had been radio silence. This wasn't like her.

He believed the Jihadi that today would be the day. The man in the chair had lost his composure when Gerry was ripping up the Koran. He was rearing up at this infidel who had perpetrated such cruelty with The Book. So he had blurted out something.

Something true.

Gerry went over it again and again in his head. He closed the laptop and put it into his backpack. The two lads were still sleeping, which was merciful. Outside the birds were giving the industrial estate an alarm call. Gerry O'Donnell, an only child, had always liked his own company. Especially at times like this.

He walked into the office and Stan stirred. He looked up, but

Gerry gestured him to put his head back down and get some sleep. Stan didn't need any further encouragement.

There was a small holdall on the desk. It offered up a task to Gerry that would keep him busy, keep him from overthinking. The bag held their arsenal of weapons, with the exception of the Glock that was sitting in the waistband of the Glaswegian's trousers. His old comrade in Cavan hadn't let him down. When they had called by there had been no questions asked.

The woman of the house had viewed the men in the van with suspicion. She knew the look of trouble and she had spent too many years visiting himself in Port Laoise to want any of that shite back again.

He hadn't been gone long when his battered old Volkswagen Passat swung around into the back of the house. Benny had gotten out and handed Gerry an old holdall. The Glaswegian hadn't inspected it, but had acknowledged the nod from the fella. With that the van had sped away with Gerry at the wheel.

They were two hours away from that man's house when they pulled in for fuel in a place that looked like it hadn't heard of CCTV. Gerry inspected the contents of the bag. As he had suspected his old buddy had never fully got with the decommissioning program. The first item was made for Stan. A Ruger GP 100 .357 magnum revolver. Blued with an ergonomic grip. The six inch barrel on the Model 1704 would make it more accurate in the steady hands of the big Pole.

There were also two venerable Browning hi-power nine millimetre automatic pistols. This had been the standard sidearm of the British forces during the war in the North and quite a few of them had found their way into the IRA's hands. Gerry looked at the automatic pistol and wondered where it had been since it had left the factory. He had promised Maria that he would never handle one of these things again. Gerry put the weapons back in the bag and walked out into the main garage area and over to a bench that was up against the wall.

The Browning hi-power disassembles very quickly if you know what you're doing. They were both in good condition. Wherever these weapons had been stored near Benny Scullion's house, it must have been dry and free of damp. It was like the man to have sourced a good dump. He was a top class operator in his day.

Gerry rummaged and found a can of three-in-one oil and drizzled some onto the barrel and inside the top cover. Those are the two main working parts of any automatic pistol. When the weapon was reassembled Gerry worked the slide back and forth several times. The chances of a malfunction was as close to zero as possible, if the ammunition was in good condition. That was an unknown variable. However, they looked OK.

The Glock 19 in his waistband was, like the Ruger, very new. He made an educated guess that they had both been purchased at gun shows in the USA. It was a procurement operation that old Belfast buddy had been involved in after the first ceasefire in 1994. The order was put in for high quality short arms; new with no history, to be stashed for the eventuality of dealing with Dissidents and providing close protection for the Leadership.

He started to load some rounds into the magazines for the Brownings. Gerry was in charge of the weapons; indeed, he was in charge of this whole shooting match. He had decided against issuing the Ruger because he wanted to keep the noise down when they entered the house in Phibsborough. For all of the benefits of the big revolver, quiet it wasn't. This would be Jack's weapon.

He was hit with an idea. He put the magazine on the bench and walked over to the van. The sliding door was open and the big man was a beached whale on the airbed. Gerry gave him a gentle nudge. Jack stirred.

"Brew?" asked Gerry.

"What time is it?"

"Time we were up, big fella."

Jack manoeuvred himself out of the sleeping bag and struggled to get out of the van. He was clearly in a lot of pain.

"Mind if Nurse O'Donnell has a look at your arse?"

"Fuck off."

"I'm serious Jack. You look fucked."

"Fuck off."

Jack was leveraging himself upright by using each side of the door frame in the van. It was clear to Gerry that he was in agony.

"Do you have any more of those pills left that the doctor gave you?"

Jack nodded.

"Take them then."

Jack rummaged in the pocket of his leather jacket and Gerry fetched a bottle of water from his pack. He offered the bottle, but Jack threw back the tablets without any liquid assistance. Gerry had never understood that ability. He needed a deluge down his throat.

"Good. They'll help with the pain. You were better last night."

"You a doctor now?"

"You're a delight in the morning honey. I regret not moving in with you when you asked me," simpered Gerry.

"Fuck off, you," said Jack hobbling over towards the office and the softness of the sofa.

Stan emerged and was immediately looking to be tasked.

"Over here," said the Glaswegian to the big Pole.

"OK gaffer."

"Used one of these before?" asked Gerry, as he produced the big Ruger.

"No."

"Well, we can't go to the shooting range and practice, but you'll be fine big fella I reckon... A bit of a kick on it. Powerful bastard it is. Accurate though."

Stand looked at the revolver that was nestling on Gerry's upturned palms.

"It's yours. Get familiar with it. It is unloaded. Keep it that way for now. The rounds are in that bag."

Jack was adjusting himself onto the couch as he waited for the painkilling medication to kick in. Gerry had quickly checked the sleeping bag and the airbed and there was no sign of blood. Karim had done an excellent job in less than ideal circumstances.

"Look big fella. You're not in any shape for this. You've done your bit."

"I've got shot in the arse by my own side!"

"If we get close to these boyos we'll need to be moving quick enough and you..."

"And I'm a fucking cripple! That it?"

"No. You're wounded. You were in combat. Look, the two of us. The lad and me. We'll fix this. Anyway the cops are on the lookout for ya."

"Let me drive the van."

I thought you were banned from driving?"

He got eye contact with the big Dubliner and they both bent over laughing as one. It was helpless funeral giggles. The absurdity of their situation encapsulated in one moment. It was bargaining time.

"Ok. You ride in the back of the van. Out of sight. Anything kicks off then you're the surprise package coming out of the side door. The signal will be me hitting the horn probably just after I've slammed on the anchors."

Jack nodded.

"You got enough of those pills to get you through today?"

"Hundred percent, wee fella."

"Anyway, if my buddy in Bangladesh doesn't pop up were going nowhere."

"What you mean?"

"My hacker girleen. She should've been back to me by now. She isn't answering her mails. Not like her big man. Bad feeling about this."

"And?"

"Until we knew we had those sim cards we had the square root of not very much. If those boyos switch on their phones and if Yas is on the ball then we can pick them up. That's if she's located the batch. That was the last message that she replied to. This isn't like her at all."

Jerome Pelfrey had only slept fitfully on the sofa in his office. Today would seal this operation one way or another. He had processed all of the eventualities and all of them led back to a scenario where Scully would get his National Security Bill through the Irish parliament. Ideally he would be made Prime Minister as well. That's what was in it for him. That was how they had ensnared him initially. He had been in Philadelphia on a Saint Patrick's trip and he had been sized up by a seasoned hand from Langley. The assessment was that

Scully was aching to be the top guy in Ireland. This wasn't just burning ambition; this was a whole oil field going up in flames.

Then the NSA had dropped some high grade dirt on Scully into the CIA's lap. That stuff was able to seal the deal. After that the Company owned him. They'd had no idea of his sexual preferences when they had first started to assess him. Without that information, he might not have moved beyond a minor agent of influence. Useful, but not a game changer. However, now he was a vital part of getting the equivalent of the US Patriot Act imposed as industry standard throughout the European Union. Little itty bitty Ireland would be the test case for Europe.

The more he thought about it, the more he believed that it would be a career defining-triumph if the derided policy wonk with the famous father had a Prime Minister of an EU state as an asset. The contractor was highly experienced and totally deniable. Nothing led back to the Company or, more importantly, to Pelfrey himself.

Anas Iqbal got out of the car. He was immediately greeted with cheers. A young man with Rastafarian locks but a West of Ireland complexion approached him and embraced him. It was a sea of smiling faces and clapping hands. He was led to the side of the flat-bed lorry that was serving as a makeshift stage. There were several wooden steps placed there to allow someone to get up onto the platform. As he ascended the steps and heard the cheering it felt like a gallows. In that moment suicide seemed a reasonable option.

Akash Mizrah trembled with anger as he stood in his living room and towered over his daughter.

"You will not bring shame on this family, Yasmin!" he roared.

He had been conflicted for several years about his daughter. The heart condition he had been diagnosed with meant that he couldn't work, and Yasmin's salary was important to the family. But she was now notable in the community in that she was unmarried and not producing children.

"You will obey me and marry the husband I have found for you. This should have happened a long time ago. But I was weak. You will soon be too old to have children."

Yasmin burst out laughing and Akash Mizrah snapped. With blinding spend the back of his right hand connected with the cheek bone of his one and only daughter. Yazmin's mother trembled, but didn't speak out. Something inside Akash Mizrah's ferociously intelligent daughter snapped. She had known this day would come, but it had never been certain until that moment.

Yasmin stood up to leave the room, but her father blocked her path. "Sit down!" he commanded.

Yasmin tried to move around him, but he grabbed her by the wrist. She twisted and yanked herself free with a speed and strength that surprised her father. It was decision time. She moved to her bedroom and her father sped after her. There was only one thing she needed and she couldn't leave without it. Her mind was racing and she lifted her small backpack from the bedroom floor. It contained her laptop; and that was everything for her.

She was almost out of the door when her father yanked the backpack to pull her back into the house. The computer spilled out as the five foot one inch hacker was spun around. She heard her mother scream from the living room but all she could focus on was the sight of the laptop hitting the concrete floor of the hallway. The sound of plastic shattering was like a knife going into her.

She wriggled out of the backpack and was halfway down the first flight of stairs in the apartment block before her father could move. This was not how she had planned her escape.

"Friends, comrades…" started Anas Iqbal.

He only had those words out and the cheering started. The lawyer had been introduced by one of the organisers as "Ireland's leading human rights lawyer". However, he didn't need any introduction to this crowd of determined activists. He was their hero. Iqbal had represented a few of them in court pro bono for charges connected to the attempted blockade of Shannon airport. His supporters were quick to point out that Scully had a legal profile created by his crappy TV show. However, their guy was the real deal. A human rights lawyer working at the coalface.

The assembled crowd was an eclectic bunch, but they all wanted the US presence at Shannon gone. If Iqbal was a rock star for this crowd then Justice Minister Scully was the devil incarnate. The lorry was in Shannon industrial estate. This was the closest the Gardaí would allow them to get to the airport itself because of the current security situation.

Just as Iqbal was ascending the steps, a Lear jet was taking off. One of the supporters near the airport messaged Liam Coyle, one of the organisers, to say that it was on the list of suspected planes used by the Americans. He stepped forward to the microphone and announced the news just before Iqbal was going to speak. It was if the US intelligence community was a warm-up act for the human rights hero.

The irony made Iqbal's' stomach turn over.

Muhammad Bokhari had dreamed of this day and finally it was at hand. Allah was wise to have created this set of circumstances, he thought. His men were loading the weapon into the hired van. It was heavy and awkward to negotiate into the vehicle, and at one point it almost slipped to the ground.

"Be careful brothers. It is not God's plan that we fail today."

"Allah Akbhar!" his men replied in unison.

They were all true soldiers of Allah thought Muhammad Bokhari and he smiled. He felt blessed.

Abdullah Muhammad walked out of the bungalow in Foxrock to witness the preparations for the attack. He embraced with Muhammad Bokhari.

"My brother, I confess the sin of jealousy that at the end of this day you will be probably be in Paradise Inshallah. I am needed for God's plan after today," smiled Abdullah Muhammad.

"The infidels will feel the might of God today," said Muhammad Bokhari.

"And this young man will definitely be in Paradise today. He is chosen by Allah," said Abdullah Muhammad, turning back and gesturing towards Hassan.

The youth stood in the doorway that led to the kitchen of the bungalow. As the men at the van cheered their approval of him he seemed to shrink back into the building. Abdullah Muhammad moved towards him and put and arm around the teenager.

"Embrace him, brothers. He has been given an important job by Allah and will be rewarded in paradise this very day."

"Allah Akbar!" shouted the men, all veterans of the war in Syria and highly skilled with the weapon that they had loaded into the van.

The Russian had been given his brief and he would obey it, but it made him uneasy. He didn't like orders that were so loose that things could go awry. An assassination was a very clear objective. The target is dead then the mission has been accomplished. Now he was a bodyguard for a group of maniacs who didn't know he was there. If they spotted him they were as likely to try and kill him.

He knew these type of men from the war in Chechnya. They had no fear of death and indeed they preferred to die than live if they were fighting for their God. However, the thought of more zeroes being added to his account in Tortola provided sufficient incentive to overlook his misgivings.

He couldn't have been more different from the men in the van that he was now following at a discreet distance.

Gerry sat in the passenger seat of the van, which was still inside the garage, and looked at the laptop screen. What he had thought was a stroke of luck, finding the sim cards in the holdall, was for nothing if he couldn't raise Yasmin. He knew that he didn't have the skillset or the time to what was required. Crucially, he couldn't think of anyone else with her cyber abilities that he would trust with this job. He knew that the opposition would be trawling the dark web looking for any indication of who was responsible for the Phibsborough operation.

Jack came out of the office. He was moving more easily. The medication was managing the pain, thought Gerry. It was one worry that could be put to the back of his mind. At least for now.

Even for someone born and reared in the city, the throng of Dhaka could be overwhelming. Yasmin had run out into the street and stopped for a second to feel inside her jogging bottoms for her cell phone. She only realised her head was uncovered when two young women walked past her. They were both wearing Hijabs and they quickly looked away when Yasmin stared back at them.

She took out her phone. It was on 20% battery. If it died she was in even more trouble. She prayed that Masud would answer. He had been pretty much off the grid since his close friend Nazimuddin Samad had been hacked to death in 2016. However, they had kept in touch privately as Masud had been forced to keep off the left wing Bangladeshi forums where he had made a real username for himself. Samad was a law student who had expressed secular views online and who had been killed in Dhaka for offending Islam.

She sent Masud a message through Signal and in doing so knew that he was her only chance.

Gerry manoeuvred the van out of the garage and Stan stood at the side operating the roller shutter. When the vehicle was fully out of the building the big Pole pressed the button and the metal started on its downward journey. Gerry stopped the van and jumped out. He went back inside and did a once over. Nothing had been left that he could see.

Jack met him on the way out.

"We're grand," said Gerry.

"Hundred per cent."

"I have to check next door."

Jack looked at him, needing an explanation.

"Just to check that I didn't leave any mess in there."

"Ah. Jaysus." Jack had almost forgotten.

The cheering had died down very quickly and the silence was of the stunned variety. Anas Iqbal explained in great detail why the recent attacks on Irish soil by "Islamo-Fascists" had made him reconsider the entire subject. Yes, he was still for human rights, but...

Somewhere in the crowd, one young man shouted the lawyer down. It was a releaser cue. Like a chain reaction the booing travelled through the crowd like an emotional forest fire. On the other side of Ireland Gareth Scully smiled as he looked at the live feed of the demonstration on his mobile phone. He had waited a long time to bury Mr Human Rights Lawyer. The fact that Anas Iqbal was publicly committing reputational suicide by reading a speech that

Scully himself had drafted made the politician smile even more as he relaxed in the conservatory of his Dalkey home.

Gerry pulled the van out onto the main road and headed in the general direction of the city centre. He still hadn't heard anything from Yasmin. Without her help all he had was a partial address in Foxrock. It would have to do.

As he was taking the Mercedes van around the first roundabout from the industrial estate he saw Stan produce the Browning hi-power and check the magazine for rounds.

"That's not the weapon I gave you big lad," said Gerry.

Stan nodded.

"Where's the revolver I gave you? The three fifty-seven?"

"Mr Jack has that. He said he liked that one. He said he knows that weapon."

"Grand," said Gerry and his thoughts again turned to where the fuck his Bangladeshi comrade was.

She had never been off the grid in the two years they had been operating together.

Hassan did not speak to the taxi driver after telling him his destination. The young man with the English accent got into the back seat, put his earphones in and looked out of the window.

Jimmy Fanning glanced at the kid in the rear view mirror and he was glad that he had a hire. It would make up for the shite morning he had spent waiting in the rank. This bombing shite had wrecked the trade in the city centre, but he still had to make a living.

The earphones allowed Hassan to listen to a sermon from the Imam in Dewsbury who had recruited him to the cause of Allah. He needed to hear his holy words at difficult times. It was natural to fear death, said the Imam; that was God's divine test for the holy and righteous.

Yasmin's phone vibrated in her pocket as she weaved between pedestrians and the chaos that was Dhaka's traffic. It was Masud! The message on Signal was brief and unequivocal.

"RP. One hour. Usual place."

She knew exactly where she had to get to; a park bench under a huge tree where Masud had confided the truth of his life to his cyber comrade. He told her he was in love with a boy at college. He hoped that the object of his affections felt the same way, but in the Islamist atmosphere of modern Bangladesh, coming out was a form of suicide. Yasmin reciprocated by telling him about her plan to get away before she was put into an arranged marriage.

Jimmy Fanning stopped at the drop off at Terminal 2. He hadn't asked the young man what terminal when he got into his taxi on Dame Street. The Dubliner looked in the mirror and the lad was miles away. Kids and their feckin' music, thought the sixty-two year old.

"Here you are son! Terminal 2?"

"Yes. Yes thank you. The money? Of course," said Hassan as he handed over a fifty euro note.

The Dubliner handed back twenty euro as the young man was leaving the back of the taxi.

"Your change, son!" said Fanning.

"Yes. Yes, thank you," said Hassan and smiled at the man.

Nice kid, thought Jimmy Fanning. Polite. Not yer typical skanger.

Gerry was driving, but kept glancing down at the laptop that was open and facing him. If anything came through from Yasmin there would be an audible alert. Nothing so far. In the absence of her coming back on the grid their grand plan consisted of going to a street in Foxrock and hoping that they bumped into the Jihadi brigade. Oh, and they had to avoid the Guards as they had a guy in the back of the van who was a suspect in a murder case. An easy enough Sunday, thought Gerry.

Hassan stood looking at the huddle of people retrieving bags from the Bus Éireann coach at the set down at Terminal 1. This was where he had been told to be. Dublin Airport had armed police and Irish Army guarding the entrances to the terminal buildings. They were on the lookout for a reasonable facsimile of the likely enemy; a young man of Middle Eastern or Asian appearance.

The time had come and he felt the weight of the vest under his hoodie. His light frame meant that he didn't look suspiciously bulky with the device strapped around him. He took a few steps toward the centre of the bustling throng. People were excavating their luggage from the belly of the bus and more were queuing up to board. A few more steps, then he would die a martyr. He closed his eyes. He hadn't expected the wave of terror that washed over him, but it did.

Hassan wanted to live.

Gerry had manoeuvred the van out onto the M50, heading south towards Foxrock. Stan was sitting quietly, as if steeling himself for what might be ahead of them. Gerry could sense his tension.

"You OK, big fella?"

"Dobzah," was the one word reply and the big Pole continued to look ahead.

No worries with this lad. They had a street name in Foxrock and hopefully they might spot these fuckers. They had less than when they had moved on the Phibsborough safe house. The old Peeler had come through for them on that one and now he was dead. This whole thing was GUBU on steroids, thought Gerry.

Muhammad Bokhari and his men arrived at the site without any mishaps. They didn't see any police cars and the journey there was uneventful. God was helping them get to their destination.

East Road in Dublin 3 had provided the perfect placement site for the weapon. All that was keeping them from the concreted area beside the apartment complex was a padlock on a chain. They would only need to be there for minutes. By the time anyone had a chance to phone the authorities, they would have delivered Allah's punishment on the infidels.

But first he had to check the other part of the operation. He powered up one of the mobile phones that had been acquired for this operation. Imran Umarov answered immediately. Muhammad Bokhari smiled at the reliability of the Chechen. He was the nephew of the legendary Doku Khamatovich Umarov. Muhammad Bokhari had no concerns about this young man who was sitting in an apartment in Drumcondra where he had a perfect vantage point to witness God's vengeance on the infidels.

Hassan walked away from the crowd at the bus towards the end of the pavement area and in the direction of Terminal 2. He crossed a zebra crossing and entered an empty covered area that was designed to protect travellers from the elements as they walked from the drop off point into the terminal building.

Hassan wanted privacy. He lifted his mobile phone and called then man who had set him on the path to martyrdom. He had been told to get rid of his mobile phone when he travelled to Ireland, but he had many photographs on it and did not want to lose them. It seemed such a long time ago for the nineteen year-old. Mohammed Mahmoud did not recognise the number that was phoning him, but when he answered he knew the voice immediately. Standing in the shade of Dewsbury town hall where he had been attending a meeting with local councillors, the Qatari Imam was panicked. He instantly realised that this meant trouble.

"You must not call. It is not safe."

The forty-three year old Qatari preacher knew he was almost certainly under British state surveillance.

"I need your blessing Imam."

"For what I am about to do," the teenager continued.

The Imam wanted to hang up, but didn't want to risk Hassan not following through with his orders. For reasons of security he didn't know exactly what the boy had been tasked to do or where. Already in GCHQ, the call was being logged automatically and the algorithms were piecing together the significance of a call between those two mobile phones.

Mohammed Mahmoud took a breath and said gently, "Remember our time together Hassan. You must serve God. You must serve him today. Mar Salaam."

"Mar Salaam," replied Hassan as two young oriental women walked past him pulling wheeled luggage behind them. They were chatting in a language he had never heard before. One of them was wearing a short T-Shirt that was showing off her midriff and small denim shorts. She looked at the young Englishman, got eye contact and smiled at him. A thrill of sexual desire rushed through him as he watched the young women walking, their hips moving from side to side. In that moment the weight of the suicide vest under his shirt pulled him down and he had never felt so alone and so frightened.

Imran Umarov confirmed to his leader that he was in position and could see everything that he needed to observe.

Gerry nearly yanked the van into the hard shoulder when an alert beeped on his laptop on the seat beside him.

"Fuck! Yasmin!" he shouted.

He hit the brakes to make the turn off for Ballinteer.

"Is problem?" asked Stan.

"No. It's fuckin' dobzah big fella," smiled the Glaswegian.

He brought the van to stop at the top of Ballinteer Avenue and told his passenger to go check on Jack.

"Tell him we might be in business."

Gerry lifted the laptop up and immediately logged into his Proton mail.

Without even reading her mail he replied with a, "Hello. You OK?"

The answer was almost immediate.

"Hey Irishman! Big problems here. Finally gone from home. At a friend's. I'm safe. Did you read what I sent you?"

Gerry took a second to scroll through the mail. O'Shea had left them gold dust in his will. The passenger door opened and Stan and Jack were getting in.

"You two get back inside there. I'm coming in there too. This is too public for you, Jack," ordered Gerry as he jumped out, cradling the laptop.

The big Dubliner nodded and Stan followed.

Hassan walked back towards the bus set-down area where another vehicle was disgorging its human load and another set of passengers were waiting in line. He felt tears in his eyes as he slid past people and, quietly and unnoticed, reached into his hoodie.

Bokhari checked his mobile phone for news from the airport. That would be their signal. In the age of Twitter there was no such thing as a press blackout, and once the attack had taken place the whole world would know within a few minutes.

Jack eased himself back into the only seat in the back of Gerry's customised van.

"You in pain?" asked Gerry.

"I'm grand" snapped Jack.

Clearly he wasn't, but right now, they had bigger problems. Gerry balanced the laptop between his knees as he sat cross-legged. He read through Yasmin's mail twice and then looked up.

"Want to know what your old Peeler sent you?" said Gerry, looking at Jack.

"Course ah fuckin' do."

"Well according to this, Mr Man of the People McMillan is a Free State tout. Been that way for years."

"Bollox," said Jack, clearly not buying it, "He's a selfish cunt. Loves himself, but he's no tout."

"This says that he was a problem before England." Gerry looked up and got eye contact with Jack as he said those words.

Jack looked straight at the Glaswegian: "Leeds?"

"Well, someone was a problem there, big fella," said Gerry in a neutral tone.

"Ah fuck it!"

"What?"

"I went to him about this. After the Luas."

Gerry didn't miss a beat. He was way ahead of his old comrade.

"So you go to McMillan about getting the Army to sort out these boyos. You then speak to the oul Guard. He ends up stiffed and you're in the frame. And McMillan isn't a tout?" said Gerry with an admonishing flourish.

"I'm a fuckin' eejit! No wonder I got fucking scooped!" Jack's anger was being directed at himself. Then, right on cue, the Gobshite started to whisper some advice.

"Anyway. We're a bit further forward. There's more here about who's who in the Guards. O'Shea reckoned that Keegan, the top man, is a straight arrow."

"Big deal," said Jack scornfully.

"She's still working on the phones. Hopefully she gets something on them. OK, let's head over to that street in Foxrock. It's still our only shot."

"Are we fucked?" asked Stan.

"Well you may very well say that. I, on the other hand, couldn't possibly comment," said Gerry in his best Westminster accent.

"Is that mean fucked?"

"The situation is desperate but not hopeless, big fella."

"Dobzah."

The Glaswegian was sending Yasmin another mail when a breaking news alert pinged on his desktop. Gerry sat back, the energy draining from him. Jack immediately spotted that something was wrong.

"What is it, wee fella?"

"Ah fuck it!"

"We fucked?"

"We are indeed buddy. Utterly fucked."

"WHAT?"

"Suicide bomb at the airport. Dozens dead. We're too late, big lad."

"Fuck!" roared Jack and kicked out at the van door before crumpling in agony as pain shot right up into his embarrassing wound.

Muhammad Bokhari smiled and looked across at the driver of his van.

"Hassan is in Paradise. It is time to do God's work"

"Allahu Akbar!" said Abu Mohammad, an English-born Libyan who had served the Caliphate in Syria.

It was unlike Gerry O'Donnell to be stuck for a plan, but he was now thinking of Jack's predicament. The big Dubliner was scrutinising his old comrade.

"What is it, Gerry?"

The Glaswegian was taken aback by Jack using his name. It was so unlike him.

"I'm thinking about how we get you out of this fit up for O'Shea."

"WE don't, but I can get the two of you out of this shite."

"What?" said Gerry, genuinely puzzled.

"Look. My DNA is all over O'Shea's gaff in Terenure. There was bad blood between us. I'm just told I can't see my kid. He's in the Luas. I go off the edge and take it out on an old Peeler. Case fuckin' closed. Drive me to the nearest barracks."

"No chance!" said Gerry, anger rising in him at the fatalism of his old comrade.

"Let's face it, wee lad. I've made an arse of the whole thing," said Jack, laughing at his own joke.

Gerry didn't get the humour and Stan looked on bemused.

"See that oul DNA? Thanks to John Wayne here I bled all over that house in Phibsborough." The big Pole put his head down.

Gerry was listening as Jack laid out the reality of the situation.

"There's two stiffs in Phibsborough and I'm already in the frame for O'Shea."

"But…" Gerry started, but the big Dubliner cut across him.

"Wee lad, I'm a lifer out on licence. They don't need to hang that much on me till I'm back in for the duration."

"You are fucked gaffer," said Stan quietly.

The Dubliner smiled and patted Big Pole on the back in an approving way.

"Top of the class, Stanislav. Gaffer is fucked and then a bit more."

"Bollox…" said Gerry quietly, admitting defeat in the situation.

"There is one thing you can do for me, wee lad."

"Name it."

"Drive this thing over to Tallaght. I'm going to try and see the wee fella before… before I set this stuff right."

"No problems," said Gerry, sadness flooding through him.

The big, bad-tempered man in the seat in front of him had a level of courage and duty he could never match, although he had never said that to him.

Then Gerry's brain kicked into gear.

"First, we better dump this gear. She calls the Guards and we're sitting in a van full of shorts…"

"Good shout. Dump arms it is then," said Jack, looking at Gerry and smiling.

The Glaswegian nodded in acknowledgment. He hoped that his comrade would get something in Tallaght other than grief and he thought of his own son. Maria wouldn't forgive this, he knew that. He had broken the most sacred promise to her. Shit, what a mess.

"OK, let's go lads."

Stan took the cue and slid open the van door to let in the August sunshine. Gerry was closing the laptop lid when it pinged. He flicked the touch pad and saw it was Yasmin. She had found them.

"WAIT!" said Gerry.

"What?" asked Jack.

"We're back in business if you're up for it."

Gerry closed the van door behind him and assumed the lotus position with the laptop balanced between his knees. Stan tried to lean over to see the screen, but Gerry gestured with his hand to sit back down. Yasmin was online and had sent him a file, which he opened. What was in front of him was like Google Maps, only much smarter. Gerry looked at the two locations that were pulsing on the map of Dublin. That was where two of the sim cards were.

"What you got?" asked Jack.

Gerry re-adjusted his seating on the floor of the van and turned the laptop around to give a presentation to the other two men.

"That batch of phones? Two of them are on and they're here," said Gerry, gesturing to the screen with his index finger. Jack leaned forward to read the map.

"Fitzroy Avenue? That's Drum C."

"OK. We go to that one first?"

"No chance."

"Why?"

"That place will be crawling with Peelers because of the match."

"Match?"

"Mayo and Kerry. Semi-final."

Gerry looked at the two pulsing circles at both locations.

"House in Drumcondra. Vacant ground in East Wall," whispered Gerry, his mind trying to process the variables. Then he recalled the Jihadi in the garage.

"The vengeance of Allah will fall from the sky."

"Yeah. Has to be," Gerry said to himself.

"WHAT?" asked Jack, exasperated.

Gerry looked up at his old comrade.

"It's a mortar attack! On Croker!"

"Holy Jaysus."

"We go now. We stop them," said Stan.

"Fuckin' right, big lad," said Gerry.

He closed the laptop quickly and with purpose. Stan slid the door open and stepped out. Gerry followed him, but turned to Jack and got eye contact with him.

"Against enemies foreign and domestic. Right?"

"Hundred per cent," smiled Jack.

Muhammad Bokhari had insisted on the larger weapon for the operation. That meant that even one or two rounds would do much more damage. The 2B14 Podnos eighty-two millimetre mortars were more numerous and easier to transport. However, the veteran of the Syrian campaign knew that the lethality of the one twenty millimetre round was what was required. He request was acceded to.

The rusty chain held by a padlock was no match for the brand new bolt cutters. They were onto the vacant lot within seconds. It was overlooked by several apartment blocks. Yes, they would be discovered, but not until they had delivered the rounds. A skilled crew could fire twelve rounds a minute from this 2S12 "Sani" one twenty millimetre heavy mortar.

This group of men had delivered rounds in the heat of battle in Aleppo. They would do God's work with skill and precision. Muhammad Bokhari was out of the passenger seat and onto the tarmac in an instant, and slapped the side door of the van.

"Allahu Akbar!" he shouted.

The side and the two rear doors burst open and his men swung into action as they repeated the chant back in unison. The mortar weighed 190.5 kg, and was rolled down metal rails on two large pneumatic tyres.

Bokhari called the Chechen and he was in position. If the crew had aligned the weapon incorrectly then he would tell them. The first shell burst over Clonliffe Road. Thirty minutes earlier it would have been full of football fans heading into Croke Park. However, there were still plenty on the thoroughfare to breath in the deadly toxin.

Imran Umarov saw the yellow cloud appear in the sky and looked at the street map on the small table at the window. He gave the corrections. The next round, Inshallah, would drop right inside the stadium. They knew this was the time when the Irish President would be on the field.

It was God's will.

Jack didn't know the route they were taking to get to East Wall. He just knew that they weren't hanging around. The wee lad certainly knew how to throw this van around, he thought. His brain was also going at a speed. He rummaged in his pocket and got out the phone that Gerry had given to him in Letterkenny.

Jack tried to remember the number and dialled it. It wasn't correct. Fuck it. The van went over some mighty bump in the road and the phone nearly flew out of his big hand.

The card. Wallet. He found Tommy's business card in his wallet and dialled the number.

"Hello?" answered the taxi driver, clearly on a hands-free.

Jack could hear the engine of the car. There was no time to be secret squirrel about this.

"Tommy boy. It's Jack."

"Jaysus. Big fella! You right?" answered Tommy Noonan, slightly frightened.

"In a tight fix here buddy."

"Just name it, lad."

"Remember that chat we had in Slattery's years ago?"

"Do surely."

"It's that time."

"Grand job. Just a second."

Jack listened to what sounded like the vehicle coming to a halt and a conversation then ensued.

"…Look, I'm not charging you, you're halfway fucking there, now OUT OF THE FUCKING TAXI!"

There was the sound of the door slamming shut and then engine being gunned.

"Another satisfied customer," said Tommy.

Jack chuckled.

"You're a mighty man, Noonan."

"Where to, sir?"

"East Road, East Wall. We're on our way there now."

"We?"

"Me and my Squad."

"On my way now!"

"We're in a green van. Donegal plates. Call this number when you're close Tommy."

"Will do, skipper."

The Russian was watching these madmen from a distance. He had parked on East Road, a few hundred yards from where the Jihadis had burst into the vacant lot. His brief was to prevent anything from happening to them. This was easy money, he thought, and his mind wandered to his extraction. The apartment would need to be forensically swept, but he was usually careful. With luck he could be in Berlin the day after tomorrow for some R & R.

Muhammad Bokhari has relaying what Umarov was saying to the crew word for word. Akbar Choudry was listening intently and carefully re-aligning the mortar. The next one had to be perfect. It was the time. It had to be now.

John Mulrennan from Roscommon had spent the Sunday morning recuperating from a heavy night with some of his buddies from DCU. As they were studying Biotechnology they'd joked that they knew the exact chemical makeup of what they were throwing down themselves during happy hour in town. When he awoke in his apartment the world was taking revenge on him. He stumbled into the kitchen in the hope that there was some OJ left in the fridge.

The twenty year old from Castlerea heard a thump outside and couldn't place the sound. He looked out over the balcony and his hungover brain couldn't initially process what he was looking at. The university student gawped at the scene from an action movie being played out in front of his disbelieving eyes.

The crew was reaching into the van for another mortar round when a green Mercedes van swung into the square. Bokhari saw the front of the van lunge down as it screeched to a halt. As the doors swung open the only sound was the van's horn splitting the air. There were weapons in the Jihadi's own vehicle and, although startled, the men turned and reached for them. It was a few seconds advantage, nothing more, but in a fight situation tiny advantages can become decisive if capitalized upon.

Between the Glock and the Browning Gerry and Stan had eighteen rounds of nine millimetre to deal with six enemies. In theory that was enough without a mag change, but close quarter battles rarely adhere to textbook theories.

Aleksander Mikhail Vasiliev was re-arranging his equipment in the holdall when he looked up and saw the worst-case scenario a hundred and fifty metres in front of him. He acted with blinding speed and gunned his car towards the Jihadis.

He was speeding towards the men he was tasked to protect when a Nissan Qashqai pulled out of the car park of an apartment block. The driver was on his mobile and simply wasn't looking. Aleksander Mikhail Vasiliev hit the brakes, but his passenger wing hit the Japanese crossover SUV. The airbag detonated and filled the space between driver and steering wheel.

Because he froze, Muhammad Bokhari was the first to die. Stan's aim was true even as he was falling from the van onto the tarmac. The Browning hi-power that Gerry had meticulously cleaned cycled smoothly with no stoppages. In an upward trajectory four rounds hit the Jihadi in the thigh, abdomen, sternum and throat. He was dead before his bulk had come to rest of the tarmac.

Akbar Choudry leapt from the back of their van and crouched with an AKS-74U short barrelled assault rifle. This gun could be a game changer in the right hands. The rounds ripped through the driver's door that had swung open and then the weapon arched upwards taking out the windscreen. The last round of his initial burst flew over the vehicle and he tied to steady himself.

Gerry, belly to the ground under the door, aimed the Glock 19 and sent two rounds at the crouching man. One of them was wide by a few inches, but the other entered his lower ribcage and the hollow point ammunition did what it said on the box. He wasn't dead, but Akbar Choudry was on the floor with a punctured aorta.

Hussein Iqbal seized a mortar shell and reached to drop it down the tube.

Stan was nearest to him.

"Stan, get him!" shouted Gerry.

Hussein Iqbal raised his GSh-18 Russian automatic pistol to stop the big Pole in his tracks, but three rounds from a Glock zinged past him, hitting their van and making him instinctively put his head down.

Inside the van, the Gobshite was in full flow.

"Just sit here. They're out there getting hurt. Guys get booze sent into prison. You can get anything you want in there. Pauline might visit with the kid. She'll come round in time. No point in dying for this shite."

Choudry's burst had narrowly missed Jack's head when it hit the van. He looked up at the holes in the vehicle that would have killed Gerry if he had been sitting in the driver's seat. Best sit tight, said the Gobshite.

Stan hit the Jihadi like a rugby player on steroids. As the Iraqi toppled over, the Polish ex-paratrooper followed through, turning his attention to grabbing the mortar bomb. He didn't know what was in it, but he knew that dropping the thing probably wasn't a good idea. Hussein Iqbal went into a frenzy of clawing and biting under the big Pole as Stan wrestled the mortar round away from him and stretched out his arms.

Muhammad Tirmizi had darted around the Jihadi's van when the action had started and seized his moment to emerge. He too had a GSh-18 9mm Russian pistol and aimed it at the man wrestling on the ground. A bullet whizzed past his head and he ducked down and came up firing at the shooter. He was a combat veteran of Aleppo and many other battles in Syria.

The first round hit Gerry O'Donnell in the pelvis, the second in the left deltoid area and the third he was sure was a head shot. The man crumpled to the ground and he moved forward to make sure.

John Mulrennan had not moved an inch. He stood and gawped as the side door of the green van slid open and a big man stumbled out firing a large pistol.

Once the Roscommon lad snapped out of his shock, he went back into his bedroom get his mobile.

The jacketed hollow point ammunition from the 357 magnum thudded into Muhammad Tirmizi's body and threw him backwards. As he arced through the air life had already gone from him.

The big Dubliner moved quickly, ripping his stiches open, towards Stan, who was trying to keep the mortar bomb away from Hussein Iqbal's frantic grasp. Jack yanked Stan up by the waist band of his jeans and the big Pole managed to hold onto the bomb. Without a word Jack put the last two rounds from the Ruger into Hussein Iqbal. It was over.

"Put that thing away, son," said Jack to Stan, gesturing to the mortar round that he was cradling in his well-developed arms.

The big Pole went inside the van and saw that there were a rack of identical rounds. He put it back and left the van.

Jack was standing over Gerry's body.

"Ah fuck, wee lad," said Jack and started to sob.

Stan went over the big Dubliner.

"We have to go, gaffer."

Jack lowered himself slowly onto one knee beside Gerry.

"Ah shite…" was all that Jack could manage.

The guilt he felt inside for listening to the Gobshite when his best friend in the world was fighting for his life was too much to bear. Big Jack Dempsey was still thinking of proper words to say when most of his brain exploded out through where his face had been.

Stan hit the deck and the Russian searched for another target for his VSS suppressed sniper rifle. The ex-paratrooper from Krakow dived for cover, bent double as he had been trained in the Close Quarter Combat course in the airborne. He ran, zig-zagging to get behind the van. Before he came to rest a huge force hit his lower right leg and spun him round in mid-air. He screamed in pain as he hit the tarmac with a thud and the automatic pistol span out of his grip.

The Russian had loosed off three silent subsonic rounds before he had found his target. The man on the ground was clearly no amateur, but now he was finished. Aleksander Mikhail Vasiliev stood up, took a couple of steps forward and shouldered his weapon. He could see the helpless man looking straight at him through his scope. The target was acquired.

It was an execution.

Just as he squeezed first pressure onto the trigger, Tommy Noonan's car hit him full force and propelled him into the air like a circus tumbler. By the time he hit East Road, life was already ebbing from him. Tommy Noonan jumped from his car and aimed a kick at the Russian's head. It flopped to the side, utterly lifeless.

"Cunt!" exclaimed the taxi driver.

"Help!" cried Stan.

Tommy Noonan covered the ground to the stricken bleeding man as quick had his sixty-five year old legs would carry him. He had tunnel vision as he ran to the aid of the Pole, but something caught the corner of his eye. It was the corpse of Jack Dempsey.

"Ah Jaysus, Jack!" said Tommy Noonan.

The grief stopped him from going near the bag man's corpse like there was a force field was around it. Tommy Noonan was snapped out of it as the sound of police sirens filled the air.

"Come on, son," said Tommy Noonan, helping Stan onto his one good leg. "The Free Staters are on their way."

He was able to support Stan to hobble a few steps, but it was clearly not working. The big man was too heavy and Tommy was too old. The sirens were growing louder.

"Wait here," said Noonan.

Stan balanced himself against the van as Tommy Noonan backed up the taxi at high speed. The tyres crunched to a halt. The passenger window came down electronically and the driver shouted: "Get in the back seat, those fuckers are close!"

Stan hopped over to the car, opened the door and dived head long into the car. The door was still open. Tommy Noonan set off and Stan struggled up to grab the door and finally pull it shut without falling out.

"Why you help me?" asked Stan as the taxi made good speed away from the scene of the gunfight.

Tommy Noonan didn't take his eyes off the road. He just made a lights before they turned red, not that he would have stopped.

"What?" asked Noonan.

"You help me. Why?"

"I swore an oath."

In the apartment, John Mulrennan looked down at his phone and saw that he had just acquired over ten thousand followers on Twitter.

Epilogue

Jennifer Jaeger was so excited about catching up with her friend Molly O'Reilly that she was sitting in the Plough and the Stars at least forty minutes before they had agreed to meet. The Philadelphia native was wearing an Eagles jacket, stonewashed jeans and Nike trainers. It was a dress-down Saturday for the working reporter. When Molly finally made it in to the Irish pub that was her home from home, Jen Jaeger stood up and waved like a groupie.

"Hey you!"

She caught Molly's eyes immediately. It wouldn't have been difficult, given that Jen Jaeger had changed her hair again; this time to Parakeet and Turquoise with a flash of pink across the fringe of her close-cropped hair. Molly O'Reilly smiled at her as she gave her a hug and sat down.

"I saw you on The Bill Marr Show, oh my fucking God!" gushed Jen Jaeger.

"JJ, in here, I'm just plain Molly O, old Seamus' daughter," smiled Molly.

"They say you're gonna win a Pulitzer Prize for this stuff. Way to go!"

"Yeah, maybe."

"I mean. Our government? The C I fucking A?"

"Yeah, pretty crazy stuff. Then again, no one would have believed all that NSA stuff before Ed Snowden," said Molly quietly.

"For sure" said Jen.

"Let's order breakfast honey. I'm not watching my Bhoys slaughter Sevco on an empty Irish stomach!"

"Molly O, you and soccer!"

Eamonn Keegan walked into Gareth Scully's office accompanied by two uniformed officers. The Justice Minister looked up with a panicked start, hunched over a portable shredder.

"Well, I didn't think that fat useless cunt Gaffney had it in him," said the tall Donegal man.

"Still, he was just a cog. It was you who was turning the big wheel in this, Minister."

"How dare you speak to me like that," blustered Scully.

Keegan placed an Olympus VN-741Pc on the desk and pressed the button. There was the ruffle of static, but the sound quality was surprisingly good for an office Dictaphone. Scully heard his own voice speaking to Gaffney. The Justice Minister then slumped in the chair and stared in front of him into a middle distance that had no future.

"Gareth Alexander Scully, I am arresting you on suspicion of…" were the last words that the Justice Minister heard.

Two young Gardaí who had come into the room just behind Keegan moved on the Donegal man's signal. The pinch of the handcuffs on Scully's wrists was the feeling of his world ending.

"One other thing, Minister," said Keegan.

Gareth Scully looked up at Keegan for some hope, for some glimmer of a deal.

"An Taoiseach sends his regards."

He was the last to arrive, and as he was ushered in to the living room by the driver and the man who had accompanied him. Liam McMillan took a sharp intake of breath. People who were household names in the Republican movement were sitting on sofas and chairs, and there was a kitchen chair in the middle of the floor. That was clearly intended for him. It was the seating arrangement for a court martial.

Jerome Pelfrey's flight across the Atlantic had been like a VIP rendition, and the irony wasn't lost on him when the Lear jet touched down in Virginia at an airfield used by the Company. A vehicle was waiting to take him straight to Langley. He hadn't been allowed to go to his home or to contact anyone. Severe protocols were in operation. During the debrief, which had lasted three days, nothing physical had been done to Pelfrey. However, he was questioned again and again by skilled interrogators working in shifts. He wasn't suspected of treason, and he was one of their own.

However, this operation inside the European Union had gone massively south and there was a lot of ass covering going on. But now, sitting outside the Director's office waiting to be called in, he was about to find out if he truly was untouchable CIA royalty. His father had been in the Company throughout the rise and fall of Nixon, and he wondered how all that would have played out in the era of blogs and the worldwide web.

"You gonna believe some fucking blog and not me?" thundered Liam McMillan to the man who was sitting directly opposite him.

McMillan had first met this man in the New Lodge Road almost half a century ago, but he'd never wanted to meet him under these circumstances. His reputation within the Movement for dealing with "internal housekeeping" was fearsome. The white-haired man, now a grandfather, took his thumb and his bent fore-finger and scraped out his bottom lip in an unconscious gesture, looking at the floor. Then he looked up and got eye contact with Liam McMillan.

"There are a lot of details out on the internet. A lot of details. Our people are asking questions," said the man.

"This is a fucking stitch-up! I'm telling ya, it's the fucking Brits. They're spinning ye a yarn!" shouted McMillan.

The big man in the corner hadn't said a word. The questioning seemed to be at an end, and McMillan had issued denial after denial. The man took his index finger and rubbed the ribbed of his nose; an unconscious mannerism he wasn't even aware of. As ever, he thought before he spoke. That was why he'd survived so long and risen to such prominence. Just before he spoke, he took a little intake of breath through his nostrils, that characteristic sniff that made everyone aware he was about to speak. McMillan was scanning his face for any indication of what he was thinking, but that was a forlorn hope. This man did inscrutability very well.

"I think we'll need to manage this situation carefully. For the optics. This isn't the old days." As he finished speaking, he looked up and got eye contact with Liam McMillan, and the TD knew he was finished.

Doctor Karim Bessaoud was meditating on the magical properties of coffee in the midst of another marathon shift, when the door to the small staffroom burst open with SWAT team urgency.

It was Rose O'Hagan from the ICU.

"Doctor!"

Karim didn't need any further explanation. He reacted with Pavlovian predictability. As he approached the room where the patient was, he heard words he had come to love in the previous few months from a voice he thought he'd never hear again.

"For it's a grand old team to play for! For it's a grand old team to see…"

Karim rushed to the bedside and Gerry O'Donnell was in full voice like he was back at Celtic Park. Karim looked down at the man in the bed. His eyes were closed, but he was now clearly emerging from his coma, and still singing. The Moroccan responded instinctively.

"Allahu Akbar. Allahu Akbar."

Rose O'Hagan, also reacting to childhood training, made the sign of the cross.

"Thanks be to God," she said.

The doctor turned and smiled at her, and she smiled back.

Karim thought to himself that it would make an interesting aside in a future professional conference that a Neurosurgeon from Morocco operating on a Glaswegian in Dublin had enlisted the clinical assistance of the James Connolly Celtic Supporters Club to come in twice a week to sit by a man's bed and sing Celtic songs to him. It is proven that people even in the deepest coma can hear, and if they hear something that is emotionally important to them, then it can stimulate recovery. For all his skill on the operating table and in the post-operative care, it just might have been the Celtic songs that had got through to what had seemed a lost cause. Karim leaned over very close to Gerry O'Donnell's ear.

"Welcome back, my brother."

Karim straightened up. He turned to Rose O'Hagan and said, "If there is any further development, let me know immediately."

"Yes Doctor," said the nurse.

As the Moroccan left the room, the young guard who had been dozily on duty in a plastic chair was standing and blocking his way.

"Doctor, is the patient awake?" asked the guard.

"Intermittently. He is showing signs of recovery, but he is not well enough to be questioned," said Dr Bessaoud.

"My orders are to…"

"Your orders are your orders, but the patient is not fully conscious and aware. And I will tell you when he is, and when he is well enough to speak to anyone. He is my patient. Is that clear?"

"Yes, yes, Doctor."

Karim walked in to the small private room and smiled when he saw that Gerry O'Donnell was sitting up eating a piece of toast.

"Salaam alaikum," said Gerry.

"Wa alaikum salaam," replied Karim, smiling.

Gerry proffered the cup of tea as if to say "Sláinte".

"The staff tells me you had a good normal sleep."

"Yeah, grand. I think I had a dream this morning. Really daft dream. Not sure. It's all fuzzy."

"That is all normal, you're making good progress. You are a tough man, Brother Gerry."

"Don't know about that. I think I've got you to thank for still being here."

"Ah, you're made from tough people. And God has smiled on you. This I am sure."

"There was one thing, though…" said Gerry hesitantly.

"Yes?"

"I had this mental dream. I mean really mental dream. It's probably nothing, but you're the guy that does the brain work."

"What was it?" said Karim, now playing the interested clinician.

"You're gonna laugh at this, but I thought it was you singing the Celtic song to me. You don't even know what that is. Don't laugh, but when I first opened my eyes, I thought I might be in Paradise. Ah," said Gerry O'Donnell, laughing at himself.

"No, but you're making enough progress for me to take you there. I made it there last week."

"Eh?" said the puzzled Glaswegian.

363

"It was against Aberdeen. We won 2-0, but it should have been more. They packed a midfield and tried to stop us being inventive. Oh Gerry, the singing in Paradise is wonderful," enthused the Moroccan medic.

"Sorry?"

Gerry O'Donnell looked stunned. He was still trying to take all this in.

"Doctor? Karim? How long have I been out?"

"More than four months, but God has sent you back to us. He has a plan for you. This is good."

Gerry O'Donnell was bringing his thoughts together. He asked the question that had been in his mind for a couple of days.

"Jack?"

"He's with God," said the Berber, with sadness in his voice.

Sadness washed over Gerry O'Donnell, and he sunk back into the pillow, not knowing what to say. Karim Bessaoud reached out an arm and pressed onto Gerry's shoulder.

"Brother Jack was a good man. In time, everyone will know that."

"I hope so."

Gerry looked up, tears starting to emerge in his eyes.

The door opened and in came a nurse. Karim left Gerry's bedside and went over to her. He stooped down as she reached up to whisper something in his ear. He nodded and she left and closed the door.

"I have a surprise for you, and I think it will aid your recovery."

Gerry tilted his head to one side in a mannerism that asked for more information. Just then, the door opened. And there she was, standing in the doorway, smiling at him like she had the first time when he had sat beside her at the Albergue in Galicia. In that moment, everything, absolutely everything, was OK in Gerry O'Donnell's world. A small bundle then exploded past her and leapt up onto the bed, throwing his arms around his father.

"PAPA!"

Gerry O'Donnell simply couldn't speak.

Maria walked forward, smiling.

"Hey Chico. ¿Cómo estas? We have missed you."

"God is good, God is good," smiled Karim.

Mary Reilly coped with her grief the only way she knew how. She kept her routine and she worked hard. The whole insane saga had taught her that there were no prizes for hiding your feelings; the man she had grown to love would now never know how she felt about him. Jack Dempsey was the last person she thought would have left a will and everything in order, but he had. Mary Francis Reilly was now the owner of a thriving security company. Money had been put in trust for his son Pádraig, and one of the clauses in the will was that Mary Reilly would make sure that it was carried through when the child came of age.

Once the guards had left her in peace and her office was no longer a potential crime scene, she got on with the job of organising the corner that had been Jack's. She took a quiet Saturday to go through drawers and find things that made her smile, and made her quietly weep. But the weeks passed into months and Jack's clutter, just like Jack, was gone. She had recruited some new guys to the firm, and she would occasionally ask herself whether or not Jack would hire this one or that one. It usually worked well enough. She was getting some invoices in order when the door opened and in stooped a sight for her sore eyes.

"Well, look who the cat dragged in," smiled Mary Reilly.

"I back."

"Well no shit, Sherlock. And here's me thinking you were hiding out somewhere."

"Everything OK?"

"Everything's grand, Sonny Jim," chirped the diminutive Dubliner.

"I mean, no more trouble? Police?" asked Stan hesitantly.

"Ah, they were here looking for ya," said Mary matter-of-factly.

"They were?" Stan was clearly worried.

"Yeah, they wanted to know where you were the day that Jack and all of that shite…"

"Asking about me? Wanting me?"

"As soon as they knew where you were they didn't want to see you. I told them you'd got hurt in the nightclub bombing and you'd, ah, gone away to rest."

"You told them where I was?" said Stan, both alarmed and puzzled.

"Yeah, they wanted to check where you were on the day it all happened and I told them – well, I just told them the truth."

"You told them…" asked Stan, still standing with his hands jammed in his black bomber jacket pockets, his brow knitted in concern.

Mary looked up from her desk and smiled.

"Well, I just had to tell them all the details. Bit embarrassing."

"What did you tell them?"

"Just that you were with me all day."

"You give me ali-"

"Alibi. It's called an alibi, son."

"Yes, you, you cover for me. Thank you."

"Anyway, if they do ask you, you'll just need to tell them that you were with me."

"Yes, I will."

"That you were with me that day, and all we did was fuck. All day. Kinda mental."

"What?" Stan's jaw dropped.

"Yeah, you were a beast. Hardly let me go to the toilet. Animal, you were," smiled Mary, bursting out laughing.

"You tell the Police that?"

"Well, they believed me, Sonny Jim, so well, you never know," said Mary Riley, breaking up laughing. She stood up, walked across the floor of the small office and gave Stan a big hug.

She looked him straight in the eyes.

"It's great to see you back, son. It's great to see you back."

"Dobzah," said Stan.

Gerry O'Donnell was sitting up in his hospital bed when the door opened and in walked two men, both over six foot tall. Although they weren't in uniform, Gerry O'Donnell knew coppers at first glance. They stood at the bottom of his bed. One, who was clearly in charge, was wearing a thigh-length plain black waterproof jacket, dress slacks, polished black shoes and a black polo-neck sweater. Their plain clothes couldn't have gotten any plainer if they tried, thought Gerry. The man looked at O'Donnell to make sure that the patient sitting in the bed with the turban-like bandage around his head was fully compos mentis.

When he was satisfied he asked, "Are you Gerard Patrick Joseph O'Donnell?"

"Well, actually, one is Richard John Bingham, 7th Earl of Lucan if one must know. Are you one of my tenants?" said Gerry in his best Sandhurst accent.

"Gerard Patrick Joseph O'Donnell?" continued the policeman, ignoring the insolence of the suspect in the hospital bed.

"I suppose you're not gonna accept no for an answer on that one, are ya?" smiled Gerry.

"Just answer the question please, sir," said Eamon Keegan.

"Yeah, yeah. The very same," said Gerry O'Donnell with a resignation in his voice.

"Gerard Patrick Joseph O'Donnell normally resident in Gortahork, County Donegal?" asked the Garda Commissioner.

"Yeah, that's the one. Now, what can I be doing for you gentlemen?"

"Mr O'Donnell, do you recognise me?"

"Wait a minute now, your face is familiar. Daniel O'Donnell concert? Donegal town, a few years ago? Things got kinda crazy?" said O'Donnell in his best sarcastic voice.

"I'm not in the mood for fucking joking."

"And I'm not really in the mood for fucking anything. I've half my fucking head missing. Or haven't you noticed?"

"I'm Eamon Keegan, Garda Commissioner. This is my colleague…"

"Fuck, not just any ordinary peeler to slap the handcuffs on me! Colour me impressed!"

"You're not being arrested, Mr O'Donnell," said Keegan. Gerry O'Donnell, was blindsided, but tried to hide his surprise.

"Well, that's a bit of good news. It was you at that Daniel O'Donnell concert, wasn't it?"

"Mr O'Donnell, I think you can probably assist in cleaning up a mess. In fact, calling it a mess doesn't really do it justice."

"I'm not sure I can help anyone in the state I'm in, Mister Commissioner," said Gerry O'Donnell, at this point completely flummoxed as to how this conversation was going to go.

"Did you get a look at the vehicle that hit your van, Mr O'Donnell?"

Gerry O'Donnell was totally bemused at this line of questioning and he was beginning to be even more uneasy than when he thought they were just in to arrest him for being at the mortar site, and the small matter of all those dead Jihadis.

"Can't say that I did. Am, but I think it had Syrian registration plates, if that's any help," said O'Donnell.

Keegan's Garda driver, a sergeant originally from Galway, burst out laughing and then supressed the mirth as his boss shot him an angry glance.

"Mr O'Donnell, I have one awful mess to clean up here. While you were in your coma this state has had the biggest crisis since the Arms Trial in 1970. Arresting you would make it a lot worse. From the very top it has been decided that it wouldn't be in the national interest to have you in a court room situation."

"Well, anything to help the forces of law and order. You know me."

"Well, I know a fair bit about you, Mr O Donnell. I was reading your file this morning. Unfortunately there are some large gaps in it, and I don't know if that's a testament to your abilities as a terrorist or the failings of this police force decades ago."

"I have no idea what you're speaking about, Mr Commissioner, sir, but I'm more than willing to help you, of course, as a law-abiding citizen," said O'Donnell, smiling.

"Look, O'Donnell, let's cut to the fucking chase here."

"Go ahead," said Gerry, all business-like.

"You were involved in a road traffic accident down around East Wall. The other vehicle didn't stop. It wasn't your fault. The medical records here will show nothing about a bullet wound, and we'll get you well and shipped back to Donegal."

"Whatever you say, Commissioner," said O'Donnell, genuinely puzzled at what was going on.

"But I do have to ask you some questions."

"Thought you might."

"Were you ever in touch with a member of this Force called Tony Byrne?" asked Keegan, looking forward and getting eye-contact, scanning for any flicker of hesitation or stress, the way police officers do when they're questioning a suspect.

"No, can't say it rings any bells," said O'Donnell in the relaxed way that people do when they're telling the truth.

Keegan scanned Gerry O'Donnell's face as he sat up in the hospital bed. He was still that street cop in the bad lands of Moyross and he didn't need a Master's Degree from anywhere to spot someone lying.

"Grand job," said Eamonn Keegan.

The policeman turned to leave the room, but stopped and turned back and said:

"Just one other thing."

"This isn't an episode of 'Colombo' is it? Because you don't have the old raincoat for that," said Gerry.

"Now that you're back in the land of the living, it would make my life a whole lot easier if someone would call off that fucking blogger. The one that seems to know more about this case than I do. Not that you probably know anything about that Mr O'Donnell."

"I'm always happy you help the authorities."

Keegan didn't reply, but this time did turn and leave the room and his driver closed the door behind him.

Three Months Later

Pauline Duffy was walking down her garden with her son when she saw a man with a black, woollen beanie hat and a green outdoor jacket, accompanied by a small boy about the same age as her son, opening her gate.

"Pauline?" asked Gerry O'Donnell.

"Who's asking?" asked Pauline Duffy with some alarm in her voice.

"Sorry. I should have said. My name's Gerry. I – I left a voice message and I…"

"Oh! You're the friend of…" said Pauline, nodding down towards her son.

"Yeah. The very one."

"You better come in, then."

Gerry felt it was time to do the introductions to the little people. "This is my fella here."

Right on cue, his son proudly stated, "Me llamo Felipe."

"Jaysus, is he foreign?" asked Pauline, putting her key in her front door and opening it.

"Sure he's as Irish as the hills, this fella."

"And you're Scottish?"

"Nah, not really. Not in any way that it matters."

"You'd better come in."

Pauline had been hoping for some me time. Her plan for that morning had been to take the wee fella over to poor Siobhán's mother. She'd sort of adopted the wee fella since everything had happened, and well, she wasn't going to have any grandkids from Siobhán; God love her.

Little Pádraig didn't stand on ceremony, and immediately struck up a relationship with the new lad.

"I've got the new PlayStation!" said Jack Dempsey's son.

Gerry looked at the little fella and realised that, for all the court wrangling, a DNA test would have been a complete waste of money. The little lad was the absolute spit of his old comrade.

Gerry's son followed the little fella into the living room, and there was the immediate sound of two busy little boys getting around the serious stuff of playing. Pauline looked in their direction, looked back at Gerry and smiled. She tilted her head in the direction of the kitchen. Pauline moved towards the kettle and flicked it on.

"Tea?"

"Ah go on, ye will," said Gerry O'Donnell in his best Mrs Doyle voice, and Pauline had a giggle.

The sound of the socialising from the living room got louder as there was some electronic crash, and the sound of Jack's son yelling, "YES!"

Gerry planted himself on one of the bar stool type chairs at the breakfast bar. Pauline smiled.

"Those two sound like they've been besties for years."

"Yeah, my little fella's an only child. He loves meeting new potential brothers."

"Yeah, my fella's gonna be an only child as well," said Pauline, thinking out loud.

"Ah sure, you're still young," said Gerry reassuringly.

"No, that fella will do me."

"Ah well, you never know," said Gerry, closing the conversation off.

"You didn't say what it was when you left the message?"

"Yeah, yeah. You're right. I didn't think it was maybe something for a voicemail," said Gerry as he unzipped his green Ventile jacket and reached in to the large map pocket inside. He pulled out a brown envelope.

"Well, it's that Fianna Fáil moment, honey."

Pauline looked at him, not getting what he was on about as he put the envelope on the breakfast bar.

"What's this?" Pauline was both puzzled and slightly alarmed.

"It's some money. It's not mine. It was Jack. Some chats we had before…Well, before, you know."

Pauline Duffy didn't know what to say.

"Well, um…"

"Look, I don't know your situation and it's none of my business, but, uh, sometimes cash transactions are handy, right?" said Gerry, smiling.

"I don't know what to say."

"You don't need to say anything. I'm just doing what I promised Jack I would."

"Thanks."

"See, you do know what to say."

"Yeah."

"There's some more where that came from, but that might give you a help just now."

"It's not been easy, trying to keep him from all that shite with his father. All over the fuckin' media."

"Yeah, I know."

"Thing is, I didn't really know him."

"Well I did. He was a hell of a man. Difficult bollocks, though," said Gerry, lifting the mood. Pauline Duffy burst out laughing, and then the tears started to come.

"What will I tell him when he's bigger?"

"When the time's right, you'll know. And you can always call on me."

Gerry reached into his mobile phone cover and took out a business card. He pushed it across.

"Anything that bothers ya, anything you need help with. I'm sure you've got family here, but anything you think you really need, if I can help, don't hesitate to contact me. OK?"

"What you doing this for?"

"Doing what?"

"Well, being here, helping, giving over money."

"Wasn't my money. I'm just passing it on."

"But helping. What you helping for? Helping us? Me? Me and the wee fella?"

"Well that's easy. I swore an oath," smiled Gerry.

Pauline Duffy was scrutinising this man sitting across from her and trying to assess who he really was. Then she snapped out of it.

"Jesus, I haven't even made you that tea."

"Ah, you're grand."

"No, I offered you a cup of tea."

"Ah, I don't have time now. Just a flying visit, if you'll pardon the pun."

"Sorry?"

Gerry flicked back the cuff of his Ventile jacket and looked at a diver's watch.

"I have to get to the airport to meet a friend."

"Ah, OK. Should be OK this time of the day, traffic-wise."

"Yeah, I don't wanna be late for her. She's never been here before. First time on our little island."

"Where's she coming from? Somewhere exciting? Spain?" said Pauline, genuinely nosy.

"No," said Gerry, smiling. "She's coming from Bangladesh."